SURRENDER

the

DAWN

MaryLu Tyndall

BARBOUR
PUBLISHING

Scripture quotations, unless otherwise indicated, are taken from the King James Version of the Bible.

Scripture quotations marked NASB are taken from the New American Standard Bible, © 1960, 1962, 1963, 1968, 1971, 1972, 1973, 1975, 1977, 1995 by The Lockman Foundation. Used by permission.

Cover image: Faceout Studio, www.faceoutstudio.com
Cover photography: Steve Gardner, Pixelworks Studios

Published by Barbour Publishing, Inc., P.O. Box 719, Uhrichsville, Ohio 44683, www.barbourbooks.com

Our mission is to publish and distribute inspirational products offering exceptional value and biblical encouragement to the masses.

 Member of the
Evangelical Christian
Publishers Association

Printed in the United States of America.

ABOUT THE AUTHOR

MARYLU TYNDALL

MaryLu Tyndall dreamed of pirates and seafaring adventures during her childhood days on Florida's coast. She holds a degree in math and worked as a software engineer for fifteen years before testing the waters as a writer. Her love of history and passion for storytelling drew her to create the Legacy of the King's Pirates series. MaryLu now writes full-time and makes her home with her husband, six children, and four cats on California's coast, where her imagination still surges with the sea. Her passion is to write page-turning, romantic adventures that not only entertain but expose Christians to their full potential in Christ. For more information on MaryLu and her upcoming releases, please visit her website at www.mltyndall.com or her blog at crossandcutlass.blogspot.com.

❖ DEDICATION ❖

To anyone who has ever felt like a failure.

"I am the Light of the world,
he who follows Me will not walk in the darkness,
but will have the Light of life."
JOHN 8:12 NASB

❖ CHAPTER 1 ❖

March 26, 1814
Merchants Coffee House, Baltimore, Maryland

M iss Channing, no privateer in his right mind would accept money from a woman investor. It is simply bad luck."

Raucous laughter—all male—shot through the tiny coffee shop that smelled more like ale and sweat than coffee.

Wrinkling her nose beneath the odor and bracing her heart against the mounting impediment to her well-laid plans, Cassandra rose from her seat. "That is merely a foolish superstition, Mr. McCulloch. I assure you, my money is as good as any man's."

Snickers and grins interspersed with the occasional salacious glance continued to fire her way. But Cassandra brushed them off. After an hour of sitting in the muggy, male-dominated room, listening to various merchants selling shares for the equipping of their vessels into privateers, she had grown numb to the attention.

When the customs agent had finally announced eight shares offered at two hundred dollars each to be invested in the *Contradiction*—a one-hundred-and-three-ton schooner out of Dorchester, housing one long nine gun, ten men, and captained by Peter Pascal—Cassandra had raised her hand. With her one thousand dollars, she could purchase over half the shares rather than be one of many investors in a larger, better-equipped ship. Owning more of a privateer meant higher returns. And she definitely was in dire need of higher returns.

Mr. McCulloch shoved his thumbs into the pockets of his trousers and shot Cassandra the same patronizing look her mother often gave her younger sisters when they failed to comprehend what she was saying. "Aye, your money is good, Miss Channing. It's the mind behind the coin that begs concern."

"How dare you, sir! Why, you are no more. . ." Cassandra clutched her reticule close to her chest and spat out, "My money and my mind are equal to any man's here."

Again laughter pulsated through the room.

"It's the comely exterior of that mind that I'm partial to," one man yelled from the back, prompting yet another chorus of chuckles.

Cassandra narrowed her eyes and scanned the mob. Did these men honestly believe they were amusing? Most of them—with the exception of a few unsavory types loitering around the fringes of the assembly—were hardworking merchants, bankers, shop owners, mill workers, and farmers. Men who often tipped their hat at her on the street. Her gaze locked with the wife of the coffeehouse proprietor, scrubbing a counter in the right corner. Sympathy poured from her eyes.

Mr. McCulloch scratched his head and gave a sigh of frustration. "A share in any privateer gives you a voice in its affairs. A business voice, miss. A voice that needs to be schooled in matters of financial investments and risk assessment."

The men nodded and grunted in approval like a band of mindless lackeys.

Cassandra tapped her shoe on the wooden floor, the hollow echo thrumming her disdain through the room. "A mind like Mr. Nash's here, I presume." She gestured toward the gentleman standing to her right. "No offense, sir"—she offered him a conciliatory smile—"I'm sure you have acquired a plethora of financial wisdom while shoeing horses all day."

The low rumble of laughter that ensued was quickly squelched by a scowl from Mr. McCulloch.

"And Mr. Ackers." She nodded toward the stout man sitting at the table next to hers. "Surely you have become a master of investment while out tilling your field?"

The proprietor's wife emitted an unladylike chortle that drew all gazes her way. Her face reddening, she disappeared through a side door.

"Besides," Cassandra huffed. "What business decisions need be made for a privateer already armed, captained, and ready to set sail?"

No reply came—save the look of complete annoyance shadowing the customs agent's face.

Cassandra pursed her lips. "Let me make this very easy for you, sir. You need investors, I have money to invest." She clutched the silk reticule until her fingers ached. "I am not without good sense, and I assure you I will seek out advice from those more experienced should the need arise."

"We cannot trust that you will do so."

"That is absurd!"

"Trouble is, miss, there's not a man among us who'd be willing to partner with you."

Nods of affirmation bobbed through a sea of heads.

Cassandra scanned the crowd, making eye contact with as many of the men as she could. "Is there no man here brave enough to stand with me?"

The hiss of coals in the fireplace was her only reply.

Mr. McCulloch sifted through the stack of papers before him. "Perhaps we could allow you to invest a much smaller percentage in a privateer if you promise to forsake your voice in any decisions and if the other shareholders would agree to it." His beady eyes swept over the mob, but not a single gentleman spoke up.

Cassandra batted her gloved hand through the air. "I will not accept a smaller percentage, sir."

"Then I fear we are at an impasse." Mr. McCulloch plucked out a pocket watch, flipped it open, and stared at it as if it contained the answer to ridding himself of her company. His gaze lifted to hers. "Miss, your father was a good man. I am sorry for your loss. But not even *he* would risk the bad luck that would surely come from aligning with a woman in any seafaring venture."

Tears burned in Cassandra's eyes, but she shoved them behind a shield of determination.

Mr. Parnell, a worker at the flour mill, gave her a sympathetic smile.

"Perhaps you should marry, Miss Channing," Mr. Kendrick, the young banker assisting Mr. McCulloch, said. "A woman your age should not be unattached." A wave of interested eyes engulfed her. "Then with your husband's signature, you may invest in whatever you wish."

Cassandra's blood boiled. She wouldn't tell them that she had no intention of marrying any time soon, and certainly not for the sole purpose of investing in a privateer. "Any man I marry will allow me to do with my money as I see fit, sir."

Again, a quiver of laughter assailed her.

Withdrawing a handkerchief from within his waistcoat, Mr. McCulloch dabbed at the sweat on his bald head. "If you don't mind, Miss Channing, we have serious business to discuss."

An angry flush heated Cassandra's face, her neck, and moved down her arms as a hundred unladylike retorts flirted with her tongue. Tightening her lips, she grabbed her cloak, turned, and shoved her way through the crowd as the man began once again taking bids for the *Contradiction*.

Contradiction, indeed. This whole meeting was a contradiction of good sense.

After turning down several gentlemen's offers to walk her home, Cassandra stepped from the shop into a gust of March wind that tore her bonnet from her hand. Too numb to chase after it, she watched as it tumbled down South Street as if all her dreams blew away with it. Perhaps they had. Perhaps her dreams had been overtaken by the nightmare of this past year.

Yes, only a nightmare. And soon she would wake up and be comfortable and carefree as she once had been. And her country would not be at war. And her father would still be with her.

But as she watched the sun drag its last vestiges of light from the brick buildings, elm trees, and the dirt street, her dreamlike state vanished. It would soon be dark, and she had a mile to traverse to reach her home.

Through a rather unsavory section of town.

Swinging her fur-lined cloak over her shoulders, she shoved her reticule tightly between her arm and body, pressed a wayward curl into her loosely pinned bun, and started down the street, nodding her greeting toward a passing couple, a single gentleman, and a group of militiamen as she went. The snap of reins, the clomp of horse hooves, and the rattle of carriage wheels filled her ears as she wove between passing phaetons and horses. An icy breeze tore at her hair and fluttered the lace of her blue muslin gown. She drew her cloak tighter around her neck. A bell rang in the distance. A baby cried. Sordid chuckles, much like the type she'd just endured in the coffeehouse, blared from a tavern along Pratt Street. Was the entire town mocking her?

Up ahead, the bare masts of countless ships swayed into the darkening sky like thickets in a winter wind. Most were abandoned merchant ships. Some, however, were privateers, while others were merchantmen that had been issued Letters of Marque to board and confiscate enemy vessels—both forbidden investments to her.

8

Simply because she was a woman.

The briny scent of fish and salt curled her nose as she turned down Pratt Street. Dark water caressed the hulls of the ships like a lover luring them out to sea. Where they could damage British commerce and put an end to this horrendous war. But the blockade kept many of Baltimore's finest vessels imprisoned in the harbor. Only the fastest privateers could slip past the fortress of British ships capping the mouth of the Chesapeake and only then, during inclement weather. The rest remained at sea, hauling their prizes to ports along the Eastern Seaboard where they sold them, along with the goods in their holds, for considerable sums of money.

Which was precisely why Cassandra needed to invest the money left to her by her father and brothers in a privateer. She patted the reticule containing the banknote for a thousand dollars—all the wealth her family had left in the world. Now what was she to do? Cassandra swallowed down a rising fear. Investing in a privateer had been her last hope. How else could a single woman with no skills provide for a family? Cassandra's mother and sisters depended on her, and she had let them down.

❖

Luke Heaton trudged up the companionway ladder and emerged onto the main deck of the ship—his ship. Or his heap of rot and rust, to be more precise. Setting his hammer atop the capstan with a thud, he shuddered against the crisp air coming off the bay.

Biron looked up from the brass binnacle he was polishing. "Did someone die?"

Luke gave a sardonic chuckle and grabbed the open bottle of rum from the top of a barrel. Plopping down on the bulwarks, he took a swig and wiped his mouth with his sleeve. "Yes, this ship. All she's good for is a watery grave."

Biron continued his polishing. "At least she stays afloat."

"But not for long. She's got two gaping holes in her hull."

"They can be fixed." Biron shrugged, but the encroaching shadows stole his expression. Setting his bottle down, Luke struck flint to steel and lit the lantern hanging from the main mast.

"What of the rotten spars, rusty tackles, and frayed sheets?" Luke ran a hand through his hair.

A twinkle lit Biron's brown eyes. Or was it merely the lantern's reflection? "All repairable."

The ship teetered over an incoming wavelet, and Luke stretched the ache from his back. An ache formed from working all day belowdecks trying to transform this heap into a swift sailing vessel. "Repairable yes, but with what, is the question." Luke took another sip of rum. "How did I ever end up with this old bucket?"

"You won it in a game of cards, if I recall."

Yes, the hazy memory returned. Along with another more disturbing one—another card game the following night when he'd lost all the money he intended to use to repair and equip his new acquisition.

The *Agitation* was indeed living up to her name.

Luke huffed out a sigh and fingered the rim of the dark bottle. A gull squawked overhead, taunting him, while the waters of Baltimore Harbor slapped the hull in laughter. The smell of rum along with his own sweat combined with the scents of wood, tar, and salt. He loved the sea. Had wanted nothing more than to return to her after his captain and best friend, Noah, had cast him from his ship.

Luke shifted on his seat as the memory stung him. The year he'd spent as Noah's first mate on his privateer, *Defender,* had been the best year of Luke's life. But he'd gone and ruined his first opportunity to make an honorable living, as he had done to everything else he touched. Even so, the experience hadn't been a complete loss, for privateering had left Luke with a love of the sea, a love for his country, and a yearning for the riches he could make in the trade. But now with no money and a broken-down hull of a ship, that dream began to sink beneath the murky waters of the bay.

"I should sell her."

Biron's gray-lined hair shimmered in the lantern light. "What? And give up?"

"Don't be a fool, old man." Luke stood and began to pace. "Where am I going to get the money to fix and arm her as a privateer?"

"Perhaps God will provide."

"Humph. God, indeed." Luke would expect no help from the Almighty—even if He did exist.

Ceasing his scrubbing, Biron looked at Luke with understanding. "I know your responsibilities weigh heavy on you, Cap'n."

Responsibilities. Luke gazed at the sliver of a moon smiling at him in the eastern sky. Was that what he would call John? Perhaps. Yet, he was so much more than that. A responsibility Luke would never forsake. And one he hoped with everything in him, he was worthy of.

Biron spit on his rag and began rubbing the binnacle again. "It is a good thing you have someone dependin' on you, or you'd while away your time in taverns, wastin' your money on wenches, wine, and whist."

"At least I find I am good at those."

Biron chuckled and shook his head. "My guess is that you are good at many things, Cap'n. If you'd just believe in yourself—and in God."

"I'm not your captain yet." Luke eyed his friend. Sturdy as a ship's mast and just as weathered, Biron had been at sea his entire life. Tufts of gray floated across his dark hair like clouds across a night sky. "Why do you stay with me, old man?"

Biron scratched his whiskers. "You promised work for this aged seaman, and I'm holding you to it, Cap'n." He smiled.

Luke took another swig. "I wouldn't place your bet on me. I'll no doubt disappoint you."

Biron set down his cloth and stood, stretching his back. "Ah, I wouldn't be too sure about that, Cap'n." He winked, tugged at his red neckerchief, and made his way over to Luke. "It grows late, my friend. I'll see you in the morning." With a moan, he hefted himself onto the dock and gazed up at the night sky. "You never know what tomorrow will bring." He turned around and winked at Luke. "Or even tonight."

❖

A sudden chill struck Cassandra. She hugged herself. In her musings, nighttime had spread a cloak of darkness over the city. With the exception of a sailor sitting on the deck of his ship by the dock, an old man ambling down the street, and a couple disappearing in the distance, no one was in sight. Facing forward, she hurried along.

Footsteps sounded behind her.

Her chest tightened. She quickened her pace.

More shuffling. The crunch of gravel. A man coughed.

She glanced over her shoulder. Two bulky shadows followed her.

Air seized in her throat. She hurried her pace and nearly tripped on the uneven pavement. The footfalls grew louder. Grabbing her skirts, she started to run. Where were the night watchmen? Why, oh why, had she been foolish enough to bring all of her money with her? *Lord, please. . .* her prayer fell limp from her lips. God had never answered her petitions before. Why would He now?

She crossed Light Street. A cat meowed.

A man jumped out of an alleyway in front of her.

Cassandra screamed and spun around. The two men approached her. Shadows swirled over their faces, masking their features. "What do you want?" Her voice came out as a squeak.

"We wants what's in yer purse there, miss."

❖

Luke took another swig of rum and squinted into the shadows where Biron had disappeared. Across the street, a lady walked alone. Two, maybe three men crept behind her. Foolish girl. From her attire, he could tell she wasn't one of the tavern wenches. What was she doing wandering about the docks so late? Luke flipped the hair from his face and slowly set his bottle down. The ship eased over a ripple and the bottle shifted, scraping over the oak planks. The men continued their pursuit. Luke shook his head. The last thing he needed was more trouble. He shouldn't get involved. He should stay on his ship. But the rum soured in his stomach. *Oh, lud.* With that, Luke shot to his feet. Searching the deck for his sword, he sheathed it and leaped onto the dock. The woman started to run. Another man leapt out in front of her. They had her surrounded.

❖

Cassandra's pulse roared in her ears. Her legs wobbled. She would not allow these ruffians to steal all that kept her and her family from starvation. Her terror quickly turned to anger. She jutted out her chin. "Well, you cannot have it, sir!"

"If you give us the purse, there'll be no trouble."

"Oh, I assure you gentlemen, if you do not leave this instant, there'll be more trouble than you can handle."

The men exchanged mirthful glances then broke into fits of laughter.

Cassandra ground her teeth together. She grew tired of being laughed at. Tired of being told what she could and couldn't do.

One of the men, a short, greasy-looking fellow, approached, hand extended. She recognized him as one of the men at the coffeehouse. "Give it up, miss."

"You'll have to pry it out of my dead hands."

The slimy man grabbed her arm. Pain shot into her shoulder. "If ye insist."

❖ CHAPTER 2 ❖

Cassandra struggled against the man's grip. "How dare you!" She pounded her reticule atop his head. Tossing up his other arm to fend off her blows, he ducked and spewed obscenities, while his companions held their stomachs in laughter.

Fury pinched every nerve into action. She would not lose this money. She could not lose this money. Her life and the lives of her family depended on it.

The man's grip tightened. Pain spiked through her arm and into her fingers. They grew cold and numb. Raising her leg, she thrust her shoe into his groin. He released her and doubled over with a groan. The other men stopped laughing. Thick fingers grabbed her arms on both sides. She screeched in pain.

"That's enough out o' you, miss. Now hand over that purse!" The man to her right—who looked more like a toad than a man—shouted, sending a spray of spittle and foul breath over her. Strands of hair hung in his bloated face as his venomous eyes stabbed her with hatred. He reached for her reticule.

Cassandra thrashed her legs. Her thrusts met nothing but air. The men on either side of her tightened their grips. She cried out in pain. Her palms grew moist. Toad-man released her and yanked the purse from her hands.

Somewhere a bell rang, chiming her doom.

"Give that back to me at once!" Cassandra grasped for her reticule, but the man jumped out of her reach and gave her a yellowed grin in return.

All hope spilled from Cassandra, leaving her numb. This couldn't be happening. "Please," she begged. "It's all I have."

"Not anymore." The bald man on her left lifted his beak-like nose and chortled.

She kicked him in the shin. He cursed and leaned over, pinching her arm even tighter and dragging her down with him.

The toad chuckled.

When Cassandra righted herself, she saw the tip of a cutlass slice through the darkness, cutting off toad-man's laughter at his neck. The sharp point pierced his skin. A trickle of blood dripped onto his grimy shirt. He froze. His eyes widened. Cassandra's gaze traced the length of the blade to a tall, dark-haired man at the hilt end, his face hidden in the shadows. "Return the lady's reticule, if you please, sir," a deep, yet oddly familiar voice demanded.

Cassandra released her breath. Her thrashing heart slowed its pace. Dare she hope for rescue?

"And you." The dark man nodded toward the beak-nosed ruffian still clutching her left arm. "Release her and back away, or your friend will forfeit his head."

A salty breeze swirled around them like a tempest, as if some unknown force were examining the proceedings. Despite the chill of the evening, a trickle of sweat slid down the toad's forehead. Beak-nose released her arm. Cassandra rubbed it, feeling her blood return.

The third man, whom Cassandra had kicked, slowly rose from the ground and slid a hand inside his coat.

Cassandra opened her mouth to warn her rescuer, but with lightning speed, he plucked a pistol from his coat, cocked it, and pointed it at the villain. "I wouldn't do that if I were you."

The third man raised his hands in the air.

Her rescuer turned back to Toad-man. "I *said* return the lady's reticule." He pressed the tip further into the man's skin. He yelped. More blood spilled.

"Whatever you say. Whatever you say." With a trembling arm, he held Cassandra's purse out to her. Snatching it, she pressed it against her bosom and took a step back, her heart slowing its pace.

14

"What are you doin', George?" Beak-nose whined. "There's three o' us and only one o' him."

"Ye aren't the one wit' a sword in yer neck, are ye, now?"

Her rescuer faced Beak-nose. A sheen of moonlight drifted over his face, over his firm stubbled jaw, strong nose, high forehead, and raven hair. Cassandra's mouth fell open. *Luke Heaton.* Her friend Noah Brenin's roguish first mate—the man he had tossed from his privateer for drunkenness and cheating at cards.

"I told you to unhand her," he demanded.

Beak-nose gave a cynical laugh that sent a tremble of fear through Cassandra. "As you wish." In one fluid motion, he released her arm and drew a sword from his belt, leveling it upon Mr. Heaton.

"What. . .ye goin' to do. . .now, hero?" Toad-man's voice came out broken beneath the tip of Luke's sword.

Beak-nose thrust his sword at Mr. Heaton. Leaping back, Luke blocked the slash with his blade. The chime of steel on steel vibrated a chill down Cassandra's back. The toad rubbed his neck and gazed at the blood on his hand as if he could not conceive from whence it had come.

With his gun still cocked and pointed at the third man, Luke met each thrust of Beak-nose's sword blow for blow. The chime of their blades rang through the night like the warning bells of Christ's Church. Cassandra gripped her throat. She should take her money and run. No man could fight such odds and win.

But how could she leave? Rogue or not, Mr. Heaton risked his life for her. She must do something to help. Frantic, Cassandra scanned the surroundings. A stack of bricks lay on the side of the building, no doubt for repairs. She grabbed one. The rough stone snagged her silk gloves as she crept toward Toad-man.

Beak-nose brought his blade down once again on Mr. Heaton. Moonlight glinted off the metal as grunts filled the air. Leaping out of its path, Heaton swung about and drove the man back with a rapid parry. The *whoosh whoosh whoosh* of his blade filled the air. His last swipe sent Beak-nose's sword clanging to the ground. He quickly snatched it up. But before he could recover, Mr. Heaton lunged toward him with a ferocious assault that sent the man reeling.

Taking advantage of the moment, the toad drew his sword. Cassandra gasped. She raised her hands to strike him with the brick. He swung around, growling, and shoved her aside. Arms failing, she dropped the brick and tumbled to the dirt. Pain shot up her back.

With blade extended, Toad-man advanced toward Luke. Still holding his pistol in one hand, Mr. Heaton fired at him. He missed. The crack pierced the night air as the smell of gunpowder bit Cassandra's nose. The toad emitted a vile chuckle. Tossing the weapon down, Mr. Heaton swung his cutlass in his direction. He ducked beneath Toad-man's clumsy slash then met his advance with such force, it spun the man around. Sweeping his sword back to the left, Mr. Heaton countered Beak-nose's next attack.

Cassandra's head grew light. She glanced down the street for anyone who could help. No one was in sight. Yet Mr. Heaton seemed more than capable of handling these two men. But not capable of keeping his eye on the third man, who finally managed to extract his pistol from his coat and aim it at Mr. Heaton.

Grabbing her skirts, she jumped to her feet and retrieved the brick. Raising it above her head, she closed her eyes and brought it down on the man's head. A sharp crack made her wince. Followed by a moan. She peered through her lashes to see him topple to the ground in a heap. Her gaze locked upon Mr. Heaton's. A slight grin crossed his lips before he turned to meet Toad-man's next charge.

In fact, Mr. Heaton continued to fight both men off with more skill and finesse than Cassandra had ever witnessed. Where the ruffians groaned and heaved and dripped in sweat, Mr. Heaton carried himself with a calm, urbane confidence. Finally his blade met the toad's left shoulder, eliciting a scream from the man that quite resembled a woman's. Clutching his arm, the villain sped into the night, leaving his partner gaping at Luke, his chest heaving. He backed away, dropped his blade, and uttered, "It's not worth this," before bolting down the street.

Sheathing his sword, Mr. Heaton collected his pistol from the ground, slid it inside his coat, and slapped his hands together as if this sort of thing happened every day. He started toward Cassandra. Her heart vaulted into her throat. Perhaps she was no safer with him than she had been with the scoundrels who'd assaulted her. He was the town rogue, after all. A drunkard and a ruffian. He halted, towering over her by at least a foot, and she resisted the urge to take a step back. He smelled of wood and rum. Recognition flickered in his eyes and something else— pleasant surprise? "Are you harmed, Miss Channing?"

"No, Mr. Heaton." She gripped her reticule. "I thank you, sir, for coming to my aid."

He glanced at the man lying in a heap in the dirt. "I've never seen a woman defend herself with a brick." His lopsided grin sent an odd jolt through her heart.

"It does not always require a man's strength to defeat a foe."

"Indeed." He chuckled. "Then perhaps I should have left you to your own devices. No doubt you could have pummeled them all unconscious."

Cassandra narrowed her gaze. "Perhaps I could have."

"Nevertheless, miss, you shouldn't walk about town at night without benefit of an escort."

"Lately, there are many things I'm told I should not do."

He swayed slightly on his feet and the smell of rum once again stung her nose. "Indeed. I suffer from the same malady."

"I doubt our situations are comparable." She glanced at the dark frame of a schooner tied at the dock. "How did you come to my rescue so suddenly? I did not see anyone else about."

"I was working on my ship when I spotted you across the street."

His ship. But she'd heard no one would hire him as a captain. "A privateer?"

Mr. Heaton gazed at the vessel bobbing in the harbor and sighed. "Alas, she could be one day." He gestured toward her reticule. "What is it you have in your reticule that would lure such rats from their holes?"

She eyed him suspiciously, wishing she could see the details of his face more clearly. "Nothing of import." She gripped it tighter. "I had business at the Merchants Coffee House." A chill prickled her skin. Surely this man wouldn't attempt to rob her after he'd defended her so admirably. She took a step back. "I thank you again, Mr. Heaton, but I really must be on my way."

"Allow me to escort you home." Closing the distance between them once again, he proffered his elbow. His massive chest spanned her vision even as his body heat cloaked her in warmth. Her breath quickened.

"There is no need." Turning, she waved him off. "I'm sure there are no more ruffians afoot." *Except you, perhaps.*

Mr. Heaton fell in step beside her. "Nevertheless, I would never forgive myself should any harm come to you, especially carrying such a fortune."

Shock halted her. "What did you say?"

One dark brow rose. "They wouldn't accept your money, would they?"

Cassandra flattened her lips.

Mr. Heaton scratched the stubble on his chin. "I was aware of the proceedings at the coffee shop tonight, miss. I would have been there myself looking for investors if I'd thought anyone in town would take a chance on me as captain." Sorrow weighed his voice.

Cassandra took in this news and allowed it to stir excitement within her. If only for a moment. But no. Even if he would take her money, Mr. Heaton was not a man to be trusted. She clutched her reticule closer and started on her way.

Clearing his throat, he walked beside her. "You have nothing to fear from me, Miss Channing. I am no thief. A gambler, perhaps, even a libertine, but no thief." He stumbled but quickly leveled his steps.

Cassandra shook her head. How on earth had he managed to wield his sword so skillfully in his condition? She stopped and faced him. "You are drunk, sir."

"Ah, yes." He gave her a rakish grin. "How could I forget? Apparently, I'm also a sot."

Cassandra searched for a glimpse of his eyes in the darkness, but the shadows denied her. How could he joke about such a disgusting habit?

"Wondering how I managed to fend off three men?"

"Two." She lifted her chin. "I took care of one of them."

He chuckled and reached up as if to touch the loose strands of her hair.

She began walking again. "Please leave me be, Mr. Heaton. I thank you for your assistance. Good night."

"You should see my swordplay when I'm sober, miss," he shouted after her.

"I'd rather not see you at all, Mr. Heaton."

She heard his footsteps behind her. Turning right onto Howard Street, she quickened her pace. Without the street lights—kept in darkness due to the war—she could barely make out the gravel road. The crunch of her shoes on the pebbles echoed against the brick warehouses on her right. One glance over her shoulder told her that Mr. Heaton still followed her, though he remained at a distance. If his reputation wasn't so besmirched, she might find his actions quite chivalrous. Instead, suspicion rankled her mind.

Down Eutaw Street, Cassandra halted before her small yard—the shadow of a two-story brick house loomed behind a garden of red roses and goldenrods. She swung about to say good night and nearly bumped into Mr. Heaton.

"Oh, forgive me, Miss Channing." Yet he didn't step back as propriety demanded. Turning, she headed up the stone path to the door.

"If you're seeking a ship to invest in, Miss Channing, mine is quite available." His boot steps followed her.

She faced him. "I am seeking a reputable ship, Mr. Heaton. With a reputable captain." She feigned a smile. The lantern light perched outside her door reflected a devilish gleam in his eyes—blue eyes. She could see them now, mere inches from her own face. Her heart took up a traitorous thump. "Preferably a sober one."

"I've been at sea my whole life. Sober or not, I'll make a good captain and bring you a fortune in prizes. Ask your friend, Noah."

"I have," she said, lifting a brow. "He warned me to stay away from you."

Mr. Heaton chuckled and tugged on his right earlobe. "He did, did he?" His eyes scoured over her as if assessing her for some nefarious purpose. "Good advice, I'd say." A sad smile tugged on his lips. "Well then, I bid you good night, Miss Channing." He bowed slightly and turned to leave.

Slipping inside her door, Cassandra closed and bolted it, then she leaned back against the sturdy wood. No matter if his was the last privateer in the city, she would never align herself with Mr. Luke Heaton.

❖ CHAPTER 3 ❖

The sound of Mr. Heaton's boots crunching over the gravel as he departed drifted in through the window to Cassandra's right, while her mind whirled with the events of the evening. A muddle of emotions knotted in her gut: from anger to terror back to anger again and finally settling on an odd feeling that heated her face and tightened her belly—a feeling she could not name.

A jumble of wheat-colored curls flew from the library door, followed by a screech that burned Cassandra's ears. Darlene barreled down the hallway with Mr. Dayle fast on her heels. Or as fast as the young footman could be with four-year-old Hannah clinging to his leg like a barnacle to the hull of a ship. Dexter, their sheepdog, flopped in after them, barking.

A groan sounded from within the closed parlor to Cassandra's left.

"Cassie, you're home!" Darlene shouted, but before Cassandra could wrap her arms around her sister, the child slipped behind her, hiding in the folds of her gown.

Shuffling over the wooden floor like a sailor with a peg leg, Mr. Dayle halted before Cassandra. Dexter sat by his side and stared up at them— though Cassandra couldn't be entirely sure the dog could see anything through the curtain of fur covering his eyes. His tongue hung from his mouth. Giggles drifted up Cassandra's back and over her shoulders to bounce off Mr. Dayle's rather bedraggled, yet comely face. Light from the

20

chandelier spilled on his blond hair, thick mustache, and fair eyebrows, making him appear to glow. "My apologies for not meeting you at the door, miss, but there appears to be something wrong with my leg."

"Indeed?" Cassandra forced her brows together. "I hope it isn't serious." She gazed down at Hannah, wrapped around his trousers, her thumb in her mouth and a smile flickering across her blue eyes.

"Hmm." Cassandra leaned over. "Appears to be an anchor of some sort—a red-haired anchor."

Mr. Dayle glanced down. "Egad, what is this that has grown upon my foot?"

Dexter chomped on a fold of Hannah's gown and began tugging her away from Mr. Dayle, growling.

Hannah inched her thumb from her mouth just enough to emit a giggle before she thrust it back inside.

"You wouldn't happen to know where Miss Darlene ran off to?" Mr. Dayle brushed dust from his gray coat. "She made quite a mess in the library, and when I insisted she clean it up, she disappeared."

Cassandra tapped her chin. "Young girl about six years old with light hair and green eyes?"

"Yes, that's the one."

Both girls giggled. Darlene poked her face out from between the folds of Cassandra's skirt.

Dexter released Hannah's gown and barked.

Mr. Dayle hunched over like a monster. "Ah, there you are." Grabbing Darlene, he swung her into his arms, her lacy petticoat fluttering through the air.

Hannah leapt to her feet. "Me too! Me too!"

Cassandra laughed. There were some things worth coming home for.

"Cassandra, is that you?" Her mother's sharp voice sliced a hole in the happy moment.

And there were some things not worth coming home for.

Mr. Dayle released the girls and set them down on the floor.

"Thank you for being so good to them, Mr. Dayle." Cassandra drew her sisters close. "I know they can be"—she glanced down and brushed curls from both girls' foreheads—"rather difficult to handle."

Dexter forced his way in between the two girls and lifted his paw up on Cassandra's skirt. She patted him on the head. "And you too, Dexter."

"My pleasure, miss." Mr. Dayle bowed slightly then winked at the girls, eliciting further giggles. "Your mother was not feeling well tonight, and Margaret and Mrs. Northrop were otherwise engaged."

"And I'm sure you have your own duties—"

Darlene whispered something in her younger sister's ear, and the two started toward the stairs. Cassandra grabbed Darlene's arm. "Oh no, you don't. You both stay here with me." She faced Mr. Dayle again. "I'm sure you have more than enough to attend to without playing nursemaid to my sisters." Since Cassandra had been forced to let most of the staff go last month, poor Mr. Dayle held many roles at the Channing home: gardener, footman, butler, steward, and apparently nanny when the occasion called for it. But the tall man in his thirties never once complained.

Mr. Dayle smiled. "I'm happy to help."

"Cassandra!" Her mother's voice sounded like a bugle stuffed with a wet rag.

"She's in the parlor." Mr. Dayle gave her a sympathetic look before he clutched Dexter's collar and led the dog down the hallway. "I'll put him outside, miss."

Kneeling, Cassandra wrapped her arms around her sisters.

"Cassie, Cassie." Hannah climbed into Cassandra's lap while Darlene kissed her on the cheek.

"Come on, girls, let's go see Mama, shall we?" Cassandra attempted to straighten Darlene's gown but it remained hopelessly wrinkled. "And your hair, Dar. It's a tangled mess."

"I'm sorry, Cassie." Darlene pouted, but a devilish twinkle shone in her green eyes.

Cassandra ushered the girls down the hall and through wide doors to their left. The smell of tallow mixed with her mother's jasmine perfume assailed Cassandra as she led her sisters to the floral sofa across from their mother. Cassandra gave them her sternest "stay where you are" look.

"Where have you been, Cassandra?" Sitting like a stiff washboard on her velvet upholstered settee, her mother threw a hand to her chest. "I was so worried, my palpitations returned."

"Forgive me, Mother." Cassandra kissed her cheek and took her seat in a chair beside the fireplace. No sooner had she set her reticule down on the table, than Hannah tore from the sofa and crawled up in her lap. Spreading the girl's gown over her dangling feet, Cassandra embraced her youngest sister, inhaling her scent of lavender soap, fresh biscuits, and a pinch of mischief. Light from numerous candles perched on the tables and across the mantle set the room aglow, bringing out the rich colors in the mahogany furniture, and the exquisite burgundy and gold tones of the oriental rug that graced the center of the floor.

"I was detained, Mother. It could not be helped."

Her thoughts shifted to Mr. Heaton, and the odd warmth washed through her again. Plucking out her fan, she waved it over Hannah's face. "Detained by what, dear?" Her mother came alert. "Did something happen? You do look flushed."

Cassandra reached over and touched her mother's hand. "No. I am quite all right, Mother."

"Well, *I* haven't been quite all right." Her mother dabbed the stiff, perfectly shaped curls framing her face. Her voice emerged as sour as her expression. "While you were out traipsing around town, doing—oh my heavens, I cannot imagine what any proper lady could be doing out at this hour—your sisters have been very naughty."

Cassandra's gaze flashed to Darlene, who slouched into the cushions. Hannah stuck her thumb back into her mouth.

Her mother continued, "Darlene caught a frog. A frog! And she put it in Miss Thain's soup. Of all the things to put into soup! Can you imagine?"

Setting her fan down on the table, Cassandra bit her lip to keep from laughing. Her wayward sisters needed no further encouragement in their mischievous pranks. What they needed was a firm hand, which had disappeared from this house when their father ran off to fight the British in Canada two years ago.

"Needless to say, upon finding the frog, Miss Thain ran screaming from the kitchen and knocked over the meat pies she had prepared for supper. Which that filthy mutt proceeded to eat." Her mother grabbed her ever-ready handkerchief from the table and fluttered it about her face. "Most horrible. Most horrible. All we had to eat were scraps of cold chicken left over from yesterday's meal."

"And some fresh biscuits, Mama," Hannah piped in.

"Yes, dear, but hardly enough for a proper supper."

Darlene lowered her chin. "I'm sorry, Mama." Her loose hair fell in a tangle around her face. "I thought the frog was hungry."

The slight edge of humor in her voice—barely perceptible to most— told Cassandra that her sister was not sorry at all.

Her mother tightened her lips. "Hungry indeed." Her voice sounded so much like the creatures in question that Cassandra once again had to force down a laugh.

"Oh, where is my tea? My poor head." Lifting jeweled fingers to rub her temple, her mother studied Cassandra. "She takes after you, my dear."

Cassandra kissed the top of Hannah's head and tried to shove aside the rebuke. Mainly because it was true. She had always been the difficult child—the rebellious one. Always questioning, investigating, wanting to figure things out on her own, do things on her own. Now, as she looked at Darlene, she saw the same free spirit.

"Perhaps if you punished her more often, Mother?"

"Punish? She doesn't listen to me. She never has. She only listened to her father and he is. . ."

Mrs. Northrop entered with a tray of tea.

"Oh, thank goodness, my tea."

The housekeeper set the tray down on the walnut table that stretched between the sofas and chairs. Brown strands sprang from beneath the servant's white mobcap, which seemed barely able to restrain her thick hair. With her small head, pointed nose, long neck, and round figure, the woman reminded Cassandra of an ostrich she'd once seen in a painting. After she poured tea for Cassandra and her mother, she swung the pot toward the girls' cups.

"No." Cassandra's mother touched the housekeeper's arm, staying her. "Please put the girls to bed, Mrs. Northrop."

"Aye, mum." The woman's smile slipped slightly, but she quickly brought it back into position. Turning, she gestured for the girls to follow her.

After a bout of complaints, Darlene trudged from the room while Hannah scrambled from Cassandra's lap to follow her.

"I'll be up later to kiss you good night," Cassandra said. "Oh, Mrs. Northrop, have the girls clean up the mess they made in the library, if you please."

The housekeeper nodded in reply.

After the girls left, Cassandra leaned back in her chair and sipped her tea.

Her mother pressed down the folds of her silk gown then shot worried blues eyes her way. "Please tell me, Cassandra, that you did not throw away the rest of our money on a privateer?"

"No, I did not, Mother."

"Thank goodness."

"They wouldn't accept a woman investor." Cassandra chafed at the memory.

Her mother dabbed her forehead with her handkerchief. "At least there's some sense left in the world."

Setting down her cup, Cassandra rose and held out her hands to the flames crackling in the fireplace. "Sense? This kind of sense, Mother, will put us in the poorhouse."

"Oh, please do not speak of such gloomy things, dear."

Cassandra spun around. She wanted to be angry at her mother for her nonchalant attitude toward their financial woes, but the look of pain on her aged face stopped her. "I must speak of them, Mother. For I have to find a way to make a living for us."

"No doubt this war will end soon, and your brothers will return." Her mother's forlorn gaze drifted to the window as if searching for her missing offspring.

Outside, darkness gripped the city, much like England gripped America. Cassandra released a heavy sigh. "As much as I'd love for our country to defeat Britain and send those pompous redcoats home in shame, we cannot count on that happening anytime soon."

"But your brothers said they'd return in a year."

"And it's been a year, Mother. We have no idea where they are." An ache formed in Cassandra's heart. Or *if* they are. Yet she wouldn't voice her deepest fears to her mother, knowing how the possibility tormented her.

"Then you must get married, Cassandra. It is our only hope. It's the only way to ensure our survival." The quiver in her mother's voice brought Cassandra around to face her.

"I don't want to get married."

"What about Mr. Crane?" Her mother's cultured brows rose in excitement as if she hadn't heard Cassandra. "He's made his interest known for many months. It's fine time you gave him a little encouragement."

Cassandra shuddered at the thought of the overbearing man.

"And he owns that successful newspaper, the *Baltimore Register*. Why, I imagine he makes over five hundred dollars a year."

"So, I'm to throw my life and my happiness out the door for five hundred dollars a year?"

Tears glistened in her mother's eyes, and she fell back into her chair. "Oh, why did Phillip leave us? And then my boys. Oh, what will befall us?"

25

Cassandra eased beside her mother on the settee. "Never fear, Mother. We must plan for the worst and expect the best."

"How much money do we have left?"

"One thousand."

"Is that all?" Sitting up straight, her mother waved her handkerchief over her face. "What of the money your brothers got from the sale of our merchant ship?"

"We squandered it this past year, Mother." *You squandered it.* "We can no longer afford luxuries: oriental rugs, the latest hats and gowns from Paris, expensive perfumes. We cannot attend theater each week. We are no longer successful merchants."

A look of confusion, or perhaps shock, claimed her mother's features, though Cassandra had told her mother this same thing a dozen times.

"I fear if I do not find a way to invest our money," Cassandra continued, "it will be gone in just a few years."

"Oh dear, my head." Her mother fell back onto the couch. "You know I cannot bear such burdens."

Cassandra clasped her mother's trembling hands. "Don't overset yourself, Mother. I'll find a way."

"How? We are only women."

"I've a mind equal to any man's."

She flashed Cassandra an incredulous look. "Surely you see that you must get married soon. In fact, I insist on it, Cassandra. Do you want to send us all to the poorhouse?"

Tearing her gaze from the lack of confidence in her mother's eyes, Cassandra turned instead to the portrait of her great-grandfather, Edward Milford Channing, hanging above the fireplace. The man had come to Baltimore in 1747 with barely a coin in his pocket. With nothing but his wit, persistence, and hard work, he'd started his own merchant business, which he had passed on to Cassandra's father. The Channings were survivors. They were strong, independent, and hardworking. And Cassandra was as much a Channing as the men in the family. She rose from her chair and lifted her chin. "It will not come to that, Mother. Mark my words, whatever it takes, I will find a way for this family to survive."

❖ CHAPTER 4 ❖

Crossing the rickety bridge that spanned Jones Falls River, Luke continued down Pratt Street. An odd lightness feathered his steps. Why, he could not fathom. It certainly couldn't be Miss Channing. She'd done nothing but turn her pert little nose up at him. And after he'd saved her life! Luke smiled. What a treasure. What a spitfire! If he'd known it was Miss Channing he was rescuing he would have dispatched the villains sooner—if only to have more time alone with her.

A sea breeze frosted around him as he turned down High Street. Tightening his grip on his overcoat, he hunched against the cold as laughter blared from a cluster of men under the porch overhang of Spears Tavern. Through the windows, an undulating sea of patrons made the small building seem like a living, ghoulish specter. Fiddle music accompanied by strident singing floated with the lantern light onto the street.

"Is that you, Heaton? Come join us!" a man Luke recognized as Ackers, a local merchantman, shouted from the porch.

Jake, a chandler, who stood beside him, lifted his mug toward Luke. "There's a game of Gleek awaiting you, my friend."

"Not tonight, gentlemen," Luke shouted in passing. No. Tonight he had a desire to get home early.

Though he didn't quite know why.

The few coins in his pocket jingled their plea for a chance to reproduce upon the gambling table. But somehow he felt it would taint the lingering memory of his brief time with Miss Channing. Ever since Noah's fateful engagement party two years ago, Luke's eye had oft found its way to the charming red-haired lady. But his gaze was all he would risk offering her. She was far too much a lady to be seen with the likes of him. Too much of a lady to entertain his advances. Luke knew his place. The only women who tolerated his company were tavern wenches, and they only did so for the coin he tossed their way. Up until tonight, Miss Channing had not spoken two words to him. But what a voice she possessed. Like an angel's.

An angel's voice wrapped around a fiery dart!

Lud, such bravery! Where other women would have swooned, she fought against her attackers like a tigress. And when she could have run, she'd chosen to stay and help him. He'd never seen such valor in a woman.

But why had she risked being accosted by strolling about town unescorted? Didn't she have brothers? Two older ones, if he recalled. Another reason why Luke had stayed away.

Besides the fact that she would outright reject any attention on his part.

Which she had definitely done tonight. Then why did his heart feel as full as a sail in high wind instead of as heavy as an anchor? It made no sense at all. But what did it matter? If the lady possessed an astute mind—which it appeared she did—she would no doubt avoid him henceforth and with even more determination.

By the time Luke reached home, his feet dragged as much as his quickly sinking spirits. He still had no money, a rotten bucket of a ship, and his brief time with Miss Cassandra Channing had come to an end.

No sooner had he shut the front door of his small house, however, than a *thump thump thump* sounded, and John hobbled into the room. "You're home early!" The boy, who reached just above Luke's waist, gazed up at him with so much affection, all Luke's problems retreated out the door behind him—at least for the moment.

Luke tousled the lad's hair and returned his embrace as the smells of broiled fish and fresh biscuits enticed his nose. "Nothing can keep me from my favorite brother."

Mrs. Barnes entered the foyer, wiping her hands on her apron. "Apparently many things can. This is the first night this week you've made it home for supper."

John released Luke, a flippant grin on his lips. "And I'm your *only* brother."

Luke clamped John in a headlock and ground his knuckles into his brother's thick brown hair. "You'd still be my favorite if I had a hundred brothers."

Mrs. Barnes clicked her tongue. "Come now, Luke. You're messing up his hair."

"Oh, I would indeed enjoy having so many brothers." John giggled. "Then I wouldn't be so lonely during the day."

Shrugging out of his coat, Luke hung it on a peg as he ignored the guilt sinking in his gut. Gray eyes that reminded him so much of their mother's flashed an admiration toward Luke that he knew he didn't deserve. That, coupled with the look of censure firing from his housekeeper, nearly sent Luke back outside to join his friends at the tavern. Nothing like a drink to drown out the voices constantly berating his conscience.

As if reading his mind, Mrs. Barnes ambled toward him, hooked her arm with his, and led him down the hall and into the dining room. "Now sit and talk with your brother while I bring in supper."

Leaning down, Luke planted a kiss on her wrinkled forehead and gave her a beguiling smile. "What would I do without you?"

A red hue crept up her face as it always did when he kissed her. She slapped his arm and wagged a finger at him. "Your charm doesn't work with me, Luke." Shaking her head, she turned toward the kitchen. "You forget how often I took a strap to your bottom when you were but a child, and I'll do so again if needs be."

Despite her threat, warmth flooded Luke. He had indeed received many a swat from Mrs. Aldora Barnes as he had grown to manhood. Not one of them undeserved. Truth be told, the old housekeeper had been more of a mother to him than his real mother, who had so often been gone on trips with his father to "redeem the dark-hearted savages."

Redeem the savages, indeed.

John stared up at him wide eyed. "I think she means it."

Luke chuckled. "Then I shall have to behave myself, won't I? As you will, as well."

John shrugged. "I always behave."

Pulling out one of the chairs, Luke dropped onto the soft cushion and eyed his brother. Yes, John did always behave. So unlike Luke. John's face twisted as he limped over and struggled to sit in the chair next to Luke's. He stretched out his leg before him, the steel brackets bending the boy's trousers at odd angles. Where one leg was thick and strong and normal, the other was thin and frail and twisted to the right. Luke cringed. He should have been the one with rickets, not his kindhearted brother. "How does your leg fare today?"

"Good." John rubbed his withered thigh.

Always the same response no matter what discomfort the boy was enduring.

"When I get a new brace, I'll be able to walk much faster," John continued. Then casting a glance over his shoulder, he leaned toward Luke and whispered, "Perhaps I can come with you on your ship then?" Excitement sparked in his eyes.

Luke fingered a spoon on the table. "I'm afraid it won't be seaworthy for quite some time." *If ever.* He shifted his gaze from the disappointment tugging on John's face. The boy loved the sea as much as Luke did—had repeatedly begged Luke to take him out on Noah's ship, the *Defender.* But of course that was not possible. A privateer was no place for a lad, especially a crippled one. And with Noah losing his own brother in a ship accident some years ago, he wasn't about to risk Luke's. After a while, John had stopped asking. Until Luke had won his own ship in a game of Piquet two weeks ago, resurrecting the boy's petitions. If John had anything in common with Luke, besides his love of the sea, it was persistence.

"Shall we make a bargain?" Luke said. "If I ever get my ship seaworthy, you may come sailing with me." Luke knew he shouldn't make such a promise, but the chances of acquiring enough money to repair the *Agitation* were less than impossible. And the look of delight now beaming in the boy's eyes was well worth the risk.

"You promise?" John held out his hand. "A gentleman's honor."

Luke chuckled and took John's hand in a firm grip. "Aye, I promise." Though he cringed at pledging upon an honor he did not possess.

Mrs. Barnes swept into the room, her arms loaded with platters of steaming food. "What's this we are pledging to each other?"

"Nothing, Mrs. Barnes." John gazed at the broiled fish, biscuits, rice, and platter of sweet pickles and fried greens that Mrs. Barnes set upon the table. He licked his lips.

Luke's stomach leapt at the succulent smells, reminding him that he'd imbibed nothing but rum all day. While Mrs. Barnes said a prayer over the food, Luke glanced over the dining room, small by comparison with other homes: whitewashed walls devoid of decoration, save three sconces wherein candles flickered; a small brick fireplace with a cloth of painted canvas before it; a chipped wooden buffet that lined the wall beneath a rectangular window framed by dull linen curtains. A silver service tray complete with teapot, china cups, and silverware sat upon it, should company grace their home. Which rarely happened.

Luke clenched his jaw. He'd wanted to do more for his brother. So much more.

"And Father," Mrs. Barnes continued, "thank You for bringing Luke home to us tonight."

Luke flinched. Candlelight flickered off the old woman's face, casting her in a golden glow that made her look much younger than her sixty years.

"Amen," John repeated then eagerly helped himself to a piece of fish.

Their meal passed with laughter and pleasant conversation, during which Luke listened with rapt attention to John's rendition of his visit to the town library that day with Mrs. Barnes. Embellished with mad adventures that involved fighting off a band of gypsies and an encounter with a fire-breathing dragon, the story could match any found in Aesop's fables. The lad had an overactive imagination. And Luke wondered if perhaps he'd be a writer someday. Whatever he did, he'd no doubt be far more successful than Luke.

Then, per John's request, Luke regaled them with one of his adventures at sea, all the while wondering whether he'd ever have any new stories to tell.

Soon after, Luke found himself sitting beside John as he lay in bed.

"You know you don't have to tuck me in. I'm not a baby anymore," John huffed.

"No, you're not." Though he had been just one year old when the responsibility of parenting had fallen solely on Luke. "You're almost a man. I can hardly believe it."

"Will you work on your ship tomorrow?"

"Yes, if you work on your studies with Mrs. Barnes."

John's face soured. "But they are so boring. I want to be with you."

Luke raised his brows. "If you're going to be a sailor, you must be able to read and write and calculate numbers. Every captain I know who is worth his salt has a good education."

31

"Truly?"

"Indeed." Luke drew the coverlet up to John's chin.

"Will you come home tomorrow for dinner?" The pleading in John's voice stung Luke.

He wiped the hair from John's forehead. "I'll try."

John gave him a placating smile that said he didn't believe him. The boy was growing up too fast. Luke planted a kiss on his forehead then mussed up his hair. "Get some sleep."

Grabbing the lantern, Luke headed for the door.

"I love you, Luke."

Luke halted, emotion clogging his throat. "I love you too, John."

Down in the parlor, Mrs. Barnes filled Luke's mug with coffee then poured herself a cup and sat down in her favorite chair—a Victorian rocking chair—beside the fireplace where simmering coals provided a modicum of heat. A wooden clock sat on the mantel, its time stranded at 9:13. Luke stared at it, willing the hands to move. But they remained frozen in place. Hadn't it been working fine just that morning? *Lud.* That was all Luke needed. Something else broken in his broken-down world.

"I'm glad you came home tonight," Mrs. Barnes said. "That boy adores you."

Luke sipped the hot liquid, enjoying the exotic smell more than its bitter taste. Yet the coffee soothed his throat and settled in a pool of warmth in his belly. "He means the world to me."

"Then come home more often."

"You know I can't."

"Can't? Or won't give up your gambling and drinking?" Mrs. Barnes set down her cup on the table beside her and picked up her knitting as if she hadn't just chastised her employer. A large Bible perched proudly beside her steaming mug. Luke never saw her without it.

"I win more than I lose." Luke shifted his boots over the wool rug, trying to rub away the guilt.

Mrs. Barnes gazed at him from kind brown eyes that seemed far too small for her round face. Gray curls, springing from her mobcap, framed her like a silver halo. "I know a great deal of responsibility was laid upon your shoulders at only seventeen, but—"

"And I have kept us alive since," Luke interrupted, his ire rising.

"I'm not disputing that."

Leaning back in his chair, Luke glanced over the parlor, which boasted of chipped paint, threadbare curtains, and secondhand furniture. "I know this isn't the most comfortable place to live, but it's all I can afford at the moment."

"You know I don't care about that, Luke. I'm concerned for your soul."

"My soul is fine."

"Hmm." She continued her knitting. "If only you'd settle down. Pick an honorable trade."

"I have. A privateer. If this war continues much longer, I can make a fortune."

"You sound as if you wish the war would go on."

"Absurd." Setting his cup down with a clank, Luke rose and began to pace. "I know firsthand what the British are capable of. I hate the blockade. I hate their intrusion onto our land. I want to fight as much as the next man. Only at sea."

Needles flying, Mrs. Barnes joined one strand of white yarn and one strand of black together in a chaotic pattern that made no sense. Much like the pattern of Luke's life.

He stomped about the room, trying to settle his agitation. "When I sailed with Noah, I took great pride in thwarting the British cause by capturing their merchant ships."

"Yet you are no longer with Captain Brenin."

Halting, Luke avoided looking at the censure he knew he would find on Mrs. Barnes's face even as he braced himself for her lecture. Everyone in town knew why Noah had relieved Luke of his duties.

But instead, she gave him a gentle smile. "If privateering is where God is leading you, Luke, then by all means, pursue that course."

Luke warmed at her encouragement. "As soon as I get the funds to fix my ship."

"What happened to the money you had in the bank?"

Luke lowered his chin as silence permeated the room.

"Your parents would not approve of your methods of procuring money. And neither does God."

"My parents followed God and look where it got them." Luke gazed at the rippled, pink skin on the palm of his right hand. "I'm doing things differently. I'm doing things my way. Besides, I'm not hurting anyone with my actions."

"Except John."

"He misses me, that's all." Luke shrugged. "I'll make it up to him when I fix my ship. Teach him to sail. We'll become merchants together after the war."

"That would be nice." Yet her tone held no confidence.

Luke parted the curtains. Aside from a few twinkling lights emanating from nearby homes, nothing but an empty, dark void met his gaze. Empty like his many promises to John. "Why do you stay with us, Mrs. Barnes? Surely your skills and experience could land you a better position in a proper home."

"Why, I wouldn't know what to do in a proper home." Her warm smile reached her eyes in a twinkle. "Besides, I love you boys as if I birthed you myself. And I promised your mother I'd look out after you."

Luke made his way back to his chair, drawn away from the darkness by the love in this precious woman's face. "You are family now, Mrs. Barnes. Which is why I allow you to speak to me with such forthrightness." He winked and slid back onto his chair.

Dropping her knitting into her lap, Mrs. Barnes leaned forward and patted his hand as she always did to comfort him. "Love can only be expressed in truth."

The wise adage drifted through Luke, finally settling on his reason. Love and truth. Two things he didn't know much about.

Mrs. Barnes gazed at the red coals. "The doctor came today."

Leaning forward, Luke planted his elbows on his knees.

"He said there shouldn't be any additional malformation due to the rickets."

"That's great news." Luke nearly leapt from his seat, but Mrs. Barnes's somber expression stifled his enthusiasm. "What else? Will the leg ever heal?"

Mrs. Barnes took a sip of her coffee then wrapped her hands around the cup. "In time, perhaps. The doctor cannot say for sure. But he did say John needs a new brace."

Luke nodded, swallowing down resurging fears for his brother's future. A new brace cost money. Money he didn't have.

"He gave me a bill." Anxiety burned in her eyes. "And the rent is due by the end of the week."

"How much?"

"Including the doctor bill, forty-eight dollars."

Luke ground his teeth together. He had only two silver dollars in his pocket—barely enough to provide food for the week. A sudden yearning for rum instead of coffee screamed from his throat. Picking up his mug, he gazed at the brown liquid swirling in his cup. Around and around it went like a brewing tempest at sea.

A tempest that was surely heading his way.

❖ CHAPTER 5 ❖

"Wake up, miss. Wake up." The sweet voice bade entrance into Cassandra's sleep.

She denied it permission.

It rose again. "Wake up, miss." Followed by the shuffle of curtains, then the clack of shutters. A burst of light flooded Cassandra's eyelids. Her ladies' maid began singing a hymn—something about a fount of blessing and streams of mercy.

Cassandra could not relate. She rolled over. "I'm not feeling well, Margaret."

"But Mr. Crane is here, miss."

Struggling to sit, Cassandra squinted into the sunlight blaring through the window. "Oh bother." She rubbed her eyes. "Mr. Crane?"

"Yes. Remember your mother invited him over for coffee and cakes this morning?"

Tossing her quilt aside, Cassandra swung her legs over the edge of her mattress as her stomach turned to lead. Yes, now she remembered. She had wanted to forget—which was probably why she had forgotten.

Swinging open the armoire, Margaret chose a saffron-colored muslin gown then pulled two petticoats from the chest of drawers in the corner, laying them gently on Cassandra's bed. "Come now, miss, surely the man can't be that distasteful?" She planted her fists atop her rounded waist

SURRENDER *the* DAWN

and smiled at Cassandra. Cheeks that were perpetually rosy adorned her plump, cheery face while strands of black hair escaped from beneath her bonnet.

With a groan, Cassandra hopped to the floor, raised her arms, and allowed Margaret to sweep her night rail over her head. "There's nothing wrong with Mr. Crane. I simply do not wish to marry him."

"Well, miss." Margaret folded her sleeping gown. "Perhaps you should give him a chance. He might improve with time."

Grabbing a stool from the corner, Margaret placed it beside Cassandra and stepped onto it, holding up the first petticoat. Few women were shorter than Cassandra's mere five feet. But dear Margaret, at only four foot eight, made up for her small stature with an enormous heart. Cassandra shrugged into her petticoat. "I doubt I'll find anyone as agreeable as your Mr. Dayle."

Margaret's rosy cheeks turned crimson. "Aye, he's a good man, to be sure. But I suspect the Lord has a kindly gentleman chosen just for you."

Cassandra let out an unladylike snort. "God has better things to do than play matchmaker for me, Margaret. And even if I believed He was involved in my life—which I doubt He is—I would prefer He provide me with a privateer rather than a husband."

"Who says He can't do both, miss?"

Twenty minutes later, Cassandra burst into the breakfast room situated at the back of the house. Silverware and crystal decanters sitting atop the table glittered in the sunlight pouring in through the closed french doors. The aroma of butter, spicy meat, and aromatic coffee whirled about her.

Tossing down his serviette, Mr. Crane rose from his seat and smiled her way. Tall, thin, with neatly combed brown hair, the man was not without some appeal. His attire was fashionable and clean, save for the occasional ink smudge on his skin. In addition, his manners were impeccable and his pedigree spotless. As Cassandra's mother loved to remind her at every turn. Speaking of, her mother, dressed to perfection in a cream-colored gown that was crowned at the neck and sleeves with golden ruffles, sat at the head of the table. Cassandra did not miss the scowl on her face. "Mr. Crane has some urgent business to attend to this morning and could wait no longer for you to join us."

"I am glad you proceeded without me." Cassandra circled the table and helped herself to a cup of coffee from the serving table, passing over

37

the odd-smelling battercakes and blackened sausage. Turning, she found Mr. Crane's eyes latched on her. "Do have a seat and finish your meal, Mr. Crane." She took a chair across from him. "I hope you'll forgive me. I fear I had a rather hectic day yesterday."

Children's laughter accompanied by the bark of a dog echoed from the back garden.

Mr. Crane flipped out his coattails and sat. "Of course, Miss Channing. I understand women need their rest."

Cassandra tapped her shoe on the floor and scoured him with a pointed gaze. "I was just telling your mother of the happenings down at the *Register*." He chuckled and lifted a piece of battercake to his mouth. After a moment's pause, his lips twisted into an odd shape as he continued chewing.

Cassandra smiled.

Which he must have taken as encouragement to continue his dissertation of the newspaper business.

Searching the table for sugar, Cassandra sighed when she remembered they'd been out for months. She sipped her bitter coffee, trying to drown out the man's incessant babbling.

Thankfully, after a few minutes, Miss Thain, the cook, entered the room. Eyes downcast, she cleared the plates, bobbing and curtseying at every turn.

Mr. Crane stood. "Would you care for a stroll in the garden, Miss Channing?"

"It's a bit cold, isn't it?" Didn't the man say he had an appointment?

"Don't be silly, Cassandra," her mother said. "I'll have Margaret bring down your cloak." She hurried off, returning in a moment with Cassandra's wool cape.

After sweeping it around her shoulders, Cassandra followed Mr. Crane through the french doors into the back garden. Warm sunlight struck her face even as a chilled breeze sent a shiver through her. Though nearly spring, winter seemed unwilling to release its grip on the city. To her left, Mr. Dayle chipped through the hard dirt in preparation for a vegetable garden. Beside him a small stable housed their only horse. To the right, smoke rose from the smokehouse where Miss Thain made the bread and smoked the meat—or where Miss Thain *attempted* to make bread and smoke meat. A small stone path wound among various trees and shrubs whose green buds were just beginning to peek from within gray branches.

Darlene darted across the path in front of them, Dexter on her heels, and leapt into one of the bushes. "I found you!"

With an ear-piercing scream, Hannah leapt out from among the branches, twigs and lace flying through the air. Darlene barreled into her, and the two girls toppled to the ground in a gush of giggles as Dexter stood over them and barked.

Mr. Crane's face scrunched. "Shouldn't the children be attending their studies?"

Cassandra smiled. What an excellent reason to rid herself of this man's company. "Of course, Mr. Crane. I quite agree. Since we were forced to let the nanny go, I'm afraid many of her duties have fallen to me." Ignoring the look of alarm on his face, she continued, "If you'll excuse me, I should get the girls cleaned up and ready for their lessons with Mrs. Northrop." She faced the gardener. "Mr. Dayle, would you please see Mr. Crane to the door?" Then with barely a glance in Mr. Crane's direction, Cassandra started toward her sisters, who were still tumbling on the grass.

"Oh, no, no, no, my dear." Her mother's shrill voice halted her. The older woman dashed into the yard, gathered the children up like a hen escaping a storm, and ushered them inside the house, shouting, "I'll attend to the girls. Carry on, carry on." Dexter followed after them but a closed door barred his passage. The poor sheepdog slumped to the ground and laid his head onto his front paws.

With a huff and a smile so stiff she felt her face would crack, Cassandra turned back toward Mr. Crane.

He cleared his throat. "Very good. Shall we sit?" He gestured toward an iron bench beneath a maple tree.

Reluctantly, Cassandra sat. The cold bars leeched the warmth from her body. Or was it being so close to Mr. Crane—who took the seat beside her—that caused her to shiver? He wasn't such an unpleasant fellow. In fact, he'd always been quite courteous to her. But something in his eyes, in his subtle gestures, pricked at her distrust.

Or maybe she didn't trust anyone anymore.

"Miss Channing." He rubbed at his fingers as if he'd just noticed the ink stains upon them. "Your mother. . .I mean to say, I have asked. . ." His face reddened and he chuckled. "Do forgive me, Miss Channing. I'm usually not this inarticulate."

Oh, bother. He was going to ask if he could court her! "Do not vex yourself, Mr. Crane. Perhaps we can talk some other time." Cassandra stood, her gaze darting about the yard, seeking escape. He grabbed her wrist and stood. "Please, Miss Channing, don't leave. What I am trying to say is, what I'm making a terrible mess of saying is, I have asked your mother's permission to court you and she has said yes."

The sharp smell of ink bit her nose. Cassandra tugged from his grasp and took a step back. Expectation and vulnerability filled his eyes—so different from the confidence and hint of sorrow burning in Mr. Heaton's eyes the night before. "Mr. Crane. I am deeply flattered. But my mother has misspoken. I am in no position to entertain suitors at this time. With my father dead and my brothers missing, surely you can see that I have more pressing matters to contend with."

He wrung his hands once again. "If that is all that concerns you, Miss Channing, I have your solution. I'd be honored if you'd allow me to assist you with your pressing matters. It is too much for a lady to handle alone."

Cassandra stiffened her jaw. "A lady can handle whatever a man can as long as she is given equal opportunity, sir."

He started to chuckle, but when his eyes locked with hers, his laughter withered on his lips.

Mrs. Northrop's head popped out from around the corner then disappeared. Mr. Dayle, still working in the garden, cleared his throat.

Cassandra studied Mr. Crane. For one fleeting moment she considered asking him to invest her money in a privateer. But that idea dissipated when she realized she'd be forced to not only trust him, but she'd be forever bound to him if he agreed. "I am grateful for your concern, sir, but I cannot allow such kindness when I have nothing to offer in return."

"Oh, but you do, my dear." Tugging on his lacy cravat, he lifted pleading brown eyes to hers.

Cassandra nearly shriveled at the look of desire and desperation within them.

He frowned. "At least give me a reason to continue casting my hope in your direction."

"I can give you no such reason, sir. I can only say that my future is yet unknown."

He lowered his chin. "That alone gives me hope."

Truly? Cassandra sighed. Would nothing put the man off?

"I shall bid you *adieu*, then." Taking her hand in his, he placed a gentle kiss upon it, bowed, then headed toward the house. Mr. Dayle leapt to escort him to the door, giving her a sympathetic look in passing.

Shielding her eyes, Cassandra gazed up at the sun halfway to its zenith. A dark cloud that seemed to come out of nowhere drifted over it, swallowing its bright light and sending a shadow over her face and a shiver down her back. An evil foreboding? For once upon a time, Cassandra's future had appeared bright and glorious, but now it seemed nothing but dark and dismal.

It was this war. This horrendous war. And the bedeviled British who had stolen her father, her brothers, her future, and who now wanted her country. But she could not let them. She must invest in a privateer. It was the only way to ensure her family's future and aid in defeating the tyrants who were intent on stealing her freedom.

Making her way to the solarium at the north side of the house, she opened the door to a burst of warm, humid air, perfumed with gardenias. Her precious gardenias. Oh, how she loved gardening—a hobby that she'd often neglected this past year. Though even without daily care, the plants seemed to thrive. Inhaling their sweet fragrance, she fingered the delicate white petals as she made her rounds, examining each bush, before sitting on the wooden chair at the far end. Reaching underneath a workbench, she pulled out a small chest. Inside was a pipe.

Her father's pipe.

Holding it to her nose, she drew in a deep breath of the sweet, smoky scent that always reminded her of Papa. She closed her eyes and pictured him sitting in his leather chair in the library, smoking his pipe while he read one of his two favorite books—John Moore's *The Practical Navigator* or the Bible.

"Oh Papa, I need you."

She could see him glance up from his book and smile at her as he took the pipe from his mouth. "Ah, my little Cassie cherub. Come see your papa." Dashing to him, she would leap into his outstretched arms and crawl into his lap. During those precious moments snuggled within his warm, strong arms, she had felt safe and loved.

Like nothing could ever go wrong.

"Papa." Tears slid down her face, trickling onto the handle of the pipe. "Why did you leave me? I don't know what to do."

No answer came. Just the chirp of birds outside the solarium and the distant sound of her sisters' laughing. Ah, to be young again—too young to be burdened with cares, too young to be forced into a marriage she didn't want. Cassandra dropped her head in her hands. She could not put her mother or Mr. Crane off for long.

The lingering memory of her father disappeared, leaving Cassandra all alone.

Another man's face filled her vision. A man with hair as dark as the night and beguiling blue eyes.

And she knew she had no other choice.

❖ CHAPTER 6 ❖

Luke waded through the muddy bilge in the hold of the *Agitation*. After hours trying to repair the rent in the hull, he should have grown accustomed to the stench, but it still stung his nose and filled his lungs until it seemed to seep from his skin. Setting down his hammer, he shook the sweat from his hair and scanned the chaotic rubble he called his ship. Even if he could afford building materials, without a crew to assist him, it would take him months to get her in sailing shape. Who was he trying to fool? He snorted. Perhaps his time would be better spent investing his last two silver dollars in a game of Piquet.

As if in response, the ship creaked beneath an incoming wave, and a beam fell from the deck head into the squalid muck with a splash. Luke stared at it, benumbed, wondering if he should bother to pick it up. He needed a drink. Grabbing the lantern, he headed for the ladder when a voice calling his name floated down the rungs as if heaven itself were summoning him home.

Which was not possible. If his time on earth was at an end, it wouldn't be heaven's voice he heard.

"Hello! Mr. Heaton." The angelic call trilled again as a slight footstep sounded above.

Slogging toward the hatch, Luke extracted himself from the mire and vaulted up the ladder, finally emerging from the companionway into a burst of sunlight and an icy breeze that caused him to both squint and shiver.

Setting down the lantern, he stared at the elegantly attired figure before him, delight overcoming his confusion when Miss Channing formed in his vision. The fringed parasol she held above her cast a circle of shade over her saffron gown. An emerald sash glimmered from high about her waist while a woolen shawl crowned her shoulders. A breeze sent her auburn curls dancing about her neck as she stood stiff like an unyielding paragon of Baltimore society, casting her gaze about the wreckage as if afraid to be sullied by her surroundings.

"Oh my." She turned her face away from him and took a step back.

He glanced down at his bare chest and smiled at her reaction. Then his eyes landed on the ship's bulwark undulating beside the dock, and he wondered how she'd managed to jump onto the deck without tripping on the flurry of petticoats peeking at him from beneath her gown. Nevertheless, he would not the curse the fortune that gave him another chance to speak with this enchanting lady.

"Welcome to the *Agitation*, Miss Channing," He gave a mock bow. "To what do I owe the pleasure of your visit?"

"If you'll don a shirt, I shall be happy to tell you." The pomposity in her voice deflated his hope that she made a purely social call.

"I am working, and it is hot belowdecks. If you'll state your business, I'll happily relieve you of my unclad presence." He cringed at his curt tone, yet she deserved it. Standing there with her pertinent chin in the air and her shoulders thrown back as if she did him a service by merely speaking to him.

Not to mention that he still felt the sting of her blunt dismissal the night before.

Rum beckoned to him from the capstan. Licking his lips, Luke brushed past her, noting the hesitation, perhaps fear, flickering on her face. Yet she held her ground. Grabbing the bottle, he took a swig and turned to face her. The pungent liquid did nothing to dull the emotions storming through him.

A ship's bell rang, and the scent of roasted pig floated to his nose from one of the taverns across from the docks. A growl churned in his belly, quickly silenced by another gulp of rum.

Miss Channing cocked her head. A breeze fluttered the fringe on her parasol. "Are you always heavy into your cups this early in the day, sir?"

Luke raked a hand through his hair and gazed at the sun high in the sky. "Aye, as often as the occasion permits."

She huffed her disdain, and an odd twinge of regret stung him. "Forgive my manners, Miss Channing. Would you care to sit?" He gestured toward a crate stacked beside the quarterdeck. "However, I fear all I have to offer you to drink is rum."

"No, thank you, sir. I do not intend to stay long." She shifted her parasol and the sunlight angled over her face, setting her skin aglow like ivory pearls he'd once seen in the Caribbean.

Luke swallowed. He knew she was a beauty, but standing here among the squalor of his ship, she stood out like a fresh flower in a dung heap. He lifted the bottle again to his lips, but thinking better of it, he set it down. "What may I do for you, Miss Channing?"

Emerald green eyes met his. Her gaze dipped then sped away as if she couldn't stand the sight of him.

Luke shifted his wet boots over the planks and snapped the hair from his face. Part of him wanted to toss her from his ship for her insolent attitude. Another part of him didn't want her to ever leave.

A pelican landed on the wheel on the quarterdeck. Letting out a squawk, the bird turned his head and gazed at them with one black eye.

Miss Channing smiled. "Your captain, I presume?"

Luke chuckled. "I'd hire him on the spot if he could get this tub out to sea."

The deck tilted and she stumbled. Leaping for her, Luke grabbed her elbow.

"Thank you." She tugged from his grip and shifted her gaze to the stern of the ship, then over the bay where the sunlight set the rippling waters sparkling like diamonds, then at the taverns lining the docks—anywhere, it seemed, but on him. "I have a proposition for you, Mr. Heaton."

Luke raised his brows as a dozen improper thoughts filled his mind. "Indeed?" He crossed his arms over his chest. "I shall be happy to oblige you."

She faced him now, her eyes widening. "I didn't mean. . . Oh, bother." Lowering her parasol, she snapped it shut, and Luke got the impression she might pummel him with it. No doubt he deserved the beating.

Balancing over the teetering deck, she stepped back from him. "I meant for your *services*, Mr. Heaton."

He grinned again, enjoying the pinkish hue that climbed up her neck and onto her face.

She tapped her right shoe over the planks. "You smell of rum and rot."

"And you smell of gardenias." He eased toward her, drawing in a deep whiff, hoping her sweet scent would chase away the foul air from the hold.

She leveled her parasol at him like a sword, her eyes flashing.

Waves slapped against the hull. A carriage rumbled by on the cobblestone street.

"Are you calling me out, miss?" Luke could barely restrain his laughter. "Parasols at dawn?"

Her eyes narrowed. With a swish of her skirts, she swerved about and headed toward the wharf.

Cursing himself for behaving the cad, Luke started toward her. To apologize, to shower her with flattery, to do anything to keep her from leaving.

She halted and faced him. With a wiggle of her pert little nose, she glanced over the deck. "This is the worst ship I've ever seen."

"Is that what you came to tell me?"

"No, Mr. Heaton, I came here to hire you as a privateer."

❖

Cassandra watched the sardonic gleam in Mr. Heaton's eyes disappear beneath a wave of shock. He ran a hand through the slick black hair hanging to his shoulders and chuckled.

He chuckled.

"I fail to see the humor, Mr. Heaton." She also wished she failed to see his tanned bare chest, gleaming in the sunlight. Though she did her best to avert her eyes, they kept wandering back to his well-shaped biceps, thick chest, and rippled stomach that hinted at his strength beneath. Warmth sped through her as she remembered the ease with which he'd dispatched her assailants the night before.

"My apologies, Miss Channing. I seem to recall how ardently you dismissed my offer last night."

"Things have changed."

"Well, they must have grown quite dire indeed for you to come crawling to the likes of me."

"I never crawl, Mr. Heaton, and my circumstances are none of your affair. Are you or are you not interested in a partnership with me?"

A smile formed on his lips—a disarming smile that no doubt had melted a thousand female hearts. "I am honored that you would ask."

"Save your honor, Mr. Heaton, I had nowhere else to turn."

He held up a hand. "No need to shower me with flattery, miss." His blue eyes gleamed mischief. "But what of your brothers? Have they sent their sister to do a man's work?"

Cassandra ground her teeth together. "I do not need my brothers, nor do I need a man to engage in a business deal any flubberhead could handle."

One side of his mouth curved upward, yet a glimmer of admiration passed through his eyes. "Yes, I can see that."

"As I can see that I'm wasting my time." Grabbing her skirts, she started for the railing.

He clutched her arm. "I agree to your proposal."

Relief sped through her, easing the tight knot between her shoulders. Facing him, she stepped back, putting distance between them. "Very good. I have made arrangements to meet with Mr. Brenin tonight to draw up the necessary papers."

"Lud, such confidence! Were you so sure I would say yes?" He scratched the stubble on his chin and stepped toward her.

She poked him with the tip of her parasol. The man had a way of disregarding propriety's distance, causing her stomach to twitch. "Since you already extended the same offer to me last night, yes, I was. Although I must say, I was unsure whether to accept it."

Even now she wasn't sure she had complete control of her wits.

"What, pray tell, convinced you to accept? My hospitality?" He gripped the bulwark. A chip of rotted wood loosened and fell to the water with a splash. He shrugged. "No doubt it was my fine, seaworthy ship."

Cassandra raised a hand to her mouth to cover her smile even while her insides churned with apprehension. What was she doing? Not only was this man untrustworthy, but this ship would be better off at the bottom of the sea. Yet, hadn't Noah just told her he'd inspected it recently and, aside from some necessary repairs, found it sound?

"Your silence tells all, Miss Channing," he said. "It seems life has cast a cloud of desperation on us both."

"Though I doubt for the same reasons, Mr. Heaton."

His dark, imperious gaze swept over her, making her legs turn to porridge. Confusion spun in her mind. Was she doing the right thing? Should she risk her family's survival on this man?

But what choice did she have?

Yet beyond the roguish facade, a spark of sincerity lingered in his eyes.

"Do you think you can put aside your usual nighttime activities to meet at Mr. Brenin's house tonight? We can sign the papers and I'll see to your payment then."

"I believe I'll have time for both, miss."

"Then I shall see you around seven o'clock."

Stepping up on the bulwarks, he leapt onto the dock then turned to extend his hand.

Against her better judgment, she took it. His strength and warmth seeped though her gloves, sending a jolt up her arm. After he settled her on the wharf, she snagged her hand away, nodded her thanks, and hurried down the dock.

A voice as smooth and as deep as the sea called after her, "Until tonight, Miss Channing."

❖

The teacup rattled on its saucer. Cassandra set it down on the table. Amber liquid sloshed over the rim. "Oh, bother. Please forgive me, Marianne."

Marianne Brenin laid a gentle hand on Cassandra's arm. "Whatever is amiss tonight, Cassandra? You've been a bundle of nerves since you walked in the door."

"Have I?" Cassandra drew a deep breath. Could it be that she was about to give the remainder of her family's money to a man she had no reason to trust? A nervous giggle rose in her throat.

Marianne's brown eyes twinkled from within a face aglow with happiness. Happy indeed. She had a wonderful husband, a beautiful son, and a promising future.

Across the room, Noah tossed seven-month-old Jacob into the air. Giggles bubbled through the Brenin parlor, bouncing off walls and causing all within to grin.

Noah stopped to look at his wife with such deep adoration that Cassandra felt as though she was intruding. She looked away. A yearning tugged at her heart. Would a man ever look at her the way Noah looked at Marianne?

As if lured by her husband's loving gaze, Marianne rose and made her way to him. Swinging an arm over her shoulder, Noah drew her close, swallowing up Jacob between them, and planted a kiss on her forehead.

Marianne ran her fingers over her husband's jaw then suddenly spun around, her face as red as an apple. "Oh, do forgive us, Cassandra. When Noah returns from a long voyage, I often forget when there are other people in the room."

Cassandra couldn't help but smile at her friend's happiness. "I seem to recall you once saying you'd rather boil in oil than marry Noah Brenin."

Noah stared agape at his wife, his lips curving in an incredulous smile. "You don't say?"

Marianne pressed down the folds of her lavender gown. "It was something like that. I truly don't remember."

"Such a thing for Mama to say." Noah tickled Jacob until the boy burst into giggles again.

"We weren't exactly fond of each other back then," Marianne said.

Noah kissed his wife on the cheek and whispered in her ear until her giggles matched their son's.

The loving scene played before Cassandra like a surreal fairy tale. Her mother and father had never expressed such affection, never even offered each other a kind word or loving glance. Until Noah and Marianne had married, Cassandra had not realized that a husband and wife could cherish each other so deeply.

The languid face of Mr. Crane filled her vision and chased her cheery thoughts away. If this investment fell through, she'd be forced to marry him.

Destroying any chance to know the kind of love that filled this home.

Cassandra stood, hoping a turn about the room would settle her nerves, but she bumped into a table, nearly toppling a small carving of a Baltimore clipper. "There I go again." She settled the wooden figure.

Taking Jacob into her arms, Marianne gave Cassandra a curious look as she sat down once again on the settee. "Surely it isn't Mr. Heaton's imminent arrival that has you so. . .hmm. . .so agitated?" She gave a coy smile.

Cassandra clasped her hands together to avoid afflicting further damage. "Don't be absurd, I care not a whit whether Mr. Heaton will be here or not. I simply want this business concluded." Heat flushed her face, and she plucked out her fan. Her eyes took in her reticule lying on the table. "My family's future rests with this investment."

"Are you sure you wish to align yourself with such a man?" Jacob grabbed one of Marianne's curls. Wincing, she extracted it from his chubby fingers.

"Now, love." Noah strode to the service table against the wall and poured himself a sip of Madeira. "Luke is our friend."

"And he is a good friend. But a business partner?" Marianne slid her loose hair behind her ear and clutched Jacob's hands as he reached for it again.

Noah sampled his wine then took a seat beside his wife. "I cannot presume to give you advice in this matter, Cassandra, but I will say that no matter what he may appear to be, Luke is a good man."

Cassandra fanned her face so rapidly, a strand of her hair loosened from its pin. Hadn't she seen some goodness in Mr. Heaton's eyes earlier that day? Something that bade her trust him? "Yet you relieved him of his duty on board your ship?"

"Aye, to teach him a lesson." Noah held his glass of Madeira out of Jacob's reach. "Truth be told, I miss him. He was the best first mate I ever had. But he couldn't control his drinking, and I wanted him to realize how damaging the habit had become."

Cassandra recalled the smell of rum hovering around Mr. Heaton last night and the way he drank on his ship earlier that day. "I fear your plan has not succeeded." Snapping her fan shut, she slid into a chair beside the settee. "Oh, bother. Perhaps I *am* making a mistake."

"Even with his drinking," Noah said, "Luke can handle a ship better than most men I've seen."

Marianne handed Jacob a doll, which he promptly stuffed into his mouth. She lifted her brown eyes, full of concern, to Cassandra. "Have you prayed about this decision?"

"Prayer has never done me much good."

"I used to feel that way." Marianne kissed Jacob's fuzzy head. "I know you've been through a lot. But you must believe God loves you and has all your concerns in His hands."

"Indeed." Noah smiled at his wife. "He's more than proven that to us."

Cassandra was about to say that God seemed to shower some people with blessing while ignoring others, when a knock at the door silenced her.

"Mr. McCulloch," Mr. Sorens, the Brenin butler, announced. Cassandra released a nervous breath as the city customs agent sauntered into the room, wearing a stylish coat of taffeta, a cravat too large for his tiny neck, and brown trousers.

Noah stood to greet him as the butler continued, "And Mr. Luke Heaton."

Dressed in the same black breeches and leather boots he'd been wearing earlier, Mr. Heaton strode into the parlor as if he were the owner of a fleet of ships instead of a lone crumbling heap of wood and tar.

Thank goodness the man had donned a shirt, though the picture of his firm chest was forever imprinted on Cassandra's mind. His eyes locked on hers and remained far too long for her comfort. She shifted her gaze away only to find Marianne and Noah regarding her with suspicion.

Turning, Noah extended his hand. "Good evening, Mr. McCulloch. Thank you for coming."

"My pleasure, sir." Mr. McCulloch's disapproving gaze landed on Cassandra. "I see you have found a captain willing to accept your investment."

"I have, sir." Cassandra thrust out her chin.

"Hmm." He gave Mr. Heaton a cursory glance. "Shall we proceed?"

Jacob looked up from his doll and spotted Mr. Heaton. A huge smile split his mouth as he lifted his chubby hands toward him and strained to be free from his mother's grip. Approaching the child, Mr. Heaton swept him up in his arms and lifted the boy high in the air.

Cassandra stared, dumbfounded, at the sight of their mutual affection.

"Jacob just adores Mr. Heaton," Marianne said with a smile.

Mr. McCulloch cleared his throat. "I have another obligation this evening."

"Absolutely, sir." Noah directed the man to sit then turned to the butler. "Mr. Sorens, will you please take Jacob up to my mother's chamber. She promised to read him a bedtime story."

Mr. Sorens frowned, folding the loose skin beneath his chin, and approached Mr. Heaton, who attempted to untangle the boy's clinging fingers from the collar of his coat. Finally he placed the whining lad into the butler's arms, and with a grunt, the man ambled from the room.

Mr. McCulloch withdrew a stack of papers, a quill pen, and a bottle of ink from his satchel and set them neatly on the table before taking his seat.

Noah sat down once again beside his wife. Mr. Heaton, however, after declining the chair offered him, stood beside Cassandra—so close, she caught his rugged scent of wood, oakum—and rum.

Snapping his attention to one of the documents, Mr. McCulloch rambled through a list of questions directed to Mr. Heaton regarding the tonnage, rig, proposed armament, and number of crew on his vessel. After a bond amount was agreed upon, the customs agent scribbled on the document and gazed at him above the spectacles sliding down his nose. "And the name of the ship, sir?"

"*Agit*—"

"*Destiny*," Cassandra interrupted.

Luke gazed down at her, brow furrowed.

"Well, which is it?" Mr. McCulloch flipped his pocket watch open, glanced at it, then snapped it shut.

Luke made a gesture of deference to her.

"*Destiny*," she stated with finality. She didn't need any further agitation in her life. She needed to create a future, a destiny for her and her family. And to be able to do so on the backs of the British oppressors made it all the sweeter. Opening her reticule, she withdrew the banknote and laid it on the table.

Luke knelt, dipped the pen in ink, and scrawled his signature over the contract then handed the pen to Cassandra.

She poised the pen over the spot awaiting her mark. The quill feathers fluttered beneath her rapid breath. Her heart seized. Jacob's laughter tumbled down from upstairs. Like the countdown to a duel, the grandfather clock in the foyer tick-tocked the final minutes before the deadly shot.

Or the deadly agreement.

Mr. McCulloch sighed.

Cassandra rose to her feet, pen in hand. "Before I sign this contract and hand over my money to you, Mr. Heaton, I have one more condition."

Eyeing her, he folded his arms over his chest. "Which is?"

"That during the time of our partnership, you will cease all drinking and gambling."

❖ CHAPTER 7 ❖

Luke felt his forehead crease. Give up drinking and gambling? Was Miss Channing mad? He didn't know whether to laugh at or berate her foolish request. He chose the former. All eyes shot his way as his chuckle bounced through the parlor—unaccompanied.

Miss Channing's eyes turned to green ice. Luke cleared his throat as Noah arose from his seat. Marianne's brows lifted, and Mr. McCulloch bore his first smile of the evening.

Miss Channing's shoe began a *rat tat tat* on the floor.

"An excellent idea, Miss Channing." Noah tugged on his waistcoat and gave Luke a victorious smile.

Luke growled inside and rubbed his right earlobe. He was tired of people telling him how to live his life. He'd had his fill of that growing up with missionary parents. Their list of oppressive rules still rankled his soul. "Lud, have you lost your senses, miss?"

"No, sir, I have not," Miss Channing retorted. "In fact, I believe I have finally found them. Perhaps you should attempt to find yours."

Luke shifted his gaze over his friends to seek some measure of sympathy, but the satisfied smirk remained on Noah's lips.

"My ability to captain my ship has nothing to do with how I choose to entertain myself." Luke's gaze latched on the banknote on the table. He licked his lips. Thoughts of John and Mrs. Barnes stabbed his conscience.

They'd be out on the street within a fortnight if he did not procure the rent. And no one else was foolish enough to invest their money with him. Yes, *foolish* was the word that came to mind when he gazed into those sparkling emerald eyes—foolish and brave and determined.

And exquisitely beautiful.

"Well, what will it be, Mr. Heaton?" the customs agent said. "I don't have all night." Again, he flipped open his pocket watch and stared at it as if wishing it could transport him to another place.

Miss Channing placed one delicate hand on her hip. "I'll not have you besotted while out at sea, Mr. Heaton, putting the crew, the ship, and my investment at risk."

Luke ground his teeth together. "I assure you, miss, besotted or not, I'm the best captain you'll find in Baltimore." He glanced at Noah. "Present company excluded, of course."

Noah nodded with an amused smile.

"Nevertheless, I'll not have my money squandered on rum and ineptitude." Miss Channing snatched the note from the table. Determination glinted in her eyes.

Luke clenched his fists as the decree built an iron cage around his will. But he had no choice. He couldn't let John down again. He owed him a life, a future.

Not a legacy of failure.

All eyes were on him. Miss Channing held the banknote before her like a gold doubloon before a pirate—like a last sip of rum to a man long deprived of drink.

Which was precisely what it meant to Luke. He shifted his stance. "Very well. I promise not to partake of drink while I'm sailing. But when I come ashore, I will do as I please."

Marianne touched Miss Channing's arm and nodded. "That certainly seems fair enough."

Miss Channing pursed her lips. "No rum on board the ship at all."

"My crew will not like that, miss."

"I care not a whit what your crew likes, Mr. Heaton. Those are my terms."

Luke swallowed and stared down at the woven rug beneath his boots, then across the bemused faces of his friends before finally shifting his gaze to Miss Channing. "Very well, you have my word."

Mr. McCulloch cleared his throat. "Do say you'll sign the papers now, Miss Channing?"

But instead of the satisfied smirk Luke expected to see on her face, she turned to Noah and Marianne with a look of apprehension.

Noah nodded. "Mr. Heaton's word is good, Cassandra."

Luke flinched at the compliment even as his heart swelled. Noah had never expressed such faith in him before. A sudden sense of unworthiness struck him. Could he live up to such an affirmation?

With a sigh of resignation, Miss Channing leaned once again over the document. Her hand trembled, sending the pen's feathers quivering. She didn't trust him. But how could he blame her when he didn't trust himself?

Snatching the signed documents, Mr. McCulloch stuffed them inside his satchel and bid them good evening as he charged out of the parlor, yelling over his shoulder that he would see himself out.

Miss Channing held the banknote out to Luke. He tugged on it. She wouldn't let go. Her gaze skittered from him to Noah, then Marianne. Her chest rose and fell beneath the lace trim of her saffron gown. Finally she relinquished it into his hand, following it with her eyes all the way into Luke's waistcoat pocket.

But what was one thousand dollars to the great Channing merchant business? Surely she had plenty more where that came from.

Grabbing her reticule and fan, Cassandra embraced Marianne, thanked Noah, and headed toward the foyer as if she couldn't get away from him fast enough. She halted at the parlor door and turned to address him. "I should like to come see the ship when she's ready to sail."

Luke gave her a mock bow. "I am at your service."

Miss Channing's eyes narrowed.

"I'll walk you out." Marianne broke the tension, moving to her friend's side and weaving her arm through Cassandra's.

After the ladies departed, Noah gave Luke that same look of reprimand he'd often given him as captain aboard the *Defender*.

Ignoring him, as he always had, Luke sauntered toward the service table and lifted the bottle of Madeira. "May I?"

"No sooner do you promise Miss Channing you'll avoid alcohol, than you run straight for a drink."

"I am not at sea." He lifted his goblet. The sweet wine soured as it slid down his throat.

"Perhaps one day you'll learn to handle life's afflictions without numbing your senses."

Luke raised his brows. "Why would I want to do that?"

"It doesn't take away the pain."

"No, but it dulls it enough to bear."

Noah crossed his arms over his chest. "Do right by her, Luke."

Luke met his stern gaze. He had every intention of honoring their agreement. But what he wouldn't tell his friend was that no matter how hard he tried, Luke could not guarantee that he wouldn't fail her as he had everyone else in his life.

"I probably shouldn't inform you of this, but"—Noah nodded toward the note in Luke's pocket—"that's all the money Miss Channing has left in the world."

Luke shrank back. "What of her brothers? The Channing merchantmen?"

"Gone—both her brothers and the ships." Noah sat back down on the settee and stretched his legs out before him. "The brothers to Canada to fight and the ships sold to provide for the family in their absence. You didn't hear?"

Luke shook his head. "No doubt they'll return soon."

"Perhaps." Noah scratched his jaw. "Perhaps not. Who knows with this mad war?"

Luke poured himself another glass. His gut churned. Taking money from a rich merchant was one thing, but taking all the lady had was quite another. Didn't she know he was not dependable? Of course she did. It was why she had hesitated, why she had demanded he refrain from drink. Luke slammed the Madeira toward the back of his throat. He hated responsibility, avoided it as much as possible. Then why did it always seem to find him?

"You are now the only one keeping Miss Channing and her family from poverty." Noah's sobering declaration rang through the room like a ship's beat to quarters before a battle.

"You should have warned her."

"Perhaps. But I have a feeling God has caused this arrangement with Miss Channing. That in some way, the association will lead you both to your destiny."

With a huff of frustration, Luke faced his friend. "Don't include me in your mad prophecies. There is no divine destiny for men like me."

Noah stretched his arm over the back of the settee and smiled. "We shall see."

Luke tore his gaze from the knowing look in his friend's eyes. Despite all of Luke's past mistakes, his shortcomings and blunders, this time he could not fail.

❖

Gripping the shears, Cassandra strolled through the solarium studying each gardenia plant as she went. It had been two weeks since she'd signed over the last of her family's fortune to the town rogue. She nearly laughed at how silly that statement sounded. She *would* laugh at the absurdity of it all if her stomach weren't tied in knots and her blood ringing in her ears. A condition that had started that morning when a messenger from Mr. Heaton had summoned her to inspect the new privateer, *Destiny*, that afternoon.

Surely it was a simple case of nerves brought on by the critical nature of her investment and not the fact that she would see Luke Heaton within an hour. For the sooner the ship set sail, the sooner her chances of catching a prize and the sooner the money would start flowing in. Then Cassandra could pay off her creditors. She didn't know how much longer Mr. Newman would extend her account at the mercantile or Mr. Sikes at the chandlers or Mr. Roberts at the cobblers or if Mr. Kile at the Bank of Baltimore would call in the loan she took out against their property. If any of them demanded payment before her investment with Mr. Heaton paid off, her family would be on the streets.

Stopping, she clipped a dead branch from one of the plants then stooped to cut off a faded flower. She wished she could rid herself of her problems as easily. Drawing a deep whiff of a fresh blossom, she brushed her cheek over its soft petals. The sweet fragrance filled her lungs, luring her eyes closed as she dreamed of happier days when her father was alive and both her brothers were home. Gregory, two years her senior, had inherited their father's flaming red hair and the temper to go with it. But he always came to Cassandra's defense on any issue and never allowed gentlemen callers unless he'd first scrutinized them at length. And Matthew, sweet docile Matthew, who, though only a year older than Cassandra, possessed the wisdom of an ancient scholar and the kindness of a saint. How many evenings had they curled up together in her chamber as children with a candle and a copy of their favorite book, *Keeper's Travels in Search of His Master*, reading late into the night of grand adventures in foreign lands?

The loud clank of the solarium door followed by childish squealing jarred Cassandra from her memories. She opened her eyes to a flash of blond hair and a flutter of petticoats as Darlene darted past her then wove in between a row of plants and disappeared. Hannah barreled in after her, her wide blue eyes scanning the room.

"Darlene, Hannah!" Margaret's voice flew in from outside.

Setting down the shears, Cassandra fisted her hands at her waist. "Now, you girls know you're not allowed in here."

Giggles burst from the far corner. Ignoring Cassandra, Hannah dashed toward them. Dexter loped into the solarium fast on the girl's heels as she threaded in between two of Cassandra's newly planted sprouts. The clumsy sheepdog bumped into a wooden table. The pot sitting atop it teetered. Cassandra stretched out her hands toward it as a scream stuck in her throat.

Dexter's bark joined screeching laughter from the far end of the solarium as the pot crashed to the floor, sending chips of clay, clods of dirt, and the small plant shooting over the stone tiles.

Cassandra halted. She heard Margaret's gasp behind her. Silence swept the children's laughter away, replaced by the patter of feet and paws as the two girls and Dexter slowly emerged from behind a row of plants, a look of dread on their faces.

"Oh miss, I'm so sorry." Margaret knelt by the broken pot and began to pick up the pieces. "We're sorry, Cassie," Darlene said, her chin lowering.

Hannah stuck her thumb into her mouth and nodded as her eyes filled with tears.

Cassandra laid a hand on Margaret's arm. "Never mind that now. I'll take care of it." She turned to chastise the girls, but Darlene grabbed Hannah and darted out the door, leaving only Dexter to take the brunt of her anger. He gave a rueful whine.

Margaret's pudgy cheeks reddened. "I was trying to collect them for their studies, miss, but they got away from me."

"It's quite all right, Margaret." Cassandra sighed. "I don't believe General Smith himself could corral those girls."

As Margaret's laughter filled the room, Cassandra glanced out the mist-covered windows. "Where is Mrs. Northrop?"

"In the house." Margaret clutched Dexter's collar and led him out the door. "Which reminds me, Mr. Crane arrived just a moment ago and your mother is asking for you." Sympathy deepened her tone.

A sour taste filled Cassandra's mouth, and she doubted it was due to the overcooked oatmeal she'd had for breakfast. "Well, I simply can't stay and socialize. I'm meeting Mr. Heaton at his ship in an hour."

"Indeed? Are you sure it's safe to be alone with him?" Margaret teased.

"Of course. He's my new captain. I must trust him." She had to trust him.

She didn't trust him.

"Besides, we won't be alone. His crew is there." Cassandra stepped out and closed the door.

"I shall pray for your safety, miss, and for God's wisdom," Margaret said.

"Thank you, Margaret. I suppose your prayers couldn't hurt." Though she doubted they'd do much good either.

Back in the house, an odd smell coming from the kitchen curled Cassandra's nose. Waving it away, she drifted past the library on her way up to her chamber. Whispered voices drew her gaze into the room where she spotted Mr. Crane and Mrs. Northrop, their heads bent together in some sort of parley. What on earth would Mr. Crane have to say to the housekeeper? Cassandra halted by the edge of the doorway to listen, but she couldn't make out their words. What did it matter, anyway? She should thank the housekeeper for keeping the man occupied and away from Cassandra. And perhaps giving her a chance to sneak out without speaking to him.

Hurrying up the stairs to her chamber, she checked her reflection in her dressing glass, donned her gloves, grabbed her fur-lined pelisse and parasol, and tried to make a quick exit out the front door before her mother noticed.

"You would simply not believe what this war has done for newspaper sales." Mr. Crane's tone blared like a dissonant trumpet from inside the parlor. "Our sales have increased a hundredfold. Everyone is scrambling for recent news from the battlefronts."

Halfway across the open doors, Cassandra tiptoed onward, not daring to peek inside the room lest she draw attention her way.

A teacup rattled on a saucer. "Oh Cassandra, dear. Where are you going? Mr. Crane has come to call on you."

Cassandra closed her eyes, silently chastising herself for not leaving by the back door. Pasting on a smile, she spun around. "I have an errand to run, Mother." She nodded toward Mr. Crane, who had risen from his seat with a rather baffled look on his face. "Mr. Crane, how nice to see you."

"Alone?" he asked incredulously.

"Yes," Cassandra replied, stepping just inside the room. "Mr. Dayle is otherwise occupied and it is broad daylight. I will be quite safe, I assure you. Now, if you don't mind." Cassandra turned to leave.

"Don't be ridiculous, dear." Her mother's harsh tone turned her back around. "You are being quite rude. Come and sit for a while."

"I fear I cannot, Mother. I have an appointment."

"With whom?"

Cassandra bit her lip. She had not told her mother of her investment yet. Had not wanted to vex her overmuch. But perhaps this would be the best time. With company present, her mother would surely not dive into her usual hysterics, and perhaps Mr. Crane could help allay her fears.

"With Captain Heaton," Cassandra blurted out. "I've invested in his privateer and they are to set sail on the morrow."

Mr. Crane flinched.

Her mother's jaw fell open and appeared to be stuck in that position. Leaning back on her chair, she threw a hand to her forehead. "Tell me you didn't."

Cassandra took a deep breath. "I did. And it will pay off, you'll see. I guarantee we shan't have any further troubles." Yet she heard the uncertainty in her own voice.

"Mr. Luke Heaton?" Mr. Crane seemed to have found his voice, although it came out slow and garbled. "The scoundrel Heaton? The man who drinks and gambles his money away?"

Cassandra lifted her chin. "Yes, that's the one."

Her mother picked up the small bell from the table beside her and rang it profusely. "I need some tonic."

Straightening his gray waistcoat, Mr. Crane approached Cassandra wearing the look of a schoolmaster instructing a foolish child. "This is quite preposterous, Miss Channing. Why would you go to such lengths when the solution to your problems stands before you?"

Cassandra forced a smile. "You are too kind, sir, but as I said before, I cannot in good conscience accept your offer."

"Stubborn girl." Her mother rang the bell again. Its shrill *ding ding ding* hammered on Cassandra's guilt. "Do you see why my nerves are strung tight, Mr. Crane? Perhaps you can talk some sense into her?"

Mrs. Northrop appeared in the doorway. Her eyes locked with Mr. Crane's before she sped to her mistress, bottle of tonic in hand.

As she poured a splash into the elderly woman's tea, Mr. Crane eased his fingers over his neatly combed hair. "Well, the least I can do is escort you to your appointment."

"That isn't necessary." Cassandra moved to her mother and planted a kiss on her cheek. "I shall be back within the hour, Mother."

Picking up her cup, the older woman sipped her tea then waved Mrs. Northrop off, avoiding Cassandra's gaze and instead seeking out Mr. Crane. "Yes, sir. Please do accompany my daughter. With your business sense, perhaps you can assess the terrible risk she has placed on our entire family and determine some way of escape. . . ."

"But, Mother. . ."

"I insist." Her mother slammed down her cup. Some of the golden tea sloshed over the rim and pooled in the saucer.

Cassandra's stomach sank. "Very well."

Grabbing his hat from the sofa, Mr. Crane set it atop his head. "It will be my pleasure."

Cassandra gripped her parasol and followed him out the door. *Oh, bother.* Mr. Crane and Mr. Heaton together in the same place?

It was going to be a very interesting afternoon.

❖ CHAPTER 8 ❖

Spreading the chart over the binnacle, Luke pointed at the spots where various shoals and sandbars transformed the Chesapeake Bay into a dangerous maze.

Biron Abbot shook his head. "It's not the shoals that bother me, Cap'n. It's those bloody British. How are we to slip past twenty of His Majesty's finest ships?"

Luke gazed up at the gray clouds rumbling across the sky. The welcome sting of rain filled his nostrils. "You're the praying man, my friend. Why don't you ask your God to keep this storm up through the night? Or better yet, pray for a fog so thick not even the Royal Navy will dare to stir a wave to chase us." Luke chuckled.

"Aye," young Samuel Rogers interjected from Luke's other side. "And if they should spot us, we can batter them with grapeshot and sail away 'fore they can catch us, eh, Cap'n?"

Luke couldn't help but smile at his new quartermaster. A few golden whiskers on the boy's chin joined his stiff stance as proud evidence of his budding manhood. At only seventeen, the boy had more experience at sea than most of the men Luke had managed to recruit—*bribe* would have been a more fitting word. Yet the lad's experience had not tempered his youthful enthusiasm and courage. Qualities much desired in a successful privateer.

Although at the moment, Samuel behaved more like a midshipman as he stood at attention before Luke. Old habits died hard, Luke supposed, for the lad had served aboard the USS *Syren* for eight years.

"A tempting idea," Luke replied. "Yet I have no desire to engage an enemy warship." No, he'd already attempted that foolhardy feat when he'd been Noah's first mate on board the *Defender*. And they'd barely escaped with their lives. An act of God, Noah had called it. Luke shook his head. More like good fortune that the USS *Constitution* had been there to pick them out of the sea. Good fortune that always seemed to come Noah's way.

But never Luke's.

No, Luke would not count on God or good fortune but on his skill and determination. It was all he had left.

From his spot on the quarterdeck, he surveyed his ship, where most of his crewmen were hard at work putting the finishing touches on the vessel: scrubbing the newly caulked deck, polishing the brass, tarring the lines, greasing the mast. Aside from young Samuel, Luke had been unable to convince any decent sailors to join him. Consequently, he had resorted to hiring criminals, drunks, and gamblers—men just like him. He only hoped they'd perform with bravery and skill when the occasion called for it. But, perhaps like him, they saw privateering as their last chance to turn their life around, to make a fortune and a respectable name for themselves.

To stop a legacy of failure.

A stream of men carried crates and barrels filled with supplies for the journey, from the wharf onto the main deck then down the open hatch into the hold. Luke's gaze landed on two crewmen standing at the prow of the ship, talking—the two men he'd asked to fix the loose railing on the starboard waist.

"Biron, order those men back to work at once."

"Aye, aye, Cap'n." Biron leapt down the quarterdeck ladder with more agility than his fifty-two years should have allowed and began barking orders.

A chilled wind rose from the bay and swirled about Luke, dragging down his spirits. Thunder growled in the distance as the weight of responsibility sank heavy upon his shoulders. Not only was this his first voyage as captain with ultimate authority on board the ship, but it was a voyage in which he must succeed.

For Miss Channing's sake, for John's, and for his own.

Luke folded up the chart and handed it to Samuel. "Take this below to my cabin."

"Aye, Cap'n." The boy saluted.

"No need to salute me, Sam. You are no longer in the navy."

He saluted again then laughed at his own mistake before darting away.

Dark clouds stole the remainder of the sun, portending a storm that would bring Luke the cover he so desperately needed to slip past the British blockade. Though his ship had been ready for two days, he and his crew had been forced to wait idly in the bay while a fortune beckoned to him from the sea. So, when Luke had spotted a tempest brewing on the horizon that morning, he thought it best to summon Miss Channing for her requested inspection. Not that he hadn't wished to summon her before. In fact, he'd been unable to get the infernal woman out of his thoughts since that fateful night when he'd saved her from those ruffians. He glanced over at the spot where he'd first seen her across Pratt Street hurrying past the Hanson warehouse. A vision of her pummeling one of the scoundrels with a brick filled his mind, and he couldn't help but smile. Yet as he continued to stare at the spot, his smile sank into a frown as another figure emerged—a tall man dressed in a dark-blue tailcoat with red collar and cuffs and a black crown shako on his head—marching straight toward Luke as if he were marching across a battlefield.

Luke cursed under his breath. Lieutenant Abner Tripp. What did the man want now? Glancing around for a bottle of rum, Luke cursed again when he remembered he hadn't brought any on board. With a groan, he made his way to the main deck just as the lieutenant halted on the wharf beside the ship, his fists stiff by his side, and his narrowed eyes seething at Biron, who was demanding to know his business.

"What is the meaning of this, Heaton?" Lieutenant Tripp shouted.

Luke snapped the hair from his face and approached the port railing. "The meaning of what?" He gave him a cocky smile.

"The meaning of using my ship as a privateer."

"Your ship?" Luke rubbed the stubble on his jaw. "If I recall, I won her from you in a game of Piquet."

Swerving about, Biron shook his head. No doubt as a warning for Luke to stop goading the man.

Which Luke would be happy to do if the rodent would simply leave.

Instead, the lieutenant took up a pace along the wharf, glancing over the ship's masts, sails, rigging, at the crew working, and finally landing on one man in particular who hung over the port side, painting the new name on her bow.

"You called her *Destiny*? Bah!" He ceased his pacing and gripped the pommel of the army saber hanging at his side. "You have no destiny, sir, but to die penniless and alone in your own besotted vomit." Spit flew from his mouth.

Luke's hand twitched beside his cutlass, longing to draw it once again on this buffoon. "I would watch what you say, Lieutenant. My temper has limits. Surely you have not come to receive a twin on your other cheek?"

Chortles burst behind Luke as a spike of white lightning lit up the sky.

Lieutenant Tripp rubbed the pink scar angling over the left side of his face, opened his mouth to say something, then seemed to think better of it.

Luke crossed his arms over his chest. "I would assume you'd be happy to see your former ship put to good use against our common enemy."

"I will only be happy, sir, to see you and it at the bottom of the ocean. You stole my ship and all my money." Wind tore over the lieutenant, fluttering the fringe of the gold epaulette capping his left shoulder.

"Won," Luke corrected him as the ship rose over an incoming wave.

"My fiancée left me."

"I fear I cannot take credit for that, Lieutenant."

More laughter sprang from behind Luke. Even Biron's face cracked into a smile.

Lieutenant Tripp's long, pointy nose seemed to grow in length, and his hand dropped to his saber once again. "I demand satisfaction, sir."

Silence overtook the ship as the crew stopped their work and gazed expectantly at the brewing altercation.

"Now? When I'm ready to set sail?" Luke smiled. He had no desire to further humiliate this man. Why didn't the beef wit simply count his losses and go?

A maroon hue, as red as the plume fluttering atop Lieutenant Tripp's shako, crept across his face. "So, it's true what they say then?"

"And what is that?"

"That without your rum, you are a coward. A miserable sot who preys

65

on innocent women and cheats at cards." His thin lips began to tremble. "A coward who sat back whilst his parents were butchered by savages."

Fury seared through Luke. His vision blurred. In two strides, he flew up on the bulwarks and leapt onto the dock. His crew tossed cheers behind him. All except Biron, who shouted for him to stop.

Fear flooded the lieutenant's eyes. He took a step back. Luke clutched the hilt of his cutlass, intent on teaching the man another lesson, when the flutter of a lacy parasol floating atop a blue muslin gown caught the corner of his eye. Drawn to the vision like a drowning man's glimpse of land, he halted.

Miss Channing strolled down the wharf, a sour-faced dandy at her side.

Relief softened Lieutenant Tripp's features. He glanced over his shoulder at her, then back at Luke, his face as hard as granite once again.

His right eyelid took on an odd twitch before he spun on his heels and marched down the wharf, causing it to wobble beneath his anger. He halted before Miss Channing and her gentleman dandy.

Luke grabbed the hilt of his sword again and started for them. If Tripp dared to lay a hand on her. . .

❖

No sooner had Cassandra turned down the dock where *Destiny* was anchored than she spotted Mr. Heaton and another man in a military uniform engaged in what appeared to be a heated battle. Dressed in black breeches stuffed within tall Hessian boots, a white shirt, and black waistcoat, Mr. Heaton stood before his ship as if he, alone, would defend the vessel to his death. Cassandra's heart jolted at the sight of him then seized when she saw him grip his cutlass and start for the man. But then his eyes locked upon hers and he stopped. A smile curved his lips, and he bowed toward his adversary as if they were the best of friends.

The man, whom Cassandra could now see was a lieutenant in the army, charged her way. Oblivious to all, Mr. Crane continued the incessant chattering he'd smothered her with since they'd left the house, only ceasing when the lieutenant halted before them and cleared his throat.

"Are you Miss Channing?" The lieutenant's face was pink and bloated, and his eyes skittered here and there, unable to focus.

"I am."

"I understand you have invested in this privateer?"

Cassandra's gaze shot behind the man to Mr. Heaton, who stormed toward them as if he'd changed his mind about not killing the lieutenant.

The man glanced over his shoulder. His eyelid twitched. "You have made a grave error, miss."

Mr. Crane chuckled. "As I've been trying to tell her—"

"Mr. Heaton is a failure and his privateer will be a failure as well," the lieutenant interrupted then straightened his coat and marched away before Cassandra could answer him, leaving ill tidings swirling in his wake.

Cassandra shuddered, wondering why he would say such a thing. His words of doom thundered over her, much like the dark clouds churning above, making her feel like a little girl alone in the midst of a storm—a storm that could sweep her and her family out to sea.

A growl bellowed from the sky in confirmation of her fears.

Until she turned to face the confident look on Mr. Heaton's face. Pushing Mr. Crane aside, he took up a stance between her and the departing lieutenant. "Did he harm you, Miss Channing?"

A sense of being protected overcame her—a feeling she hadn't felt in quite some time. It warmed her from head to toe. "Why, no."

"He merely told her the truth." Mr. Crane's chortle spun Mr. Heaton around. He eyed the man as if he were a bothersome gnat. "And you are. . . ?"

"Forgive me," Cassandra interjected. "This is Mr. Milton Crane. He is the proprietor of the *Register*."

"Hmm," Mr. Heaton huffed. "You are too early, sir."

"Early?" Mr. Crane's face scrunched.

"To report on *Destiny*'s outlandish success." Luke faced Cassandra and winked. She felt her knees weaken. Then he waved off Mr. Crane, saying, "Come back in a month," before he proffered his elbow to Cassandra.

Shifting her parasol to hide her grin, she accepted Mr. Heaton's arm.

Mr. Crane's footsteps followed them. "You mistake me, sir. I am escorting Miss Channing."

As they approached the ship, Cassandra spotted a man hanging over the bow, putting the finishing touches on the word *Destiny* painted in bright blue on the hull.

"I see you have come armed," Mr. Heaton said.

"Mr. Crane?" Cassandra said. "My mother insisted he accompany me."

"I was referring to your parasol, miss." His dark eyebrows rose above a grin. "Him"—he gestured over his shoulder—"I can handle."

Cassandra's giggle was instantly silenced when she halted and found the eyes of at least two dozen rather shabby-looking men latched upon her from the deck of the *Destiny*. Swallowing down a lump of unease, she threw back her shoulders. These men were in her employ and the sooner she made that clear, the better.

After leaping onto the ship, Mr. Heaton turned to assist her. Ignoring his hand, she closed her parasol, clutched her gown, and stepped onto the teetering deck. She would show this man and his crew that she was not some delicate flower to be plucked and squashed. Yet even as she lifted her chin in victory, the deck tilted and she stumbled. Mr. Heaton gripped her elbow to steady her.

Refusing to look at the grin that was surely on his face, Cassandra turned to inform Mr. Crane that he need not wait for her when he tumbled onto the deck behind her and took his spot at her side.

An older gentleman approached them.

"Mr. Biron, assemble the men, if you please," Mr. Heaton ordered.

"Aye, aye, Cap'n." The man blew a whistle, sending the men on deck and the ones pouring from the hatches scrambling to form a straight line from bow to stern.

While she waited, Cassandra took the opportunity to study the ship. The chips in the bulwarks had been repaired, the wooden deck had been stripped and recaulked, the broken spoke on the capstan was restored, lines were coiled neatly beside belaying pins, and the brass atop the railheads, wheel, and belfry gleamed. She gazed upward to see that one of the sails had been replaced with fresh canvas. The scent of tar and wood filled her lungs.

She dared a glance at Mr. Heaton standing before his men, fists at his waist, dark hair blowing in the breeze, his shoulders stretched with the authority of a captain. She couldn't recall smelling rum on him as he'd escorted her to the ship. Could it be the man intended to keep his promise? For the first time, Cassandra allowed a smidgeon of hope to form within her that Mr. Heaton might prove his reputation wrong and become a great privateer.

As if in defiance of that hope, an icy wind tainted with the sting of rain whirled around her, and Cassandra drew her pelisse tighter about her neck.

"Gentlemen, may I introduce to you Miss Cassandra Channing," Mr. Heaton shouted after all the men had assembled. "She is half owner of this privateering venture."

Crane snorted then coughed into his hand.

"And"—Mr. Heaton's dark gaze snapped to Mr. Crane—"she is here to inspect our fair vessel."

Then leading her to the bow, he proceeded to introduce each crewman. Some barely glanced at her, their faces reddening at the introduction. Others brazenly took her in as if she were a sweet pastry—their salacious scrutiny promptly squelched by one look from Mr. Heaton. The stench of unwashed bodies permeated the air, but she resisted the urge to draw a handkerchief to her nose.

One man dared to spit to the side and say, "Bad luck to have a woman investor."

"Indeed." Mr. Crane's annoying voice buzzed from behind Cassandra.

Ignoring him, Mr. Heaton started for the sailor as if he intended to shove him back, but Cassandra stayed him with a touch to his arm. "Well, I hope to prove you wrong, Mr. Nelson." She smiled, and the sailor seemed befuddled for a moment before he smiled back.

"And this is Biron Abbot, my first mate." Luke stopped before the older gentleman, a rough but kindly looking man who reminded Cassandra of Reverend Drummond. He dipped his gray head. "A pleasure, miss."

The ship lurched over a wave, and she pressed the tip of her parasol onto the deck to keep her balance.

Mr. Heaton moved to the next man. "And Mr. Joseph Keene, my boatswain."

Cassandra nodded at the handsome man who was at least fifteen years her senior. Dressed in colorful silk and lace, he looked more like a pirate than a sailor. His disarming smile, coupled with the mischievous twinkle in his eye, did nothing to dissuade her opinion. He took her hand and placed a kiss upon it as the jewels on his fingers glinted in the daylight.

Mr. Heaton pushed between them, breaking the contact, and moved on to the next man. "Mr. Zachary Ward, my gunner."

Completely bald to the top of his head, yet with a veritable lion's mane flowing down the back, the man presented such an odd sight that Cassandra would have laughed if he wasn't looking at her with hatred burning in his eyes.

She took a deep breath and shifted her parasol into her other hand.

She would not let him intimidate her. "Are you familiar with cannons, Mr. Ward?"

"Aye, miss. Was in the American navy, I was."

"Indeed, why are you still not enlisted?"

"Cashiered, miss, for blasphemy and drunkenness." His tone held no remorse.

Cassandra turned to Mr. Heaton. "You seem to be among friends."

A hint of a smile played on his lips.

"Of all the. . . ," Mr. Crane announced with alacrity. "This is preposterous. These men are not fit to sail this ship. Surely you can see that, Miss Channing."

Ignoring him, Cassandra studied the gunner. "But I sense you have changed your ways, Mr. Ward?" Her approving tone stripped the defensive wall away.

"That I have, miss." He dipped his head.

She leaned toward him with a smile. "Good for you, sir."

"This is ludicrous," Crane whispered over her shoulder. "These men are wastrels and thieves. Why, they'll do nothing but rob you blind."

Cassandra cringed. Though she tried to prevent Mr. Crane's words from affecting her, they crouched around her budding hope like a pack of wolves around a newborn lamb. Mainly because there was truth in his assessment. Indeed, these men were not the finest gentlemen she'd encountered—probably not the finest sailors either—but Mr. Heaton was the captain and for now she must trust his judgment.

Luke scowled. "The lady has a mind of her own, Mr. Crane. Please allow her to use it."

Cassandra shot him a curious gaze. She had never heard a man declare such a thing. Did he mean it, or was he simply trying to slip into her good graces? Yet when his eyes locked with hers, they held understanding, not insincerity.

Turning his back to Crane, Mr. Heaton took Cassandra's arm and moved her to the next man. "Mr. Samuel Rogers, my quartermaster."

The young boy's wide grin reminded Cassandra of her brother Matthew. Nothing pretentious, no pomposity or hidden meaning lurked in his expression. His long sandy hair was pulled behind him in a tie, and his sparkling blue eyes held a thirst for adventure.

"Aren't you a bit young to be going on such a dangerous journey?" she asked him.

"No, miss. I was born on a ship. Spent me whole life in the navy till I quit last year to become a privateer."

Cassandra couldn't help but admire his enthusiasm—the same she'd seen in her brothers before they'd left to fight in Canada. Did fate have the same thing in store for this young man? "But doesn't war frighten you?"

"No, miss. I love fightin'. I hope to be a pirate someday."

Thunder rumbled in the distance.

"A pirate. Good heavens!" Mr. Crane chortled. "Surely you've heard enough, Miss Channing."

Cassandra spun around. "I have not, sir. If you have, I suggest you leave."

A gust of wind tossed his neatly combed hair into a spin even as his mouth tightened into a thin line. "I am only looking out for your interests."

"Look out for them in silence, if you please." Cassandra turned around to find Mr. Heaton gazing at her with a mixture of ardor and amusement.

He led her onward. "And lastly, Mr. Nyle Sanders, our purser."

With tablet in hand, the small man—who, with his pointy nose and tiny dark eyes hidden behind a pair of spectacles, reminded Cassandra of a rat—greeted her kindly, with nary a glance her way.

"Dismissed!" Mr. Abbot shouted. Cassandra jumped at the abrupt command then watched as the men dispersed as quickly and haphazardly as they had assembled, their bare feet pounding over the wooden deck.

Mr. Crane grabbed Cassandra's arm and drew her to the side. "Miss Channing. Please end this charade. Anyone can see that this is nothing but a ship of villains and reprobates. Do not be so naive to assume you'll see a penny's return on your investment. I urge you to demand your money back and flee this ship of doom at once."

❖

Luke grabbed the hilt of his sword, longing to slice off Mr. Crane's annoying tongue. It was either that or Luke feared he might toss the man overboard. This dandy was nothing but a puffed-up, implacable fribble.

"Too late, Mr. Crane." Miss Channing released a sigh of annoyance. "The money has already been spent. So, you see, your complaints do nothing but cause me discomfort."

71

"Well, I certainly did not mean. . . ," Mr. Crane stuttered. His cheeks swelled, but before he could finish, Miss Channing swept her pretty face toward Luke, her auburn curls dancing over the fur trim of her pelisse.

And with her sweet smile, all thoughts of murdering Mr. Crane vanished.

In fact, Luke had been amazed at how well she handled herself in front of the motley group of vagrants he called a crew. About as civilized as a band of hungry bears, they were likely to frighten even the most stalwart of women. Yet Miss Channing had greeted each one of them as if they were members of the town council. She neither shrank back from their licentious glances nor took offense at their snide comments. Lud, instead of passing them by with a lift of her nose as he had expected, she'd even asked them questions that went beyond her interest in them as an investment.

"Will you show me the armament you purchased, Mr. Heaton?" Her smile reached her eyes, and at that moment he believed he'd show her anything she wished.

"Armament, ha!" Mr. Crane tugged on his cravat. "I doubt you could have procured anything decent for this waterlogged tub."

Luke gave the man one of his most imperious gazes, the kind that sent men cowering in the taverns. It had the same effect on Mr. Crane. Clearing his throat, he moved to the other side of Miss Channing.

Luke waved at the carronades mounted on the starboard railing. "As you can see, I purchased eight carronades, four on each side." He pointed toward the other group lining the port side of the ship. "And one lone nine at the prow."

"Is that all?" Mr. Crane snorted with disdain. "Hardly enough firepower to catch a fishing boat, let alone a merchantman."

Enough was enough. Luke's gaze landed on the broken railing, and he found himself suddenly glad the lazy crewmen had not followed his orders to fix it.

"No, Mr. Crane. We also installed two eighteen pounders below-decks. You can see their muzzles jutting out from the gun ports if you look over the starboard railing."

"Eighteen pounders! Preposterous! On a schooner?" Mr. Crane snorted.

"See for yourself." Luke shrugged one shoulder and gestured with his head toward the railing.

Stomping toward the spot, Mr. Crane peered over the edge. "You taunt me, sir. There is nothing there."

Miss Channing's brow furrowed.

"Of course there is." Taking a spot beside the buffoon, Luke pointed over the side. "Can't you see them?"

Mr. Crane leaned on the faulty piece of railing. With an exasperated sigh, he angled the top half of his body over the side. *Crack! Snap!* A chunk of the wood broke from the railing and dropped into the bay.

Mr. Crane's arms flailed before him. His eyes bulged. He let out a broken shriek as he toppled over and splashed into the dark water below.

❖ CHAPTER 9 ❖

C assandra stepped inside the captain's cabin and took in the masculine furnishings. A sturdy oak desk guarded the stern windows. Charts, a logbook, quill pens, a quadrant, and two lanterns spread across a top that was marred with divots and stains. Rows of books stood at attention on two shelves to the right, a mahogany case filled with weapons lined the opposite wall, and one velvet-upholstered chair stood before the desk. The smell of tar and whale oil and Mr. Heaton filled her nose as he ducked to enter the room behind her. Mr. Abbot followed on his heels, wearing a smirk that had lingered on his lips ever since Mr. Crane had fallen overboard.

And though Cassandra tried to stifle her laughter, another giggle burst from her mouth at the vision of Mr. Crane being pulled from the bay by a fisherman. Afterward, he had simply stood there, dripping like a drowned possum and shaking his fist in the air before he turned and marched away.

"You really should have tossed a rope over for him." Cassandra turned to face Luke.

A mischievous glint flashed in his blue eyes. "Why? He had overstayed his welcome."

"You are incorrigible," she huffed.

"So I am told."

Mr. Abbot chuckled. "I fear you have made another enemy."

"A growing list." Mr. Heaton rubbed his right palm. Pink scars lined the skin, making Cassandra wonder what had happened to cause them.

"The men are asking when we will set sail," Mr. Abbot said, lingering at the open door. Thunder shook the ship as the *tap tap* of rain pounded on the deck above.

"As soon as it's dark." Mr. Heaton stomped toward the shelves as if looking for something then halted and turned back around with a sigh. "I have an errand to run first."

"What errand? We have all our supplies loaded." Mr. Abbot tugged on his red neckerchief and glanced at Cassandra. "Shouldn't we leave while the storm is upon us?"

"I must say good-bye to someone."

Cassandra's gaze shot to Mr. Heaton. The way he'd said the words with such affection, it had to be a woman. She knew of his reputation. Of course a man like Mr. Heaton would have a love interest in town, perhaps many. Then why did her insides burn at the thought?

Sitting on the edge of his desk, Mr. Heaton crossed his arms over his chest. "Biron, order the men to repair that railing at once."

Cassandra flinched. She opened her mouth to ask the elderly man to stay—to not leave her alone with this rake—but he had already slipped into the companionway. The thud of his boots soon faded beneath the caress of the waves against the hull.

She should leave as well. She had seen the entire ship and now the captain's cabin. There was no reason for her to stay.

Except for the pull of Mr. Heaton's eyes as he allowed his gaze to wander over her. Not in a bawdy way as his crew had. But as someone staring at an object of great beauty that he could never possess.

No one had ever looked at her that way before. And it made her feel, all at once, like both a princess and a prig. As if she were precious and yet too pretentious to touch. She approached the chair, putting it between herself and Mr. Heaton, and ran her hand along the carved back. "I suppose Mr. Crane deserved the embarrassment. But do forgive him, Mr. Heaton. I fear it is only jealousy that drives his peevish behavior."

"So, he has some claim on you?"

She pursed her lips, shocked at his bold question. "I don't see how that's any business of yours."

He grinned then gestured for her to sit.

"No, I cannot stay. I should not stay." She glanced at the door, thankful Mr. Abbot had left it open.

Standing, Mr. Heaton approached her until only the chair filled the space between them. A space that instantly heated and crackled beneath some unimaginable force. "Do you fear being alone with me, Miss Channing?" A mischievous glint flashed in his eyes.

Thunder growled. Though he towered over her, she did her best to lift her gaze to meet his. "Should I?" Yet she knew the tremble that coursed through her had nothing to do with fear.

The sheen over his eyes softened, and he raised a hand to touch her face. Cassandra leapt back with a gasp.

He frowned. "I am many things, Miss Channing, but I would never hurt a woman. In fact, I am quite fond of women."

Cassandra tightened her grip on the handle of her parasol. "So I've been told."

He rubbed the back of his neck. "My reputation bothers you."

"Not in the way you might think." *No, in every way possible.* Even in ways she dared not admit. "I only care that you keep your focus on privateering."

"Fortunately for us both, I have the ability to focus on many things at once."

Indeed Cassandra could see many things in his eyes now—sorrow, admiration, yearning. The realization confounded her and set her heart racing. She glanced at the charts spread across his desk. "In what direction do you intend to sail?"

A strand of his black hair slid over his jaw. Glancing over his shoulder at the desk, he eased it behind his ear. "South along the coast and then across the Caribbean trade routes. That should afford us the best chance of crossing hulls with a British merchantman."

Beyond the stern windows, lightning flared across the sky as rain splattered the panes, running down in silver streams.

"And when do you expect to return?" she asked.

"As soon as I catch a prize."

"Soon then, I hope."

A devilish grin curved his lips. "You will miss me?"

A wave of heat flooded Cassandra. "Don't be absurd. My interests lie purely in my investment." She shifted her gaze to the door. "I should be going."

"I'll have Mr. Abbot escort you home."

An odd disappointment settled on Cassandra that Mr. Heaton would not do the honor himself. "It is still light. There is no need."

"There is for me."

"Very well." Cassandra gripped her parasol and made her way to the door. She faced him. "Then I wish you a safe journey, Mr. Heaton."

A touch of sadness softened his eyes. "Never fear, Miss Channing. I will protect your investment with my life."

❖

"Why do you have to go?" John's gray eyes clouded like the storm brewing outside their small house.

Luke drew him near. "Because I must take care of you and Mrs. Barnes."

"Can't I go with you this time?" John gazed up at Luke. "You said if you ever fixed your ship, I could come."

Mrs. Barnes sat in her cushioned rocking chair by the fireplace, sorrow furrowing her brows.

Luke led the boy to the sofa. "Yes, I did. But not on a privateering mission. It's far too dangerous."

John hung his head. "Lots of boys my age work on ships."

The truth of his words stung Luke. Was he being overprotective of his brother? His eyes met Mrs. Barnes's, seeking her advice, but she continued her knitting with a gentle smile on her lips as if she trusted Luke to make the right decision. He huffed. When had he ever made the right decision?

Grabbing John by the back of the neck, he drew him close and stared at the yellow and red flames spewing and crackling like mad demons in the fireplace. A picture of his mother running toward him formed out of the blaze, her face screaming in terror. She handed him a white bundle—a bundle that contained one-year-old John. "Keep him safe!" she shouted above the roar of the fire. "Keep him safe!" Then the inferno swallowed her up.

That was the last thing she had ever said to him.

No, he couldn't risk John.

Luke moved to the sofa and John slumped beside him.

Pain spiked through Luke's right ear. Ignoring it, he gave John his most authoritative look. "Yes, lots of boys your age work on ships, but they don't go out on privateering missions on their first voyage." Yet,

77

perhaps it *was* time to teach John how to sail. To see how he could handle himself on a wobbling ship with his brace. Perhaps, in due time, it would even help strengthen his leg. "I'll tell you what. I'll take you out on the ship when I return."

John lifted his gaze, his eyes sparkling. "When? When will that be?"

"I don't know. But when I do return, it will be with enough money to pay off our debts and buy us all a proper dinner at Queen's Tavern."

John grinned. "Did you hear that, Mrs. Barnes?"

"I did, indeed." The creak of her rocking chair filled the room, but she didn't look up from her knitting. Two balls of thread, one black and one white, sat in her lap.

"What are you making, Mrs. Barnes?" Luke asked.

She gave him a knowing smile. "Oh, I know it doesn't look like much now, but it will be beautiful. You'll see."

Beyond the windows, darkness swallowed up the city. Luke knew he needed to go. He glanced at the clock on the mantle—9:13. Stuck on 9:13 for the past sixteen days—ever since the night he'd first met Miss Channing. It was as if that meeting had stopped time, or perhaps it had set into motion some otherworldly clock, starting a sequence of events that would lead to his destiny, as Noah had said. *Destiny*, the name of his ship. Choking down a bitter chuckle, Luke shook his head. What foolishness had consumed his mind? And he hadn't even had a sip of rum.

❖

Luke stood at the quarter rail, telescope to his eye, scanning the horizon off *Destiny*'s bow. Nothing but the fuzzy blue line dividing sea from sky met his gaze. Lowering his scope, he shielded his eyes against the noon sun and glanced up at the crewman at the crosstrees. "Are you sure, Mr. Kraw?"

"Aye, Cap'n!" The shout returned. "Off the starboard bow."

The announcement of a sail had sparked hope in Luke—hope that had been deflated over the past two months of scanning the Eastern Seaboard for British merchantmen. So far, they had encountered three fishing boats, one whaler on his way north, a French Indiaman, one American privateer, and a British warship of eighty guns. Thankfully, they'd been able to outrun the latter. Now, five long days had passed since they'd seen anything but endless azure sea in every direction.

Beside him, Biron gripped the railing, tufts of gray hair blowing in the wind beneath his hat. "Dear God, let it be the prey we seek."

The ship bucked over a wave. Luke adjusted his stance and lifted the scope once again. A crowd of white sails popped over the horizon. "There she is."

"What do you make of her, Mr. Kraw?" he shouted, noting that his crew had stopped their work to stare at the intruder. He hoped Biron's prayer had been answered, for the men had been none too happy these past months. Their supplies were dwindling as quickly as their spirits, and it had become hard to discipline the unruly lot, especially without any rum for incentive. *Very much appreciated, dear Miss Channing.* The endless days and nights would have passed with much more tranquility and glee with a drink in hand. Luke licked his lips, searching for a hint of the spicy taste he so loved but seemed to have nearly forgotten.

When they'd set out from Baltimore Harbor, Luke's success in sneaking past the British fleet under cover of the storm had sent a huge wave of confidence throughout the crew. The success had not only bolstered Luke's hopes, but had given him confidence to believe that perchance he was not destined to be a failure at privateering as he was at everything else.

The thought encouraged him, for he wanted nothing more than to shower Miss Channing with wealth. To solve all her problems and see admiration and appreciation beaming in her eyes, instead of the mistrust and fear he constantly saw now. Ah, what a treasure she was! Hair the color of burgundy framing glowing skin that housed a pair of fathomless emerald eyes. He would sail around the world and back to possess such a woman.

But what was he thinking? He was so far beneath her in everything that mattered—integrity, honor, education, status, morality—that it still baffled him that she had aligned herself with the likes of him.

"Should I head for them, Cap'n?" Samuel said from his position at the wheel.

"Not yet," Luke said. A blast of hot air tore across the deck, cooling the sweat on his neck and brow. He gazed up at the courses glutted with wind and slapped the scope against his open palm where scars taunted him with a past failure.

His biggest failure of all.

The ship crested another wave and slammed down the other side, sending foam over her bow. The smell of salt and fish stung Luke's nostrils.

"A fair wind today. We should catch them with no problem," Biron stated.

Luke raised the scope again. The ship headed their way. He could make out the square shape of her hull and her three masts reaching for the sky. A good-sized ship. But was she a merchantman? And if so, was she British? For as tempting as it would be to attack any prize that came their way, Luke was no pirate. Though he had begun to think he wasn't beyond such measures if another month passed without satisfaction.

"Steady as she goes, Sam." Luke glanced at Mr. Keene who was standing on the main deck. "Ready the men to go aloft, Mr. Keene, should we need further sail."

"Aye, Cap'n." Mr. Keene shouted orders across the deck, the lace at his sleeves and collar flapping in the breeze. The top men leapt into the shrouds and raced up the ratlines to their posts just as Mr. Ward, the gunner, emerged from below, his eyes sparking with expectation.

Beside Luke, Biron bowed his head in prayer.

"Say an extra one for me, will you?" Luke whispered.

"You can talk to the Almighty just as well as I can," his first mate mumbled.

Luke snorted. "God won't listen to me."

"At least you're admitting He exists." The man continued praying.

Luke didn't know what he believed. If he admitted God existed, then he'd have to admit He was a cruel overlord. A God who cared not a whit for orphans or widows or the poor—or young boys with rickets. Raising his scope, he studied the oncoming ship.

"She's a British frigate!" The call came down on them like hail before Luke could even focus.

His heart stopped.

"And she's bearing down on us fast!"

His crew froze in place.

"Foresheet, jib, and staysail sheet, let go! Helms a-lee!" Luke fired off a string of orders ending with, "Mr. Ward, ready the guns, if you please." Not that they'd do any good against a frigate, but the preparation would keep up the men's spirits. Not Luke's. He knew exactly what he was up against. And unless he could outrun her, he and his men and his ship didn't stand a chance.

"So much for your prayers." He snickered toward Biron.

His first mate shrugged. "I suppose God has other plans."

"Yes, to see me destroyed, no doubt." Luke turned and marched away before Biron responded. Taking the wheel from Sam, he turned the ship about.

"She's picking up speed," Mr. Kraw yelled from the crosstrees.

"And she's got the weather edge," Samuel groaned as he took the wheel back.

Which meant she had the advantage of the wind. Sweat broke on Luke's brow as visions of being impressed into the Royal Navy assailed him. He'd rather die than allow that to happen again.

Releasing the wheel, Luke barreled onto the main deck as Biron barked orders to the men. The ship vaulted over a wave. Salty spray showered him, stinging his eyes. He gripped the port railing until his knuckles whitened as he gazed at the oncoming enemy. Closer now. Even though Luke had brought the ship around and raised every inch of canvas to the wind. The British frigate was a fast bird, indeed. And one that intended to swoop down and gobble up *Destiny* and her crew for supper.

Just as he imagined the fowl carnage in his mind, a plume of orange shot from the enemy's bow. "All hands down!" Luke shouted over his shoulder. His crew toppled to the deck, covering their heads with their arms. All save Luke and Mr. Ward, who exchanged a harried glance. Luke would not cower, and he assumed his gunner had seen too much action in his lifetime to be intimidated by so slight a volley.

An ominous *boom* cracked the sky. The shot struck the sea just twenty yards off their larboard quarter, shooting spray at least five feet into the air. Too close.

Far too close.

Luke's stomach dropped. He swung about, trying to settle his racing heart. His crew scrambled to their feet. Two dozen pairs of fearful eyes settled on him, waiting for him to issue an order.

Waiting for him to save them.

Luke rubbed the scars on his palm and swallowed. With each passing moment, each moment in which he hesitated, the faith in their eyes faded beneath a rising tide of terror. His own terror rose to grip every sinew and fiber of his being. Not a terror of the British, but a terror of failing these men who had put their trust in him.

Biron approached him, concern sharpening his features. "Your orders, Captain?"

Luke's blood pounded in his ears. He glanced at the oncoming frigate then over at his crew.

Another thunderous roar shook the sea, followed by a spray of seawater not ten yards off their stern.

And anger took the place of fear.

Anger and a determination to not fail without giving it all he had. "Lay aloft and loose top foresail!" Luke bellowed then turned to the helmsman. "Hard about, Sam!" He scanned the deck for the gunner. "Mr. Ward, man the starboard guns and be ready to fire on my order." Though he hoped they wouldn't have to.

The bald man grinned, his eyes sparking like embers. "Aye, Cap'n."

Luke faced forward. Biron took a spot beside him. "You'll outrun them." He gave Luke a knowing look that defied their harrowing circumstances. Luke rubbed the wet railing with his thumb then slammed his fist on the hard wood. "Let's hope so. This old bucket of a ship must have some fight in her yet."

Minutes passed like hours. Luke's legs ached from the strain of standing on the heaving planks. Sweat streamed down his back. Tension strung across the deck as tight as the lines that held the sails in place. Aside from his occasional orders in regard to direction and positions of sails, no one spoke. When they weren't adjusting sail, the crew kept their eyes riveted on their pursuer. The frigate fired again. No one bothered to duck this time. The shot plunged into the raging seas. Luke rubbed his aching eyes. Did they deceive him or had the iron ball struck the water farther away this time?

Smiling, Biron grabbed Luke's shoulder and shook him.

"We're outrunning them!" Samuel yelled from the wheel, while Mr. Keene slid down the backstay and nodded his approval to Luke.

The crew shouted "huzzahs" into the air.

Luke's muscles began to unwind. Removing his hat, he ran a hand through his moist hair and studied the frigate. The white foam curling on her bow indicated she still pursued them, but her diminishing size said she was losing the chase.

"Fire a salute to their heroic effort, if you please, Mr. Ward," Luke said with a grin.

Mr. Keene chuckled. "I like the way you think, Captain."

The gunner happily complied by lighting his matchstick to the touchhole of one of the carronades mounted on the larboard quarter.

The gun roared a proper adieu to the British ship, sending acrid smoke back over the crew and a tremble through the timbers. With his nose still burning from the smell of gunpowder, Luke completed the farewell with a wave of his cocked hat and a mock bow.

The enemy responded with a guttural blast of one of their own guns before veering away.

Minutes later, Luke raised his scope to see the frigate fading against the setting sun. Releasing a deep breath, he stuffed the glass into his belt and addressed Biron standing beside him, "Lower the royals and stays, and tell Sam to set a course three degrees south by southeast."

"Aye, aye, Captain." Biron touched his floppy hat.

His emotions a turbulent whirl of relief, thankfulness, and budding confidence, Luke took the companionway down to his cabin.

He could sure use a drink about now.

❖ CHAPTER 10 ❖

I beg your pardon, Mr. Stokes." Cassandra dropped her gaze to the goods she'd deposited on the mercantile's counter: a one-pound bag of oats, a six-yard bolt of calico to make new dresses for the girls, a tin of coffee beans, a sack of rice, whale oil for the lanterns, and ten fresh apples. All necessities.

Mr. Stokes eased a lock of hair over the bald spot near his temple. "I'm sorry, Miss Channing, but I cannot extend your credit any further until you make a payment." The look in his eyes spoke of genuine sorrow. "With the blockade, the store isn't doing well, and I can't provide for my young ones on credit."

Cassandra closed her eyes for a moment. Just a moment to gather her thoughts and her resolve.

Someone behind her shouted, "If you can't pay, step aside, miss. I don't have all day."

Ignoring him, Cassandra opened her eyes and leaned forward. "Please, Mr. Stokes. Just one more time. I'm expecting a huge return soon on an investment."

Mr. Anderson, one of the dock workers, sidled up beside her. "If you're waitin' for Luke Heaton t' come back wit' your money, you'll be waitin' a long time." He grinned, revealing a single gold-capped tooth. "Why, I'd gamble all my earnings that he took off wit' your money and is right now, piratin' in the Caribbean."

Chuckles shot through the room and pierced her heart with as much pain as if they'd been real darts. Nevertheless, Cassandra straightened her shoulders and faced the man. "Yet word about town is that you're not too good at gambling, Mr. Anderson, so I don't believe I'll take you up on that bet."

Save for a single chortle sounding from the back of the crowd, the room grew silent. A woman in the corner who'd been choosing apples from a bin drew her two children to her skirts.

Mr. Anderson frowned and fumbled with his hat, spearing Cassandra with seething eyes, before he glanced over the crowd and lumbered out the door. Facing Mr. Stokes, Cassandra gave him one last pleading look, but he crossed his arms over his work apron and shook his head.

"Thank you for your time," she mumbled and turned to make her way to the door, avoiding the pitiful gazes that followed her outside. Bursting onto the muddy street, she fought back the burning behind her eyes and lifted her chin to the warm rays of the sun making its descent in the western sky. June's hot, muggy air swamped around her, bringing with it the scent of fish and salt from the bay, luring her to the docks. A group of militiamen dressed in white trousers and dark-blue jackets marched by. The sergeant at their head smiled at her, tipping his hat.

She returned his smile, but her thoughts were on Mr. Heaton. She prayed he hadn't absconded with her money as the man in the store had said.

She pictured him sitting in a tavern somewhere in Barbados, a voluptuous wench on his lap, gambling with the gold doubloons he'd acquired as a pirate. Laughing, as he lifted his glass of rum toward her in a mock toast.

Grinding her teeth together, Cassandra marched onto the street. A horse neighed. She looked up to see the snorting nostrils of the beast just as the rider jerked the reins to avoid her.

"Look out where you're going, miss," the gentleman scolded her as he tried to settle the animal.

"My apologies." Cassandra swung around and nearly bumped into a couple crossing the road. The fashionable lady draped on the gentleman's arm scowled at her.

"Forgive me." Cassandra shook her head, trying to scatter thoughts of Mr. Heaton as she continued to the other side. The bare masts of ships swayed above the roofs of warehouses and taverns like wagging fingers, chastising her for her stupidity, yet luring her toward them nonetheless. Before long, she found herself standing at the edge of the wharf where *Destiny* had been docked. Of course, there was another ship there now— one of those infamous Baltimore clippers, known for their swift speed.

A bell rang in the distance. A group of fisherman passed, tipping their hats in her direction and leaving the sharp smell of fish in their wake. Sailors working on a ship tied at the next dock stopped to stare at her.

Ignoring them, she closed her eyes.

A warm breeze sent her curls dancing over her neck, tickling her skin. She pictured Mr. Heaton standing tall and confident on the wharf, broad shoulders stretched beneath his shirt, black hair blowing in the breeze. She could still hear his deep voice that reminded her of the soothing sound of a cello. Had she been fooled by his charm like so many others? Had she made a mistake that would cast her and her family onto the streets?

She drew a deep breath of the brackish air. *What am I to do?* Her family couldn't survive much longer on vegetables from the garden and fish Mr. Dayle managed to catch in the bay. And her poor sisters with only tattered clothes to wear. A sob caught in her throat, and she thought of praying. But when had that ever done her any good? After all the prayers and pleading to God to bring her father and brothers home, still they were gone. Her father forever.

She had never felt so alone.

"Miss Channing." The calm voice snapped her eyes open, and she turned to see Reverend Drummond beside her. "I didn't wish to startle you." He smiled and gazed at her with such kindness, Cassandra nearly released the tears pooling in her eyes. Instead, she turned and brushed them away.

"You didn't, Reverend. I was just. . ."

"Praying?"

She shook her head and gazed down at the reticule in her gloved hands. "No."

"Honesty. Very refreshing, Miss Channing, but then I can always count on you for that."

She smiled at him.

He glanced over the multitudes of ships swaying in the bay. "Waiting for someone?"

"No. . . Yes. I await the arrival of the privateer I invested in." A cannon blast thundered from Fort McHenry. Cassandra squinted at the sunlight glinting off the water, searching for an incoming ship. But no sails appeared. No doubt they were only testing the guns.

"Ah yes. Mr. Heaton's ship, *Destiny*." Reverend Drummond gave her an odd look.

Cassandra flinched. "How did you know?"

He chuckled and scratched his gray beard. "There's not much that goes on in this town that doesn't end up being broadcast in the taverns where I minister each night."

Cassandra nodded. "It's been two months. Shouldn't Mr. Heaton be back by now?"

"Not necessarily, Miss Channing. You cannot predict where and when he'll come across a British merchantman." He proffered his arm. "Can I walk you home? It isn't safe for you to be here alone."

Laughter spewed from a tavern down the street, confirming his words. She slid her arm into his. "Perhaps you're right, Reverend."

They strolled down Pratt Street in silence, reminding Cassandra of the times she and her father had walked around town, arm in arm. Happier days, when she had felt loved and secure.

After a while they chatted of Rose, Cassandra's friend and Reverend Drummond's niece, who rarely left their farm at the edge of town. They chatted of the blockade, the British raids on the countryside, battle news from Canada, and the reverend's charity hospital.

Finally, they stopped before Cassandra's house. A splash of maroon and tangerine set the western sky aglow with such peaceful artistry that it seemed as though war and death and struggle could never exist alongside such beauty.

As if reading her mind, Reverend Drummond said, "If you and your family need anything, Miss Channing, please come by the church. Part of my job is to help those in need."

She gazed down at the stain on his waistcoat and knew that though Rose had inherited some wealth from her father, the Drummonds gave most of their earnings away. His forehead folded into lines that were straight and true, just like the man standing before her. Truth be told, she *did* need supplies. Embarrassment heated her face at the thought of accepting charity. But no, they were not that desperate. Not yet.

"Thank you, Reverend, but I will find a way."

"There is no shame in accepting help, lass. God provides in many ways."

A hot wind stirred her mother's garden full of mayflowers, honeysuckles, and roses, wafting their sweet scent over Cassandra. "I have yet to see evidence of that."

"Because you do not believe."

"How can I believe when, despite my prayers, everything has been torn from me?"

"Does that mean that God is not with you?"

Cassandra gazed at him, confused. "What else could it mean?"

"Hmm." Wisdom and genuine concern burned in his eyes.

Cassandra tightened her grip on her reticule and gazed at the house across the street. Through the brightly lit window she caught a glimpse of Mr. Simpson hoisting his young son into the air. Father, family, love, all the things she used to possess. "God has abandoned me just like my father and my brothers. Now, it is up to me to care for my family."

Reverend Drummond laid a hand on her arm. "God never abandons His children, lass. It is we who so often abandon Him."

Cassandra gave a tight smile, tired of the man's empty platitudes. "Thank you for walking me home, Reverend." She turned to leave. "Give my best to Rose."

"I will, lass, and I'll be praying for you."

Cassandra shut the door on the reverend's statement. She didn't want to hear it. Didn't want any prayers lifted on her account. For she didn't want to give God another chance to ignore her.

"Cassandra!" Her mother's shrill voice filled the foyer before her visage appeared around the corner, clutching her gown.

Normally unaffected by her mother's histrionics, Cassandra tightened at the look of terror firing from her eyes. "What is it, Mother?"

"It's Hannah, dear. She's fallen terribly ill with a fever."

❖ CHAPTER 11 ❖

Luke coughed. His lungs filled with smoke. He couldn't breathe. He leapt from his bed. Brilliant ribbons of red and orange fluttered beneath his chamber door. A gray mist slid in through the crack like an unwelcome specter. Jumping into his trousers, he darted for the handle. Pain seared his hand. He leapt back as the stench of burning flesh turned his stomach. Someone screamed. Bracing for the pain, he grabbed the handle again and flung open the door. Flames sprang for him, crackling and chortling. Heat scorched his bare chest.

"Mother! Father!" he yelled, darting into the inferno. Hot coals branded his feet. Pain sizzled up his legs.

"Luke!" He heard his name in the distance. Perhaps they were already outside. Black smoke smothered him. Gasping for air, he dropped to his knees. He crawled into the front parlor, peering into the room. No sign of anyone. Someone bumped into him from behind. He spun about to see the lacy hem of his mother's nightdress.

Jumping to his feet, Luke batted away the smoke and saw her face twisted in horror. She coughed and thrust a white bundle into his arms. "Take John."

She kissed the top of John's head and gripped Luke's arm, a mixture of sorrow and terror etched across her face. "Take care of him, Luke. Promise me." Streaks of gray soot streamed from her eyes. Then she disappeared into the smoke.

"Mother!" Gripping John, Luke barreled over, coughing.

"Your father!" His mother's raspy voice echoed back over him.

Turning, Luke held his breath and rushed toward the front of the house. John began to wail. Shifting him to one arm, Luke darted through a hole in the flames, shouldered the front door, and barreled outside. A blast of crisp night air slapped him and swept the smoke from his face. He tumbled down the porch stairs and onto the dirt. Gasping, he turned to face the house. John's whimpers faded. Poking his head from within the white folds, the child stared, mesmerized by the insidious ballet of yellow and red lights dancing over their small cabin. The fire burst through one of the front windows with a mighty roar, sending a spray of glass over the porch.

Movement caught Luke's gaze, and he turned to see the lithe dark figure of an Indian standing at the edge of the clearing. The native raised his spear in the air and released a war cry that sent chills down Luke. Then he faded into the shadows of the forest.

"Mother! Father!" Luke started for the burning home, but a wall of heat halted him.

John began to cry. Pressing the child tightly to his chest, Luke put his head down and dashed for the house again. He must save his parents.

He would not allow them to burn to death!

Luke jerked upright in bed and struck his head on the bulkhead. Pain shot through his neck. Pressing a hand to the ache, he gasped for air. Sweat dripped off his chin onto his coverlet. The familiar creak and groan of the ship filled his ears.

A nightmare. Just another nightmare.

An odd glow penetrated his closed eyelids even as warmth spread over him. Prying his eyes open, he peered toward the source. The bright figure of a man stood by his cabin door. His entire countenance blazed, yet he did not burn. Luke's heart crashed against his chest. Was he still dreaming? The man's clothing seemed to ripple with life like an ocean of liquid silver under a heavy wind. Luke squinted and held up a hand to block the light, but he couldn't make out the man's face, only the trace of a lingering smile on his lips.

There was something familiar about him.

Luke opened his mouth to ask the man who he was when the vision slowly faded and disappeared. An odd pain throbbed in Luke's right earlobe.

Pound. Pound. Pound. "Cap'n!" The door burst open and Biron dashed inside. "Cap'n."

Luke shifted his gaze from Biron to the place where the luminous man had stood. "Did you see him?"

"See who, Cap'n?" Biron glanced over the cabin.

"Nothing." Luke rubbed his eyes. "I'm just seeing things."

"Well, we aren't seeing things on deck. We spotted what looks to be a merchantman." Biron's eyes flashed. "And she's flying the Union Jack."

Moments later, while shaking the fog of sleep from his head, Luke leapt onto the main deck, marched to the railing, and lifted the scope to his eye. White sails floated like puffs of cotton against the orange glow of dawn. Shifting the glass, he focused it on the ensign flying at her gaff. The red crisscross against a blue background of the Union Jack formed in his vision. He scanned what he could see of the hull. No gun ports, but two brass guns lining her railing on the port side gleamed in the rising sun. From the size of her, she appeared to be a brig. A merchant brig. And she was running fast before the wind.

He lowered the scope. "Make all sail, Biron!" he shouted, turning to seek out his first mate and nearly knocking him over in the process. Biron's aged face crinkled in excited anticipation.

Luke winked. "And clear for action."

Swerving about, Biron bellowed across the deck, "You heard the captain. Make all sail, gentlemen! Up topsails and stays. Clear the deck!"

With an excited gleam in his eye, Mr. Keene, who was standing amidships, piped the crew to quarters. Men swarmed over the ship, some leaping into the shrouds and scrambling aloft to set sail, others clearing away barrels and ropes and anything that wasn't bolted down, while the rest dropped belowdecks.

Destiny rose and plunged over a wave, sending sparkling foam over her bow as her decks buzzed with excitement. Shaking the hair from his face, Luke drew a deep breath, gathering his courage and wit—he'd need every bit to succeed.

Mr. Ward emerged from the companionway and headed straight for Luke, his tiny eyes aglow like the bundle of burning wicks in his hands.

Luke restrained a laugh at the man's enthusiasm. "Ready the larboard guns, if you please, Mr. Ward."

The gunner cracked a smile before turning to shout orders down the hatches. Soon men emerged from the waist hatch carrying round shot, powder bags, langrage, and grape from the magazine. Other sailors grabbed muskets and pikes from the arms chest and ran up the shrouds to take their places at the tops.

Luke gazed aloft. Loosened topsails thundered and flapped hungrily, seeking their airy breakfast as the crew hauled upon the halyards. Suddenly the canvas gave a hearty snap as its belly gorged with wind. *Destiny* sped forward, cresting a massive wave. Balancing his boots on the heaving deck, Luke swung about as sea spray slapped his face. He shook it off and ran a hand through his hair.

Nigh a mile before them and under a full press of sail, the merchantman fled for her life. Ribbons of foam shot from her stern. Yet *Destiny* gained on her. Luke leapt onto the quarterdeck and nodded toward young Sam. The boy's hands gripped the wheel, his eyes alight with excitement. "Steady as she goes, Sam. Keep us positioned off her larboard quarter."

"Aye, aye, Cap'n."

The wind roared in Luke's ears and tore at the loose strands of his hair. He shoved them into his tie and fisted his hands at his waist. Scanning the deck, he watched as Mr. Ward's men hovered over the guns, loading and priming them while the gunner stood ready with his handful of slow-burning wicks. Above him, the men in the tops, those who weren't trimming sail, held their muskets at the ready should they move in close enough to spray the enemy deck with deadly shot.

Luke shifted his gaze to the brig. She sat low in the water, which meant her hold was full of cargo. Wealth for him and Miss Channing. He had to do this. He could not fail. Wind whipped past him bringing with it familiar taunting voices.

You couldn't even save your parents. How can you win a sea battle?

Shaking them off, Luke swallowed down a burst of dread and clenched his fists. *God, help me,* he breathed more out of impulse than as an actual prayer, but like every request he'd made of God, his words were quickly swept away in the wind.

After two hours of running hard before the wind, *Destiny* came within range of the merchantman. Dark clouds bunched on the horizon, stirring the sea like a witch's cauldron. The sting of rain spiced the hot wind spinning around them. The change in weather did nothing to ease Luke's fears. "Bring in the studding and topsails," he ordered Biron. No sooner did the first mate repeat the orders than a yellow flash followed by a puff of gray smoke shot from the brig's stern. A second later, a thunderous boom cracked the sky.

"Hit the deck!" Mr. Keene yelled. The crew halted and stooped, arms braced over their heads.

The shot splashed impotently off their starboard bow.

Luke gripped the railing. "Bring us athwart her stern, Sam!"

"Aye, aye, Cap'n."

Stomping across the main deck, Biron spouted orders that sent the men aloft to trim the sails to the wind.

"Aim for his rigging, Mr. Ward," Luke shouted.

"Aye." With a crazed look in his sharp eyes, and his hair flailing about in the wind, the gunner looked like the ghost of some ancient sea battle.

The ship tacked to starboard. Sails thundered above. Luke spread his boots on the heaving deck and took up a position behind the guns. He squinted as the sun glinted off the polished brass. Biron came up alongside him, dabbing his neckerchief across his forehead.

As *Destiny* came around, bringing her larboard guns to bear, the stern of the brig rose from the sea like a barnacle-encrusted whale. Crewmen scurried around a stern chaser perched on her railing. But they would be too late. Luke hoped. Though he couldn't be sure. For one well-placed shot could damage his rigging beyond repair. A blast of hot wind struck him even as the low rumble of thunder laughed at him from the horizon.

"On my command, Mr. Ward."

The gunner distributed the burning punks to the men at each gun.

Destiny leveled out keel to stern as she glided past the brig.

"Fire!" Luke yelled.

Smoldering sticks flew to touch holes atop the guns. Four deafening roars shook the ship from stem to stern, flinging a broadside of grape and langrage at the merchantman. A wall of gray smoke crashed over Luke, stinging his eyes and stealing the air from his lungs. Coughing, he spun about, cupped his hands, and shouted aloft, "Unfurl tops!" Then charging onto the quarterdeck, he turned to Sam. "Hard to starboard, Sam."

"Hard to starboard, Cap'n," the boy repeated and the ship jerked, the deck canted, and Luke clutched the quarter rail to keep from falling. White foam hungrily licked the starboard railing. The blocks creaked and groaned from the strain.

Another ominous *boom!* sounded behind them. Luke turned to gaze at the enemy. A spiral of smoke drifted from her stern. The shot struck a rising wave twenty feet off their larboard quarter. Luke's crew cheered.

Raising the scope, Luke studied the brig. Sailors raced frantically across her deck. Her main topmast was shot away. Rigging and sails cluttered the deck below.

"Bring her about, Sam." Luke lowered the glass. "Let's give the British another taste of American hospitality."

Sam's eyes sparkled. "Aye, Cap'n."

Several minutes passed as *Destiny* maneuvered for another round. The ship creaked and complained like an old woman, yet she held tight beneath a full set of sail. Pacing the main deck, Luke gazed at the men in the tops adjusting canvas then down at Mr. Ward's gun crew as they prepared the starboard guns and elevated the quoins beneath the gun breeches to aim once again for the brig's rigging.

The eyes of every crewman shot to Luke, awaiting his next command. This time, not a trace of doubt could be seen within them. *You always fail.* The insidious voice clawed over Luke's soul, tugging on his newfound confidence.

No. Drawing in a deep breath of air tainted with gunpowder, Luke lengthened his stance. No. Not this time.

Destiny swooped athwart the brig's stern once again. Only this time, the enemy was ready. Luke could make out her crew lighting the touchholes of two stern chasers.

"Fire!" Luke bellowed just as two yellow flashes speared out from the brig.

Boom boom boom boom! Destiny's four carronades belched black madness, sending wave after wave of thick smoke back over the deck. The timbers trembled beneath Luke's boots. Coughing, he shouted orders to veer to larboard. The direful swoosh of shot sped past his ears, parting the haze and striking wood with an ominous crunch. More shots screeched past him like hail. The sound of canvas ripping filled the air. A scream of agony. Luke's heart clenched. Fear crowded in his throat.

When the smoke cleared, he marched to the railing and glanced over the main deck. He spotted Biron.

"Damage report."

White eyes, stark against a black-sooted face, stared up at him. "A few tears in the sails and rigging, sir, and the aft bulwark is crushed. Mr. Rockland's arm was nicked. Nothing else of note."

Luke nodded, relieved, then raised his scope and found men dashing over the enemy brig in a state of frenzy. Their entire main mast had cracked and fallen in a tangle of sailcloth cordage and shattered spars, spreading over their deck like a giant spiderweb of confusion.

Luke snapped the hair from his face and smiled. "Bring her about, Sam! Stations for the stays!"

Luke had her. One more broadside and the British merchantman would be his.

Destiny hauled on the wind as the brig began firing once again—the Englishmen shooting wildly and hitting nothing but sea. Which meant they were desperate and frightened. Good. Luke marched across the deck as the ship flew through the heavy seas, plunging into the rollers and shooting spray into the air in brilliant showers. Soon they came within fifty yards alongside the brig.

Mr. Ward's brows raised in anticipation.

"Hold on. Steady now," Luke said.

Mr. Keene crossed his arms over his embroidered waistcoat, a smile of victory on his face.

"But they're preparing to fire on us, Cap'n," Mr. Ward said.

Luke's glance took in the men aboard the brig, frantically buzzing around their guns. But Luke was a gambling man. And he gambled that in their haste, the brig's gun crew wouldn't hit their target. The seas had grown rough and their shot must be timed perfectly with the roll of the waves. They would waste it, and then Luke would have them.

He hoped.

He rubbed the sweat from his scarred palm and gripped the railing.

The thunderous growl of the brig's three guns sliced the darkening sky. But the shots sped overhead and landed in the churning waves off *Destiny's* larboard side.

"Fire!" Luke yelled and the carronades roared, pummeling the brig with yet another broadside of grape shot.

Smoke once again clouded Luke's vision, but distant screams of agony accompanied by the crack and snap of wood told him their shots had hit their mark. When the haze cleared, he smiled at the sight of the Union Jack being lowered in surrender.

The air returned to his lungs. Wiping the sweat from the back of his neck, he felt the tension slip from his body. He had won his first battle. If there was a God, Luke would thank Him for the victory.

If there was a God.

A cheer rose from his crew as all eyes shot to him. "Let's hear it for Captain Heaton!"

"Hip hip hurray. Hip hip hurray!"

Though his insides swelled at their approval, Luke raised his fist in the air. "For America!"

"For America!" they shouted in unison.

"Put the helm down and bring us alongside her, Sam," Luke ordered.

Biron slapped Luke on the back. "That's some fine sailing, Luke. Your first prize."

Luke stared at the brig as she lowered her sails. "I hope there'll be many more."

❖

Luke gazed out the stern windows in his cabin, rising and falling over the moonlit horizon. The *tap tap* of rain struck the glass and slid down in chaotic streams. Though the rough seas had not abated, he and his crew had still managed to board the brig, assess her damage, round up her crew, and inventory the cargo.

Mr. Sanders cleared his throat, and Luke spun around.

The purser adjusted his spectacles and read from a parchment in his hand. "Glass, white lead, coffee, flour, sugar, silk, Holland duck, burgundy wine, and rum, Cap'n." Greed sparkled in the man's oversized blue eyes.

"That should bring us a fair price." Biron commented from his seat in the velvet-upholstered chair. "Not to mention selling the brig itself."

"Aye." Mr. Keene rubbed his jeweled fingers together. "I'm beginning to like this privateering."

"Me too!" Sam punched the air. "You sure took it to those Brits, Cap'n. I never seen anything like it." Admiration beamed in his eyes.

Biron passed a stern look over the three men standing in a line before the captain's desk. "We aren't in this trade just for the money, gentlemen. Our country is at war. And each British merchantman we capture means less money in our enemy's coffers."

Thunder rumbled in the distance as the ship pitched over a wave, swinging the lantern hanging on the deck head and casting shifting shadows over the cabin.

Luke nodded and circled his desk. "I quite agree." Though he needed the money—needed it desperately—he hated the British tyrants even more. "We must do our part to frustrate the plans of the enemy or one day we will wake up and find our liberties stolen from us."

Mr. Sanders continued staring at the list, clearly unmoved by the patriotic speech. "Would you like me to add up the value of the cargo and conjecture on what we can expect to receive?"

"If you wish, Mr. Sanders." Luke leaned back against his desk and crossed his booted feet at the ankle.

The slight man pursed his thin lips. "We may not get what we hoped. The government takes a huge share in custom duties, I'm afraid." He looked up and tugged on his cravat. "Perhaps we should appoint one of the men as prize master and send him and the ship to port while we capture another one."

"Thank you, Mr. Sanders," Luke said. "You are dismissed."

With a scowl, the purser scurried from the cabin.

Mr. Keene cocked his head toward the door. "The man makes a good case, Cap'n. Why not continue the hunt while your luck is high?"

"Not luck, providence, Mr. Keene," Biron interjected in his usual confident tone.

Ignoring him, Luke sighed. "Because I have matters to attend to at home first."

Sam's face twisted into a pout, and Luke raised a hand to silence him. "I promise we will set out again within the month."

"What matters could be more important than money?" Mr. Keene cocked a smile that made him seem more callow than one would expect of a man over forty. "Ah, I know." He pointed a finger toward Luke, flinging his soot-stained sleeve through the air. "A woman?"

Luke flattened his lips. "None of—"

"If it is a woman," Mr. Keene interrupted, "my dear captain, might I remind you that the more money you have, the more women you can attract."

Sam chuckled at the man's display, but Luke studied Mr. Keene as an uncomfortable feeling of familiarity swamped him. "It depends on what type of women you wish to attract." Luke said the words before he even knew from what cultivated corner of his conscience they had hailed, for he certainly had never been meticulous about the sort of female companionship he had kept before.

Biron smiled his approval.

Luke cleared his throat. "Mr. Keene, will you do me the honor of taking command of the British merchantman?"

Mr. Keene's dark eyes flickered. "Of course, Cap'n."

Sam fidgeted in his spot as if he could hardly stand still. Though Luke knew what the boy wanted, he hesitated to send him along with Keene. The man's company could only besmirch Sam's innocence. But Luke couldn't keep the two apart forever. "Sam, you may go with him as his second in command."

"Thank you, Cap'n." The lad grinned. Mr. Keene grabbed him by the neck and fisted a hand playfully over his hair the way Luke often did with John.

A longing to see his brother filled Luke's soul until it ached. A mist covered his eyes, and he turned to gaze at the charts spread across his desk. "Biron, as soon as we are done here, divide the prisoners between the two ships and lock them up below."

Sam's laughter faded. "Where are we heading, Cap'n?"

"We'll sail for Wilmington first thing in the morning and sell the ship and cargo there." Luke faced forward again.

"And then?" Mr. Keene shifted his stance. "The crew is asking."

"We'll find a place to anchor safely. I'll assign a few men to stay with the ship and the rest are free to head over land to Baltimore. Unless the men prefer to stay in Wilmington until I return. It's up to them."

Keene's eyebrows leapt. "To spend our shares on women and wine."

Samuel grinned and threw his shoulders back. "Aye." His voice came out deeper than normal.

Mr. Keene chuckled. "You're too young for such pleasures, boy."

"No, I'm not." Sam shot a glance at Luke. "Am I, Luke? You took up drinking and gambling at my age, didn't you? I heard you tellin' Biron."

Luke shifted uncomfortably on the edge of his desk. Suddenly his vile habits didn't seem so appealing. In fact, they sickened him. Concern rose within him for this young, impressionable lad. Associating with crude sailors would do nothing to produce the qualities esteemed in a true gentleman. And for some reason Luke wanted more for the boy. In truth, he suddenly wanted more for himself.

"Mr. Keene is right, Sam. You'll go home and visit your mother and father. I'm sure they are anxious to hear how you are faring." No, he would not have Sam fritter away his time and money drinking and womanizing, ending up an empty-handed failure in ten years.

Just like Luke.

Sam frowned and scuffed his shoe over the deck. "Yes, sir."

Mr. Keene grabbed the boy by the arm, winked at Luke, and headed out the door.

After they left, Biron opened his mouth to say something when a knock on the door sounded. A sailor entered, bottle of rum in hand.

"Mr. Sanders's compliments, sir. He sent over a crate of rum from the brig." The sailor set the bottle on Luke's desk.

At the sight of the amber liquid, Luke's throat became a desert. "Thank you, Mr. Willis. That will be all," he managed to squeak out.

With a nod, the sailor left and closed the door behind him.

Luke rubbed his stubbled jaw. The rum teetered in the bottle like liquid gold with each movement of the ship. He hadn't had a sip in over two months. During the first week, he'd trembled so badly, he'd thought his brain would shake loose. Didn't he deserve a drink after winning the battle today? After all he'd endured?

Biron quirked a brow. "You promised her."

Luke nodded.

Thunder growled outside the windows. Wind whipped pellets of rain against the glass as if God, aware of his weakening resolve, was warning him to stay away from the tempting liquid.

Or perhaps it was just a portent of coming doom. For the mantle of success that lay temporarily across Luke's shoulders was sure to slip off soon enough.

❖ CHAPTER 12 ❖

Cassandra laid the back of her hand over Hannah's forehead. Heat radiated from the child. Still feverish. Hannah moaned, and Cassandra wrung out a cloth in the basin and dabbed it over the little girl's face and neck before laying it atop her forehead again. Streams of bright sunlight rippled over the bed in defiance of the sickness within, highlighting Hannah's damp red curls as they formed delicate patterns across her neck. The little girl turned her head on the pillow and let out a ragged sigh.

Dexter, lying across the bed at Hannah's feet—where he'd remained since she'd taken ill—lifted his head at the sound but then laid it back down on outstretched paws with a moan.

The tap of Cassandra's mother's slippers as she paced at the foot of the bed joined Hannah's mumbles and Margaret's whispered prayers in a grim melody that only further darkened Cassandra's spirits.

"Oh, what are we to do?" her mother said.

Cassandra turned in her chair to see her mother wringing her hands then spinning about to cross the room again. Fair curls, which were usually strung tight around her face, hung loose over her cheeks. Her blue eyes skittered to and fro from within a pale, droopy face, and though it was nearly midday, she still wore her nightdress and robe.

Cassandra approached her, touching her arm, halting her in her worrisome trek. "She will be all right, Mother. Don't vex yourself so."

Margaret stopped her prayers and looked up from where she knelt on the other side of the bed as if expecting Cassandra to share some profound revelation.

But Cassandra had none. In truth, she didn't know whether Hannah would survive. It had been three weeks since she'd taken ill, and although she had seemed to be recovering the past few days, last night after the medicine ran out, the poor girl had taken a turn for the worse.

Her mother's lip quivered. "How do you know that?" Tears glistened in her eyes. "I have lost my husband and most likely both my sons. I cannot lose my daughter."

Margaret gazed lovingly at Hannah then bowed her head again over her open Bible.

No! Cassandra stomped her foot. There would be no further tragedy in this house. Not if Cassandra had anything to do about it.

She took hold of her mother's shoulders. "You won't lose her, Mother. Hannah is strong. She will recover."

"But Dr. Wilson said there was nothing he could do. She needs the medicines." A tear spilled from her mother's eye. She batted it away. "And we can't afford any more."

Drawing her mother close, Cassandra wrapped her arms around her. The scent of jasmine swept the foul odor of illness from Cassandra's nose—if only for a moment—as her mind spun, seeking an answer. But there was none. She had run out of money weeks ago.

Margaret raised her head. Her misty eyes found Cassandra's and they exchanged a sympathetic glance, making Cassandra wonder how her maid fared reliving a tragedy that must be so fresh to her heart.

"The silverware." Cassandra stepped back from her mother.

The elderly woman wiped her swollen face. "What do you mean, dear?"

"We still have that silver serving set, do we not?"

"No, we sold that last month." Her mother frowned.

"Oh, bother." Cassandra bit her nail and took up her mother's pace. "What of the china oil lamps?"

"Gone."

"The painted plates from France?"

Her mother shook her head.

"All of it?" Cassandra knew her mother had sold some household items last week in order to buy the medicine and some additional food, but she hadn't realized just how much they'd lost.

Hannah groaned and Margaret eased a lock of her hair from her face. Her mother sniffed. "Yes. Everything of value."

Cassandra rubbed her temples. Something tickled her neck. Earrings. Unhooking them, she held them out. "I have these."

Her mother's eyes widened. "And I have my pearl ones. They are all I have left."

"Run up and get them for me, Mother, will you? And any other jewelry you can find."

With a nod, her mother sped out the door, her robe fluttering behind her.

Cassandra knelt by the bed and took Hannah's hand in hers. Placing a kiss on the heated flesh, she glanced at Margaret. "I know this must be hard for you."

Her lady's maid swallowed and lowered her chin. "My sweet baby Grace is in heaven now. A far better place." Though her voice trembled, the conviction within it bespoke of firm belief.

"How did you ever recover?"

"With God's help, one day at a time." Margaret smiled.

Cassandra gazed at Hannah, her ashen skin covered with red blotches, her damp hair clinging to her forehead, her hand limp within Cassandra's. "I would never forgive God if He took Hannah."

Margaret reached over and touched her arm. "Yes, you would. You would come to realize, as I have, that God is good and loving and whatever happens is for our best."

How could a child's death be good for anyone? Cassandra swallowed down her anger. "I'm not like you, Margaret. I don't believe whatever some reverend tells me. I want to find things out for myself. And the more I look for God, the further away He seems."

Margaret closed her Bible and ran her hands over the leather as if the book were the most precious thing in the world. Sunlight rippled over the leather binding, making it glow. "Perhaps you're the one pushing Him away."

Cassandra swallowed. Hadn't Reverend Drummond just said the same thing? Standing, Cassandra waved the thought away. "It doesn't matter!" She exhaled a long breath, noting the worry in Margaret's gaze. "Can you sit with her while I'm gone?"

A putrid smell wafted in through the door. Margaret wrinkled her nose. "What is that?"

Cassandra gave her a wry smile. "I asked Miss Thain to make some soup for Hannah."

"When she gets well enough to partake of some, we'll have to pray it doesn't make her ill again." Margaret's eyes sparkled playfully. "How long will you be?"

"As long as it takes to sell our earrings and get the medicines from the apothecary."

A loud crash sounded from below.

Closing her eyes, Cassandra gathered her resolve. What else could go wrong today? Before she made it to the door, footfalls sounded on the stairs, and Mr. Dayle's harried figure filled the frame. He glanced from his wife to Cassandra, his features twisted in fear.

Cassandra's throat went dry. "What is it, Mr. Dayle?"

"It's Miss Darlene."

Cassandra fisted her hands at her waist. "What did she break now?"

"No." He shook his head, catching his breath. "That was but my clumsiness. I knocked over a vase in my haste."

Cassandra's heart took up a rapid pace. "Then what is it about my sister?"

"Miss Darlene has gone missing."

❖

Luke tossed the stable owner a small pouch of coins and turned to watch the few of his crew who had traveled with them to Baltimore splintering toward the taverns that lined the street. Young Samuel slipped in between two sailors turning left.

"Sam!" Luke called.

The boy halted and turned.

"Isn't your home in the other direction?" Luke jerked a thumb toward his right and raised his brows.

"Ah yes, you're right, Cap'n. My mistake." Sam smiled then turned and darted down the avenue, his chortle bouncing on the wind.

Mr. Keene appeared beside Luke. "You should let the boy do what he wants."

On Luke's other side, Biron scratched his whiskers and stared at Luke as if waiting to see how he would answer.

"He's a good boy." Luke crossed his arms over his chest. "Smart, skilled, and disciplined. He's started on a good path in life, why send him down a wrong one?"

Mr. Keene huffed. "There's nothing wrong with a man enjoying himself after working hard." Then settling his red-plumed hat atop his head, he winked and sauntered away.

Biron tugged at his neckerchief and gestured toward Mr. Keene. "I'd watch out for that one, Captain. He's all charm on the outside but he's got a temper as fierce as any I've seen."

Luke noted the man's arrogant swagger before he disappeared into the crowd. Remorse sank like a brick in his belly. "Reminds you of someone, doesn't he?"

Biron snorted. "I'll admit, he's like you in many ways. Yet, not in others. There's something sinister in his eyes." Biron poked Luke in the chest. "You've got a good heart in there. You just don't know it yet."

"The only thing that keeps my heart the slightest bit good is John." Luke raked a hand through his hair. He gazed over the ships bobbing in the harbor. Nearly the same group of ships that had been there when he'd left nearly three months ago—still landlocked by the British. But one thing had changed. The weather. Though the sun was setting, June's muggy heat refused to release her hold on the city. Luke stretched his neck to a slight breeze flowing in from the bay, but it was barely enough to cool his skin. The smell of horseflesh, fish, and a hint of honeysuckle drifted past his nose. Baltimore. He was home.

"I'm proud of you for keeping your promise to abstain from rum," Biron said.

"I may be a gambler, cheat, and drunken sot, but I'm no liar." Luke grinned but Biron's face remained stoic as he gazed down the street where carriages, horses, and people on foot headed home for the evening.

Luke studied his first mate and saw the dread in his face, the prospect of going home to an empty house. He knew the man's wife had died in childbirth some years ago. "If you'd like to come home with me, I'm sure my housekeeper has a savory dinner prepared."

"No, you go on." He leaned toward Luke. "I think I'll go join the crew and keep them out of trouble."

"A tall order for just one man," Luke called after him with a laugh, resisting the urge to follow his men to the rum he could now smell on the wind.

Biron turned and pointed to the sky. "I have all the help I need."

Lud, God again. Luke started down the street, wincing at the pain spreading down his legs from the long horse ride. He skirted a group of ladies and tipped his hat in their direction, barely noticing them. Their flirtatious giggles brought his gaze around to see them smiling over their shoulders at him. Facing forward, he kept moving. When had he stopped flirting with every lady he saw?

A vision of a petite lady with burgundy hair and emerald eyes filled his mind. His spirits lifted knowing he'd see her soon. He couldn't wait to give her her share of the prize money. And watch the mistrust blossom into appreciation on her face. He had more than proven himself to her—and to himself and his crew. Perhaps his success would engender her trust and, dare he hope, a hint of affection? He shook his head, hoping to dislodge such fanciful notions. Miss Channing deserved a far better man than he would ever be.

Darting between two carriages, he crossed the street and stepped onto the cobblestone walkway. The setting sun spread its golden feathers over the treetops in a final farewell for the day. He had hoped to see Miss Channing tonight, but it would be inappropriate to call on her so late without an invitation.

Besides, a stench he could not describe emanated from his clothes. He needed to wash and don fresh attire before he saw her. And he longed to see John and Mrs. Barnes and tell them of his success.

Success. Luke shifted his shoulders beneath the odd-fitting cloak. Had he truly found something he was good at? A way to redeem his name and help his country?

Even as he mulled over the new sensation, two ladies approached him, children in tow. As soon as they spotted him, they drew their children into their skirts and scurried across the street, as if he would snatch their little girls and turn them into tavern wenches on the spot.

Luke frowned. His mantle of success slipped off one shoulder. Maybe it would never fit at all. Turning, he headed toward his favorite tavern, his lips suddenly parched. It wouldn't hurt to have one small drink before he headed home. His promise to Miss Channing rose to scold him as it had so many times aboard his ship. But he was on land now. Free to do as he pleased.

Entering the open-aired room, he was greeted by several patrons seated at tables or standing at the serving bar. "Hey, Heaton, where you been?"

"Busy," he replied as he headed for the bar. Grant, the owner, set down a glass of rum before Luke, anticipating his request. With a nod of thanks, Luke grabbed it, flipped a coin on the counter, and made his way to one of the open windows. Perching on the ledge, he propped up his boot and gazed outside, ignoring the calls to join various games. The chink of coins and slap of cards beckoned to him from a table in the corner, like the melody of a siren. The same men inhabited each table, each corner, drinking and playing the same games, night after night. Luke took another sip of rum. The pungent liquid warmed his throat and belly as familiar scents of spirits and sweat curled beneath his nose, making him wonder if he'd ever left Baltimore at all. Had he only dreamed of sailing away and capturing a prize? He shifted his back against the hard window frame and patted his waistcoat to ease his harried mind. The thick bulge of dollars reassured him that it had not been a dream. Nevertheless, they pleaded to be freed from his pocket. Yet. . .

He glanced at a circle of men playing a game of Gleek by the bar. He knew each one of them, and none were good at the game. Not like Luke. If the cards went his way, he could double his fortune and give Miss Channing twice her share.

No. He turned away. He could not risk it. He had worked too hard these past few months to risk it. With a sigh, he gazed out upon the street and sipped his rum as a breeze wafted over him, cooling his skin and stirring a loose strand of hair over his cheek.

Across the way, a man emerged from the alleyway beside a brick warehouse, dragging a young girl behind him.

"Let me go! Let me go!"

Luke could barely make out her scream above the fiddle music and the chatter of the men in the tavern.

The man stopped, shouted something at her, and then continued to drag her to a horse tied to a post at the edge of the street.

"Help!"

Perhaps just an unruly child and her father. Yet something pinched Luke's gut. He scanned the surroundings. Though people stared at the altercation, no one made a move to help.

Slamming the rum to the back of his throat, Luke cursed his obnoxious conscience, slid down the other side of the window onto the porch, and charged across the street. He grabbed the man's arm and spun him around. "What are you doing?"

The man, who was taller than Luke's six-foot-one frame, gazed at him as if he were not worthy of an answer. "Taking my daughter to her mama."

"I'm not your daughter!" Light hair the color of wheat tumbled over the girl's shoulders in disarray while green eyes fired his way. She tugged from the man's grasp and stumbled backward. "He's trying to steal me." Tears slid down her cheeks.

The man spat to the side. "Don't listen to her. She's misbehaving." He leaned down to grab the girl again. "Now be gone. This is no business of yours."

The girl kicked the man's shin. He moaned. Tightening his grip on her, he dragged her past Luke, pushing him aside.

Luke grimaced. "I'm making it my business." He drew his sword and pricked the man's back with the tip.

Halting, he slowly faced Luke, rage thundering across his face.

Leveling the blade at the ogre's chest, Luke gestured toward the girl. "Prove she's your daughter and I'll leave you be."

"I don't have to prove nothin' t' you." The man's narrowed eyes fired.

A crowd began to form around them. Men poked their heads out of the windows of the tavern. The music stopped.

The sun absconded with the remaining light, leaving them in shadows.

Luke pressed the tip of his cutlass into the man's chest. A speck of blood blossomed on his stained shirt. "Apparently you do."

"Very well. Have it your way." The ogre released the girl and shoved her aside. She tumbled to the ground in a flurry of lace. He raised his hands in surrender, but his eyes held no compliance. Then leaping backward, he reached inside his coat and pulled out a pistol.

Before he could cock and fire it, Luke barreled forward and knocked it from his hand with the hilt of his sword.

Yelping, the man grabbed his wrist. The shock on his face exploded into fury.

Out of nowhere a rock flew and struck the man's head. A trickle of blood spilled down his cheek. He scoured the surroundings with his maddening gaze, his fierce eyes locking upon the girl. He started for her, but Luke thrust his sword in between them, halting him.

Murmurs spread through the crowd. A man yelled, "Finish him off," from the tavern.

Finally, the ogre grunted, spit to the side, speared Luke with a look of fury, and then dashed away.

Luke turned to find the little girl holding another large rock—at least large for her tiny hands. She dropped it and ran to him, hugging his leg. "Thank you, mister."

Peeling her from his breeches, Luke knelt and examined her from head to toe. Aside from stains and tears in her gown, she appeared unharmed. "Are you all right?"

She nodded. Her lip trembled as if she was trying to keep from crying. The crowd dispersed behind them. The fiddle resumed its off-key ditty.

"What are you doing out here alone?" Luke asked.

"I was trying to find Dr. Wilson's house." She rubbed her eyes.

"By yourself?"

"Yes, my sister is very sick and Mother and Cassie aren't doing anything." She brought her lips into a pout. "I know I've been to his house before. But I got lost."

Something in her green eyes and the sassy tilt of her mouth struck a familiar chord. Luke stepped back to study her. "How long have you been wandering around the city alone?"

She shrugged. "I don't know. But my stomach's making lots of noise."

"Mine too." Luke chuckled. He'd grown tired of shipboard food after the first week and had been looking forward to Mrs. Barnes's cooking again. He glanced down the street, but the villain had disappeared. "Did you know that man?"

The girl shivered. "No. He grabbed me and told me he and his wife were moving far away to the frontier and they needed a daughter."

Luke hugged her. "It's all right now. Tell me where you live and I'll take you home. How does that sound?"

Wiping her eyes with the back of her hands, she nodded. Luke rose to his feet and took her by the hand. "My name is Luke. What is yours?"

"Darlene, Darlene Channing."

❖ CHAPTER 13 ❖

C assandra dragged her feet up the stairs to her house, numbness overtaking them with each step. How had they lost her? Disappeared without a trace? It seemed impossible to even consider. Taking her arm, Mr. Dayle assisted her up the final step. "We'll look for her first thing in the morning, Miss Channing. Never fear. I'm sure she's somewhere safe."

But where? Halting on the porch, Cassandra turned and gazed over the fading colors of the flower garden, the dirt street before their house, and the city beyond. Buildings of all shapes and sizes wove a haphazard pattern down to the bay where ships rocked limp and useless in the dark waters. Night, like a shadowy bear, hovered over Baltimore, waiting to pounce.

Terror strangled Cassandra's heart. They'd searched all afternoon for Darlene, down every street, every alleyway, in every shop, inquired at all their friends' homes.

The girl had simply disappeared.

"Perhaps the night watchmen will find her." Mr. Dayle's voice lifted in his usual cheery optimism.

"Perhaps." Cassandra breathed a silent prayer that felt more like an inward groan. They had alerted the constable who had consequently alerted each watchman to be on the lookout for Darlene during their nightly shifts.

"To think she's out there alone and frightened." Cassandra wiped away a tear. "I should be helping them search."

At first furious at Darlene for being such a troublesome chit, Cassandra had swept through the town like a storm, determined to punish the girl severely when she found her, Then, after the first hour of searching produced no sign of Darlene, fear had crept over Cassandra like a cold fog.

"You're far too exhausted, miss." Mr. Dayle turned her to face the house. "I'll move much faster without you."

"What am I to tell my mother? I cannot face her." Cassandra stepped toward the door, hesitating.

Mr. Dayle opened his mouth to respond when voices trickled out the parlor window on a shaft of flickering light. Her mother's voice. And a man's. Shaking her head, Cassandra gripped the door handle. She had left her mother nothing but a whimpering, sobbing ball curled up in her bed. Was Darlene home?

Cassandra swung open the door to Mrs. Northrop just reaching for the knob. "I thought I heard you, miss." She smiled and took Cassandra's wrap. "The most marvelous news. Miss Darlene has come back to us!"

Flinging a hand to her throat, Cassandra released a hearty sigh. She shared a smile with Mr. Dayle as he closed the door. A male voice that seemed oddly familiar emanated from the parlor. Confusion took over Cassandra's relief, followed by anger. "Who is here?" she demanded from the housekeeper.

Not waiting for an answer, Cassandra brushed past Mrs. Northrop and stormed into the parlor.

And found Mr. Heaton perched on the sofa across from her mother.

She sat as though a pole had been inserted into her spine. Her expression matched her stiff posture. The air thinned in Cassandra's lungs. She closed her eyes for a second then opened them, expecting a new scene to appear in her vision rather than the one that made no sense at all.

Before she could inquire as to what was going on, Darlene leapt from the chair beside her mother's and flew to Cassandra. "Cassie, Cassie!"

Kneeling, Cassandra pulled the girl into her arms and showered her neck with kisses then nudged her back to examine her. No cuts or bruises and only a few stains and tears on her gown. Cassandra's anger returned. "Where have you been? I was so worried."

Mr. Heaton rose from his seat as if to explain. His presence filled the room and ignited a tempest in her belly.

Ignoring him, Cassandra focused on her sister.

"I'm sorry, Cassie." Darlene thrust out her bottom lip. "I went to get Dr. Wilson for Hannah."

"Can you imagine, all by herself?" Cassandra's mother whined. "Oh, my poor head." She batted the air around her with her handkerchief.

Darlene sniffed and lowered her chin, but Cassandra wasn't buying her sister's penitent act. An act Cassandra had perfected when she was Darlene's age. Standing, she straightened her shoulders. She would have to deal with her sister later.

"Mr. Heaton, what on earth are you doing here?" she asked. "Tell me you didn't lose the ship. I fear I cannot stand any further disasters tonight."

"Quite the contrary." His smile was sincere, lacking its usual sarcasm.

"He saved me, Cassie." Darlene slid her hand in Cassandra's and dragged her to the sofa.

Where Mr. Heaton stood.

Too close. Cassandra could smell the sea on him, along with wood and rum and something else that curled her nose. She retreated a step and laid a hand on the back of a chair for support.

"I was kidnapped! You should have seen him make quick work of that villain." Darlene scrunched her face into an evil twist.

"I had a bit of help." Mr. Heaton chuckled.

Cassandra's brows drew together at the affectionate exchange that passed between them. "What vill—"

"Oh, it truly was quite heroic, Mr. Heaton." Her mother's words did not match the look of suspicion she cast his way. "We are deeply in your debt." She picked up her bell. The strident *ding ding ding* only added to Cassandra's befuddlement.

Mr. Heaton bowed. "My pleasure, madam."

Circling the chair, Cassandra sank into it before her legs gave out. Mrs. Northrop entered with a tray of tea and her mother's tonic.

Darlene inched to stand beside Cassandra's chair. "I got lost, Cassie, and then this evil man grabbed me." She demonstrated by clutching her arm, eyes wide. "He told me he was taking me to be his daughter."

"Oh my." Cassandra leaned forward, hand covering her mouth.

"Then Mr. Heaton fought him off."

"He did?" Cassandra lifted her gaze to Mr. Heaton. A grin quirked his lips.

"Then I threw a rock at him." Darlene flung her hand in the air.

"Such behavior for a young lady," her mother said with scorn as Mrs. Northrop poured tonic into her tea and handed her the cup.

"Your sister has quite the aim. She struck him square on the head." Luke lowered himself to the sofa. "Reminded me of someone else."

"Oh, to think how close we came to losing you." Cassandra's mother sipped her tea then set the cup down as her eyes misted over. She beckoned to Darlene and the girl dashed into her embrace.

As Mr. Heaton smiled at the scene, Cassandra allowed herself a longer glance his way. Dirt marred his breeches and waistcoat, while black smudges lined his once-white shirt. Gunpowder? Strands of loose hair spilled from his tie, while at least two days' stubble peppered his chin. His rugged masculinity stole the breath from her lungs. Indeed, he looked more like a pirate than a privateer. No wonder her mother was swooning so.

Waving Mrs. Northrop's offer of tea aside with a *No, thank you,* Cassandra attempted an even tone, despite the torrent of emotions spinning within her. "That still doesn't explain what you're doing in town, Mr. Heaton."

He leaned forward, elbows on his knees, his blue eyes sparking. "I have good news."

Cassandra swallowed. She needed good news. Mr. Dayle appeared in the doorway. "Hannah is asking for you, Mrs. Channing."

"Oh, good." Cassandra's mother rose from her chair and took Darlene's hand.

Hannah. Renewed fear swamped Cassandra. She jumped from her seat. "How is she?" Cassandra started for the parlor doors then turned. "Forgive me, Mr. Heaton, but I'm afraid we cannot entertain guests at the moment. My other sister is quite ill."

Her mother gave her a reassuring look. "Never fear, Dr. Wilson is with her now, dear."

Cassandra stared at her in disbelief. "But we can't aff. . . How?"

Her mother waved her handkerchief in Mr. Heaton's direction. "Mr. Heaton brought him along with the medicines she needs."

Cassandra flinched, shifting her gaze between her mother and Mr. Heaton. "I don't understand."

"I'm sure Mr. Heaton will explain it to you." She turned to face him. "Good evening to you, sir. We are very grateful for your kindness. Mr. Dayle will see you out."

Cassandra cringed at her mother's tone—a tone she used to dismiss servants. "In a moment, Mother. I wish to speak to Mr. Heaton before he leaves."

The matron of the house pinched her lips as she raked Mr. Heaton with one of her disapproving glances. "Very well. Mr. Dayle, please stand by. Darlene, come." She tugged upon the girl, who cast a final grin over her shoulder at Mr. Heaton.

Mr. Dayle took up a spot just outside the open parlor doors.

Cassandra spun around to face Mr. Heaton. "I am all astonishment, sir."

"I hear that quite often." His gaze assessed her.

"But rarely as a compliment, I'm sure." Cassandra bit her lip, unsure why she was playing the insolent shrew when this man had saved her sister's life.

But he seemed to take no offense. Instead, he cocked his head and grinned. "Then can I assume your meaning was of the rare kind?"

"Indeed." Cassandra made her way back to her chair. "I cannot thank you enough for saving Darlene."

"Do all the Channing women wander about the streets at night?"

"Not all." Cassandra fingered the mahogany carving on the back of the chair.

He took a step toward her. "When she struck the villain with a rock, I had no doubt she was your relation." Humor rang in his voice.

Cassandra couldn't help but chuckle. "Indeed, I fear Darlene is far too much like me." She gazed up at him and her knees weakened. Weaving around the chair, she quickly slipped onto its soft cushion for fear of falling. "You brought the doctor. How did you know?"

"Darlene told me about her sister. And being familiar with Dr. Wilson, I took the liberty of calling on him. Then together we interrupted the apothecary's evening meal so he could prepare the proper medicines."

"I don't know what to say. I will repay you, of course."

"There is no need."

"I do not take charity, Mr. Heaton."

"You won't have to anymore."

❖

Luke reached inside his waistcoat pocket and pulled out a piece of foolscap. Unfolding it, he pressed it on the table. He watched her, anxious to see her reaction at the numbers scribbled across it and totaled at the bottom.

He couldn't help but watch her.

Her demeanor, her expressions, her words all combined into a fascinating play being acted out before him—a play in which numerous actors skittered across the stage of her eyes. How he longed to see admiration make its debut, perhaps, dare he hope, even ardor.

She examined the paper. Her eyes widened then narrowed in confusion.

Luke could contain himself no longer. "I captured a prize."

She looked up at him. "I see that." She shook her head, sending her red curls dancing. "I don't know what to say."

"You don't have to appear so surprised, Miss Channing." He laughed.

"Forgive me. I meant no offense."

Luke reached inside his waistcoat and pulled out a leather sack. Untying it, he counted out her share and laid it on the table.

Miss Channing's chest began to rise and fall rapidly. She picked up the notes and stared at them as if they were the most beautiful things she'd ever seen. "Ten thousand dollars." Her eyes met his, shimmering emeralds. "I cannot believe it."

Luke swallowed down his own emotion and pointed to the document. "We caught the British merchantman *Hawk* and sold her and her entire cargo in Wilmington for one hundred thousand dollars. US customs took twenty thousand, and I split half of the remainder among the crew. I took my share and that leaves you ten thousand." He pointed to the final number on the document.

"I heard privateering was lucrative, but I had no idea just how lucrative. Do you know what this means to me, Mr. Heaton?" Now, finally, admiration made an appearance in those green eyes. The sight of it set Luke aback, initiating a torrent of feelings he dared not entertain.

He cleared his throat. "I cannot promise you this amount on each voyage. I was lucky. Many privateers sail for months before acquiring a prize."

She smiled, a genuine, unassuming smile that showered him in warmth. "Where is *Destiny* now?"

"In Elizabeth City to the south. We found anchorage there and purchased horses for the two-day ride to Baltimore."

Miss Channing sifted through the bills, shaking her head as if she still didn't believe her eyes. She attempted to speak but her voice choked.

Luke grabbed his hat from the arm of the sofa. "I should allow you to attend to your younger sister. I was sorry to hear of her illness." He didn't want to go—could easily sit here all night staring at Miss Channing—but remembering her mother's curt invitation to leave, he didn't want to overstay his welcome.

Miss Channing led him to the front door. Opening it, she followed him outside onto the porch. A blast of evening wind gusted over them, enveloping him in her sweet scent of gardenias. He faced her, light from a lantern hanging on the porch sparkling in her eyes.

She smiled again. "You smell like rum." Her tone was playful, yet accusing.

Luke cocked a brow. "Yes, I had one drink, my first in nearly three months."

Disbelief shadowed her face. Then taking a step back, she wrinkled her nose.

He shuffled his boots over the porch, suddenly wishing he'd had time to clean up before seeing her. "My apologies. I just rode into town a few hours ago."

"Quite all right, Mr. Heaton. How long will you be staying?"

"A few weeks. The crew needs a rest. They'll get restless when their pockets are empty again." He glanced over the city, blanketed in darkness, then back at her.

"And you, when will you get restless again?" One side of her lips curved slightly as her gaze probed him.

Which gave him the impetus to toy with her. "That depends."

"On what?"

If you'll allow me to court you, spend time with you, get to know you. "If I have some reason to stay." When concern creased her face, Luke regretted his bold words.

Their footman, still standing in the foyer, glanced his way. "You have saved me and my family, Mr. Heaton." Her tone had regained its metallic formality. "For that I will be eternally grateful. If I can ever help you, please don't hesitate to call." Luke took her hand in his and eased her back toward him, longing to regain a trace of her former tenderness. She trembled and her breath hastened. Was she as affected by him as he was by her? Only one way to find out. He lowered himself to whisper in her ear. "Perhaps a kiss of gratitude?"

Tugging her hand from his, she retreated into the house. "Good evening, Mr. Heaton."

And slammed the door in his face.

❖ CHAPTER 14 ❖

Flinging open the damask curtains, Cassandra rubbed her eyes and squinted at the radiant glow of dawn. Pulling her robe tight about her waist, she studied the morning breeze dancing through the leaves of the maple and birch trees outside her window. She'd hardly slept a wink the past two nights. In fact, with candle in hand, she'd crept down to the solarium more than once to check on the ten thousand dollars she'd hidden in her father's chest. If only to reassure herself that she hadn't dreamt up receiving the fortune from Mr. Heaton.

One thing she knew for sure, however, was that she hadn't dreamt up the rake's inappropriate request for a kiss. Outrage consumed her at the memory. How dare he treat her like one of his common wenches, as if he could purchase her affections with the toss of a coin! She reached up and brushed her fingers over her neck. Then why had her insides melted at the waft of his warm breath over her skin? And her stomach flutter as if a thousand fireflies flew within it?

No doubt it was just the excitement of receiving so much wealth. In one night, her life had gone from poverty, sickness, and shame, to life, health, and a promising future.

All because of the town rogue.

The door opened and Margaret slipped inside humming her favorite hymn. Strands of black hair sprang from her mobcap. "Oh miss, I didn't know you'd arisen." She placed the basin of steaming water on the vanity, then gazed at Cassandra. "Whatever are you thinking, miss? I've never seen such a glorious expression on your face."

Cassandra shook off the uninvited smile. "Nothing."

"Or *who* were you thinking about? I should say."

The heated flush that had begun moments before on Cassandra's neck moved onto her face. She swung about to face the window.

Margaret made her way to the bed and began straightening the sheets. "That Mr. Heaton presents a rather handsome figure, does he not?"

"I hadn't noticed," Cassandra lied.

"Then you must be the only lady in town who hasn't."

Cassandra gave her maid a coy smile. "Well, perhaps I have noticed. But what does it matter? You know his reputation as well as I."

Margaret finished making the bed and shrugged. "I never put much value in town gossip, miss. Besides, he's shown you nothing but kindness."

"Mother disapproves of him."

"And you?" Margaret cocked her head and smiled.

Cassandra moved to the bed and gripped one of the wooden posts. "I haven't made up my mind yet." Her thoughts drifted to the money, and she lifted her hands to her mouth as tears of relief burned behind her eyes. "We are saved, Margaret. I can hardly believe it!" She hadn't allowed the reality to settle firmly in her heart. Not yet. Mainly because her thoughts had been consumed with Hannah. What difference would all the money in the world make if Hannah did not survive? Yet, after sitting by her sister's bedside, spoon-feeding her broth and cooling her forehead with wet rags, Cassandra had watched the little girl finally drift into a peaceful sleep late last night. An hour later, a touch to her forehead indicated her fever had abated.

Margaret took her hands. "Yes, miss. We are saved."

"We have enough money to last us twenty years if need be."

"God has been good to you, miss."

Cassandra pulled away. "I don't know why God would bless me in this way but neglect to save my father." She moved to the chair of her vanity and sat down with a huff.

"He's always been with you, miss. He won't let His children starve. Look what happened to me and Mr. Daley. After our baby died and we had to sell the chandler shop to pay the doctor bills, we would have been living out on the street, begging for food." Margaret stepped behind her and began unraveling Cassandra's long braid.

"I hired you, not God," Cassandra reminded her.

"God can use anyone, miss." Margaret leaned over and smiled at Cassandra in the dressing glass. "Even the town rogue."

Cassandra stared at her reflection, longing to believe Margaret's words, longing to believe that God was still with her and looking out for her—that she wasn't the only one standing between her family and complete ruin.

"I checked on Hannah this morning," Margaret offered as she picked up a brush and began running it through Cassandra's hair. "She is sleeping soundly. Another blessing from God." She began humming once again, and the words Cassandra had often heard accompanying the tune chimed in her head.

Come, thou Fount of every blessing
Tune my heart to sing Thy grace
Streams of mercy, never ceasing
Call for songs of loudest praise. . .

After sweeping up Cassandra's hair and fastening it in place, Margaret stepped toward the armoire and flung open the doors. "What are your plans today, miss?"

"I'm going into town to pay off all our debts and purchase some much-needed food and supplies." The thought pleased her immensely. Finally she'd not have to endure the looks of pity cast her way from proprietors and citizens alike. Finally, she could hold her head up high in the knowledge that she was as capable as any man to provide for her family.

As soon as she finished dressing, Cassandra slipped into the solarium, sat down on her stool, and unlocked her father's chest. Withdrawing the stack of bills, she placed them in her lap and grabbed her father's pipe. Drawing it to her nose, she breathed in the spicy scent that always invoked her father's image with such clarity.

"Papa, I've done it. I've provided for the family!" She caressed the bills and pressed the wad against her chest. "I wish you were here to see this. Wouldn't you be proud of your little girl?"

"Ah, my Cassie girl." She envisioned her father, pipe in hand, looking up from his chair in the library. "I've always been proud of you." He smiled and gestured her forward and Cassandra closed her eyes and imagined his beefy arms engulfing her in strength and warmth. Tears burned in her eyes, but she forced them back. Today was not a day for mourning. Today was a day of celebration.

After counting out enough bills to cover her errands, she tucked the rest into the bottom of the chest beneath the stack of her father's letters. Then after one more whiff of his pipe, she placed it atop the missives, closed the lid, locked it, and slipped the key into her pocket.

❖

Stretching, Luke entered the dining room and tousled John's hair as the boy sat slopping down a bowl of oatmeal. "I smell coffee."

John beamed up at him then spooned more of the creamy cereal into his mouth.

Mrs. Barnes strode into the room from the kitchen, carrying a tray of biscuits, sausage, and cheese, their decadent scents ambling in with her. "Finally you're awake."

Luke yawned. "Never thought I'd miss my lumpy old mattress." Pulling out a chair, he sat and poured himself a cup of coffee.

"It's good to have you back." Mrs. Barnes slid the platters onto the table.

Finishing his oatmeal, John pushed the bowl away and turned to face Luke. "Tell us how you captured that merchantman again."

Luke sipped his coffee. "I already told you, you little scamp." Several times, if he recalled. In fact, Luke had spent the entire day yesterday with John and Mrs. Barnes, regaling them with his adventurous tale. All the while John had sat mesmerized, gazing at Luke with admiration—the same admiration on his face now.

"Quite the story." Mrs. Barnes's eyes crinkled. "Praise God He kept you safe."

"Praise God for the money I gave you, Mrs. Barnes." Luke retorted. "Now you can pay off our debts and buy yourself a new gown."

"Oh my." Mrs. Barnes laid a hand on her wrinkled cheek.

John giggled.

Luke glanced down at John's leg. "And we can afford that new brace for your leg."

"And then I can go with you on your ship," the boy stated as if there would be no argument.

Mrs. Barnes's hawklike gaze scoured Luke from above a pair of wire-rimmed spectacles.

He rubbed the stubble on his chin and looked back into John's expectant gray eyes. John was ten years old. A good age to learn how to sail. It was time Luke stopped babying him.

Take care of him, Luke. His mother's last admonition echoed in Luke's mind. *Take care of him.*

But that didn't mean to hide the boy from the world. Luke wouldn't always be around, and John needed to grow up. Needed to learn how to fend for himself.

Luke sipped his coffee and set the cup down with a clank. "I don't see why not."

John leapt from his seat and stood at attention before Luke, reminding him of Samuel. "I'll be real good, you'll see. I learn things fast."

"I know you will. You're my brother, after all." Luke swallowed a burst of pride.

"You can't be serious?" Mrs. Barnes's red cheeks swelled. "He's just a boy. And we are at war."

"There are many boys his age out at sea. Besides, we encountered relatively little danger on my last trip."

"But you can't be sure that the next trip will go so well."

"I can't be sure of anything in this life." Luke grabbed a biscuit from the pile and took a bite. His parents' murder had taught him that. There were no assurances of safety, no guarantees that people wouldn't get sick—he glanced down at John's deformed leg. That money wouldn't run out. That he wouldn't be dealt another bad hand.

That loved ones wouldn't burn to death.

Pain throbbed in his right ear, and he lifted a hand to rub it. No, life was nothing but a chaotic matrix of haphazard events. And it was only how a man dealt with those events, good or bad, that defined his success. Success that Luke had only just begun to taste.

Mrs. Barnes clasped her hands before her smock. "But that is no license for carelessness, Luke."

"Is it careless or prudent to teach the boy to sail?"

"Sail, yes, but privateer. . . You could be shot at."

John's eyes bounced between Luke and Mrs. Barnes. "Truly?" Excitement raised his voice.

Mrs. Barnes let out an exasperated sigh.

Luke stood. "Never fear, Mrs. Barnes. I have no plans to engage a British warship." He gave her a mischievous smile and leaned to kiss her cheek.

She shook her head.

"Now, if you'll both excuse me," Luke said. "I have business in town."

"Do you have to go?" John slunk back into his chair.

"Yes. You listen to Mrs. Barnes and do your studies. I'm your captain now. If you disobey me"—Luke hunched over and narrowed his eyes, doing his best pirate impression—"I will make ye walk the plank."

John giggled. "Aye, aye, Captain."

Luke headed for the front door, the *slip-tap* of Mrs. Barnes's slippers following him.

"What business do you have?" she demanded.

Luke swept the door open and stepped outside. "I'm not gambling, sweet lady, if that's what you fear. I'm helping Noah bring cannons to the fort." He headed down the pathway. "Although I may attempt my hand at cards this evening," he shouted over his shoulders with a wink.

With an exasperated snort, she waved him off. "You are incorrigible." Then chuckling, she closed the door.

❖

Cassandra stepped out from the mercantile, her mother, Darlene, and Mr. Dayle following behind her. She lifted her face to the hot sun. Summer's warm abundance was at full swing. Not just in the weather, but in Cassandra's family, in her life, in her heart. Until now, Cassandra hadn't believed in fresh starts. She hadn't believed in miracles. But today, anything seemed possible. The scent of sweet ferns drifted by her nose. A bell rang in the distance accompanied by the *clip clop* of horses' hooves over the cobblestones.

"Where are we going now, dear?" her mother asked as Darlene slipped her hand within Cassandra's.

Cassandra glanced down at her list. "Let's see. We've paid the mercantile, the chandler, blacksmith, millinery, cobbler, and the seamstress. Now all we've got to do is pay the butcher and then buy something delicious for dinner. Perhaps a chicken to make some soup for Hannah. And also some cinnamon to settle her stomach."

Turning, she glanced at Mr. Dayle who was already loaded down with packages and sacks. "Just a few more stops, Mr. Dayle."

"No bother, miss."

Her mother patted her tight golden curls. "Oh, I would so love some new fabric for a gown. I haven't had one in months."

"Can we wait on that, Mother?" Cassandra headed down the brick pathway. "I don't want to spend money on luxuries just yet."

"But we have so much money." Her mother tugged at her white gloves with a whine.

For now. But it would be gone in a flash if Cassandra allowed her mother full rein to buy whatever she wished. Why, the entire amount would be gone within the year. And if Cassandra's brothers never returned, and Mr. Heaton never captured another prize. . .

And Cassandra never married—which appeared to be a greater possibility with each passing year.

"We must make it last, Mother. You don't want us to end up destitute again, do you?"

"No, of course not, dear. But we should enjoy our success." She furrowed her brows at Cassandra. "What has happened to you? You used to live life so vivaciously, with reckless abandon."

"I seem to recall that you detest that about me."

"Well, I did. I do," she mumbled. "I simply do not see why you must change now."

Halting, Cassandra gave her mother an incredulous look. "I took on the support of the family, Mother. I had to grow up."

"Oh, pish." Her mother plucked out a handkerchief and began dabbing her neck. "You are so much like your father. He never let me buy anything."

"Father took good care of us." Cassandra proceeded down the walkway.

Friends and acquaintances waved at them as they made their way through the crowds. A few stopped to stare, their heads dipping in conversation as they passed. No doubt discussing Cassandra's recent privateering success. Baltimore kept few secrets. But Cassandra didn't care. Whether they approved of her business venture or of whom she had chosen to align with, she had done what few women had. She had provided for her family. More than provided, in fact.

With her head held high, her list and reticule in one hand, and Darlene holding the other, Cassandra sauntered down Baltimore Street.

"Mr. Heaton!" Darlene slipped away from Cassandra and dashed down the street.

"Darlene, ladies do not run!" her mother yelled after her, but to no avail.

"Oh, bother." Holding her hat down against a blast of hot wind, Cassandra stormed after the girl, weaving in between people, horses, carriages, and wagons, leaving a trail of angry rebukes in her wake. "Pardon me." Cassandra attempted to placate one angry footman who sat atop a fancy phaeton as he jerked his horse out of her way. She continued onward. Then she saw him.

Dressed in his usual black breeches, white shirt, and black waistcoat, Mr. Heaton was perched on the seat of a wagon beside Noah and Marianne. Spotting Darlene, he yanked on the reins and leapt to the ground just as the little girl halted before him. He leaned down and laid a finger on her nose, giving her one of those smiles that would melt any female heart. Then straightening his back, his eyes met Cassandra's and an odd moment of understanding stretched between them before he graced her with the same smile. Only this one held a hint of desire that made her stomach spin.

"You're looking lovely today, Miss Channing," he said when she approached.

Cassandra tugged her sister away from him, remembering the ease with which this swaggering rake thought he could procure a kiss from her. "Save your flattery, sir. I am not a woman easily swayed by idle words."

"Then pray tell, miss, what *does* sway you?" He cocked his head with a smile.

Noah cleared his throat.

"Forgive me, Noah." Cassandra gazed up at her friends. "Marianne, so good to see you."

"And you." She dipped her head, a knowing grin on her lips.

"Darlene, how many times have I told you to not run off like that?" Her mother's shrill voice blasted over them from behind. Shielding her eyes from the sun, she greeted Marianne and Noah.

"Good day, Mrs. Channing. Mr. Dayle," Marianne said.

"Congratulations on your privateering success, Cassandra." Noah took the reins and stilled the horse.

"I believe it is Mr. Heaton you should congratulate," Cassandra said.

"Indeed," Noah replied. "But the credit goes to you for choosing a good captain."

Luke rubbed his palms and looked away as if embarrassed by the compliment. Sunlight turned his hair into liquid obsidian.

"Do forgive us for not getting down," Marianne offered, "but we must be on our way."

"Where are you heading?" Cassandra peered in the back of the wagon where thick sheets of canvas covered up whatever they were hauling.

"Naval guns." Mr. Heaton flipped an errant strand of hair from his face and squinted in the sunlight.

Noah tipped his hat up and glanced toward the bay. "Major Armistead and General Smith asked us to strip them from any idle ships in order to reinforce the fort."

Cassandra's mother plucked out her fan. "Oh my, he doesn't expect an attack on Baltimore, does he?"

"Just a precaution, I'm sure, Mrs. Channing," Noah said.

Cassandra turned to Mr. Heaton. "I had no idea you were so patriotic."

His eyes smiled. "There is much you don't know about me."

Darlene tugged on Cassandra's skirt. "Can Mr. Heaton come for dinner?" She looked up at him. "We're having a celebration tonight."

Cassandra's mother groaned. "I'm sure Mr. Heaton has far more"— she scanned him with disdain—"interesting things with which to entertain himself."

Mr. Heaton's shoulders seemed to sag.

Embarrassed by her mother's impudence, Cassandra took a step toward him. She owed him a great deal. Certainly the least she could do was offer him a decent supper. As a bachelor, he no doubt rarely partook of a home-cooked meal. Besides, the prospect of getting to know him better was not completely without appeal.

Though why she dared not ponder overmuch.

"What could be more interesting than a fine meal?" Cassandra asked. "Isn't that right, Mr. Heaton?" Yet even as she said it, Cassandra could not in good conscience apply the description to Miss Thain's cooking. "I insist you join us."

Darlene smiled up at Luke and grabbed his hand.

"That's quite impossible, dear." Cassandra's mother snapped her fan shut. "I've already invited Mr. Crane for supper tonight."

Cassandra's stomach soured. "You did? When?"

"Why yesterday, dear. He came to call on you, but you were busy attending to Hannah."

"Oh, bother." Cassandra tapped her foot. It would never do to have them both to dinner. Especially after Mr. Heaton had all but pushed Mr.

Crane into the bay.

By the look of amusement on his face, Mr. Heaton was no doubt enjoying the same memory.

"How is your sister faring?" His tone sobered to one of true concern.

"Much better, thank you." Cassandra eyed him curiously.

Marianne grabbed her husband's arm. "We're very happy to hear it."

A breeze swirled around Cassandra, cooling the perspiration on her neck. Laughter shot from a group of men across the way. Oh, what did it matter if Mr. Crane was coming? It should be up to Mr. Heaton to decide if he wished to endure the man's presence or not. She wished she had the same choice. Besides, Mr. Heaton would offer a pleasant diversion from Mr. Crane's annoying ways. "Do say you'll come to dinner, Mr. Heaton."

His pointed gaze shifted from Cassandra to her mother and back to Cassandra as if considering the genuineness of the invitation. He must have decided the offer was sincere—at least on Cassandra's part—for he dipped his head and said, "I'd be happy to accept."

Ignoring her mother's groan and shrugging off the odd delight that drifted through her, Cassandra gazed up at her friends still seated on the wagon. "And you must come too, Marianne and Noah. We have much to celebrate."

The couple exchanged a loving glance. "Some other time perhaps." A pink hue blossomed on Marianne's cheeks. "This is Noah's last night in town before he sails out again."

"Oh, I see." Cassandra's face heated, and she shifted her gaze, noting a twinkle in Mr. Heaton's eyes.

"Very well, then." Cassandra cleared her throat, suddenly anxious to leave the awkward scene. "I should allow you to attend your business. Good day to you all." Tugging Darlene away from Mr. Heaton, she turned and headed down the street. "Seven o'clock sharp, Mr. Heaton," she shot over her shoulder.

"See you tonight," Darlene shouted as they made their way once again across the street.

Cassandra bit her lip. Mr. Crane, Mr. Heaton, and Cassandra's mother all eating at the same table. Yes, this would be a very interesting evening, indeed.

❖ CHAPTER 15 ❖

Luke waited for the ladies to take their seats before sinking into his chair around the oblong table covered in white linen. Pewter dishes, crystal goblets, and silver platters glowed beneath the light of several candles perched at the center. From her spot at the head of the table, Mrs. Channing glared at him with the same disapproving scowl she'd worn since Luke had first entered the house and been led into the parlor. Where he'd been curtly reintroduced to Mr. Milton Crane, the foppish cur who now took a seat beside him. The man had grunted that he'd already had the pleasure of Luke's acquaintance, but both his spiteful tone, and the way he assessed Luke as if he were a spoiled piece of meat, spoke otherwise. Thankfully, Crane's pride forbade him to mention his swim in Baltimore Bay for Luke doubted he could apologize for something that still brought a smile to his lips.

And though Miss Channing had attempted to include Luke in the pre-dinner conversation—an action that endeared her to him even more—the banter between her mother and Mr. Crane would not permit a word.

Luke cared not a whit that Mrs. Channing did not approve of his presence in her home. It was a chance to see Miss Channing and get to know her better. And for that, he'd happily tuck his pride away for the evening.

As it was, Luke had been content to stand by the hearth and gaze upon Miss Channing seated on the settee, her cream-colored gown spread around her, her delicate curls the color of fine wine lingering about her neck, and her green eyes sparkling as she politely listened to the boorish discourse. Not an ounce of powder or rouge marred her glowing complexion, which always seemed to redden when her eyes met his.

When the housekeeper announced dinner, Luke was fast to Miss Channing's side to offer her his arm. After glancing toward Mr. Crane, she took it and even graced Luke with a small smile in reward. However, Mr. Crane's face twisted in irritation as he spun around and offered his arm to Mrs. Channing while Darlene sped up on Luke's other side and slipped her hand in his.

"Seems you have an admirer." Miss Channing laughed. "One of many, I'm sure."

Darlene gazed up at Luke, and he squeezed her hand. "He's just my friend, Cassie." Her tone of admonishment brought a smile to Luke's lips.

Now, as the housekeeper and another woman of slight figure entered the dining hall and filled the table with steaming platters, Luke dared a glance at Darlene and Miss Channing, who both sat across from him. He promised himself to don his best behavior and prove to them—and to Cassandra's mother—that he was not the cad the town thought he was.

The rumble in his stomach was quickly silenced by a strange smell, emanating from the cuisine, that Luke could not quite place. But he could be sure of one thing—it bore no resemblance to anything edible. Mrs. Channing bowed her head and blessed the dinner with a prayer that, by her tone, sounded more like the recitation of marching orders for God than an offering of thanks.

"Amen." Mr. Crane slapped his hands together and reached for a bowl of boiled potatoes. After shoveling a heap onto his plate, he passed the bowl to the lady of the house and took the liberty of pouring himself a glass of wine from the carafe. "I was most pleased to hear of your good fortune, Miss Channing." He dipped his head toward Cassandra.

Grabbing a plate of what appeared to be fried fish, she handed it to Luke. "Yes, indeed, sir. We have Mr. Heaton to thank for that. As it turns out, he is quite the privateer."

Luke smiled inwardly as he grabbed the platter and slid a portion onto his plate.

Mr. Crane sipped his wine. "Isn't it just a game of luck, Mr. Heaton, this privateering?" he said without looking at Luke. "I mean to say, it's quite a gamble that you'll even encounter a British vessel, let alone one that you can catch and defeat in battle."

Luke opened his mouth to reply but the man continued, "And then she must have a bellyful of cargo to sell to make her worthwhile prey." He plucked a biscuit from a tray and passed the plate to Cassandra. "Yes, indeed, it seems but a game of chance."

"As it turns out, Mr. Crane. I'm quite good at gambling." Luke winked at Darlene as she passed him a bowl of greens. The girl giggled.

"A worthless pastime," Mrs. Channing interjected. "For charlatans and idlers."

"I quite agree." Mr. Crane huffed. "Your reputation, Mr. Heaton, does you no credit. And like all gamblers, I'll wager your luck will run out in time."

"Then you would wish ill luck on me as well, Mr. Crane." Cassandra seethed. "For my success is tied with Mr. Heaton's."

Luke raised a brow at her spiteful tone.

"Not at all, my dear." Alarm rang in Mr. Crane's voice as if he realized his error. "I merely speak in philosophical generalities. No harm done, Mr. Heaton, eh?"

Fury surged through Luke's veins while he forced a calm smile upon his lips. All eyes shot to him as if expecting an angry outburst. "I'm flattered that you have spent so much of your precious time pondering my pastimes and my reputation, sir. Perhaps you should attend to your own."

Cassandra smiled and gazed down at her plate.

Mr. Crane stretched his neck. "I'll have you know, sir, that my reputation is without blemish."

Mrs. Channing helped herself to the meat pie. "Indeed, Mr. Crane. You need not concern yourself in that regard. All of Baltimore can attest to your good name." She gave a nervous chuckle, no doubt anxious to change the topic. Her glance took in the table. "Do forgive the lack of proper dining service. I'm afraid we haven't had time to redeem our china and silverware."

"Ah, no bother. No bother at all, my dear lady." Mr. Crane lifted a spoonful of fish to his mouth then recoiled slightly as he tasted it.

"But, wouldn't you say, Mr. Crane," Cassandra pressed, "that one's reputation is never etched in stone? That it is subject to improvement over time?"

Amazed at her defense of him, Luke sought out her eyes, but she kept them locked upon Crane.

Mr. Crane gazed at her with the patronizing look of a teacher with a child. "A rarity, Miss Channing, for it is my belief that one's character"—he cast a condescending glance at Luke—"or lack thereof, is forged in one's youth."

"I do not agree, sir." Cassandra pursed her pink lips. "And I'll ask you not to further insult Mr. Heaton. He is my guest."

Luke sipped his wine, enjoying the exchange. Enjoying that this fascinating woman stood up for him. Perhaps he should thank Mr. Crane for being such a priggy bumblehead.

Mrs. Channing leaned forward, her pointed gaze landing on her daughter. "Come now, Cassandra, enough of this absurd drivel about reputations." She waved a hand through the air. "Let us enjoy ourselves."

"Nevertheless"—Cassandra flashed Luke a smile that jolted his heart—"you must give credit where credit is due. I, for one, am glad I hired Mr. Heaton as a privateer."

Luke lifted his glass toward her in appreciation of her confidence. Hearing her speak so ardently on his behalf was worth enduring the odious company of Mr. Crane.

"I am, as well," Darlene piped in as she took a bite of biscuit.

Cassandra turned to her mother. "And you, Mother? Are you quite happy to be free of financial worries?"

"Why, of course, dear." The older lady's smile was tighter than a sheet under full wind.

Mr. Crane took a bite of meat pie. His lips twisted in a knot. Grabbing his wine, he poured the remainder down his throat then set his glass down. "Well, it does seem your risky investment has paid off. For now." He poured himself more wine. "However, Miss Channing, you needn't have gone to such extremes. I readily offer you my assistance whenever the need arises."

"So generous, Mr. Crane." Mrs. Channing patted her curls.

Cassandra straightened her shoulders. Candlelight spread a delightful sheen over her burgundy curls. "I do thank you, sir, but I prefer to make my own way."

"Rubbish." Mr. Crane snickered, pushing his food around the plate with a fork. "Women are best at childbearing and managing the home, don't you agree, Mr. Heaton?" He winked at Luke.

"As to childbearing, I agree they are best suited for it." Luke leaned back in his chair, noting that Miss Channing's jaw tightened. "As to managing the home, I do not think they should be forced to limit themselves to only those functions."

A look of shock and appreciation claimed Miss Channing's face.

Mr. Crane snorted his displeasure.

Luke took a bite of fish. A sour taste saturated his mouth. Miss Channing lowered her chin. Longing to bring her gaze back to him, he swallowed the bite and inquired after Miss Hannah.

He was immediately rewarded. "She is much better, Mr. Heaton. Thank you for asking."

Darlene exchanged such a warm glance with her elder sister that a lump formed in the back of Luke's throat, his thoughts flickering to John.

"I cannot wait until she has fully recovered. I miss playing with her," the little girl said.

"In fact, we expect her to be able to leave her bed very soon." Mrs. Channing took a bite of fish then dabbed her lips with her serviette.

Luke sampled the meat pie but found it no better than the fish. Even the cook aboard *Destiny* produced more palatable meals than this. "I am glad to hear of it."

Grabbing his wineglass, Mr. Crane leaned back in his chair. "Ah yes. Miss Hannah. I had quite forgotten she had taken ill."

Cassandra gave the man a look of disdain, which he seemed to miss entirely. Her mother gestured toward Mr. Crane's plate. "You did not find the meal to your liking, Mr. Crane?" Disappointment stung her blue eyes.

"Come now, Mother." Cassandra's delightful giggle lifted the spirit of the room. "I'm sure Mr. Crane is accustomed to finer fare than our humble cook can produce."

"I do not see why you keep her on." Mr. Crane flung his serviette onto the table.

Mrs. Channing's face reddened. "I'm afraid my daughter insists."

"Because, Mr. Crane." Cassandra's voice filled with venom. "She is a war widow and has no family. I'd sooner eat boiled rat every night than put her on the street. Besides, she's improving."

Crane shifted in his seat at her rebuff and refilled his wineglass while

Luke allowed this new revelation to find anchor in his mind. He knew Miss Channing was beautiful, feisty, brave, intelligent, and determined. But he had not realized until now that she also possessed the heart of a saint.

The thought made him as uncomfortable as Crane seemed to be. Yet for a completely different reason. For each new thing he learned about Miss Channing pushed her higher out of the reach of a man like him.

❖

Cassandra eyed Mr. Crane as he downed yet another glass of wine and tugged uncomfortably at his cravat. Her gaze shifted to Mr. Heaton sitting beside him with all the confidence and manners of a titled gentleman. Though she'd been concerned he would overindulge in drink, his wineglass stood half full. Though she'd been concerned he'd ignite a brawl with Mr. Crane, he'd responded with nothing but polite, albeit witty, answers to the man's insulting remarks. And how could she miss the smiles shared between him and Darlene? The young girl adored the man, just as Marianne's son, Jacob, adored him. And though the food tasted like the boiled rat she referred to earlier, Mr. Heaton forced it down with nary a complaint.

Dressed in a suit of black taffeta with silver trim, his dark hair slicked back into a tie, he had nearly stolen her breath when he'd first walked into the parlor. Even the stubble was vacant from his chin. Somehow, Cassandra missed it.

Just then his eyes found hers, a smile lingering at the corners. Flushed, Cassandra looked away.

"May I be excused, Mother?" Darlene asked. "I'd like to go see Hannah."

"By all means." Mrs. Channing lowered her glass to the table as Darlene leaned in to kiss Cassandra on the cheek then flew from the room.

Gazing after her, Mr. Crane sipped more wine. "If I may say so, that girl needs a strong hand. Word has spread through town of her escapade the other day."

"Why, I quite agree, Mr. Crane." Mrs. Channing set down her spoon. "She has been beyond control since my Phillip left. And, my word, but she gave us all such a fright."

Anger pulsed through Cassandra's veins. The audacity of the man.

131

"Though I thank you for your concern, Mr. Crane, we are quite able to handle Darlene. Besides, Mr. Heaton brought her home before any harm came to her."

"Quite the hero, eh, Mr. Heaton?" Mr. Crane's chuckle carried no sincerity.

Mr. Heaton merely smiled in return.

"Indeed," Cassandra said. "He also saved me from thieves a few months past."

Crane gulped his wine. "Odd how you seem to find yourself always in the right place and time to rescue the women of this family."

"A burden I gladly bear, sir," Mr. Heaton said.

"Perhaps you could write a story about him in your paper?" Cassandra couldn't resist toying with Mr. Crane. "He's quite the talk of the town now with his privateering success."

Mr. Crane's forehead twisted. "I'm afraid, Miss Channing, that my paper deals with more, shall we say, matters of higher importance."

"Of course it does." Cassandra's mother gave her a look of censure before she turned to face Mr. Crane. "Oh, do tell us, Mr. Crane, what stories are you working on currently?"

The meat in Cassandra's stomach hardened into a rock as the man, accepting the request with glee, began regaling them with every aspect of running a paper, from rambunctious employees, to secret sources, to the shortage of ink due to the blockade, and to the overwhelming decisions that fell on him each day. With each story, he sat a bit taller in his chair and drank a bit more. And with each sip of wine, his eyes became more glassy and his boasts more emphatic.

Blocking out his incessant drone, Cassandra found her gaze drawn to Mr. Heaton who now sat back in his chair, sipping his wine, while pretending to listen to the babbling man. More than once his eyes met hers and a smile would form on his lips. A smile that sent her heart into a frenzied beat. What was wrong with her? The man was a scoundrel, a gambler, who had more than once tried to steal a kiss from her. True, he had made her a fortune and for that she was grateful, but their relationship must end there. He was not the sort of man a lady entertained thoughts of a future with. Not the sort of man a lady could trust. And trust was of the utmost importance to Cassandra. She would not be abandoned again.

Yet the comparison with Mr. Crane—the respectable, trustworthy businessman—made her head spin. Who was the true gentleman, after all?

Mr. Crane's sharp tone snapped her attention toward him. "Your charity astounds me, Miss Channing. It's one of the many things that endears you so to me."

"Of what charity do you speak?"

"Why, of inviting Mr. Heaton to dine with you." His words slurred as he leaned forward. "In appreciation of his success on your behalf."

"And why do you consider that charity, sir?"

He adjusted his waistcoat and cast a cursory glance toward Luke. "Not to impugn your character further, sir. . ."

"Not that you could, Mr. Crane," Mr. Heaton was quick to respond.

Crane huffed. "But clearly, he is beneath such an invitation. Though I do understand your reasoning, Miss Channing. A bachelor in need of a good meal. Ah, your kind heart astounds me."

"Mr. Crane." Cassandra's blood boiled. "That is not—"

But Mr. Heaton raised a palm, silencing her. Calmly placing his glass on the table, he rose from his seat and bowed toward Cassandra's mother. "Thank you, madam, for having me in your home and for a most interesting meal." He turned to Cassandra, his eyes twinkling with ardor. "Always a pleasure." Then, facing Mr. Crane. "You sir, are a buffoon." And with that, he quietly left the dining hall.

Cassandra's mother gasped. Mr. Crane coughed, his face a bright red. Forcing down a giggle, Cassandra clutched her skirts and darted after Mr. Heaton, catching him just as he'd opened the front door to leave. "Please, Mr. Heaton."

He faced her. Moonlight turned his eyes to silver. He smelled of wood and spice.

"I must apologize for Mr. Crane. He isn't normally so belligerent."

"That's the second time you've apologized for the man."

She lowered her gaze. "He doesn't seem overly fond of you."

Mr. Heaton chuckled. "Indeed. But I believe I can handle the likes of him." Without warning, he brushed a thumb over her jaw.

His touch sent pinpricks over her face and neck. "Yes, I believe you can." Her voice came out breathless.

He leaned toward her. "Thank you, again, for the invitation."

Cassandra tried to release the breath that had crowded in her throat. "It's the least we could do to thank you."

"You owe me nothing." He leaned further and placed a gentle kiss on her cheek before Cassandra could stop him. His warm lips branded her with delight.

She couldn't move.

Then he winked, stepped outside, and closed the door behind him.

The sound of footfalls woke Cassandra from her dream and spun her around to see the back of Mr. Crane stumbling down the hall.

❖ CHAPTER 16 ❖

Luke tossed the last bit of rum into his mouth and gestured toward the barmaid for more. The pungent liquid swirled a rapid trail down his throat before plunging into his belly in a fiery blaze. He nodded at Mr. Sanders and Mr. Keene who were sitting far across the crowded tavern. Luke had seen them when he first entered, but he wasn't in the mood for conversation, especially not with his crew.

"What'll it be, Heaton?" The grimy-toothed man sitting to his left, who smelled no better than the supper Luke had partaken of that night, yelled over the raucous crowd and gestured toward the cards in Luke's hand.

Luke studied them, their images blurring in his vision. He hadn't meant to drink so much. Had intended to go straight home after dining with the Channings. But he could not chase Mr. Crane's insults from his mind. They rose like demons, taunting them with their truth. Crane may be an officious fat wit, but he was right about one thing. Luke had no business dining with such a prestigious family. Further, he had no business entertaining thoughts of calling on Cassandra. He was a drunk, a womanizer, and a gambler. Just because he'd succeeded in capturing a prize didn't mean that the entire voyage hadn't been one huge wager. With no more certainty of success than the game he played now. Simply the luck of the draw. Which, as Luke stared at his cards, he needed at the moment.

Selecting the two of diamonds, he laid it facedown on the table. "Another card, if you please."

A pianoforte chimed from the back of the tavern, overpowering the hum of conversation and occasional curses flung about the shadowy room. A throng of men began belting out a disparaging chorus. Mr. Crenshaw, a shipbuilder, sitting across from him, dealt him another card. Luke picked it up and smiled. The ace of diamonds. This might turn out to be a good night, after all.

Clara, a well-endowed barmaid who enjoyed sharing her voluptuous wealth with others, slapped down another glass of rum in front of Luke then leaned over to capture his approving glance. The sting of tobacco and perfume bit his nose, making him long for Cassandra's sweet scent of gardenias.

"I can offer you much more than rum." The barmaid's salacious slur did not have the same effect on him that it usually had.

Mr. Fairfax chuckled from Luke's right and grabbed the lady, forcing her onto his lap. "How about me?"

Giggling, she struggled to free herself and slapped his arm playfully then planted a hand upon her curvaceous hip and stared at Luke.

"Thank you, Clara, just the rum for now." He swept his gaze from her figure, suddenly finding the unabashed display unappealing.

"Perhaps later then." She pouted and sashayed away, checking over her shoulder to see if he was looking. He was. And yet he wasn't. Something else had caught his eye on the other side of the bar.

A gold epaulette glittered in the lantern light. Along with the brass buttons of a lieutenant's uniform, on top of which perched the squash-shaped head and pointed nose of Abner Tripp.

With a moan, Mr. Fairfax played a card.

Luke watched as the lieutenant stood alone at the bar and ordered a drink. This seedy tavern was not the sort of place Luke would have expected Lieutenant Tripp to frequent. He was more the posh tavern sort, places like Queen's or Grant's Tavern. In fact, it had been at Grant's Tavern that Luke had won his ship from the man in a game of Piquet.

Mr. Crenshaw tossed a coin in the pile and grinned.

Shaking the fog from his head, Luke gazed back at his cards. A breeze swirled in from the window, scattering the stagnant air and flickering the lantern's flame. If he indeed possessed the hand swirling in his vision, then it appeared his luck would hold.

The fishy-smelling man tossed his cards down and let out a belch. "That's it for me, gentlemen."

"And for me, as well." Luke snapped the hair from his face and laid his cards out faceup on the table. Gauging the men for their reactions, he reached inside his coat and fingered his pistol just in case.

Mr. Crenshaw emitted a foul word and scratched his head as if he couldn't fathom how Luke had won. He tossed down his cards. Mr. Fairfax, however, eyed Luke suspiciously. He clung to his hand as if the cards were all he had left in the world. His biting gaze shifted from Luke's cards to his own then across the other players.

Slipping his hand inside his coat, Luke gripped the handle of his pistol. How many men had accused him of cheating? An insult he could never allow to pass without calling for satisfaction. Which was precisely what had happened with Lieutenant Tripp. Normally, Luke would not mind an altercation. It kept his skill with the sword sharp while discouraging others from challenging him. Yet, tonight he found he had no desire to fight.

Finally, Mr. Fairfax tossed down his cards and mopped his sweaty brow. "Your infernal luck, Heaton."

Luck. "It's been a pleasure, gentlemen." Releasing his pistol, he reached to gather his winnings when he spotted Lieutenant Tripp parting the crowd, heading his way.

The annoying man halted before the table. "Heaton," he snorted. "Just where I expected to find you."

"But not where I expected to find you," Luke retorted with a grin.

Tripp straightened his coat and wobbled in place. "I heard of your success with my ship."

"Did you, now?" Luke leaned back in his chair. The man was drunk. It would be no fun taunting him in his condition.

Luke's three companions scooted their chairs back.

"Except it's my ship now, if you recall."

A sneer curled Lieutenant Tripp's lips. "You're nothing but a sot and a wastrel. One day of good fortune at sea cannot change that."

Luke attempted to shrug off the man's words though they sank into his gut, landing atop the ones Mr. Crane had planted there earlier that evening. "Perhaps. But what is that to you?"

"I'll have my ship back."

"So you have said." Luke sipped his rum. "You're drunk, Lieutenant.

Go home and sleep it off."

The crowd quieted as eyes shot their way. With the money he'd made, Luke could almost buy another ship and give *Destiny* back to this moron. If the man ever ceased being such a whining ninny, Luke might do just that.

The lieutenant stumbled again and rubbed the scar on his left cheek. "You will pay, sir."

Luke grew tired of the repetitious threats. He lifted his rum toward the man in a mock salute. "Perhaps. Now if you don't mind. . ." Luke waved his hand toward the door and slammed the rest of the rum to the back of his throat. Yet he had a feeling no amount of alcohol could make the peevish man disappear.

Before Luke could set down his glass, Lieutenant Tripp booted the table over, sending the coins, lantern, and cards flinging through the air, clanging and crashing to the wooden floor. He raised a pistol and pointed it at Luke. Mr. Fairfax doused the lantern flame, while Mr. Crenshaw dropped to his knees, scrambling to retrieve the coins.

The throng of excited onlookers backed away. The pianoforte stopped playing.

Luke released a frustrated sigh, set his glass on the next table, and slowly stood. The man's misty eyes wandered over him. The pistol shook in his hands.

Luke spread out his arms. "Well, shoot me then and get it over with." Certainly a deserving way for him to die. He'd given Mrs. Barnes enough money to last for years, at least until John was old enough to provide for himself. In fact, both she and John might be better off without Luke. Though his heart cramped at the pain the boy would endure at losing his only brother.

Lieutenant Tripp's eyelid began to twitch. He licked his lips. The pistol swung like a pendulum across Luke's chest. Time passed in slow motion. Only the sound of shifting boots, the hiss of lanterns, and the occasional grunt broke through the tense silence. Finally, someone yelled, "Shoot him" from the back of the mob. Others begged Tripp to put the weapon away.

A drop of sweat slid down Lieutenant Tripp's cheek as the pistol teetered in his hand. If Luke didn't stop this madness, the man might shoot an innocent bystander. Growing tired of waiting, Luke charged him, grabbed the gun, and tried to pry it from his fingers. Tripp struggled.

He clenched his teeth, growling like a rabid bear. People scattered.

Swinging back his fist, Luke struck the man across the jaw. He let go of the weapon and tumbled backward into the crowd. Uncocking the gun, Luke released a deep breath as the mob broke into a chorus of cheers and chuckles. A man emerged from among them and helped the groaning and red-faced Lieutenant Tripp to his feet.

Luke blinked. *Mr. Crane?* Luke had left him only an hour ago at the Channings'.

"Did Miss Channing toss you out?" Luke chuckled.

Crane led Tripp to a nearby chair then faced Luke. "Don't be daft. I came here to confirm my suspicions of you."

The pianoforte began thrumming again as the throng dispersed back to their depraved revelries.

"Indeed." Luke cocked his head, wondering which suspicions he meant, when Clara sidled up beside him and caressed his arm. "Are you all right, Luke?"

"Yes, thanks, love." He nudged her back.

"Miss Channing thinks you are a man of honor, sir." Mr. Crane's buzz-like voice drew Luke's gaze back to him. "A rather distorted view, I'd say, biased by the fortune you made for her. For I see that the rumors about you are true. You are a drunk." He eyed the cards lying haphazardly across the sticky floor. "A gambler, and a bully who would strike one of the great officers who protects our good nation."

The hypocrite! Fury seared through Luke, pooling in his fist still gripping the pistol, while his other hand wandered dangerously close to the hilt of his cutlass. Could he not escape this man? Only the fact that he was a friend of Miss Channing's kept Luke from drawing his sword.

"Rest assured, sir," the mongrel continued, "Miss Channing will hear of your behavior tonight"—his eyes wandered over Clara standing off to the side—"and I'm sure she will be as horrified as I am to discover just what type of man she has allied herself with."

Setting the pistol down atop a table lest he shoot the bird-witted clod, Luke forced a grin to his lips. "I have no doubt, sir." Then barreling through the throng, he blasted out the front door, only then realizing he'd forgotten his winnings. No matter. He'd have a hard time getting them from Mr. Crenshaw, anyway. Besides, what was a few dollars when he had thousands? A wall of cool night air slapped him, instantly sobering him, and making him thankful he hadn't challenged Mr. Crane. He'd dueled men with far less provocation.

But Miss Channing wouldn't approve.

And he found himself more than anything never wanting to displease her.

Yet this night had established one fact. Luke was not worthy of a treasure like Cassandra. If he continued to shower her with his attentions in the hope of gaining her affection, it would only end up causing her pain. For everything he touched became tainted—sullied. No, for Cassandra's own good, Luke must keep their relationship strictly business. And despite the torrent of feelings she invoked within him, he must do his best to stay away from her.

❖

Milton Crane led the wobbling lieutenant to a table in the far corner, away from the crowd that was still chattering about the altercation.

"That capricious blackguard," the lieutenant cursed as Crane eased him into a chair and asked him if he'd like a drink.

The lieutenant rubbed his forehead. "No, I believe I've had quite enough."

"Milton Crane." Crane held out his hand and took a seat beside the lieutenant.

"Lieutenant Abner Tripp." The man took his hand. "Thank you for your help, sir."

Even in his besotted state, there was no mistaking the pure hatred that burned in the lieutenant's eyes toward Heaton. Such passionate hatred must have its reward. And Crane knew just the thing.

"That was Mr. Heaton who assaulted you, was it not?"

Lieutenant Tripp moaned. "Yes. I should have shot him when I had the chance." He looked up, his gaze drifting back and forth over Crane. "Do you have the misfortune of being acquainted with the villain?"

"Only recently, sir. Though I am quite aware of his reputation."

"Then you've no doubt heard that he stole my ship in a game of cards, took all my money as well, and then had the audacity to call me out to a duel." He rubbed the long purple scar on his cheek.

Crane grinned. This was getting better and better. "I had not heard, sir. But I assure you, I find the man equally repugnant."

The lieutenant's eyes seemed to sober for a moment as he stared at Crane as if he too, could foresee an alliance between them.

Crane gestured with his head toward Mr. Keene and Mr. Sanders who were sitting at the next table. "You see those men. They are part of his crew."

The lieutenant shrugged. "So?"

"So, if they are like Heaton, they have no loyalty to him or anyone else."

Lieutenant Tripp slouched in his chair and shook his head.

"Mr. Heaton stands in the way of something very important to me." Visions of the scoundrel kissing Miss Channing on the cheek in the foyer of her home flashed through his mind as well as the dozens of amorous glances they had shared at dinner. The foolish girl was besotted with him. And he must put a stop to their growing affection before Miss Channing was hurt.

"And I perceive," Crane continued, "that you also seek revenge."

"You perceive correctly, sir." Tripp rubbed his long sideburns. "But I don't see what we can do about it."

"Ah, that's where you are wrong, Lieutenant. If we put our minds together, I believe we can both get what we want."

"Which is?"

"To destroy Luke Heaton."

❖

"Are you quite sure?" Cassandra turned her back on Mr. Crane and faced the window of their parlor, not wanting him to see the pain that must surely be visible on her face.

"Yes, I'm sorry to be the one to inform you, Miss Channing." His gravelly voice assailed her from behind. "I know how you admire the man. Not to mention your business arrangement with him."

Yet she doubted Mr. Crane was truly sorry at all, for not a trace of regret tinged his voice. Cassandra gazed at her mother's roses sparkling with morning dew in the front garden. "Why should I care if the man was entertaining a tavern wench?" She kept her voice disinterested, while a sick feeling clenched her gut and spiked through her heart at Mr. Crane's description of the buxom woman draped over Luke Heaton's lap last night.

"And I'm afraid he was quite drunk and gambling as well. And he got into a bit of a scuffle with a military man. Slugged him across the jaw."

Cassandra spun around, suddenly indignant at the man's jealous slurs. Why had she let him in the house again? She had woken in such high spirits. Everything in her life appeared to be going well. For once. Then why did this man's accusations of Mr. Heaton, true or not, squash her joy like a bug beneath his buckled shoe?

"I fail to see the purpose of telling me this, Mr. Crane. As long as Mr. Heaton is successful at privateering, I could care less what he does in his free time." Without thinking, she lifted a hand to her cheek where Mr. Heaton's lips had touched her skin.

Mr. Crane must have noticed her sorrow for he gave a sympathetic smile. "I thought you should know the trustworthiness of the man with whom you have invested your wealth."

Trustworthiness. Cassandra sighed. That was the crux of the matter, was it not? Cassandra's trust had been betrayed far too often and by far too many people. Never. Never would she toss her affections upon a man who, for all indications, would betray her, abandon her, and leave her all alone in the world.

❖ CHAPTER 17 ❖

Cassandra entered the Brenin sitting room and dashed into Marianne's outstretched arms. "I came as soon as I got your note. Any word?" She drew back and gazed into her friend's red-rimmed eyes.

Marianne lowered her chin and shook her head. "None so far."

Taking her hand, Cassandra led her to the sofa. "But you don't know which privateer was captured?"

Marianne sniffed and held a handkerchief to her nose. "No, only that it was a brig like Noah's and that it had just set out to sea, as he had done."

"Many of the privateers are brigs." Cassandra squeezed her hand, longing to bring the poor woman some comfort. "And there are hundreds of them out at sea."

Marianne played with the delicate lace on the edge of her handkerchief. "I hate to think of him pressed into the navy again. Or worse, sent to one of those rotting prison hulks." Her shoulders began to quiver.

Slipping an arm over Marianne's shoulders, Cassandra drew her close. "Surely God will take care of Noah." Though she didn't believe the words herself, she knew Marianne would find solace in her faith. A faith Cassandra had always envied and yet found so lacking within herself. Perhaps believing in a God who cared was just a fantasy, after all. The thought oddly weighed upon her heart with a deep sorrow.

Marianne's mother entered the room, young Jacob in her arms. "He's asking for you, dear."

Swiping her tears away, Marianne took the baby and perched him on her lap. Laying her chin atop his head, she inhaled a deep breath as if the scent of her son would bring his father back.

"Good day, Mrs. Denton." Cassandra rose, but the elderly woman waved a hand for her to stay with Marianne.

"Do not get up on my account." She smiled and lowered herself with difficulty into one of the floral-printed chairs beside the hearth.

Cassandra shook her head. Mrs. Denton suffered from far more serious illnesses than Cassandra's mother, yet rarely did a complaint pass through her lips.

Clank clank clank. The front door reverberated with the sound of the brass knocker. Marianne's face paled, and her eyes shot to the foyer. A few seconds passed, and Mr. Sorens announced Reverend Drummond just as the man ambled into the room, fumbling with his hat.

The butler cleared his throat and held out his hand. The reverend stared at him for a moment before handing him his hat. "Ah yes, good fellow. Thank you." He faced Marianne again.

She rose, hoisting Jacob into her arms. "Forgive me, Reverend, but I am quite distressed today. I was not aware you intended to visit."

He bowed toward all three ladies and greeted each one in turn. "My apologies, Mrs. Brenin, for barging in, but I just left Mr. Heaton."

"Mr. Heaton?" Marianne asked.

Luke? Cassandra nearly leapt from her seat. Why did the mere mention of his name cause such a childish reaction? It had been nearly a week since she'd last seen him at her house for dinner. A week since he'd kissed her cheek and run off into the night.

Run off into another woman's arms.

After Mr. Crane's visit, a shroud of gloom had descended on Cassandra, even as she chastised herself for such preposterous feelings. What did it matter how Mr. Heaton conducted himself? He was on land and could do what he wanted. There was no understanding between them that went beyond business. Finally after a few days, she had been able to tuck her confusing emotions away. After which, her senses returned. She needed no man. And she had informed Mr. Crane of that fact in no uncertain terms as she had swept from the parlor.

Had he hoped that after he disparaged Mr. Heaton's character, she would run into his arms and swoon? "Bah!"

All eyes shot to her, bringing her back to the present. She covered her mouth with her hand. "Forgive me. . . . You were saying?"

"Yes," Reverend Drummond continued. "I was saying that Mr. Heaton informed me of your situation, Mrs. Brenin. He is heading to the docks to see if he can uncover any information that will be of help." He took a step closer, his brown eyes brimming with concern. "And I thought I'd come by to see if I could offer you some comfort while you await the news."

"How kind of you, Reverend," Marianne's mother said.

Marianne smiled and sat back down. Jacob waved his hands in the air and grabbed his mother's handkerchief.

"What has Luke to do with this?" Cassandra stood and began to pace.

Marianne collected her son's flailing arms in her hand. "He came by as soon as he heard the news and offered to help."

"Do sit down, Reverend." Marianne's mother gestured toward a chair then asked Mr. Sorens, who had remained at the parlor entrance, to instruct Mrs. Rebbs to serve tea.

Marianne pressed a hand over her belly. "I don't believe I can drink anything right now, Mother."

"You must try, dearest. It will settle your stomach." Her mother folded shriveled hands in her lap and leaned back in her chair, a picture of tranquility, though the nervous blinking of her eyes betrayed her.

"What if it's Noah?" Marianne's voice broke into a sob. "What if he's been captured?"

As Cassandra passed by the sofa, Jacob reached for her. Gathering him in her arms, she extracted the handkerchief from his hands and handed it to Marianne.

"Noah is a competent sailor," Mr. Drummond offered, lowering himself into a chair.

Marianne dabbed at her eyes as another knock rapped through the foyer. The door squeaked open and the thud of heavy boots echoed over the wooden floor. Cassandra's heart froze. She knew the sound of those boots anywhere.

Mr. Heaton's masculine frame filled the doorway. His eyes widened at the sight of her before he greeted Mr. Drummond, Marianne, and her mother.

"Miss Channing," he said, tossing his cocked hat onto a table. "A pleasure as always." Then marching across the room, he planted a kiss on Marianne's cheek.

A kiss. Just like the one he'd given Cassandra. A casual kiss of friendship. That was all it had been. Which would explain the trollop and the fact that Mr. Heaton had not come to call on her in five days. Cassandra felt a hot flush rise up her neck at how silly she had been.

"What news?" Marianne wrung her hands together.

Mr. Heaton gave her a reassuring look. "Nothing yet. But I have an acquaintance looking into it. He'll question them immediately and come here as soon as he discovers anything of note."

Marianne nodded and squeezed his hand. "Thank you, Luke."

"It's the least I can do. Noah has been a good friend. More like a brother to me." Mr. Heaton's jaw tightened, and for a moment Cassandra detected a slight sheen covering his eyes. He cleared his throat. "I see you have family and friends around you."

His gaze brushed over Cassandra as he sat in a chair near the doorway and leaned his elbows on his knees.

Jacob grabbed a lock of Cassandra's hair and pulled it from its pin. The late afternoon sun cut a sharp angle of glittering dust across the room. It spun in a frenzied dance, mimicking Cassandra's insides. Why, when she should be focusing on comforting her friend, did the man's presence affect her so?

After several moments of silence in which everyone fidgeted uncomfortably, Reverend Drummond turned to Marianne. "Would you like me to pray, Mrs. Brenin?"

"Yes, very much." Marianne smiled and she, along with her mother, folded her hands in her lap. The reverend bowed his head. Cassandra did the same, clinging to Jacob, who with thumb in his mouth, now leaned peacefully against her chest.

"Father, we beseech You to protect Noah Brenin. Be with him wherever he is and put a shield of Your warring angels around him. Bring him home safely to his family. And, Father, protect the men who did get captured. We pray it isn't Noah and his crew. But if so, Father, help us to. . . ," he continued, but Cassandra opened her eyes. She wanted to see Mr. Heaton's reaction to the prayer, but his gaze locked onto hers—a gaze burning with such strong yearning and admiration that she dropped her chin again.

"Amens" sounded around the room.

"Thank you, Reverend," Marianne's mother said as Mrs. Rebbs brought in a tray of tea and biscuits and set it on the table.

Reverend Drummond reached over and touched Marianne's arm. "You must trust God."

"I do trust. But I also know that tragedies come our way."

Cassandra nodded. She could well attest to that. What she couldn't fathom was why God allowed such horrible things to happen to His children.

Jacob began to fuss and she wandered to the window, rocking him in her arms. Outside the shadows cast their nets over the street and houses, capturing the last rays of light and dragging them away. She tickled Jacob beneath the chin. He giggled. Kissing him on the forehead, she inhaled his sweet scent as he tried to put his fingers in her mouth. She clutched his tiny hand. No, she would never understand how a Father could hurt His own child.

The clank of spoons on china filled the room, even as the scent of mint tickled her nose.

"Yes, horrible things do happen," Reverend Drummond said. "We live in a fallen world. But if you're God's child, everything serves a purpose—a good purpose. You remember that."

Marianne sighed. "Yes. I learned that lesson well when Noah and I were impressed aboard that British frigate." She gave an embarrassed huff. "You'd think I would never forget."

Cassandra turned around to see Mr. Heaton stretching his booted feet out before him and crossing his arms over his chest. "I beg your pardon, Reverend, but no good came out of my being impressed in the Royal Navy save a sore back and a starving belly."

As if just now noticing Mr. Heaton's presence, Jacob stretched out his arms toward him, nearly leaping from Cassandra's arms.

Rising, Mr. Heaton made his way to her, but his eyes were on the boy.

"Much good came out of that, Luke." Marianne handed a cup of tea to Reverend Drummond. "You were there. We saved the USS *Constitution*."

Luke's blue eyes met Cassandra's—a trace of sorrow in them—before he took Jacob from her arms, flung the boy into the air, and returned to his seat. "Happenstance. The right place at the right time. That's all it was."

Cassandra watched as he set Jacob's feet on the floor and then held onto his hands to help him stand. His faith was even more depleted than hers. But what did she expect from a man who possessed no morals?

"Exactly." The reverend slapped his knee. "The right place at the right time. Hardly feasible unless there's a God controlling things, wouldn't you say, Mr. Heaton?"

Mr. Heaton's face hardened like granite. He placed Jacob's hands on his knees for support then released him. "No, I would not, sir. I cannot believe that. Otherwise it would force me to accept that God is a monster."

"Oh my. How can you say such a thing, Luke?" Marianne's mother gasped.

Marianne stared at him while Reverend Drummond flattened his lips. But the reverend's eyes filled with love, not the anger Cassandra had expected. "You have suffered much, Mr. Heaton. But those who have suffered much are destined for much." He smiled and sipped his tea.

Jacob wobbled and plopped to the ground on his bottom. Before he could whine, Luke swung him into his lap. "Destined for what, Reverend, more suffering?" No bitterness spiked his tone, just a defeat that made Cassandra sad.

"We have all suffered," Marianne's mother said quietly.

Mr. Heaton's gaze shot her way and his expression softened. "Indeed."

Up until now, Cassandra had not considered that Mr. Heaton had suffered overmuch. Yet, she seemed to recall that his parents had been murdered by Indians some years ago.

Marianne passed Cassandra a cup of tea. Her friend's hand trembled. Taking it from her, Cassandra sat beside her, pondering the suffering they all had endured.

Reverend Drummond scratched his beard. "God's destiny is never bad. But it is good and acceptable and perfect just as Paul says in Romans 12:2."

Marianne slid her hand inside Cassandra's as she said, "You speak the truth, Reverend. I have seen God's destiny in action. His plans *are* good." Her glance took in everyone in the room. "They don't always make sense at the time, but in the end they are always good. A very astute young boy said to me once that since I didn't know the end of the story, how could I know if the things that were happening to me were good or bad?"

Reverend Drummond smiled.

Confusion rampaged through Cassandra's mind. How could her father's death and her brothers' disappearance bring anything good to her and her family? When she looked up, she saw that Mr. Heaton seemed to be having an equally difficult time accepting Marianne's statement.

Jacob flung his arms about Luke's neck. The bewilderment slipped from his face. He smiled at the lad and allowed him to pull strands of black hair from his tie.

"It's a lovely thought, Marianne," Cassandra said. "But I have yet to see it played out in my life."

The reverend set down his cup. "You must believe God is good and that He rewards those who diligently seek Him. And you must seek Him, Miss Channing, with your whole heart."

Mr. Heaton snorted and stood.

Cassandra sipped the bitter tea, glancing at the tray for sugar but finding none. She hadn't sought God, yet she'd been rewarded nonetheless with more than enough money to pay off her debts and care for her family. Was life merely just happenstance? Just a thread of chaotic events? Or were there reasons for everything that happened? A plan? A purpose?

Yet another knock on the door brought Marianne once again to her feet. Mr. Sorens ushered in a young man dressed in a checkered shirt, pea jacket, and oiled blue trousers. The scent of fish filled the room. His eyes locked with Mr. Heaton's then glanced over the others. He smoothed down his unruly hair as if suddenly conscious of his appearance.

"William." Reverend Drummond greeted the man as if they were old friends.

Mr. Heaton shifted Jacob to his other arm. "By all means, Mr. Yates, do you have news of Noah Brenin?"

❖ CHAPTER 18 ❖

Luke eyed the sailor, who seemed as out of place in the Brenin parlor as a pirate at a cotillion. Yet his fear for Noah's fate overcame his patience. "Spill it, man, what news?"

"Ah, yes." The sailor grinned. "I have good news. The ship that was caught by the Brits was the *Rover*, not the *Defender*."

"Praise God!" Reverend Drummond shouted, leaping to his feet.

Marianne swayed as if she might faint, and Miss Channing helped her to sit back down on the sofa. Clutching her throat, Marianne released a breath. "God is good."

"Amen," her mother added.

As relief poured through him, Luke thanked the sailor, who dipped his head and spun on his heels as if anxious to leave the cultured surroundings.

"I best be going as well." Reverend Drummond searched for his hat. "I've got business to attend to." Anticipating the request, Mr. Sorens appeared around the corner, Reverend Drummond's hat in hand. Grabbing it with his thanks, the reverend called out after the sailor. "I'll walk with you, lad." Turning, he bid them all adieu, received Marianne's heartfelt thanks, and then left the sitting room. Luke could hear Mr. Drummond slapping the sailor on the back with a chuckle as they closed the front door behind them. Did the reverend hold such close acquaintance with everyone in town?

Marianne's mother rose and crossed the room to sit beside her daughter. She drew her into an embrace and together they half sobbed, half laughed, while Miss Cassandra gazed on with moist eyes. The tension that had kept the air in the room as stagnant as the doldrums released in a flurry of joy.

"Well, that saves me the trouble of having to go rescue him." Luke winked at Cassandra then knelt and set Jacob on the floor, holding him up by his hands. The boy attempted a step on his own. His wide grin, sporting three teeth and a stream of drool, melted Luke's heart. John was about the same age when Luke had taken over his care. Oh, how he wished he could go back in time and be a better father to the boy.

But God did not give second chances.

Marianne sat up and dabbed her handkerchief beneath her eyes. "He'll be walking before you know it."

"Indeed. They grow up fast." Luke's eyes landed on Miss Channing, who stared at him with an odd mixture of surprise and admiration. He warmed beneath her gaze, which she quickly swept to the window, where encroaching shadows had absconded with the light.

"When do you sail out, Luke?" Marianne asked.

"I leave for Elizabeth City tomorrow. I sent my crew ahead two days ago to prepare the ship."

Marianne's mother gripped the arms of the chair as she struggled to rise. "My goodness, the night has overtaken us unawares. I must bathe Jacob before supper."

"I will help you, Mother." Marianne made her way to Luke. With great reluctance, he relinquished the young boy. And apparently the feeling was mutual as Jacob whimpered and held out his hands toward Luke.

"Please be careful, Luke." Marianne clutched Jacob's hands to settle him. "And if you see Noah"—she looked down with a coy smile—"well, you know what to tell him."

Luke nodded.

"Oh my." Marianne turned to Miss Channing. "However will you get home in the dark?" Yet Luke caught the tiny smile peeking from the corners of her mouth.

Miss Channing stood and lifted her chin. "I am quite capable of finding my own way."

"Nonsense," Marianne's mother scoffed as she moved to her daughter's side.

"I would be happy to escort you, Miss Channing," Luke offered, ignoring the war within him—between his desire to spend time with this captivating woman and his promise to stay away from her.

Cassandra opened her mouth to say something, but Marianne held up a hand. "There, now, it is all settled." She approached Cassandra and touched her arm. "Thank you so much for coming, dear friend. I don't know what I'd do without you."

"I'm so pleased things turned out well." Cassandra clasped her hands together as if suddenly nervous.

"Mr. Sorens will see you out." Then turning, Marianne and her mother, along with a whimpering Jacob, left the room.

Luke raked a hand through his hair and raised his brows at Cassandra. Offering him nothing but a mere flick of her sharp eyes, she swept past him into the foyer, plucked her bonnet and gloves from a table, and waited for Mr. Sorens to open the door. Luke stepped onto the porch after her.

"There really is no need, Mr. Heaton." She tugged on her gloves, despite the muggy air.

"Nevertheless, I would never forgive myself should something happen to you." Luke could not explain her sudden stony demeanor. Last week at her house, she'd been kind, agreeable, and even quite complimentary toward him at the dinner table. She'd even allowed him to plant a kiss on her cheek.

Granted, he'd made himself a promise to avoid her. But now in her presence, he found himself longing to see a spark of ardor beaming from her eyes. Just a glimmer of sentiment would be enough to comfort him on his long sea voyage ahead.

But she kept her eyes from him as she stormed down the steps and out onto the street before he had a chance to offer her his arm. Lud, what an infuriating woman.

With only a quarter moon and a smattering of stars to light his way, Luke marched after her, overtaking her halfway down the street. He offered her his arm. "Unless you don't wish to be seen with me."

"I'm afraid it's too late for that, Mr. Heaton."

"Ah, that's it then, your reputation has been forever tarnished by our association." He chuckled, but she did not join in his amusement.

Instead she shot him a seething glance. "Go back to your trollop, Mr. Heaton."

Luke ground his teeth together, suddenly feeling like the cad everyone believed him to be. So, Mr. Crane had followed through with his threat.

When Luke didn't answer her, she gave an exasperated huff and hurried down the street. Somewhere, a fiddle played and laughter crackled in the air, but otherwise silence reigned on the city as thick as the night. Rubbing his jaw, Luke followed her at a distance, close enough to keep her firmly in his vision. She blazed forward into the darkness like a wild cougar, a tail of lacy petticoats flailing behind her.

No, not a cougar, an angel.

And certainly not one he could ever expect to possess.

She turned down Baltimore Street. The *clip clip* of her shoes over the cobblestones echoed off the brick walls of nearby buildings and local watering holes. Music blared from Payne's Tavern up ahead. Luke knew it well. Why was she traveling this way? Foolish woman. It would be much safer to take the long way around and avoid this section of town.

Yet still she stormed forward as if *she* were the indefatigable town rogue, not him. How the lady survived to be five and twenty defied all logic.

❖

Cassandra charged ahead, only realizing when she'd made it halfway down Baltimore Street that this was not the safest route to take at night. The jangling of a pianoforte, accompanied by a fiddle and raucous discourse, rode upon lantern light bursting from a tavern up ahead. Cursing burned her ears. She glanced over her shoulder, fully expecting to see Mr. Heaton behind her, but he was nowhere to be found. Hadn't she told him to go back to his trollop?

Yet she hadn't expected him to obey her.

Fear prickled her skin. How could he leave her all alone? Facing forward, she lowered her head and crossed the street, hoping the shadows would hide her until she could make it past the tavern, bustling with patrons, up ahead. Most of whom, she was sure, she did not wish to meet.

At least she carried no money with her this time. No banknotes. Nothing anyone would want. A shot echoed in the distance, jerking her gaze in that direction. The British? Or was it just a tavern brawl? Clutching her skirts, she quickened her pace, squinting into the darkness. Moonlight coated the buildings, trees, and cobblestone street in a ghoulish, milky sheen. The sting of alcohol and rain filled her nostrils.

Across the street, clusters of men hovered under the porch of the tavern, their heated conversations jumbled on the wind.

She was nearly past them.

A man barreled down the tavern steps, another on his heels. The first took a swig from a bottle, wiped his mouth on his sleeve, and handed it to his friend.

Cassandra sped to the shadows from a row of buildings up ahead.

"Hey there, missy!"

Her heart seized. She started to run.

"Where ye goin', missy? Come back here." The man's slurred words slinked over her shoulders and slammed into her gut.

Heavy footfalls pounded the road, growing louder and louder.

Not again. Cassandra darted forward. When would she learn her lesson?

"Missy, come join us, eh?" Insidious laughter accompanied the thump of footsteps.

Perspiration dotted her neck. She heaved a breath. One glance behind told her the two men were gaining. Ducking her head, she raced forward.

And ran headfirst into a warm, firm body.

Tar and smoke and wood filled her nostrils. *Mr. Heaton.* She glanced up, but could barely make out his smile in the darkness. He pushed her behind him then faced the villains and crossed his arms over his chest.

She peered around his back, her heartbeat steadying, then stepped beside him, fisting her hands on her hips and pasting a look of defiance on her face.

Her pursuers spotted Mr. Heaton. With wide eyes, they halted, their laughter faltering on their lips.

"Heaton, what ye doin' here?" The man's gaze shifted to Cassandra. She lifted her chin in his direction.

"The lady is with me, gentlemen." Mr. Heaton's stern voice left no room for argument.

A stream of profanity poured from their mouths. "Come on, Heaton. We was just havin' some fun. We weren't goin' t' hurt her none."

"Watch your language in front of the lady, or you'll answer to me," Luke said with authority.

154

The first man shook his head and scowled, yet he made no move. Instead Cassandra detected fear, dare she say respect emanating from him.

The other man grunted and swayed back and forth like one of the ships in the bay.

Luke waved them off. "Begone with you. There's no fun to be had here."

Turning, the two men shuffled away, passing the bottle between them as if to console themselves on their defeat.

Mr. Heaton faced her, stared at her for a moment, then proffered his elbow. "Now, will you allow me to escort you home?"

"You didn't leave me." Cassandra gaped at him, stunned.

"That is never my desire."

The wind drifted through loose strands of his hair, and for a moment the moonlight offered her a glimpse of something in his eyes that caused her breath to seize. She slid her hand in the crook of his elbow, and he led her forward. "Those men." She glanced over her shoulder to see them join a mob loitering in front of the tavern. "They offered you no resistance."

"They know me." He kept his face forward, his voice deep and resonant.

"In other words, they've seen you use a sword." Her praise brought no reaction. "Such depraved company you keep, Mr. Heaton."

"As you have informed me." He should be mad at her for her foolish behavior. He should be angry at her insults. But instead, a hint of humor spiked his voice.

An awkward silence surrounded them as they turned down Charles Street. Another shot echoed in the distance, followed by baleful laughter, yet Cassandra found no fear within her. As long as she was with Mr. Heaton. The thudding of his boots accompanied the whistle of the wind and the bells of the night watchmen in a whirlwind of emotions that reeled around her like the dust spinning on the street.

Mr. Heaton was a scoundrel, yet she always felt at ease on his arm.

A dark cloud abandoned the moon, showering them in silver light.

He was a drunk, yet he had never behaved improperly in her presence.

They turned down Eutaw Street, lined with quaint homes and decorative flower gardens. The smell of wild bergamot and fresh apple pie drifted over her nose.

He was a gambler, yet she trusted him with her investment.

Turning down the path in front of her house, Mr. Heaton stopped at the bottom of the porch stairs. Cassandra stepped up on the first tread and spun to face him. She was nearly level in height with him—nearly. The lantern light sparkled in his eyes as he placed a boot atop the step and released her arm.

He was a womanizer; then why did she feel her heart yearning for his affection?

He turned to leave.

"Thank you once again for your rescue, Mr. Heaton."

He faced her. A sad grin hovered over his lips. "My pleasure."

"So, you'll be leaving tomorrow?" She longed to keep him here. And hated herself for it.

"Riding out to the ship first thing in the morning."

"How long will you be?" Cassandra asked then realized the absurdity of the question. She laughed. "Of course you don't know that."

He gave her a quizzical look. "Will you miss me?"

"Don't be absurd." Cringing at the dishonest twang in her voice, she stared off toward the bay. "I'm simply anxious for you to catch another prize."

"Ah." He scratched the stubble on his chin and gave her one of his beguiling grins. "Of course."

Cassandra tapped her foot. "Oh, bother, Mr. Heaton. You can wipe that grin off your face. Not every woman in town pines for your affections."

"No." The sorrow in his voice nearly broke through the shield she'd erected around her heart. "Not every woman."

What was she doing? Allowing this rake to charm his way into her graces. Steeling herself against his further attempts, Cassandra pursed her lips. "Mr. Crane informed me of your ignoble activities."

"Which ones?" He jerked the hair from his face and chuckled. Moonlight drifted over a scar on his right earlobe.

"You may make sport of it all you wish, Mr. Heaton, but I hardly consider gambling, drinking, and fighting suitable pursuits for a successful privateer, much less a gentleman."

"Well, Miss Channing, you knew what you were getting when you hired me." One brow cocked, he gave her a pointed gaze. "Besides, I'm hurting no one." His eyes lowered to her lips. He swallowed.

Heat swirled in her belly. "I am not so sure, Mr. Heaton."

"Why are you so interested in what I do at night, Miss Channing? Care to join me?"

"Of course not! I'm sure you have no need of me with all your trollops to entertain you."

Propping his hand on the post, he drew close until she could feel his warm breath on her cheek. "If I were a more astute man, I'd say you were jealous."

Cassandra's heart took up an erratic beat. Lowering her chin, she gathered her resolve to put this man in his place. Then squaring her shoulders, she met his gaze and opened her mouth to give him a tongue lashing. "That's ridicu—"

His lips met hers. Firm, yet gentle. He caressed her mouth ever so briefly like the most delicate flutter of butterfly wings. Then he withdrew, hovering over her, breathing hard. Cassandra's mind swirled. She couldn't think. She couldn't breathe. She just wanted more of him. She inched forward until her lips touched his again. Her feet tingled. The world spun around her. He took control and deepened the kiss, cupping her jaw in his hand and caressing her cheek with his thumb. She drew in the scent of him, never wanting to forget this moment. He tasted of spice and salt.

The trollop barged into her dreamlike state. The one Mr. Crane had described in such detail. Her blond curls, sweet blue eyes, and buxom figure draped over Mr. Heaton.

No! The small part that remained of Cassandra's rational mind screamed. She would not be one of his many conquests. She would not attach her affections to this man, only to be abandoned.

She shoved Mr. Heaton back. Her chest heaved. "How dare you?" Then raising her hand, she slapped him across the cheek.

❖ CHAPTER 19 ❖

Pain lanced across Luke's face. He rubbed his cheek and stared at Cassandra. The woman was indeed an enigma. One minute returning his kiss with surprising intensity and the next, striking his cheek. He would never have made such advances if he'd not seen desire in her eyes. Not to mention an ardor that made his heart soar with hope. Hope that a woman like Cassandra found anything worthy of admiration in a man like him. Then, the way her moist lips shimmered in the moonlight, her puffs of warm breath, inviting him, luring him for a taste. He'd been unable to resist her. And, ah, sweet reward. He hadn't expected so passionate a response. Heat seared through his body while a pleasurable fog had invaded his mind.

What he *had* expected came later—a slap. A worthy punishment for so great a prize.

And now a mixture of horror and ecstasy battled in her eyes as she stood there, red faced with her infernal shoe tapping on the stairs.

He'd never seen a woman so lovely.

Luke rubbed his jaw again. "What, pray tell, was that for?"

"For trying to take liberties with me."

"Trying?" Luke chuckled. "I believe I succeeded. And as for the liberties, they were freely given."

"How dare you!" She lifted her hand again to strike him. He caught it in midair. "Ah, ah, ah, only one slap allowed per kiss." Caressing her hand, he lifted it to his mouth, but she snagged it from his grasp.

"Is everything a joke to you, sir?"

"Not everything." He smiled.

She let out an exasperated sigh and took a step away from him. "This is a business arrangement, Mr. Heaton, and you are nothing but a business partner. I insist you conduct yourself as such in my presence."

Luke could feel the heat coming from her flushed skin. Her chest rose and fell like the bow of a ship upon stormy seas.

"If you're certain that is what you wish." He dipped his head with an unavoidable grin.

"If I'm. . ." She flattened her lips and tore her gaze from him. "Of course I'm certain, you buffoon."

The quiver of desire in her voice belied her statement. Luke offered no response. He simply gazed at her as the moonlight caressed her in sparkling waves. He didn't know how long he'd be gone, and he never wanted to forget how beautiful she was, nor how deeply affected she seemed to be by his kiss.

"Good evening, Mr. Heaton." She met his gaze then turned and opened the door. The voices of children and bark of a dog floated from inside. Halting, she spoke without turning. "Godspeed to you, sir. Have a safe journey."

"Good evening, Miss Channing."

Then, stepping into the foyer, she closed the door behind her.

❖

"This is madness, Luke. I beg you to reconsider." The squeak of Mrs. Barnes's rocking chair increased in tempo.

"I promised John, and I won't go back on my word." Tired of the conversation, Luke set his mug of coffee down on the table and leaned forward with elbows on his knees. Mrs. Barnes's fingers flew, her needles jumping up and down like handles on a bilge pump. He studied the web of black and white threads coming together in a deranged mass. "What is that you're making again?" he asked, mainly to change the subject.

Ceasing her knitting, she glanced down at her creation. "A masterpiece," she announced with assurance. But her brief smile faded into a frown, and she laid her knitting aside. "He's far too young, Luke, and you know it." Her pleading tone reached out to strangle Luke's conviction.

Swimming eyes met his above the glimmer of her spectacles. He pulled his gaze and stared at the cold soot lining the fireplace. "He's as old, if not older, than most boys who go to sea. Besides, with his new brace, he's walking better."

"But on a heaving ship? When you could be attacked? When you probably will attack other ships?" Mrs. Barnes grabbed her cup of tea. Her hands trembled, and the amber liquid sloshed over the sides. She set it down on the saucer with a clank and folded her shriveled hands in her lap.

Luke shot to his feet and took up a pace across the sitting room. He rubbed his jaw where Miss Channing had slapped him earlier that evening. Though the memory brought a smile to his lips, he couldn't help but feel as though he were being slapped all over again by Mrs. Barnes's lack of confidence in him. But what else did he expect? Save for his one success at sea last month, Luke had been a failure at everything else.

But he *had* outsailed a frigate. He had dodged cannon blasts. He had taken a prize. Never once had his crew been in any serious danger. Despite her age, *Destiny* was a swift and agile bird. And Luke a good captain. Surely he had proven that.

"I could not bear to lose him," Mrs. Barnes said.

"And you think I could?"

"No, of course not. But your parents put him in your charge. I beg you to not make such a rash decision."

Trailing a hand through his hair, Luke faced her. "I have thought long and hard about this, Mrs. Barnes. He is ten. Brace or not, we cannot coddle him forever. He must be allowed to face life with all its dangers and heartaches. How else is he to grow up and become a man? How else is he to learn a trade so he can take care of himself someday?"

She opened her mouth to object but Luke raised a hand. "He is going."

A tremble crossed her shoulders. Chastising himself for being so harsh, Luke knelt before her and took her hands in his. "I'll keep him on a long line tied to one of the masts, so there'll be no chance of him falling overboard. When we overtake a prize, I'll send him below. He'll be fine." He kissed her bony fingers.

"I promise you, I'll bring him home safe."

❖

Luke planted his boots firmly on the quarterdeck as *Destiny* rose over yet another swell then plunged down into the murky sea. Waves crashed over the bow, spraying the air with foamy salt and sending a waterfall over the deck. A giggle sounded, and Luke's gaze shot to his brother on the main deck. He was talking with Mr. Ward, the gunner. Feet spread apart, John stumbled only slightly before he righted himself then held out his hands and dipped a bow at Mr. Ward's hearty applause.

Despite his apparent sturdiness, Luke was still glad the boy was tied to the mast with a rope long enough to allow him access to the entire deck. Aside from his initial bout of seasickness, the lad had more than adapted to life aboard the ship during the long weeks at sea. With his positive outlook, cheerful disposition, and strong work ethic, the crew took an immediate liking to John. But it was the odd relationship that had developed between him and the ornery gunner that surprised Luke the most.

Biron crossed the quarterdeck and halted beside Luke. "Courses and mains raised, Cap'n, and the horizon is clear."

Luke shielded his eyes from the setting sun as a hot gust of wind punched him. They'd been running under courses for days now. No need to unfurl the stays and topsails until they gave chase. Or, God forbid, were chased. Either way, they'd not spotted a ship in a week, which was why Luke had ordered *Destiny* on a south-by-southeast course to intercept West Indies trade routes.

Biron chuckled. "Ward's taking a liking to the boy."

"Odd. Yes."

"I wonder if he's the best influence on the lad?" Biron quirked a brow of reprimand at Luke.

"Knowing my brother, it's him who'll be influencing old Ward for the better. Perhaps, the old codger will even stop his swearing and drinking."

"Perhaps you will join him." Biron's voice was etched with sarcasm.

Luke chose to ignore it as the ship crested another wave. Bracing his feet on the moist deck, he breathed in the fresh, salty air. He loved the sea. There was freedom here upon the waves. Freedom and power. For the first time in his life, he felt in control of his own destiny.

Gripping the quarter railing, Luke glanced up at the sails, their white bellies bloated with wind. Mr. Keene stood on the main top, directing the sailors adjusting canvas, lace flapping at his cuffs and collar. His humor was vastly improved from the last voyage. As were several of the sailors. No doubt due to the bottles of rum locked in a crate belowdecks, and the money that still lined their pockets. Bottles Luke had brought aboard, despite Miss Channing's insistence to the contrary, but only on the condition that Luke would dispense the alcohol at his discretion. Which so far had only been two ounces in a cup of lemon water twice a day to each sailor. This seemed to appease the men, but it made Luke's vow to abstain while sailing all the more difficult. He licked his lips. His taut nerves and empty belly yearned for a sip. Just one sip.

Still he had kept to his word. Thus far.

Sam cleared his throat from behind them. "She still feels a bit sluggish, Cap'n."

Luke shrugged off the ill feeling that accompanied Sam's words. He'd already sent Mr. Sanders down twice to check on the hold, and both times the purser had reported nothing amiss. Perhaps it was just Sam's inexperience with such a small ship. "Just keep her south-by-southeast, Sam." Luke squinted at the sun sinking below the horizon as a breeze, bearing a reprieve from the day's scorching heat, cooled the sweat on his neck.

"Aye, aye, Cap'n."

John hobbled up on the quarterdeck with the agility of an experienced seaman.

"When can I take off this silly rope?" He made a face of disgust as the wind tousled his hair.

"When I say you can," Luke replied.

"But I'm steady on my feet now. The sailors make fun of me with this leash on!"

Biron chuckled. "Don't listen to them, boy. One day you'll be their captain and we'll see who's laughing then."

John's face brightened. "You really think so, Mr. Abbot?"

"That I do."

"You have the makings of a great sailor, John. A natural talent"— Luke raised a brow—"but you must still obey your captain."

John saluted. "Aye, sir."

"Sail ho!" The voice brayed from the tops, jerking Luke to attention.

John gripped the railing and scanned the horizon.

"Where away?" Luke shouted, lifting the scope to his eye.

"Two points off our starboard beam!" The shout ricocheted off the deck as Luke spun the glass in that direction. Excited chatter rose from the assembling crew.

Billowing sails, stark against the murky sky, came into view.

"Is she a merchantman, Luke? I mean Captain Luke." John's voice brimmed with enthusiasm.

"Hold steady there, lad," Biron interjected. "It won't matter if she is. We haven't enough daylight left to take her."

"Ah. . ." John's shoulders lowered.

Luke could relate. Patience had never been one of Luke's finest virtues either. If he possessed any virtues at all. Though he knew privateers could be out for months before seeing any action, the quicker he caught a prize or two, the quicker he could return to Baltimore to see Miss Channing. The quicker he could add another success to outweigh his list of failures. And the quicker he could prove to Mrs. Barnes that he was fully capable of taking care of John at sea.

Several minutes passed as the ship came sharper into view. Waves slapped against the hull. Sails flapped thunderously as his crew awaited orders. Luke studied her armament and the shape of her hull just as a shout from above confirmed his assessment.

"She's a Royal Navy frigate!"

John's eyes widened. "A frigate!" He begged for the glass, nearly plucking it from Luke's hand, then raised it to his eye, looking ever so much like he'd been born to captain a ship. Luke smiled. If Mrs. Barnes could see the boy now, all her worries would blow away in the wind.

Biron tugged at his red neckerchief, his gray brows colliding. "Should we run?"

Luke shook his head as the sun bade its farewell with bands of orange and maroon. "No sense. It will be dark soon." He turned to Sam, manning the wheel with as much seriousness as he had no doubt done in the navy. "Keep her steady, Sam."

John's *oohs* and *aahs* filled the air as he examined the ship through the scope. But soon darkness stole it from their view, and he handed the glass back to Luke.

"Sam, alter course slightly to the east," Luke ordered. "We'll lose them during the night. And Biron, inform the night watch to keep the lanterns cold, if you please. We don't want to give them anything to shoot at, do we?"

"Aye, aye, Cap'n," both men replied.

Untying John, Luke ushered the boy down the companionway to the captain's cabin. After a rather tasteless meal of dried meat and hard biscuits, Luke assisted John with his studies—another thing he'd promised Mrs. Barnes he would do. After going over mathematics, literature, and shipboard navigation, Luke tucked John into the captain's bed. "You're much smarter than I ever was, little brother. I was never very good at my studies."

"I know. Mrs. Barnes told me." John smiled.

Laughing, Luke tapped John on the nose, pride welling up in him. "You're also going to be a great sailor and a good captain."

"I told you I could do it." The young boy nodded.

"And you were right. I should have trusted you."

"I take after you, Luke." John grew serious. "You're a great captain. Mom and Dad would be proud."

Emotion burned in Luke's throat as he pulled the quilt up to John's chin. He doubted that was true. If his parents could see the way Luke lived his life, it would no doubt break their hearts. All the things they had warned him to stay away from, he had run out and done anyway. The gambling, drinking, the womanizing. And all the things they had told him were important, reading his Bible, praying, working hard, and trusting God, he had not done. Why? Rebellion against their rigid rules, he supposed. But it went much deeper than that. Right into the depths of their faith. Where had their devotion to God gotten them? Burned alive in their own house. But Luke didn't blame God for that. How could he blame someone who didn't exist? No, their deaths were on Luke's head. He could have rescued them, but he didn't. Instead, he had stood there like a coward.

A sudden ache sliced through his right ear, and he reached up to rub it.

"Get some sleep, John." Luke stood. "You never know what tomorrow will bring. Perhaps we'll catch a prize!"

John gave him a wide grin then turned on his side and closed his eyes as if obeying Luke would make it come true.

By the time Luke made it to his desk, John's deep breathing filled the cabin. Ah, to be an innocent child again and fall asleep without a care in the world. Sinking down onto the stern window ledge, Luke propped up his boot and gazed out the windows onto the ebony sea beyond. Boisterous laughter and a ribald ballad drifted down from above, reminding Luke that everyone—but him and possibly Biron—was enjoying some rum tonight.

Infernal woman. He leaned his head back on the bulkhead. Infernal, wonderful, beautiful woman. Though it had been weeks, his lips still burned with the passion of her kiss, her taste. The way she had melted at his touch and groaned in pleasure. She had wanted him to kiss her. And he had been unable to stop. Just as he was unable to stop thinking of her now. Did he have a chance to win her affections? He had not thought so until that night. But a seed of hope had wiggled into the hard soil of his heart—albeit a tiny seed—that a woman like Cassandra could love a blackguard like him.

❖

"Captain!" Rough hands gripped Luke's arms. "Get up."

Luke rubbed his eyes and opened them to see a worried look on Biron's lined face.

"What is it?" He sprang from the hammock.

"It's the frigate, Captain." Biron shot a glance out the stern windows where the sun's rays were just intruding into the cabin and then at John, still sound asleep on the bed.

"She's fast on our tail."

❖ CHAPTER 20 ❖

Clutching her gown, Cassandra dragged her tired legs up the stairs to her chamber. She'd been woken far too early that morning when Darlene, Hannah, and Dexter had burst into her room chasing each other in a game of privateer versus British merchantman. With sticks as swords, hairbrushes as pistols, and Dexter's thunderous barks serving as cannon blasts, the trio had pounced on her bed, oblivious to Cassandra's sleeping form. After chastising them, Cassandra had given in to their sobs and gathered them up on her rumpled coverlet where the three of them, and Dexter, had engaged in a renewed battle, only this time using pillows— the likes of which had quickly become casualties of war in a snowstorm of feathers. Cassandra had insisted they all help Mrs. Northrop clean up the mess, but now as Cassandra entered her chamber, she spotted one rebellious feather peeking at her from beneath the bed. Stooping, she picked it up and brushed it over her chin, a smile lifting her lips. Just to see Hannah well again was worth the mayhem.

A scraping sound jerked Cassandra's gaze to her dressing bureau in the far corner where Mrs. Northrop stood gaping at her, a look of terror on her face.

"Mrs. Northrop, whatever are you doing in here?"

The housekeeper waved both hands in the air. "Just searching for more feathers, miss." Her voice quaked and her gaze skittered across the chamber. "Oh, I see you've found one." Dashing toward Cassandra, she plucked it from her hand and rushed out of the room.

Cassandra stared after her. The woman's behavior was becoming more and more peculiar with each passing day.

The shrill *ding ding ding* of a bell shot through the open door, followed by her mother's pathetic howl. Then Darlene's boisterous laughter, accompanied by Hannah's yelp, barreled through the window from outside.

Perhaps the entire house was mad, after all.

Cassandra wandered to her window and sat on the cushioned ledge. Shafts of afternoon sunlight angled across the side of the house and over the top of the solarium below. The leaves of birch and maple trees fluttered in the breeze as pink Virginia creeper circled their trunks. A hot summer breeze caressed her face, swirling the scent of wild mint and thyme beneath her nose. A bell tolled from the docks, and her thoughts drifted to Mr. Heaton. He'd been gone two weeks. Not a day—no, if she were honest—not an hour passed that she did not think of him.

And his kiss. The way her insides had felt like a thousand flickering candles. The look of adoration and desire in his eyes. The shameful way she had responded.

Before she had slapped him.

Yet even her strike had not erased the affection from his gaze or the mischievous smirk from his lips. She missed him. And she hated herself for it. A niggling fear had ignited within her these past days. Privateering was dangerous business. What if something happened to him and his ship? What if she never saw him again?

Cassandra gazed down at the floral pattern on the cushions. She must not think of him. Nor of his kiss. She must not entertain thoughts of any attachment to the man. For he was a blackguard and a philanderer. Not a man to be counted on—trusted. Even if she accepted his courtship, he'd no doubt grow restless and abandon her. No, she could not depend on anyone, not ever again. For everyone had let her down. Even God.

God. Reverend Drummond and Marianne had said that God had a purpose—a good purpose for everything that happened. If that was true, if God was involved in the details of Cassandra's life, would He still listen to her prayers? Even though she had ignored Him for years?

She bowed her head. "God, if You're listening, please protect Mr. Heaton."

The sound of a throat clearing opened Cassandra's eyes. She turned to see Margaret smiling at her from the doorway. Cassandra's face heated.

"Forgive me, miss. I didn't mean to intrude, but your mother requests your presence in the parlor. Mr. Crane has arrived."

Cassandra closed her eyes. "Oh, bother." Lately, the man seemed to appear wherever Cassandra happened to be: at the chandlers, the wheelwright, the seamstress, the butcher. And when she didn't venture out, he showed up at her house. However, his usual dour mood had significantly improved these past few weeks. To the point that he was almost giddy with delight. And for some reason, that annoyed her more than his peevishness. At least he had not brought up the subject of a courtship between them again. Though if that was not his goal, she couldn't imagine why he continued to call on her family. Squaring her shoulders, Cassandra rose from her seat, pressed down the folds of her gown.

"Pardon me for saying so." The maid gave her a coy grin. "But it's good to see you praying again, miss."

Cassandra flung a hand in the air as she brushed past Margaret. "I was just praying for Mr. Heaton's safety."

"Well, if he's the one causing you to talk to God again, I hope he returns to town soon." Margaret's words followed Cassandra downstairs and settled on her heart with equal sentiment.

So did she. So did she.

Before she reached the foyer, whispers slithered over her ears. Peering over the banister, Cassandra spotted Mr. Crane speaking to Mrs. Northrop at the entrance to the long hall that led to the back of the house. Mrs. Northrop nodded and sped away, while Mr. Crane strode to the foot of the stairs, his face aglow with surprise when he saw Cassandra descending.

"Ah, Miss Channing, you look lovely this afternoon."

"Thank you, sir. What on earth were you speaking to my housekeeper about?"

His lips twisted in an odd shape before he answered. "Just ordering some tea for your mother." He proffered his arm and led Cassandra into the sitting room where her mother perched excitedly on the settee.

"Oh, there you are, dear. Isn't it nice that Mr. Crane has taken time away from his duties at the newspaper to call on you?"

Not particularly. Cassandra forced a smile and took a seat beside her mother just as Hannah darted into the room, her eyes red with tears. "Mama, Darlene hit me."

After an embarrassing glance at Mr. Crane, Cassandra's mother placed her fingers atop her temple. "Please, dearest, tell her we do not hit each other in this house."

"I did," Hannah whined.

Darlene tumbled into the room then stopped short when she saw Mr. Crane. "I didn't hit her, Mother."

"Yes, you did." Hannah stomped her foot and folded her arms over her chest.

"No, I didn't."

Cassandra's mother closed her eyes and rang her bell, while Mr. Crane examined the girls with disdain before releasing a huff of impatience.

Seeing an opportunity to relieve herself of Mr. Crane's company, Cassandra rose. "I'll take them upstairs, Mother." She started toward the girls.

"No, dear, I insist you stay and entertain Mr. Crane. I've invited him to stay for supper. Besides, Mrs. Northrop can take care of them." She rang her bell again and the housekeeper appeared, a scowl on her face.

Kneeling beside her sisters, Cassandra gave them both a stern look. "Now go with Mrs. Northrop and attend to your studies. And behave yourselves, both of you."

"I'm sorry, Cassie." Darlene feigned a pout.

"I simply cannot handle them anymore," her mother remarked to Mr. Crane after the girls left.

Cassandra spun around. "You never could handle them, Mother."

Her mother frowned. "I suppose you're right. You were equally as difficult, but at least your father was still here to help."

Cassandra's anger dissipated beneath the look of pain on her mother's face. Taking her seat again, she placed a hand on her mother's arm. "I'm truly sorry, Mother."

Her mother gave a sad smile. "You always did have a mind of your own."

Mr. Crane cleared his throat. "All those girls need is the firm hand of a man's discipline."

"Oh, you are so right, Mr. Crane. You are so right, indeed." Her mother's voice came back to life.

Cassandra leaned back in her chair, desperate to change the subject.

"How is the newspaper business, Mr. Crane?"

"Booming." He tugged at the cuffs of his coat and sat on the sofa opposite Cassandra. A breeze stirred the curtains at the windows as the clatter of a horse and carriage ambled by on the street. "War is good for the news business, you know."

Her mother chuckled. "Of course it is."

Cassandra braced herself for another excruciating soliloquy of the happenings down at the *Baltimore Register*. But instead, Mr. Crane brought up a topic that had consumed Cassandra's mind of late. "Have you heard from Mr. Heaton?"

A moment passed in which Cassandra gazed at him in astonishment, then another moment as she wondered at his reasons for asking. He had made his abhorrence of Mr. Heaton quite clear the last time they'd been together.

"Cassandra, you're being rude. Answer Mr. Crane." Her mother laughed nervously.

"No, I have not heard from him, sir. But it's only been a few weeks. It could be months before he returns."

Mr. Crane's lips fell into a frown, and the edges of his nose seemed to droop with them. "So many of Baltimore's privateers have never returned." Leaning forward, he clipped the edge of the table with his forefinger and thumb while he spoke. He did not meet her gaze, though she thought she saw a hint of a smile peeking from the corners of his eyes. "The *Eleanor*, *Phaeton*, *Pioneer*, *Tartar*, all lost at sea. And the *Baltimore*, *Cashier*, *Courier*, *Dolphin*, *Arab*, *Lynx,* and *Falcon* all captured. Ah, the list goes on."

Cassandra shifted uncomfortably on her seat.

"How true, Mr. Crane." Her mother huffed. "But at least our share of Mr. Heaton's first prize should last us a good long while."

Our share? Cassandra eyed her mother. When had it become *their* enterprise and not Cassandra's foolish venture? "Regardless, Mother, there are human lives at stake. Not to mention the fate of our country."

"I'm sure your mother meant no disrespect," Mr. Crane said. "I, for one, can attest to that feeling of security that comes from financial independence." With chin extended, he draped both arms across the back of the settee like a peacock spreading his feathers. "But I do come on another matter."

Her mother nearly jumped from her seat as if she knew of what matter he spoke. Cassandra gazed between them, unsure if she wished to hear it or not.

"Yes, Mr. Crane?" her mother said.

"No doubt you've heard about the upcoming ball at the Fountain Inn."

Cassandra's heart dropped. "I have, sir."

"Please extend me the privilege of escorting you, Miss Channing." His confident smile sent a shiver through her.

"Oh, how kind of you, sir!" Cassandra's mother clapped her hands. "Isn't it, dear?"

"Very kind." Cassandra bit her lip and avoided the man's gaze. Her eyes landed on a tea service on the table, and confusion wracked through her. Mr. Crane had said he ordered Mrs. Northrop to bring tea. With narrowed eyes, she opened her mouth to question him when an ominous crash sounded from the back of the house. Someone screamed, and the pounding of feet echoed down the hallway.

Cassandra's mother moaned. Cassandra shot to her feet and tossed a "pardon me" over her shoulder at Mr. Crane before darting from the room and down the hall as she followed the sound of sobbing coming from the kitchen. She barreled through the swinging door to see Miss Thain on her knees before pieces of broken china and a splattering of red liquid. Dexter sat on his haunches, taller than Miss Thain on her knees, and grinned—if dogs could grin—bloody juice dripping from his furry chin. The smell of pea soup and dog breath assailed her. The door swung open, bumping Cassandra as her mother and Mr. Crane joined her.

Miss Thain wiped the tears from her face. "I'm so sorry, mum. Darlene and Hannah ran through and knocked the tray from my hands. And that beast followed them in and ate the entire roast for dinner."

"Gads!" Mr. Crane said. "Of all the. . ."

Mrs. Northrop entered the room and gasped.

Growling, Dexter charged Mr. Crane and leapt upon him, forcing him back with two enormous paws upon the man's pristine coat. Pristine no longer as blood from the roast, mixed with dog saliva, sprayed over the fabric with each bark.

Mr. Crane's face crumpled in disgust. Cringing, he crossed his arms over his face as Dexter shoved him against the wall. "Get him off of me!"

"Oh dear, Mr. Crane. My apologies, sir." Mrs. Channing hurried toward him. "Dexter, get down this instant!" Her harried gaze swept to

Cassandra. "Get that monstrosity of a dog off Mr. Crane and out of here at once!"

Restraining a giggle, Cassandra grabbed Dexter's collar, tugged him from the cowering newspaper man, and led him to the door.

"How many times have I told those girls not to run in the kitchen or to allow that dog in the house!" her mother brayed to no one in particular.

"Be a good boy, now," Cassandra whispered to the dog, closed the door, and turned to see her mother nearly swooning over Mr. Crane, who had somewhat recovered from his display of cowardice. Although to be fair, Cassandra had never seen Dexter behave so violently with anyone before.

"That was to be our supper, Mr. Crane," Cassandra's mother whined. "We had purchased the finest meat we could find in town. Quite expensive, you know. And now we have nothing to offer you."

"Do not vex yourself, Mrs. Channing." Mr. Crane led her to a chair at the preparation table. "I am happy to eat porridge and biscuits if that is all you have to offer me."

"Don't be silly, Mr. Crane." Her mother dropped her forehead into her hand. "We would never think of serving such menial fare to such an important guest."

"How kind of you, madam." Mr. Crane took a step back and examined his soiled coat. He brushed his sleeves in a panicky fashion, as if the pandemonium in the house were infectious.

Miss Thain continued to sob.

"Perhaps you should take Mother to the parlor, Mr. Crane"— Cassandra offered him a sweet smile—"while I straighten this mess out."

"Yes, very well." He tugged at his cravat.

"But what are we to serve for supper?" her mother asked.

Cassandra gazed out the window where bright sunlight lit the garden in a kaleidoscope of greens, browns, and yellows. "Never fear, Mother, it is still early. Margaret and I can go to the market."

Clinging to the table for support, her mother stood and smiled. "Thank you, dear." Then clutching Mr. Crane's arm, she allowed him to lead her from the kitchen.

After they left, Cassandra reassured Miss Thain that she bore no blame for the incident and then instructed Mrs. Northrop to assist the cook in cleaning up the mess. Upstairs, Cassandra retrieved the key to her father's chest from its hiding place in the top drawer of her dressing bureau. If she was to purchase a good cut of fresh meat, she'd need some money.

With key in hand, she ventured out the back door into the garden and made her way around the corner of her house to the solarium. Inside, the warm, moist air saturated her with the smell of gardenias. She drew in a deep breath and shook her head at the madness that seemed to always plague her family. Sitting on her stool, she pulled out the wooden chest from beneath her workbench, inserted the key, and flung it open. Her heart seized.

And shattered into a million pieces.

The money was gone.

❖ CHAPTER 21 ❖

Stuffing a pistol into his baldric and his cutlass into its scabbard, Luke leapt onto the main deck. He plucked the spyglass from his belt and pointed it aft. Mountains of white sails filled his vision—floating atop the hull of a British frigate. The Union Jack flew proudly from her foremast as she bore down on them just a few miles off their stern. They were gaining fast.

Luke's throat closed. "Lud. How did this happen?"

"She appeared out of nowhere as soon as the sun broke the horizon," Biron replied, his tone filled with surprise and something else that Luke had rarely heard from his friend—dread.

Lowering the scope, Luke squinted against the rising sun and scanned the ship where his crew stood gaping at the oncoming enemy. "Get to work, you sluggards!" he barked. "Mr. Keene, make all sail. Up topgallants and stays. Drop every stitch of canvas to the wind."

Standing on the foredeck, Mr. Keene snapped out of a daze and turned to shout orders to the topmen, sending them leaping into the shrouds. Gone was the permanent smirk from his lips, the mischievous glint in his eyes. Instead fear laced his features.

Luke turned his attention to Sam, who stood ever faithful at the wheel. The lad's light hair blew in the breeze. His eyes focused forward as if willing the ship to go faster. "Four points to starboard, Sam. Steady as she goes."

174

"Steady as she goes, Cap'n," Sam replied in a terse tone.

Luke gazed up at the men unfurling the extra canvas above. When all sails were raised to the wind, *Destiny's* lighter frame should have no trouble outrunning the much heavier frigate. And on the off chance they couldn't, Luke would bring the ship alongside the coast, where they could slip into a cove that was too shallow for the frigate to follow.

Destiny flew through the water, cresting a rising swell and plummeting down the other side. Churning water leapt over the bow and rolled across the deck. The ship creaked and groaned beneath the strain. Bracing himself for the next wave, Luke raised his scope again. The frigate seemed to have picked up speed. With the wind's advantage, she glided toward them under towering peaks of white canvas, a mustache of milky foam cresting her bow.

Alarm tightened Luke's nerves.

Mr. Ward appeared on deck, followed by Mr. Sanders, the purser's angular face made sharper by fear. The gunner, however, stopped before Luke, determination stiffening his features. "Orders, sir?"

"Prepare the guns, Mr. Ward," Luke said. "And pray we don't need to use them."

As the gunner ambled away, the thunder of sails drew Luke's gaze upward as the topgallants and staysails dropped into the wind. Good. Now perhaps *Destiny* would pick up speed. No sooner had the thought brought him some comfort than a deafening clamor rained down from above.

The main and fore staysails flailed in the breeze like sheets hung out to dry, giant rents splitting them from foot to leech. Luke shook his head, unwilling to believe his eyes. Who would have done such a thing? Hadn't he ordered Mr. Keene to inspect all canvas before they'd set sail? His wary gaze shot to the boatswain as the man slid down the backstay to the main deck. He charged toward Luke.

"Captain, I don't know what happened. I inspected each sail myself before we left." The sincere look in his eyes, coupled with the terror lining his face, convinced Luke that he told the truth. The ship heaved over the rough seas. Balancing himself, Luke charged toward the railing, his mind reeling.

"Furl the damaged ones, Mr. Keene, and get below to retrieve additional canvas."

Mr. Keene nodded, but the brief knowing look they exchanged told

Luke they were of the same mind. By the time they got the additional sails hauled up on the stays, it would be too late.

Luke swallowed down a surge of dread. His thoughts drifted to John, still asleep below. Cargo more precious than silver or gold or even the ship itself.

The sun released its grip on the horizon and spread golden wings over the sea. Wings Luke needed at the moment to quicken his ship and fly away.

"Cap'n, she's still sluggish," Sam shouted from the wheel. Luke speared fingers through his hair. Scanning the deck for his first mate, he found Biron assisting the gun crew at one of the larboard carronades. "Biron, get below and check out the hold."

With a nod and a look of concern, Biron jumped down one of the hatches just as Luke turned to see a burst of yellow flame lash out from the bow of the frigate.

Too far away. They were too far away to hit them. Luke stood his ground.

Boom! The gun roared. Luke's crew froze in place and stared toward the advancing enemy.

"Clear the decks. Beat to quarters!" Luke yelled, sending the harried crew buzzing like a hive of agitated bees.

As expected, the shot fell several yards short of their stern. A warning shot. Luke raised his glass to see men scrambling around one of the frigate's bow chasers.

John emerged from the companionway, his eyes widening as he scanned the sea and spotted the British ship.

"Get below, John. Stay in the cabin!" Luke ordered as *Destiny* swooped over another wave. A spray of salty mist showered over him, stinging his eyes.

John approached him. "They shot at us." His soft voice could barely be heard over the roar of the sea.

"Aye, they did. But they are too far away. Go below, John."

"I want to be with you."

Luke gripped his shoulders. "I need you to stay in the cabin." The authority in his voice, tainted with a bit of pleading, left no room for argument from his brother. With a frown, John slipped below and out of sight.

Fear for his brother, for his crew, his ship, consumed Luke, knotting

each nerve and muscle. The sailors, who weren't in the tops adjusting sail or assisting Mr. Ward with the guns, congregated on the main deck, shifting their eyes between the oncoming enemy and Luke as if he somehow had the answer to their salvation.

Biron leapt onto the deck from below. His eyes firing the same fear that burned in Luke's gut. "The crates we thought were filled with supplies, well, most of them are filled with iron bars."

Bile filled Luke's mouth. He swallowed. "How. . . ?" But he didn't have time to consider the how or why of such an act. He glanced over his crew. All eyes shot his way.

"Gregson, Rockland, Sikes"—Luke pointed to the first men he saw—"form a line of men leading to the hold. Hoist up the iron bars and toss them overboard."

The men sped off to do his bidding. Above them, sails flapped as the top men attempted to furl them again. Off their stern, the warship plunged over waves, heading straight for them, splitting the sea in a line of noxious foam. At this rate, with no staysails and her hull heavy with iron, *Destiny* would never be able to outrun the frigate. Nor were they close enough to shore to dive into some inland estuary.

They'd be caught. And either pressed into the British navy or sent to prison in England.

And what would happen to John?

To Miss Channing?

"Guns are ready, Cap'n," Mr. Ward shouted.

Luke gripped the hilt of his cutlass. He turned to Biron. "This would be a good time to pray to your God."

The old man nodded and rubbed his gray, stubbled chin. "I've already been doing that. Perchance, He wants to hear from you?"

"I've no time for your sermons," Luke spat. Sweat beaded on his forehead and neck. If God existed, it would indeed take an act of His mighty hand to save them now.

Soon, men emerged from the hold, forming a line that led to the railing. Iron bars passed through the trail of hands, until finally, they were hoisted over the side. Their splashes could barely be heard above the gush of water against the hull.

But it wasn't enough; the frigate still gained. Luke no longer needed the spyglass to see the lines of her hull, the laughing charred mouths of her carronades, and the sparkle of brass in the rising sun.

"They're signaling for us to heave to, Cap'n!" the lookout above shouted.

"Then let's send our reply." Luke turned to the gunner. "Mr. Ward, fire as you bear."

With flashing eyes, the gunner made his way to a carronade at the larboard quarter. Pushing the gun crew aside, he waited for *Destiny* to crest another swell then he lowered the burning wick to the touchhole.

Boom! The air reverberated with the cannon's angry black belch. A tremble coursed through the ship. Her timbers groaned in complaint. Gray smoke drifted back over the deck, stinging Luke's nose. Coughing, he batted it aside and watched the shot fall impotent into the sea several yards before the frigate.

As he'd expected. But the message had been delivered. One that he hoped would deter the frigate from bothering with such small prey.

Yet it seemed to have the opposite effect, for they persisted. "Keep her steady, Sam."

"Aye, Cap'n. They're gaining." The fear in the lad's voice struck Luke in the back like a thousand needles of failure.

Making the next few minutes pass like hours. He couldn't fail. Not this time.

But you always fail, don't you? The voice slithered over Luke. He tried to shake it off, to remember his prior success, but it rooted deep in his soul.

The frigate swept within three hundred yards of *Destiny*, well within range of her guns. At least twenty dark muzzles lining her main and quarterdeck winked at them in the morning sun. Within seconds, the frigate would sweep alongside and fire a broadside that would not only cripple *Destiny*, but probably kill some of Luke's men.

But Luke had a choice. Surrender or die. Gripping the hilt of his cutlass, he scanned the deck, where his crew stood pale faced and tight. The men in the tops clung to the lines, ready with muskets in hand. The gun crews hovered over the guns, ready to hurl deadly cannon shot at their enemy. These men might have been the baseborn, outcasts of society, but they were no cowards. He guessed most of them would rather fight to the death than surrender. But the most precious thing in the world to Luke was below in his cabin.

John deserved a chance at life. A free life.

The frigate swept swiftly upon their larboard quarter. *Caboom!* One of her carronades erupted, sending an ominous echo through the sky. Another warning shot. But this one carried an unspoken message—surrender or be sunk.

British officers formed an imperious line on the quarterdeck, looking down at their sailors standing calmly in position. Even the gun crews, surrounding the twenty guns pointed at *Destiny*, stood at attention, awaiting orders to unleash hell.

"Raise the white flag, Mr. Keene," Luke managed to say through a clenched jaw. "Furl all sail. Put the helm over, Sam."

Shaking his head in disgust, Mr. Keene stomped toward Luke. "We cannot give up!"

"We can and we will."

Biron rubbed the back of his neck with a sigh but said nothing.

Relinquishing his post by the larboard gun, Mr. Ward stormed forward. "Cap'n, I ne'er surrendered wit'out a fight an' I ain't gonna do it now."

Some of the crew grunted their agreement.

"Then we will all die." Luke gazed over the men, raising his voice. "Is that what you want? To sink to the bottom of the sea?"

"Better that than serve the Brits for the rest of me life," one crewmember said.

"Or rot in a prison hulk," another man shot out.

How could Luke tell them that he agreed? That if John weren't on board, he'd be happy to die defending his country. Gripping the quarter rail, he squinted at the sun making its way high in the sky, oblivious to the horror playing out below. Oblivious to the fact that if they didn't surrender they were about to meet a watery grave.

Words, magnified yet muffled, swept over them from the frigate.

On her deck, a man in a lieutenant's uniform held a speaking cone to his lips. "This is the HMS *Audacious* ordering you to stand down and heave to at once or we will fire upon you."

They awaited *Destiny's* reply. A bitterness born of failure and fear crowded in Luke's throat. He swallowed, hoping to rid himself of it, but it resurged nonetheless. He thought of Mrs. Barnes and the promise he had made. He could not see John die.

"Raise the flag!" Luke shouted.

The men hesitated.

"Now!"

Amidst a flurry of loathing glances, his crew obeyed him, and soon with all canvas furled and all men on deck, *Destiny* slowed to a near standstill.

A cheer of *huzzah*s resounded from the British frigate as *Destiny's* white flag of surrender replaced the American flag at the gaff. Luke grew numb. He'd served aboard a frigate once before and had the scars to prove it. And he'd become a pious monk before he'd allow his brother to endure the same fate.

As the ship maneuvered to come alongside *Destiny*, Luke sent Biron below to instruct John to stay out of sight no matter what happened. Perhaps Luke could offer himself and his ship to the British on the condition they deposit his crew and John ashore. He hoped the captain was a reasonable man. Not insane as Captain Milford of the HMS *Undefeatable* had been. The memory of the sting of the master mate's switch resurrected across Luke's back. Shifting it away, he leapt to the main deck as Mr. Keene, the topmast men, Samuel, Ward, and even Mr. Sanders formed an arc of men behind him.

"You did your best," Biron said as he stood stoically by his side.

But Luke's best hadn't been good enough. He had failed. He had failed them all. Miss Channing, his brother, Mrs. Barnes, his crew.

His country.

An ache settled in his head and pulsated in his earlobe as he watched the frigate lower a boat, fill it with officers, and head their way. The foreboding thud against the hull signaled their doom and brought back memories of his capture aboard Noah's ship *Fortune*.

Two lieutenants and three marines, resplendent in their red coats, scrambled over the bulwarks, followed by several sailors, all of whom drew pistols and swords and leveled them at Luke and his crew.

The British captain emerged and landed on the deck with a brazen thump. Dressed in white breeches and a brass-buttoned blue coat adorned with emblems of his station, he sauntered toward Luke. Short-cropped, graying hair spilled from beneath his cocked hat, and eyes as hard and penetrating as blades speared into Luke.

"You are the captain, I presume?"

Luke's hopes to appeal to the man's mercy and gain quarter for any of his crew deflated beneath the man's malicious expression of victory. "Captain Heaton, at your service." He gave a caustic smile.

"Captain Raynor of His Britannic Majesty's frigate, the HMS

Audacious." He held out his hand for the sword hanging at Luke's side.

Pulling it from its sheath, Luke held it toward him, hilt first, wondering why the captain had not stayed on his ship as was the usual practice.

Raynor took it and passed it to a man behind him then snapped his fingers. "Search every inch of the ship." All but the two lieutenants and three marines separated from the group and dispersed.

"You men"—Captain Raynor waved a hand over Luke's crew—"toss your weapons in a pile." He gestured to an open spot on the deck beneath the fore rail.

A gust of wind, plump with the sting of gunpowder and fear, tore across the ship and formed into tiny whirlwinds—whirlwinds of possibility. Mr. Keene seemed of the same mind as he inched beside Luke and cast him a knowing look. The hard metal of Luke's hidden pistol pressed against his belly. He had forty armed crewmen against only fifteen Brits—only six of which stood before them now. And the HMS *Audacious* would never fire upon their own captain.

Clearing his throat, Luke glanced over his shoulder at his men, hoping his eyes portrayed his intent.

"I said, drop your weapons, sir!" the captain barked.

Swords drawn, the marines advanced. Luke drew his pistol. Behind him, the click of pistols cocking and the chime of swords rang like sweet music through the air.

Captain Raynor's eyes turned to steel. "You are outnumbered, sir. Do you all wish to die?"

"Do you?" Luke pointed his pistol at the captain's head. "For you will be the first to go."

Rays from the sun, high above them, reflected off the drawn blades and radiated in waves of heat off the deck. *Destiny's* aged timbers creaked and moaned in protest.

A British sailor emerged from below, dragging John by the collar. He halted. John's wide eyes took in the proceedings. A metallic taste filled Luke's mouth. Captain Raynor noted the change in Luke's demeanor. "And whom do we have here?"

"I found this boy hiding in the master cabin."

"Indeed?" Captain Raynor grinned and waved a hand through the air. "Shoot him."

"No!" Luke charged toward John, his only thought to save him. In a vision blurred by terror, he saw the sailor draw a pistol and hold it to John's head.

Shouts and screams muffled in a mass of confusion in Luke's ears. Something sharp pierced his neck. Pain shot into his head and through his shoulders. He froze. The tip of a lieutenant's sword jabbed him below his chin. The man's face bunched like a knot of gunpowder ready to explode. Luke knew he wouldn't hesitate to run him through.

Behind him swords clanged and a moan sounded. Then silence.

"Hold," the captain ordered. The sailor lifted the gun from John's head. Captain Raynor sauntered toward Luke. "Now hear me and hear me good, Captain Heaton. You will order your men to stand down and relieve themselves of their weapons, or I *will* shoot the lad. Are we clear?"

From the look in his eyes, Luke had no doubt the man would do just that. He nodded, and the captain ordered the lieutenant to withdraw his sword from Luke.

Turning, Luke motioned for his crew to comply, noting that Mr. Keene pressed a hand over a bloody wound on his shoulder. With groans, the men tossed their weapons onto a pile. Clanks and clinks of metal sounded like the incessant hammering of nails into a coffin. Luke's coffin.

"A noble effort." Captain Raynor clasped his hands together as if pleased at the exciting interruption. "I would expect no less from a privateer, eh?"

Rubbing his neck, Luke raised his brows. "We are but an innocent merchant ship from Baltimore on our way to pick up spices and sugar from Jamaica."

"Baltimore? That nest of pirates!" Captain Raynor grunted in disgust. "No, I think not, Captain. A privateer sailing under the same name captured one of our merchantmen off the Carolinas last month."

"A mere coincidence." Luke doubted the man would agree, especially when Mr. Keene chuckled.

"Ah, you have jesters on board." The captain's cutting eyes skewered Mr. Keene. "How nice. My men can use some diversion."

"Sir, if you please." Biron stepped forward. "We are but simple merchantmen. And we mean no harm to you or your country."

"Balderdash!" Captain Raynor's bark was as loud as a cannon's. "You are Americans and privateers. And now, you are prisoners of war."

"Blasted Brits," young Sam spat under his breath.

One of the lieutenants flashed his sword toward Sam.

Nudging the boy aside, Luke held up a hand. "No need for that, Lieutenant."

Captain Raynor cocked his head. "There is fight in you, Captain. I see it in your eyes." His glance took in the men standing behind Luke. "And loyalty in your crew. I take it you are a good captain, though perhaps not a good sailor."

The British sailors chuckled. Luke fisted his hands.

"I shall take you as a prize," the captain continued as he glanced over the ship. "Though this tub is hardly worth the effort." He gestured toward John. "Bring the lad here."

The sailor pushed John, sending him tumbling to the deck. Luke charged him, raising his fist to put the man in his place. Shouts assailed him from behind. Clawlike hands gripped Luke's shoulders and pulled him back.

"It's all right, Luke." John struggled to his feet and brushed off his shirt. The bravery in his eyes sent a wave of pride through Luke.

"Your son?" The captain's eyes traveled between them. He put a finger on his chin. "No. Your brother, I believe."

Luke struggled against the pinched grip of two British marines. "What does it matter?"

The captain turned and whispered something to a man behind him, sending him over the railing and back to the British frigate.

"It changes things a great deal." Captain Raynor took up a pace across the deck. The sun gleamed off his brass buttons and set the gold-fringed epaulettes on his shoulders glimmering as they flapped in the breeze. "You see, I'm in need of fresh supplies. And you're in a position to get them for me."

"You'll get nothing but bilge water from me."

The captain smiled. "Ah, but I will. Because, you see, I will have this boy, this relation of yours."

Luke's heart stopped beating.

"We shall make an accord, you and I," the captain continued, his voice laced with pompous humor. "You will bring me supplies every few weeks, and I'll let the boy live. And when the war is over and we've won, you may have him back."

John trembled but stood his ground.

Biron tugged on his neckerchief. "Kidnapping a boy is beyond all decency, sir. Even in time of war."

"Ah, that is where you are wrong." Captain Raynor grinned. "There are no dictums of decency in war."

"He's just a boy." Ward charged forward. "Let him be."

Mr. Keene tossed up his good arm to hold the gunner back.

Jerking free from the marines, Luke thrust himself in front of John. "Take me instead."

Captain Raynor held up a hand to stop the advancing marines from grabbing Luke again. "Ah, but would your crew commit treason for *you?*" He scoured Luke with a gaze from head to toe. "I think not, sir. But I do sense you would do so for this lad."

The deck teetered over a wave. John eased from behind Luke and stood by his side.

"I'm no thief." Captain Raynor withdrew his hat and dabbed at his forehead with a handkerchief. "I'll pay you for the supplies. You'll make money. Your crew will be happy. Your brother, or whoever he is, will live. And you'll be helping to shorten the war."

Luke's mind reeled with the ultimatum he knew he must accept. "I am no traitor."

"You already are, Captain. You and all the American rebels are traitors to England."

"And if I refuse?"

"I will confiscate your ship as prize and all of you will join the British Navy." Captain Raynor's gaze landed on John. "At least those of you strong enough to serve. The rest? We have prisons where they can await the war's end."

The man returned from the frigate and handed the captain a scrap of foolscap. "Betraying your rebel country. Or slavery for all of you—including the lad. Which do you choose?"

Luke searched his mind for some way out. "Your scheme will not work. The people in Baltimore will grow suspicious."

"You'll think of some explanation, I have no doubt, Captain Heaton. Here are the coordinates." He handed Luke the paper. "You'll meet us here in two weeks with as much food, water, gunpowder, and shot as you can carry."

"Then you'll give me the boy?"

"We shall see."

"How will I slip past the blockade?"

"Don't you anchor in other ports?"

184

"If I am to meet you in a fortnight at this location, Baltimore is the closest port with enough supplies to meet your needs." Not really. But, stationed at home, Luke could possibly elicit help to rescue John.

"Very well." Captain Raynor shrugged. "Raise the following ensigns in this order. Red, blue, yellow, and green striped, then white. That will identify you to our fleet as a supplier. You won't be harmed." He glanced up at the sky as if bored. "If I see any other ship but yours approaching, I'll kill the boy. If you do not show up within a day of our appointed time, I'll kill the boy." His eyes met Luke's. "Is that understood?"

"You bedeviled mongrel," one of Luke's men whispered from behind. Thankfully, the captain didn't seem to hear it.

Luke knelt before John and gripped his shoulders.

John swallowed. "Don't do it, Luke. Don't betray our country." His voice faltered, but his expression was sincere. "If I die, I'll go to heaven and be with Mother and Father. I'll be all right."

Amazed at the boy's courage and faith, Luke shook his head. "I promised Mother I'd take care of you, and I will. Be strong for me."

John nodded.

Luke leaned in to kiss him on the cheek. "I'll come back for you. I promise."

"How touching." The captain's voice was sickly sweet. He waved a hand. "Take him away."

A lieutenant grabbed John and shoved him toward the bulwarks. He disappeared over the side. Luke's fingers twitched. He could grab the captain's sword and thrust it into his depraved heart before anyone could stop him. But what would that do but get them all killed?

With a contemptuous snort, Raynor dipped his head. "Until we meet again, Captain Heaton. A pleasure doing business with you." The British sailors laughed. Then turning, he marched across the deck and lowered himself over the side, his men following behind him. Luke started after him, but Biron and Mr. Keene held him back.

"Not now, Captain. We'll figure out a way," Biron said.

But Luke knew there was no way.

❖ CHAPTER 22 ❖

Luke stabbed a hand through his hair and yanked on the strands until his head hurt. Spinning around, he retraced his steps across his cabin. A cascade of foul words spilled from his mouth, joining the thud of his boots.

"We'll get him back, Luke." Biron's voice held an anger Luke had never heard before.

"How?" Luke shot fiery eyes his way then scanned the line of men standing before his desk. Mr. Sanders twitched nervously and did not meet his gaze. Beside him, Sam kept repeating "Blasted British, blasted British" under his breath. Mr. Keene's jaw knotted as he leaned against the bulkhead, and Mr. Ward perched on the barrel of the twelve-pounder guarding the foot of Luke's bed, his meaty arms folded over his chest, and a look as if he could kill the devil himself storming across his face.

Destiny rolled over a wave. Her timbers creaked and groaned as the lantern hanging from the deck head cast shifting shadows over the men, creating menacing specters over the painted canvas beneath their boots.

"We'll think of something. We'll put our heads together and think of something." Biron's voice pummeled Luke's back as he continued his nervous trek. Swerving yet again, he retraced his steps and finally halted before his desk. He leaned on the oak top and gripped the edges until his fingers burned. How could this have happened? How could he have failed so miserably? His promise to his mother—his promise to Mrs. Barnes—to protect John slapped him in the face.

"Rescue a boy from a British frigate?" His laugh came out bitter. "Impossible."

"Nothing is impossible with God," Biron said.

Luke lifted a hand to his friend. "Not now, Biron. Not now." If God existed, then He had allowed this to happen. And despite what Reverend Drummond had said, Luke could not see how anything but heartache and death could come of it.

Mr. Keene shook his head. "What I can't understand is how the staysails got torn."

"Or the iron got into our supply crates," Mr. Ward growled.

Luke eyed his crew. What reason would any of them have to sabotage the ship? Even if they harbored some animosity toward him, why would they risk their own lives?

Mr. Sanders raised his oversized blue eyes to Luke. His nose twitched. "My apologies, Captain. I didn't see the iron when you sent me below."

"Not your fault." Luke rubbed the scars on his right hand. "The perpetrators hid it well. I'm the captain. I should have gone below myself." He should have done many things. The odor of whale oil and body sweat rose to join the stench of his own inadequacy.

"There was that new sailor you hired." Mr. Keene lifted a jeweled finger in the air.

"Yes, Mr. Flanders," Samuel shot out.

Dread sucked the breath from Luke's lungs. "What new sailor?"

"The man who joined us when you sent us ahead to prepare the ship." Mr. Keene's brow furrowed.

"I sent no such man."

Biron scratched his head. "You didn't hire a Mr. Flanders?"

Luke shook his head, his mouth suddenly parched. He could use a drink. "Is he still on board?"

"I ain't laid eyes on him since," Mr. Ward spoke up.

"Ward, Sanders." Luke gestured toward the two men. "Go search for him and report back to me at once."

"Aye, aye, Cap'n." They sped off, ducking beneath the frame of the open cabin door.

The deck tilted, and the men braced their boots firmly to keep from stumbling. Wind sped past the stern windows in a sinister whistle.

"What did this man have access to, Mr. Keene?" Luke asked.

"He helped load supplies, checked the lines and the canvas. . . ." Mr. Keene froze.

"Blast!" Luke struck his desk. Pain spiked into his arms. He spun around. Darkness as thick as molasses seeped through the stern windows, held back only by the occasional flash of lantern light.

"No doubt he was hired by someone else," Biron said.

"Someone who hates me." Someone like Lieutenant Abner Tripp. Hadn't the man sworn to get his revenge? Luke gazed down at the burn scars on his hand. How could he have been so foolish? He should have been on his guard. This was all his fault.

"Who?" Sam said.

Luke swerved around. "It doesn't matter."

Mr. Ward and Mr. Sanders returned, shaking their heads. Mr. Keene's face twisted with rage. "If Flanders were still here, I'd keelhaul him."

Mr. Sanders shivered, no doubt at his friend's cruel suggestion. "What will you do, Captain?"

Luke eyed his men. Misfits all of them. Would they stay with him now that his privateering career was over? How far did their loyalty extend, especially to a man like Luke? "I'm going to sell Captain Raynor his supplies."

Biron nodded. "It's the right course, Captain. For the boy."

The older man's approval settled well on Luke. "But I can't ask you all to join me. If we are caught, we'll be hanged for treason."

The only answer came from the thunder of sails above and the ravenous purl of the sea against the hull. Lantern light flickered over the men as their gazes dropped to the floor. All except Sam and Biron.

"Of course we'll join you, Captain." The boy's enthusiastic smile sent a sliver of warmth through Luke's frozen heart.

A devilish glint overtook Mr. Keene's eyes. "I'm in. Treason or not, it's a way to make money."

Luke cringed at the man's lack of scruples.

Mr. Ward scratched his bald head. "What other ship is going to hire a drunken cur like me?"

Mr. Sanders's eyes widened, and he glanced around at his fellow crewman then back at Luke. "For how long? I don't fancy a rope about my neck."

"Until we rescue John," Biron said.

"Yes." Luke crossed his arms over his chest, seeking the faith he saw so frequently in Biron's eyes. "And that won't take long if I have my way."

"That's the spirit, sir!" Sam nearly leapt. And the men chuckled at the boy's enthusiasm.

Emotion burned in Luke's throat at his crew's loyalty. "I thank you, gentlemen."

"What about the rest of the crew?" Sanders's mouth twitched.

"Biron, choose the men you believe will be comfortable with our mission and ask them to join us," Luke said, even as the fear of discovery began to gnaw at him.

"In other words, Captain, the blackguards. Those with loyalty to nothing but coin?" Biron arched his brow.

"Yes, those are the ones." Luke huffed. "The rest we'll inform that our privateering days are over and excuse them from duty when we reach Baltimore. Now, off with you." He tilted his head toward the door. "Grab your supper from the galley and then back to your posts, men."

One by one they left the cabin, leaving only Biron behind. The first mate shut the door and approached Luke, concern written on his face. "How are you holding up?"

"Not well." Luke spun around to face the stern windows, not wanting Biron to see the moisture in his eyes. "I can't imagine what John is enduring right now."

"He's a strong lad, Luke. He's got your blood flowing through him."

"But he's just a boy." Luke rubbed his ear. "And you forget I know what happens aboard a British warship."

"I haven't forgotten."

"I need a drink."

"That won't help anything right now."

Luke sighed and turned around. "How are we going to get him off that ship?"

Biron flattened his lips and released a sigh. "I don't know. With God's help, we'll find a way."

Luke huffed. God again. Lowering himself into a chair, he dropped his head into his hands. "I've lost him, Biron. I failed him and everyone else."

The ship tilted, sending lantern light spinning in circles over the painted canvas rug.

"When my wife and babe died in childbirth," Biron said, "I thought

I'd failed them both, too."

"How could you not blame God for that?" Luke didn't look up.

"For a time I did," Biron said. "But what good does that do? God has His reasons for things, and they're good reasons. For the ultimate good. I'll find out someday."

"I don't have the patience to wait that long." Luke looked up. Nor could he wait to repay Lieutenant Tripp for his part in this. "First thing I'm going to do when I get home is accept Lieutenant Tripp's challenge to a duel and send him to the depths of hell where he belongs."

"You can't do that."

"Quite the contrary." Luke snorted. "I believe I can."

"No, think, man. If you get your revenge, he'll know his plan worked. But he'll see you still have your ship, your crew. He's no dull wit. He'll figure out what you're up to."

"Not if he's dead."

Biron arched his brow.

Luke lowered his gaze beneath the look of reprimand on his friend's face. "So, I can't kill him and neither can I take pleasure in beating him to shreds?"

"No. Besides, there's far grander pleasure in being kind to the man. God's Word says that if your enemy is hungry, give him bread, if he be thirsty give him water. For thou shalt heap coals of fire upon his head, and the Lord shall reward thee."

Luke chuckled. "Why don't I just skip to dumping the hot coals on his head?"

Biron smiled. "Kindness will kill him more slowly."

"Kindness? You're crazy, old man."

"Perhaps. But hear me, Luke. If you arrive in Baltimore a successful privateer, it will drive the lieutenant mad, I assure you."

Luke studied his friend, allowing his words to form sense in his mind. Yes, perhaps the old man was wiser than Luke gave him credit. Or, this God of his was.

Biron headed for the door. "We'll be in Baltimore in a few days. Get some rest, Captain. We will think of a way to rescue John."

Luke heard him leave as the door shut again. Rest, how could he rest knowing what his brother was enduring on that frigate? Rising, he opened a drawer of his desk and pulled out a bottle of rum. He held it up to the lantern light. Mr. Sanders had brought it to him a few nights ago.

Luke had not taken a sip. Not a single sip. Wanting to honor his promise to Miss Channing. But what did it matter now? What did anything matter now? Uncorking it, he took a long draft, hoping the burning liquid would warm his gut and numb his senses. But after several swigs, he felt nothing but grief—deep seated, clawing into his soul. Lifting the bottle, he tossed it against the bulkhead. It shattered, spraying rum over his bookshelves and onto the deck. Shards of glass clanked to the floor in a glittering shower, dripping with the vile liquid.

Sinking back onto his chair, he dropped his head in his hands once more. "Oh God, what am I to do?"

Sometime in the night, he must have dozed off beneath exhaustion and grief. He dreamed of cannon blasts and smoke and men being lashed by a cat-o'-nine-tails and John crying Luke's name in echoed ripples over the sea. And in the middle of the mayhem, a glowing figure appeared. Tall and muscular, shining like bronze, with a sword hanging at his side. He said, "Never fear."

❖

Marianne shoved a roll of dollars into Cassandra's hands. "Here, take this."

"How can I thank you?" Cassandra's eyes burned. "I am so ashamed to have to ask you for help. I know you and Noah don't have a great deal of wealth." She slipped the wad into her reticule and set it down on the table.

Marianne cupped Cassandra's hands with her own. "God has blessed us. I'm happy to help you. So, not another word about it." Releasing her, she skirted the table in her sitting room and poured two cups of tea, handing one to Cassandra.

"Thank you." Cassandra warmed her hands on the cup then took a sip. She gazed out the window, where afternoon sunlight splintered the room in glittering swords.

"Now, tell me what happened." Marianne patted the sofa beside her.

"I don't really know." The cup shook in Cassandra's hands. The soothing mint turned to ash in her mouth. She lowered the cup to her lap. "No one knew where I hid the money. The chest wasn't broken so they must have used my key, which I keep in the desk in my chamber."

Marianne frowned. "It must be someone in the house, then. But who?"

Cassandra had driven herself mad the past two days trying to figure

191

out the answer to that question. All her servants had been with her for years, and she had never seen a spark of disloyalty among any of them. Visions of Mrs. Northrop standing in her chamber a few days ago sped across her mind. But no. The housekeeper had always been a bit of a snoop. Nothing unusual about that. "I fear my mother has taken to her bed with a case of headaches and hysterics, which has left my sisters to run amok through the house."

"Why didn't you put the money in the bank?" Marianne asked.

"I was careless. I had been without funds for so long, I didn't trust anyone, not even the bank." Cassandra's hands trembled, and she set the cup on the saucer with a clank lest she spilled the tea on her gown. "I've gone and ruined everything. I've put my family at great risk again."

Marianne touched her hand. "It's only money."

"It would have lasted us years."

"Luke will return soon with more, you'll see."

Mr. Heaton's name sent a spark of joy through Cassandra. "I'll pay you back upon his return, I promise. Until then, this will help me buy some much-needed food."

Marianne's brown eyes sparkled. "Word about town is that Mr. Crane is bringing your family food. A goose one night, two chickens the next, and fresh cod and crab last evening?"

Cassandra couldn't help but laugh at how quickly rumors spread in the town. "Is nothing secret?"

"Well, not when the man tells everyone that you and he are courting."

"Courting?" Cassandra frowned. "Oh, bother. We are doing no such thing. How dare he spread such tales!"

"I wouldn't be so hard on him. No doubt he considers the courtship firm since you have accepted his charity."

"Which is precisely why I needed to borrow this money. Good grief, the man keeps insisting he take me to the Fountain Inn Ball."

"Why not go with him?" Marianne waved a hand through the air, then she stopped and gazed at Cassandra as if she could see into her thoughts. "Unless you are waiting for someone else to ask you. . .someone who is perhaps out to sea at the moment?"

"Don't be absurd." Cassandra looked away. "*If* I marry it will be to a man I can depend on. A man who is stable and grounded. Someone I can trust."

"Odd. That sounds precisely like Mr. Crane." Marianne sipped her tea, a grin playing on her lips.

Cassandra made a face at her friend, though she supposed Marianne was right. Why, then, didn't Cassandra long for Mr. Crane's attention? Why didn't her heart bounce when he walked into the room? Perhaps marriage was not meant to be based on such foolish sentiments, but on mutual respect and financial and familial practicality.

If so, Cassandra would be better off alone.

"I wouldn't disqualify Mr. Heaton just yet on those counts," Marianne said.

"Who said anything about Mr. Heaton?"

"Oh, I don't know. . . . You just had that dreamy look in your eye again." A child's laughter filtered down from above, and Marianne glanced out the parlor door before she faced Cassandra with a smile. "I've seen the way he looks at you."

Why did her statement send a thrill through Cassandra?

"Mr. Heaton is my business partner, nothing more." Cassandra folded her hands in her lap.

"God doesn't always choose the men we think are best for us. Take Noah and me. For years, I couldn't stand the sight of him."

"God doesn't choose for me. If He does, I can hardly trust Him, given the bad choices He's made so far."

Marianne set down her cup. "You'll see that He is looking out only for your good in the end."

Uncomfortable talking about a God who obviously paid her no mind, Cassandra stood and made her way to the window. "Noah is not yet returned?"

"No. I do miss him so." Marianne joined her and gazed out onto the carriages and pedestrians strolling down the street. "And so does Jacob. I pray this war will be over soon and we can get back to a normal life."

"Only if we win."

"Indeed." Marianne offered her a sad smile.

And only after Mr. Heaton has caught another prize. Cassandra cringed at her selfish thought.

After finishing her tea and thanking Marianne for the money, Cassandra began her trek home. Casting a glance toward the west at the setting sun, she guessed she had enough time to visit the harbor before dark. Pulling the pelisse tight around her chest, she turned down Pratt Street. For some reason, seeing all the ships made her feel close to Mr.

Heaton. And feeling close to Mr. Heaton brought her more comfort than she cared to admit. She shrugged the sentiment away, reasoning that it was only her need for the money he would bring home. But deep down, she knew it was more than that.

She greeted several people as she made her way down the cobblestone walkway then darted across the street between a phaeton and a wagon—avoiding the horses' deposits—to the dock side of the street. Halting, she scanned the bay, its dark waters rustling against the pilings of the wharves. Salt and fish and tar filled her nostrils. A fisherman hawked his fresh catch. A bell rang and a burst of wind tore at her straw bonnet. A few dockworkers turned to look at her. Her eyes landed on a schooner anchored off Spears Wharf. It seemed familiar. She headed in that direction then crept out on the wobbling dock just far enough to see the name painted on the ship's bow.

Destiny.

❖ CHAPTER 23 ❖

Vague shapes formed behind Luke's eyelids, like shadowy specters of light and dark drifting over his eyes. A clank sounded from somewhere in the distance. The scent of coffee spiraled beneath his nose and thrummed on his rousing senses. No. He tried to push his mind back into the abyss of apathy, back into the soothing comfort of unconsciousness.

But another clank jarred him. Then the pain struck. Like a grappling hook clawing through his brain. He moaned and waved a hand around his head to see if someone was hammering on it. He touched his face. Nothing but damp flesh met his fingers. Cold and damp. And what was that stench that infiltrated the sweet smell of coffee?

Footfalls sounded, and he pried open one eye to see the blurry shape of Mrs. Barnes enter the sitting room with a tray. Setting it on the table, she sank into her favorite rocking chair with a heavy sigh. "I made you breakfast." Her voice was thick and choppy, devoid of its usual cheerfulness.

Luke wanted to say thank you. Wanted to tell her to leave him alone. But he felt as though someone had stuffed a rag in his mouth. He opened his other eye to peer at the wooden ceiling and waited until the room stopped swirling.

"I see you drank yourself into unconsciousness." Mrs. Barnes began to rock in her chair, the *creak creak* scraping holes in his wall of alcohol-induced narcosis.

Allowing memories to barge into his mind. The image of John being stolen by the British captain struck Luke first like a broadside in the gut, jarring him fully awake. Then the vision of Mrs. Barnes when he'd told her the news. The horror in her eyes, her ragged breathing, trembling lips, and the white sheen that had covered her face. Luke had grabbed her before she'd fallen and led her to a chair where she had sobbed for nearly an hour. Fighting wave after wave of guilt and battling his own tears, Luke had fumbled in the kitchen, attempting to make her some tea to soothe her nerves.

But no amount of tea or apologies or promises had been able to assuage the grief-stricken woman.

Closing his eyes, Luke struggled to sit. He felt as though a twenty-pound cannonball sat on his neck. He leaned on his knees, hoping the room would stop spinning. An empty bottle of brandy leaned on its side atop the hearth. The brandy he'd found in the kitchen. The brandy he'd intended to take only a few sips of to settle his raging soul.

Hair hanging in his face, he dared a glance at Mrs. Barnes. Her skin was even paler than last night. The lines etched across it deeper. Dark circles tugged on eyes that were red and puffy. A look of pity crossed them, and she poured him a cup of coffee that she passed his way.

Luke set it on the table, his stomach rebelling at the sight. "You serve me coffee after what I've done?" he moaned.

"You're a son to me, Luke. I love you no less than I love John."

The sound of his brother's name pierced Luke's heart. He hung his head. Not once after Luke had told her the news had Mrs. Barnes scolded him. Not once had she shouted or screamed or cursed him for what he'd done. No. She'd simply sat in her rocking chair, with her Bible in her lap, alternating between bouts of tears and gazing numbly into the burning logs of the fire.

Rebuke, shouting, even hatred, Luke could bear. But not her silence. Not her agony. So he had taken to drink to numb the pain.

"What happened, happened," Mrs. Barnes said. "Maybe John was too young to go to sea. Maybe he wasn't. You did what you thought best."

"He was good out there, Mrs. Barnes," Luke said, pride swelling within him, even now. "You should have seen him. He took to sailing as if he'd been born on a ship."

"Why wouldn't he?" The hint of a smile twitched one side of her mouth before it faded. "He's got your blood running through him."

Luke didn't want to hear that. John was nothing like Luke. John was kind and pure and good. He would make something of his life.

If Luke hadn't already sent him to his grave.

Mrs. Barnes drew her Bible to her chest and gripped it as if it held the answer to their dilemma. She stared once again at the coals in the fireplace, now black and cold. "I've been up all night praying, you see. And God has told me there is a reason this happened."

Luke shot to his feet and instantly regretted it. His head spun and his stomach lurched. "I grow tired of hearing that God has a reason for every bad thing that happens." Bile rose in his throat, but the desert raging in his mouth forbade him to swallow it down. "Bad things happen because there are bad people in the world, nothing more." Bad people, of whom he was one. "John is. . . John is. . ." He ran a hand through his hair, unable to even say the words out loud. "This is all my fault. I should have known Tripp would try something. I should have checked the sails and supplies myself." Luke sank back down onto the couch and dropped his head in his hands.

He heard the rocking chair squeak and felt Mrs. Barnes's wrinkled hand on his arm. "This isn't your fault, Luke."

He raised a shocked gaze to her. "How can you say that?"

"Not everything is your fault, Luke. Not your parents' death and not John's kidnapping." A peace Luke envied glowed from her glassy eyes. "Your pounding head is your fault. The gambling, the drinking, those are your fault." She shook her head. "Not John's kidnapping."

❖

Sitting on the stool, Cassandra unlocked the small wooden chest, replaced the key in the pocket of her gown, and opened the lid. Hope sparked in some small part of her that still believed in miracles—hope that the money would be there. But of course, it wasn't. Though she refused to believe any of her family or servants could have stolen it, that seemed the only logical conclusion. But who? It pained her to even think of it. Removing her father's pipe, she raised it to her nose and drew a whiff of the fragrant, spicy smell.

"Oh Papa, what am I to do?" Toying with the pipe, she glanced over her leafy-green gardenia bushes, the fading sunlight spilling from their leaves, replaced by the golden glow from the lantern overhead.

After purchasing enough food for a week with the money Marianne had loaned her, Cassandra had headed home, still baffled by the sight of Luke's ship anchored in the bay.

"He must not have caught a prize, Papa, for that is the only reason I can think of that he would have returned and not come to see me."

The wind whistled over the panes of glass in the solarium, and Cassandra released a heavy sigh. "And if that is true, I fear, Papa, that we are done for." She certainly couldn't borrow any more money from Marianne and Noah. And what were they to do when the food ran out in a week's time?

Her gaze landed on her father's Bible tucked within the chest. Closing her eyes, she pictured him sitting in his chair in the library, the Holy Book opened in his lap, his blue eyes, so full of life, glancing up at her as she entered the room.

"Come here, my darling Cassie," he would say as he set the book aside. And Cassandra would crawl into his lap—her favorite place in all the world. Then he would stroke her arm and kiss the top of her head and tell her how much he loved her.

The Bible seemed to glow from within the chest. Cassandra rubbed her eyes. She was seeing things. Memories of what Marianne, Reverend Drummond, and even Margaret had told her of God's love, purpose, and provision flooded her mind. But none of it could be true, could it? Not when He had taken so much from them.

A tear slipped down her cheek. "Papa, I don't know how to take care of Mother and my sisters. We have no money. Soon, no food. I haven't paid the servants in weeks. Why would someone steal from me?" She fisted her hands and pounded her lap. "Why was I so foolish to keep the money here? Oh Papa, why did you leave me all alone?"

Nothing but the rustle of the wind answered her as the last traces of sunlight slipped from sight. Cassandra drew a deep breath and straightened her shoulders. There was only one thing left to be done. If Mr. Heaton had indeed returned without a prize, then Cassandra would have no choice but to accept Mr. Crane's courtship. She would not allow her family to starve or end up on the street because of her own selfishness.

The crank of the door latch drew her gaze to the front of the solarium. Those unruly urchins. Couldn't they leave her alone for one minute? But then heavy footsteps thumped on the hard dirt, giving her pause. Her heart hammered against her chest. Cassandra peered between the leaves of a bush just as a deep voice said, "Hello."

Mr. Heaton stood just inside the door, cocked hat in hand, gazing over her bushes. Her heart took on a different sort of thump. She slowly rose. His eyes met hers. A smile lifted his lips. "Good evening, Miss Channing. I hope I didn't startle you."

Cassandra could not find her voice. Perhaps it had been swept away in the tide of hot waves that flooded her at the sight of him standing there in his black boots, brown breeches, and white shirt. Absent the neckerchief and waistcoat propriety dictated. Aside from a few loose strands, his black hair was tied behind him, and there, peppering his chin was the ever-present stubble, as if his beard were as stubborn as he.

An imposing figure so out of place among her flowers. Yet she found no fear within her. Quite the opposite, in fact.

"Why, no, Mr. Heaton," she said. "I'm surprised to see you is all."

"Your maid." He gestured toward the front of the house. "She said I might find you here."

Margaret. Cassandra flattened her lips. She would speak to her later.

He took a step toward her. "So, this is why you always smell like gardenias."

Cassandra smiled. "I love these flowers." She caressed one of the leaves. "I come here to think."

"And I have disturbed you. I hope you'll forgive me, but I come on an important matter."

It occurred to her she'd been so happy to see him that she'd not even considered that he'd come with news of a prize. "I saw your ship at anchor earlier in the day." Cassandra approached him.

"Yes, I sailed in late last night."

"How did you get past the blockade?"

She thought she saw a flicker of unease pass over his blue eyes. "*Destiny* is swift and hard to see in the dark." He would not meet her gaze.

"Did you capture a prize?"

He shook his head, and her hopes tumbled. "Not this time, miss."

Cassandra's throat burned. She fought back a flood of tears. Even if Mr. Heaton caught twenty prizes in the next six months, it would be too late to keep the house and provide food for her family. She pressed a hand over her stomach.

Mr. Heaton grabbed her elbow and leaned toward her, his face full of concern. "Are you unwell, Miss Channing?"

"Yes. . . No." Warmth spiraled up her arm at his touch, and she pulled away from him. "I had hoped"—she waved a hand in the air—"oh, what does it matter?" She eyed him. "You smell like a tavern, sir."

He frowned. "I'm on land again, miss."

"Why are you back so soon?"

"I needed supplies."

The statement made no sense to her, but she didn't inquire further.

Shifting his stance, Luke gazed out the windows onto the back garden. "I went to see Marianne today."

The odd statement jarred Cassandra, and she dared a glance into his eyes—so close she could see the lantern light flicker in their depths.

At her inquisitive look, he scratched the stubble on his chin and gave her one of his roguish grins. "Well, in truth, I hoped to see Noah, but the blasted man is still out scouring the seas for British prey." He chuckled.

"Why are you telling me this, Mr. Heaton?"

He reached inside his waistcoat and pulled out a leather billfold and handed it to her.

Cassandra shook her head. "What is this?"

"Take it, Miss Channing."

Grabbing it, she unhooked the clip and opened it to find several dollar bills—at least eighty. Confusion left her stunned. "What? I can't take this."

"I assure you, you can."

"How? I don't. . ."

"Marianne told me of your plight."

The solarium began to spin. Cassandra lifted a hand to her forehead. "But this is from your share of the last prize."

He said nothing. He just looked at her as if she were as precious as one of the gardenias blossoming beside her.

"I cannot accept this." She shoved the billfold back toward him.

He held out a hand. "I have no need of it at the moment." Sorrow crossed his face. He looked away.

"Still, Mr. Heaton, it is most inappropriate."

"If you wish it not to be a gift, you can repay me out of our next prize earnings. This should last you a few months until then."

She shifted her eyes between his but found no insincerity within them. Could this be true? Her legs transformed into noodles and she staggered.

Mr. Heaton reached out to steady her. She fell against him. "Are you all right, miss?" His warmth and strength surrounded her, and an odd sense of well-being invaded her turbulent soul. A feeling she'd not had since her father had been alive. Was it possible this rogue, this blackguard, could be trusted?

"Forgive me, Mr. Heaton, It's just that"—she stepped out of his embrace—"it's just that you have no idea how much I needed this money. I fear I had decided to take drastic measures."

His eyes wandered down to the pipe in her hand.

"Smoke a pipe?" He chuckled.

She joined him. "No! I was about to accept the proposal of a certain gentleman. . . ."

"Ah." Mr. Heaton's dark brows rose. "Mr. Crane, I presume?"

Cassandra looked down. "Yes, I fear he's become quite persistent, insisting I accompany him to some ball happening at the Fountain Inn."

He studied her with that look that held possibilities she dare not entertain. "I can see why."

Her face heated. She took a step back.

"Forgive me," he said, but the flirtatious look remained. "Perhaps you could inform him that you're attending the ball with me?"

Cassandra blinked even as a thrill sped through her. "Why would I say that?"

"Because it will give you an excuse to turn him down. And because attending with me will be far more adventurous, I assure you."

Of that, Cassandra had no doubt. She brushed a finger over one of her gardenias, trying to settle her rampant emotions. Why was she all aquiver over this rake's invitation and so repulsed by Mr. Crane's? "Then, shall I presume you are extending an invitation to escort me, sir?"

❖

Luke smiled at the coy look on her face, both thrilled and shocked that she seemed at all interested in attending the ball with him. "I am."

"But how long will you be in town?" she asked.

He shrugged and pushed an errant strand of hair behind his ear. "I will make sure I'm here for the event."

"Then I accept your kind invitation, sir," Cassandra said.

Luke gave her a befuddled look, wondering if he were dreaming. Never in a thousand years would he have ever hoped to escort a lady like Cassandra Channing to a ball.

She lowered her gaze to the billfold in her hand. "You don't know how grateful I am for this money, Mr. Heaton. I will accept it, but only as a loan."

Then it hit Luke. Like a stone sinking in his stomach. "I hope you didn't agree to my invitation because of the money."

"No, not at all." Setting down the pipe and money on a nearby stool, she laid a hand on his arm.

"Because there are no obligations attached to the gif—loan." But when he raised his eyes to hers, Luke could see his fears were unfounded, for nothing but candor flashed in their depths.

"Of course," she said. "We are partners, after all."

His gaze dropped to her lips. He licked his own and swallowed an urgent desire to kiss her. Shifting both his thoughts and his gaze away, he gestured toward the billfold on the stool. "Might I suggest you put it in the bank this time?"

"I deserved that." Her lips slanted.

He cocked his head. "And if I might make one small request?"

She hesitated, eyeing him, but saying nothing.

"Please make no mention of the money to anyone or from whence it came. We don't wish to alert the thief a second time. Even for so small an amount."

"Indeed."

Luke's heart soared at the appreciation beaming from Miss Channing's face. If only for the moment, at least in her eyes, he was no failure. At least in her eyes, he was a champion. He had failed everyone else, even himself, but he never wanted to fail her. The trust and confidence in her gaze made him want to be a better man—to become a man she could trust, a man she could love.

The way the lantern light glittered in her burgundy hair and caressed her soft cheek, sliding down her neck. . .

Luke caught hold of his wayward thoughts and took a step back, fumbling with his hat. For the first time in his life, a woman had him befuddled—unsure of himself.

Against his will, his gaze landed once again on her lips. He remembered the soft feel of them, their moist response to his kiss weeks ago. His throat grew parched, longing for just one sip. But she would think him presumptuous after she'd accepted the money. It wouldn't be right.

For once, he withdrew.

"I should leave you, miss." He started to turn away when the press of her hand on his arm stayed him. He faced her again.

She gazed at him mystified, mesmerized before her lips met his.

❖ CHAPTER 24 ❖

Cassandra had no idea what she was doing. In fact, she was absolutely sure that she could, here and henceforth, be classified as a witless hussy. Why did she force her kiss on Mr. Heaton? After he had turned away from her as a true gentleman should? Dash it all, she had thrown herself into his arms as if she were one of his tavern wenches. Yet, as soon as her lips met his and he responded by engulfing her in his embrace, she no longer cared. Reputation and propriety tossed to the wind, she drank him in as if she could never assuage her thirst. He tasted of smoke and spice. His breath tickled her cheek while his stubble scratched her skin. A plethora of delights soared through her until every ounce of her sizzled like hot coals. He cupped her face in his warm hands and kissed her deeply then placed light gentle kisses over her face and neck.

Cassandra moaned and fell against him. He stroked her hair, his chest rising and falling rapidly beneath her cheek.

She felt warm and safe and loved. And she never wanted him to leave.

"Aren't you going to slap me again?"

Cassandra shook her head, regaining some of her senses. She pushed back from him, horrified that she'd kissed him. "I don't know what came over me. Please forgive me." She lowered her chin.

His finger raised it, until their eyes met. "I fear I cannot." He looked at her as if she were a rare treasure—something to protect and cherish.

But then it struck her. How many other women had he graced with that adoring look? Kissed with such hungry fervor? He was skilled in the art of *l'amour*. As evidenced by the wake of broken hearts he left behind.

And she was a fool.

Cassandra took a step back. "This means nothing."

The smile slipped from his mouth. "To you, perhaps."

"I lost my head. It was the money, your charity." Cassandra tore her gaze from him and hugged herself against a sudden chill. "We are nothing but business partners."

"Indeed?" He cocked his head and studied her. A sigh, laden with sorrow, blew from his lips.

Cassandra fingered a gardenia petal. Her body still tingled from his kiss. Confusion galloped unbridled through her thoughts, pounding them into dust before she could make sense of them. Could she actually be falling in love with this rogue?

"You don't trust me," he said.

"I trust no one, Mr. Heaton."

"I hope to remedy that, Miss Channing." Before she could stop him, he leaned down and brushed his lips over her cheek then placed his hat on his head, opened the door, and left.

Caressing the spot on her face where his lips last touched, Cassandra watched as the shadows stole him from view.

❖

Luke stood on the teetering deck of the HMS *Audacious* as the British purser, a rather stubby fellow with a pointed chin, checked items off a list. Luke's men, aided by British sailors, hauled aboard crates, barrels, and sacks from *Destiny*'s hold, dropping them on deck for inspection before additional British sailors carried them below. Flanked by his lieutenants, Captain Raynor gazed down upon the proceedings from the quarter rail in a pompous display of dark-blue coats and cocked hats that made Luke sick to his stomach. He glanced over at the lines strung taut on belaying pins off the larboard quarter, and renewed pain etched down his back. Not two years ago, he stood in that very spot on a different British frigate, hauling lines while the master's mate whipped his back repeatedly with the rattan.

The thought shot renewed terror through his veins like shards of ice. Terror for John. Where was he? Since Luke had boarded, he'd scanned every inch of the deck. But his brother was nowhere to be seen.

And Luke had to get close to John in order for his plan to work. Close enough to pass him a scrap of foolscap containing important instructions. The scrap that now seemed to be shouting from within Luke's pocket.

"That's it, Captain." The purser lifted his gaze. Four sacks of rice, six sacks of flour, one crate of fresh fish, two pigs, five sacks of coal, ten barrels of water, twenty chickens, one crate of apples, two barrels of rum, and twenty-five pounds of gunpowder.

Gunpowder that might kill Luke's own countrymen.

The ship canted over a swell. Bracing his boots on the deck, Luke ground his teeth together and reached for his sword by instinct. Of course, it wasn't there. Nor was his pistol. He and his men standing behind him had been searched before they'd boarded the frigate. Even if his entire crew were armed, what could twenty men do against hundreds? Thunder charged through the broiling, gray sky that hung low enough to touch. A vile wind whipped across the deck, stinging Luke's nose with the scent of brine and rain.

"Very good, Mr. Garrison," Captain Raynor said. "Pay the man his due."

The purser tossed a bag of coins to Luke. He caught it and turned his attention to the captain. "I demand to see my brother."

"Demand, is it now?" The man chuckled and glanced at his lieutenants, who joined him in laughter. Lightning flashed, casting a silver glow over his maniacal expression and transforming the gray and black streaks of his hair into eerie shades of blue.

"I am, Captain, or I'll bring one of our navy's warships to our next meeting." Luke knew his threat was empty. The American Navy would never risk a ship to rescue the brother of a traitor.

"The American Navy, you say?" Captain Raynor grinned. "Last I heard you had less than ten frigates and a couple of sloops against our hundreds of warships." He shook his head. "Ah, you Americans. Entertaining at best. At the least, full of impotent threats and boasts. But alas, you may see the lad if you wish." He turned and said something to one of the midshipmen standing behind him and the man dropped below, returning in moments with John.

The instant the boy saw Luke, he broke into a huge smile that helped settle Luke's taut nerves. The man released him, and John dashed toward his brother, barreling into his embrace. Luke swallowed him up, wishing he'd never have to let go. After a moment, however, John pushed back as if embarrassed at the affectionate exchange. He glanced over Luke's shoulder. "Mr. Abbot, Mr. Keene, Mr. Ward."

"Hi there, lad," Mr. Ward said. "How are you faring?"

"I'm well." His gaze returned to Luke. "They make me work hard, but they feed me too."

Luke knelt and slipped his hand into his pocket for the foolscap. "How is your brace holding up?"

The boy nodded. "Good." He eyed Luke for a moment and cocked his head. "Don't worry about me. God is here with me."

Luke huffed. If God was here, He would have freed his brother already. But he would let the lad have his fantasy if it brought him comfort. Luke's eyes dropped to the blisters on his brother's hands and his torn trousers. He gripped the boy's shoulders. He felt bonier than before, and Luke wondered if he'd lost weight. "I'm going to get you out of here," he whispered. Sliding the note to the inside of his palm, Luke eased his hands to John's waist. "Do what the note says. I'll be waiting." He shoved it inside John's trousers.

John's eyes nodded but he said nothing. Good boy. So brave.

"Enough!" The captain's voice ricocheted over the deck. Two marines grabbed John and drew him back before Luke could embrace him once more.

Rising, Luke branded the captain with a fiery gaze. What he wouldn't give to challenge the man to a duel right now. Just the two of them. To the death, for John's freedom. Rain started to fall, bouncing on the deck in large drops as if heaven itself were sad at the proceedings below.

Plop plop plop, like the beating of a war drum. The frigate heaved over the agitated sea. Salty spray lashed across Luke's face. He shook it away.

"We shall see you in a fortnight, Captain Heaton." Raynor dismissed them with a wave of his hand. "Escort these men from the ship, if you please, Mr. Leonard."

John cast Luke one final glance before the sailor shoved him down the companionway ladder. Jerking from the marine's grasp, Luke followed his men over the bulwarks, down the rope, and onto the deck of *Destiny*.

Thunder bellowed as the lines tying the two ships together were released and the hulls slipped apart.

"Do you think it'll work, Captain?" Biron said from beside him.

"It has to. I can think of no other way to get him off that ship." Luke shook the rain from his hair then slicked back the wet strands. "Let's be on our way, Biron."

"Aye, Captain." Biron turned and shot a string of orders across the ship. "Stand by to make sail! Lay aloft, topmen! Man the halyards and sheets!"

Sam approached. "Where should I point her, Cap'n?"

"West, as if we're sailing back to Baltimore." Luke winked.

The boy saluted and raced up on the quarterdeck to take the wheel.

As Biron's and Mr. Keene's orders filled the air, Luke heard his crew scrambling over the deck. He heard their grunts as they leapt into the shrouds to raise sail, their moans as they hauled on lines. And within minutes *Destiny's* canvas caught the wind in a thundering snap and sped on her way over the rising swells of the sea.

A burst of salty wind struck Luke as he watched the frigate fade behind a curtain of rain.

Biron appeared by his side. "He's a brave lad, I'll give him that. If he reads the note and can slip away during the night watch as you told him, he should have no trouble making it over the side."

"Unless they're keeping him locked up below at night." Mr. Ward approached the railing.

Luke shook his head. "They didn't keep me in irons, why would they keep a boy?"

"Will he jump, though? That's the question." Mr. Keene joined them.

"He'll jump," Luke said. "He's my brother." Shielding his eyes from the rain, he glanced up. "It will be dark in an hour. And with this weather, most of the night watch will be hunched under their coats. Maybe God is looking out for us tonight, after all."

"He's always looking out for you," Biron said. "You heard your brother."

"Ah, it's best to count on wit, might, and money, Mr. Abbot," Mr. Keene said. "Those are the things that will never let you down."

Yet Luke wished above all else that there *was* a God to whom he could appeal tonight—that there was an almighty, all-powerful God who could swoop down and close the eyes of the British watch so Luke and his crew could rescue John.

As his men dispersed to their duties, Luke stood at the starboard railing, gazing at the turbulent, dark sea. Lightning etched a white fork across the clouds. When he was sure no one was looking his way, Luke bowed his head. On the off chance there *was* a God, Luke uttered a silent appeal for His help—for John's sake, not Luke's.

But instead of the peace Biron so often spoke of, heavy rain pelted Luke as if God spat on him in reply.

Seven hours later, Luke knew his appeal had fallen on deaf ears. After darkness had transformed the sea into liquid onyx and hidden them from their enemy, *Destiny* had crept to within a half mile of the HMS *Audacious*'s larboard quarter. The frigate had furled all sail, drifting through the darkness under top gallants alone on a southern tack. Luke leveled his scope at the quarterdeck, desperately seeking a glimpse of his brother crawling over the side. A jolly boat rocked alongside *Destiny*, manned by four of Luke's crew, ready to pluck the boy from the water.

The note had told John to jump over the side at that exact spot between one and two in the morning. Luke's eyes strained from the intense focus he had maintained for over an hour. Now, at ten minutes past two, and with still no sign of his brother, Luke's hopes began to sink beneath the murky waters.

"We should be going, Captain." Biron's voice was heavy with sorrow yet held a tenderness not often heard from the man. "They'll spot us if we linger here much longer."

"He could still come." Luke gripped the railing, not wanting to let go. Not wanting to give up. He could not allow his brother to be enslaved for one more minute, not allow himself to be a traitor to his country one more time. His knuckles ached as he peered into the darkness, searching for the one thing his heart yearned to see. But all that met his gaze was the shadowy outline of the frigate's hull, lit by the fluttering glow of a lantern mounted at her stern.

Biron tugged at his neckerchief. "You told him not to come after two in the morning. He's a good lad. He'll obey you."

"I guess he couldn't get away," Sam added.

Luke sighed, knowing they were right. If his brother had the opportunity to come above deck, he would have. "Raise topsails, Mr. Keene, and move us out of sight of this dastardly ship. Then head back to Baltimore at first light, Sam." Back to a town of patriots ravaged by British troops on all sides. Back to being a traitor to everyone he knew and everything he believed in. Back to Mrs. Barnes, once again without his brother. Back to Miss Channing.

If she ever discovered his traitorous activities, she would have nothing to do with him. And he wouldn't blame her in the least.

❖

"Cassandra, dear. Mr. Crane asked you a question." Her mother's shrill voice snapped Cassandra from her musings.

Musings about Mr. Heaton. A topic that seemed to occupy much of her thoughts of late. Wondering how he fared out at sea, wondering if he caught another prize, wondering if he was well, wondering if he thought of her as much as she thought of him.

"Oh, do forgive me, Mr. Crane. I fear my mind was elsewhere." Picking up her glass, she sipped the cool mint tea then set it down and glanced at the man across the dining table. She'd had a week's reprieve from enduring his company—a peaceful, glorious week. Well, if she didn't count the ongoing antics of Darlene and Hannah. But, at her mother's invitation, Mr. Crane had joined them once again for supper.

He dabbed the serviette over his lips. "I asked you—*yet again*—if you would honor me by allowing me to escort you to the Fountain Inn Ball?"

Cassandra dropped her fork onto the plate with a loud *clank*. "I had no idea the ball was so fast upon us."

"Cassandra, whatever is wrong with you?" Her mother's forehead wrinkled.

"Nothing." Nothing except the man sitting across from her. Everything else was going well. They had paid this month's mortgage, had food for a month, and had given the servants their back pay. Her mother had even purchased a new hat. But Luke had only just set out to sea last week. Would he catch a prize and return before her money ran out? Cassandra tried to settle her agitated nerves. Whimpering, followed by the scrape of claws on glass drew Cassandra's gaze to poor Dexter, banished to the back garden while Mr. Crane was visiting.

At the sight of the dog, Mr. Crane's nose wrinkled. His impatient gaze shot to Cassandra. "Your answer, miss?"

Thankfully, Miss Thain entered the dining room and began clearing plates, providing the diversion Cassandra needed to avoid answering the question, as she wondered how she would tell Mr. Crane that she had already accepted Mr. Heaton's invitation to the Fountain Inn Ball. Regardless of her feelings about the newspaper man, she didn't wish to wound Mr. Crane's pride. Nor his heart. Nor crush her mother's expectations. But lately it seemed, she did nothing but disappoint everyone around her. Especially herself.

Never making eye contact, Miss Thain swept through the room, gathering up utensils and platters, finally ending with Mr. Crane's half-full plate of boiled wild geese, fried potatoes, and baked beets from the garden. The fact that it neither resembled nor tasted like any of those things was no longer a shock to Cassandra.

"Thank you, Miss Thain," she said as the woman darted from the room, plates stacked up her arms.

"Now that you can afford a good cook, perhaps you should hire one?" Mr. Crane leaned back in his chair and cocked one brow.

Cassandra's jaw tightened.

"Though where you obtained additional funds is beyond me," he said. Cassandra's mother fluttered her napkin about her face. "Dreadful, simply dreadful business the way our money was stolen. And without your help those few days afterward, we would have starved."

Mr. Crane returned her smile with a forced one of his own before he faced Cassandra. "A distant, wealthy relative die and leave you a fortune?"

"I fail to see how that is any of your affair, Mr. Crane." Cassandra thought she saw a flicker of turmoil cross his eyes before he swept them away.

"Wealthy relative die?" Her mother laughed nervously. "Wouldn't that be a turn of fortune?"

Cassandra gave her mother a pointed gaze, reminding her that she'd instructed her not to say anything about where the additional money had come from.

Her mother coughed and set her serviette on the table. "Shall we have coffee in the parlor?"

Mr. Crane extended his chin. "As I said, I'm more than happy to provide whatever you need, Miss Channing."

"And as I have said, you are too kind, sir." Cassandra stood as a playful scream sounded from above stairs, followed by giggling, the stomp of tiny footsteps, and Mrs. Northrop's harsh voice.

"Oh dear." Cassandra's mother rose. "I had hoped Mrs. Northrop would have gotten the girls abed by now."

Frowning his disapproval, Mr. Crane stood and proffered his arm to Cassandra's mother, leading her down the hall to the parlor.

Cassandra dipped her head in the kitchen door to ask Miss Thain to bring coffee before she followed them.

No sooner had she sat down on the sofa and spread her skirts about her than Mr. Crane, standing at the hearth, one arm draped over the mantel as if he owned the home, brought up the Fountain Inn Ball once again.

A warm breeze swept into the room, fluttering the curtains. Cassandra gazed into the darkness creeping in from outside.

Mr. Crane cleared his throat. "The ball is in ten days, Miss Channing. Surely you have not made other arrangements?"

"But I'm afraid I have, sir." Cassandra smiled sweetly, hoping her demeanor would soften the blow. "I have agreed to be escorted by Mr. Heaton."

Her mother gasped. Grabbing her bell, she shook it vigorously.

Mr. Crane's bushy brows bunched together. His mouth dropped open. "Mr. *Luke* Heaton?"

As if there could be any other.

Miss Thain entered with a tray of coffee and set it on the table, seemingly oblivious to the incessant chiming bouncing off the walls.

"One and the same." Cassandra reached over and stayed the bell in her mother's hands.

Miss Thain's oversized eyes met Cassandra's before she lowered them and began to pour the coffee.

Cassandra's mother raised a hand to her forehead. "Oh, never mind that, Miss Thain. Please have Mrs. Northrop bring my tonic immediately."

After the cook left the parlor, Cassandra's mother glared at Cassandra. "You cannot be serious, dear. This is unheard of!"

"Isn't the man out to sea?" Mr. Crane's normally calm voice cracked.

Cassandra poured a cup of coffee and handed it to her mother, but the woman merely stared at her as if she'd lost her mind. Setting the cup back down with a *clank*, she swallowed. "He assured me he would be in town for the occasion."

"How can he assure you of such a thing? Of all the. . ." Mr. Crane gazed up at the picture of Cassandra's great-grandfather as if trying to garner some wisdom from the aged man.

"Mr. Heaton cannot predict when he is in town and when he isn't." Suspicion twisted his features.

"Dear." Her mother touched her arm. "I know you feel you owe Mr. Heaton for his success at sea, but this type of charity is simply beyond the pale."

Cassandra tapped her shoe over the ornate rug. "Yet I have given him my word, and I intend to abide by it."

Mrs. Northrop entered the room with tonic in hand. Crossing to the table, she poured a splash of the magical elixir into Cassandra's mother's coffee and left without saying a word or speaking to any of them.

Mr. Crane tugged on his embroidered waistcoat, crossed to the table, and poured himself a cup of coffee. The sharp scent of ink followed him.

From his terse expression Cassandra knew she had hurt him, but there was nothing to be done about it. The sooner he realized she could not possibly accept his hand, the freer he would be to find some other lady upon whom to shower his affections.

He tossed the coffee to the back of his throat then grimaced, no doubt from the scalding liquid. Setting the cup down, he dipped his head toward them. "I thank you for supper, Mrs. Channing, but I fear important matters draw me away early this evening." Cassandra's mother rose. She pressed her trembling hands together, a wild, pleading look in her eyes. "So soon, sir?"

"I'm afraid so." He shot a gaze so filled with outrage toward Cassandra it sent a chill down her.

As he made his way to the door, her mother eased beside him. "Forgive her, Mr. Crane. I will speak to her." Though she whispered, her words found their way to Cassandra's ears. "Rest assured, she will attend the ball with you."

❖

After Mrs. Channing saw him out, Mr. Crane made his way down the flagstone path to the street, anger tossing the putrid contents of his supper into a tempest. How dare the young tart refuse him? And for that swaggering miscreant? After all Crane had done for this family. He clenched his jaw until it hurt then turned toward the shrubbery that marked the corner of the Channing property. There as expected, the housekeeper, Mrs. Northrop, emerged from the shadows.

"What do you have for me?" he asked, settling his hat atop his head.

A breeze, ripe with the scents of honeysuckle and roses, tousled wisps of the elderly woman's hair from beneath her mobcap. She puckered her lips and gazed back at the house. "I thought you should know, sir, that it was Mr. Heaton who gave Miss Channing the money."

"Mr. Heaton again!" he shouted then slammed his mouth shut with a groan. He closed his eyes as a horse and rider walked past. "Why does she take his money and not mine?"

Mrs. Northrop stretched her already elongated neck. "She says it is only a loan until he catches another prize."

The news rankled over Crane's already agitated nerves. Catch another prize, indeed. Not if he could help it. "Anything else?"

"No, sir. But I'll keep my eyes and ears open for anything unusual like you said." She held out her hand.

Mr. Crane huffed. "I gave you five dollars last time."

"It's not easy sneaking around listening in on conversations. Mrs. Channing is getting suspicious. Besides, I took a big risk for you stealing Miss Channing's money."

"And you were handsomely paid for that."

Yet the servant's hand would not retreat. Mr. Crane plucked a couple of coins from his waistcoat pocket and deposited them atop her greedy palm—if only to buy her continued silence.

"Thank you, sir." Turning, she snuck away into the darkness.

Mr. Crane stormed down the dirt street, his mood as dark as the evening shadows around him and as turbulent as the skies above. He cursed Luke Heaton. How did the man keep succeeding at sea? Lieutenant Tripp had assured him that he'd sufficiently sabotaged Mr. Heaton's ship. Yet five days ago, the scoundrel had sailed into Baltimore harbor a victor. His ship none the worse for wear and his pockets full of coins. "To the devil with him!" Mr. Crane shouted as he turned down Lombard Street. The man was up to something. No privateer could capture a prize and return to port in that short amount of time. Nor would luck allow him to slip undetected past the British blockade more than once.

One thing Crane knew. Mr. Heaton must be dealt with. Without him in the way, Miss Channing would have no choice but to accept Crane's courtship. No, the rake was up to something.

And Crane intended to find out just what that something was.

❖ CHAPTER 25 ❖

C assandra exited the drapers, wrapped package in hand. Margaret followed her outside onto the street bustling with people, horses, and carriages. From his spot leaning against a wooden post, Margaret's husband, Mr. Dayle, lengthened his stance, picked up two empty buckets from the ground, and greeted them, his gentle smile ever present.

"Success, ladies?"

"Yes, thank you, Mr. Dayle." Cassandra tilted her head into the hot August sun.

"The gown looks glorious on you, miss." Margaret's eyes twinkled. "Mr. Heaton will no doubt be speechless at your beauty."

Warmth flooded Cassandra's face as she turned and proceeded down the walkway—warmth that had nothing to do with the sultry afternoon. "I care not what effect my beauty has on Mr. Heaton. I simply needed a new gown and the ball provided me with an excuse." Though she could ill afford the extra expense.

Margaret's giggle reminded Cassandra that she'd forgotten to chastise her maid for telling Mr. Heaton she was in her solarium alone those. . . how many nights ago? It seemed an eternity since she'd seen the man.

Felt his strong arms surround her.

His lips on hers.

More heat swamped her.

"Miss, are you all right? Your face is as red as a beet," Margaret said.

Cassandra glanced at her maid, expecting to see a look of concern. Instead she saw a mischievous grin. Opening her parasol with a snap, Cassandra stopped to cross the street. "You are incorrigible, Margaret."

"Indeed," Mr. Dayle agreed as his eyes took in his wife with affection. "My wife fancies herself a matchmaker."

"It's just that I wish everyone could be as happy as we are, my love." Margaret smiled up at him, her cheeks as rosy as her lips.

A twinge of jealousy pinched Cassandra at the adoring affection that stretched between the couple. "Well, I assure you, you are wasting your matchmaking skills with me. I have enough of that with my mother. Besides, I cannot hope for such a fortuitous match as yours. Most marriages occur out of necessity and are merely contracts of convenience by reason of wealth or pedigree."

Mr. Dayle stepped into the road, leading the way between a passing landau—overflowing with passengers donned in lace and exotic feathers— and a wagon filled with children dressed in rags sitting amongst barrels. Cassandra smiled at one of wee ones, and the little girl waved.

Margaret weaved her arm through Cassandra's. "Contracts such as the one between you and Mr. Heaton?"

Cassandra shook her head and laughed. "I surrender, Margaret." A breeze blew in from the harbor, cooling the perspiration on her neck and dancing through the lace that fringed her parasol. "Now, let's go fetch water from the spring and get home before this heat becomes unbearable. And I'll have no further talk of Mr. Heaton or any other man for that matter."

Yet, as they headed down the crowded street, Cassandra could think of nothing but Mr. Heaton. She had spotted *Destiny* anchored at bay when they passed by the harbor that morning. Odd that only he had successfully slipped past the blockade yet again. Ignoring the nip of suspicion, Cassandra settled on the fact that he was a better captain than she or the entire town had given him credit for.

He was in town! Which meant she would soon see him. Which also meant he had kept his promise to be home in time to escort her to the ball.

A group of militiamen marched by, muskets propped on their shoulders, their boots stirring a dust cloud in the street, reminding Cassandra that they were at war. But how could she forget that with the British fleet sitting just miles off their coast, repeatedly threatening to sail toward Baltimore? Not to mention the musket shots that peppered the sky many a night, waking Cassandra from a deep sleep. Perhaps she shouldn't allow herself such flighty thoughts of balls and gowns and romance during such a time as this.

She was still pondering these things when they turned the corner onto the city square, where a natural spring provided not only fresh water, but the perfect meeting place for the inhabitants of Baltimore. Several groups of people mulled about the area. Feathered bonnets and cocked hats huddled in deep conversation. Children darted here and there. Giggles and the thrum of chatter accompanied the *clip-clop* of horses' hooves and the slosh of water being collected from the spring. As Cassandra scanned the crowd, her eyes latched onto a tall man with dark hair standing with his back to her.

Her heart vaulted into her throat.

"Cassandra!" Marianne waved at her from her spot beside Mr. Heaton. Noah and another powerfully built man with brown hair and a regal bearing lifted their gazes in her direction.

Trying to avoid looking at Mr. Heaton, lest she give away her excitement at seeing him, Cassandra approached the group and gave her friend a hug.

Margaret joined her husband at the well where they waited their turn to fill the buckets.

"Noah, so good to see you. When did you get home?" Cassandra asked, avoiding Mr. Heaton's gaze.

"Two days ago." He gave his wife an endearing look. "I had a very successful voyage."

"I'm happy to hear it." She turned to Mr. Heaton. "I saw your ship in the bay."

"Indeed. I sailed in last night." He drank her in with his eyes.

Marianne turned to the other gentleman. "Oh, forgive my bad manners. This is Lieu. . .Mr. Reed. He is a friend of Rose's."

Tearing her gaze from the trance Luke placed on her, Cassandra faced the newcomer. "Rose McGuire?"

He dipped his head. "The same." Sorrow crossed his deep brown eyes. Then taking Cassandra's gloved hand, he placed a kiss upon it. "A pleasure to meet you, miss." His voice reeked of British nobility.

"How do you do, Mr. Reed. Pray tell, how do you know Rose?"

Luke snorted and lowered his chin.

Noah waved a hand through the air. "It is a long story, I'm afraid. For another time, perhaps."

The alarm firing over Marianne's face sent a prickle of unease through Cassandra, but she shrugged it off. It was none of her business.

Against her will, her gaze found its way back to Luke. "So your voyage was met with success?"

A perpetual grin sat on his mouth as his eyes kept wandering to her lips.

Sending her stomach into a whirl. *Cad.*

"Quite," he said. "In fact, I was on my way to see you about the prize money."

A burst of wind tugged at her parasol, drawing Luke's glance. A playful smirk lifted his lips as a loose strand of his hair brushed over his jaw. "Why not come for supper, Mr. Heaton? We can settle accounts then." The invitation flew from her mouth before she could ponder the wisdom of it. Yet, perhaps, if her mother spent more time with him, she would see that he was a gentleman. And one who possessed just as much charm, intelligence, and dependability as Mr. Crane.

She shocked herself with her confidence in the man.

Mr. Heaton's gaze shifted to Noah, who smiled toward Cassandra. "I'm afraid I have need of Luke tonight, Cassandra. He's assisting me and Mr. Reed with an important task."

A look of understanding passed between the men, causing her uneasiness to grow. But when she looked to Marianne for understanding, her friend gazed at her husband with concern.

"Very well, then"—Cassandra smiled—"perhaps we can discuss business when you come to call on Saturday."

Mr. Heaton's brow furrowed. "Saturday?"

"The ball?" Cassandra tamped her foot on the mud.

He flinched. "Yes, of course."

"You forgot?" She snapped her parasol shut.

Eyeing it, he backed away. And she resisted the urge to poke him with it.

The prattle of the crowd seemed to rise up around her as if, with wagging tongues and looks of pity, everyone in the square witnessed Cassandra's humiliation.

"Forgive me, Miss Channing. I've had much on my mind." An unusual sadness tugged on Luke's features.

But she would not fall for his act. All the happiness she'd allowed herself to feel these past weeks dissolved into a single drop of despair. "We only forget things that are not of import to us. I shall relieve you of your obligation to escort me." She faced her friends. Sympathy filled Marianne's eyes. Noah gave Luke a caustic look, and Mr. Reed glanced off to the side.

"Good day to you all." Then turning, Cassandra stomped away.

She heard the thud of his boots following her. He grabbed her arm and spun her around. "Miss Channing, I truly wish to escort you to the ball."

"You have an odd way of showing it, Mr. Heaton." She headed down the street.

And again he stopped her. Desperation crinkled the corners of his blue eyes. "I'm a cad, Miss Channing." He gestured toward the bundle in her arms. "I see that you've had a new gown made for the occasion. How can I make it up to you?"

"Don't flatter yourself, Mr. Heaton. This gown is not for the ball. If you'll please deduct what I owe you from my share of your most recent prize and send the paperwork and any additional funds to me by courier, I'd be obliged." Then turning, she stormed away.

Only this time, she did not hear him following.

Margaret fell in step beside her, while Mr. Dayle, with full buckets in hand, followed behind. A hundred unflattering names for Mr. Heaton sped through Cassandra's mind, empowering her steps. Reprobate, scoundrel, villain, blackguard, libertine. Clutching her closed parasol in one hand, she pressed the gown to her chest, if only to prevent herself from tossing it to the dirt as she wished.

She had no need of it now.

But she wouldn't give the insolent rake the satisfaction. She would keep the new gown for another occasion—when a true gentleman came to escort her for the evening.

Someone who would not use his charm to worm his way into her trust—to gain kisses she had given to no one else. Then, once he had obtained them, once he was satisfied with her desire for him and his insatiable vanity was fed, he abandoned her like the string of broken women before her.

How could she have allowed him to woo her? She knew what type of man he was. Fighting back tears, she turned the corner onto Market

MaryLu Tyndall

Street. Just when she had finally begun to trust him—finally begun to think he was noble and honorable. Someone she could depend on.

"I'm sorry, miss," Margaret said as they weaved their way down the busy street. "It's only a silly ball."

"It's not the ball, Margaret. It's that I counted on him. For the first time in a long time, I counted on someone. And he let me down."

Instead of uttering one of her platitudes, Margaret took Cassandra's arm in a consoling grip and walked silently beside her.

Hearing the slosh of the water as Mr. Dayle struggled to maintain their harried pace, Cassandra slowed. Besides, people were beginning to stare. She drew in a deep breath and raised her chin. "What does it matter anyway?"

Yet the tears pooling in her eyes belied her words. Why, oh why, had she done the very thing she had forbidden herself to do?

Why had she fallen in love with the town rogue?

❖

"Good evening to you, Miss Addington, always a pleasure. And Mr. Snyder." Luke shoved his hat back onto his head and backed out of the humble cottage. "I'll trouble you no further tonight."

Before Miss Addington had shut the door, Mr. Snyder, the city councilman, shouted from within his house, "What is that noise?" The sound of his buckled shoes clipped over the wooden floor. Hurrying down the front steps, Luke waited in the shadow of a tree for his friends to appear from behind the house. If the councilman caught them in his chamber, he would no doubt implicate Luke in the crime. More trouble Luke did not need. But how could he refuse Noah's help? The man was his best friend and he had saved his life on more than one occasion. Mr. Reed was another story. Luke was yet unconvinced that the British Royal Navy lieutenant meant them no harm—that his actions were in the best interest of Rose McGuire, as he professed. But Noah believed him. And that was all Luke needed to go along with the nefarious deed.

Seconds passed like long minutes as Luke peered into the darkness. Finally, the duo appeared, darting from the left side of the house, Mr. Snyder's shout following them like cannon shot. Mr. Reed pressed a bundle to his chest. Moonlight glimmered off a sword in his hand as the three men sprinted down the street without saying a word. Once they turned the corner, Noah slowed to a walk, his chest heaving. Then his

220

and Mr. Reed's chuckles filled the air.

"I take it you got what you came for?" Luke asked.

"I did." Mr. Reed's tone lifted in excitement. "Thank you for your help, Mr. Heaton, especially considering our past."

The past he referred to, as well as his British accent, still grated over Luke. The past in which Luke had been enslaved aboard the HMS *Undefeatable* where Mr. Reed was second lieutenant. "I did it for Miss McGuire, not for you."

"I thank you nonetheless, sir." Though Luke could not make out Mr. Reed's expression in the darkness, his voice was sincere.

A fleeting thought drifted through Luke's mind. Perhaps Mr. Reed could aid him in rescuing his brother. But no. That would mean confessing Luke's traitorous activities to Noah. Noah was an honorable man. A patriot. Friendship or not, Luke doubted that Noah's irreproachable conscience would allow him to do anything but turn Luke in.

"If that's all you need tonight, gentlemen," Luke said as they approached the street that led to his favorite tavern. After his meeting today with Miss Channing, he needed a drink. He knew he had crushed the bud of their relationship beneath his stupidity. He knew she would probably never forgive him. His flickering hope for any courtship between them was sufficiently doused. It was for the best. She deserved much better than him.

"I would impose on you one more time, Luke," Noah said, stopping him. "Mr. Reed and I need your help at the ball in three days."

"I'm not attending."

Noah halted and touched Luke's arm, stopping him. "Will you attend for me? Mr. Reed wishes to bid Miss McGuire one last adieu and pass along some good news."

"Why do you need me?" Luke huffed. "Another lady to distract?"

"No. A man. Mr. Snyder, to be exact."

Fisting his hands at his waist, Luke chuckled. Truth be told, he was no friend to the slimy councilman and would love to see the man put in his place. Besides, he had several days before his next rendezvous with the frigate. Since he'd already devised a new plan to rescue John, he had naught else to do but sulk about and drown his sorrows with rum. Now that he was not attending the ball with Miss Channing, what would it matter if he aided Noah and Mr. Reed?

"You can count on me."

❖ CHAPTER 26 ❖

Struggling for a breath, Luke tugged upon the silk neckerchief Mrs. Barnes had elegantly tied around his neck. How did men continually wear these infernal things? He gazed down at the suit of black lute string trimmed in velvet that he'd borrowed from Noah. Though it fit him perfectly, he felt like an overprimped fop. Lifting the glass to his lips, he sipped the wine punch and gazed at the display of pomposity spread across the dance floor and hovering in cackling clusters about the room. Baltimore's finest citizens attired like peacocks, men in their silk-embroidered waistcoats, ladies in the latest gowns, adorned with colorful sashes and glittering jewels. Their hair alone, twined with pearls and golden pins, must have taken hours to fashion.

Biron appeared beside him. "Cheer up, Captain. You look as though your ship just sank."

"You know I despise these functions." Luke snorted as a malodorous cloud of perfumes stung his nose. His first mate adjusted his velvet waistcoat and smiled at a passing lady. Luke had never seen the old man in anything but his dirty breeches, gray shirt, and red neckerchief. Nor had he ever seen him so chipper. In fact, he'd been completely surprised to discover that Biron was attending the ball at all.

"You wouldn't despise such grand affairs if you were escorting Miss

Channing." Censure rang in Biron's voice.

Just the sound of her name sent pain sprawling across Luke. "Certain things are worth enduring for women like her."

"And for friends who need your help," Biron added, a twinkle in his eye.

"Aye, which is why I'm here dressed like a stuffed pig and feeling like a fool." Luke sipped his drink again, noting the wine was getting quite low. He would need a refill soon if he was going to endure this night.

"It feels indecent to be here amongst all this luxury," he said. "Enjoying my wine, when John is no doubt huddling belowdecks, lonely and hungry, aboard that frigate."

"Aye, Captain, but there's naught to be done about it now. It's better to be here helping your friends than sitting in some tavern, flooding your belly with rum and losing what's left of your money." Biron's eyes lit up. "Besides, the scenery here is much more appealing."

Luke huffed. Perhaps his friend was right.

The quadrille ended, and the couples bowed and curtseyed to each other as they moved from the dance floor. Several ladies peered at him above silk fans.

"Ah, to be young and as handsome as you are, Captain." Biron dipped his head toward the giggling ladies, shocking Luke.

"I've never known you to desire the company of the softer gender."

"In truth, after my wife died, I had no interest, but the older I get, the more I'm findin' the need for companionship. God said it isn't good for man to be alone. And I do believe He was right."

"So, *that* explains why you came tonight."

"Aye, look at all the sweet angels floating about the room."

Luke chuckled as his eyes landed on Mr. Keene, dressed in his usual pomp, at the edge of the dance floor, kissing the hand of a young lady who seemed barely old enough to be out in society. She tugged her hand from his grip, her eyes pools of pain and betrayal, before she clutched her gown and flew away like a wounded bird.

Instead of following her to make amends for whatever caused her distress, Mr. Keene immediately veered his gaze to another lady standing off to his side and shrugged. The woman laughed and gave him a coy come-hither glance. Which the man immediately obliged. After a few seconds, in which it appeared the lady scribbled Mr. Keene's name on her dance card, he turned, spotted Luke and Biron, and headed their way.

"What was all that about?" Luke asked.

Mr. Keene raised his eyebrows in innocence. Luke pointed with his drink to the door on the far side of the room where he'd seen the troubled lady exit. "That young woman. She seemed vexed."

Mr. Keene clasped his hands behind his back. "Ah yes, Miss Melody. She was under the mistaken impression that we were courting." He chuckled.

Biron scratched his head. "Hmm. I wonder how she came to that conclusion."

"I have no idea. You know how women can be." Mr. Keene gave a sensuous smile to a passing lady, who returned it with a wave of her fan. "I suppose I called on her on a few occasions."

"Just called on her?" Luke asked.

"I suppose I may have kissed her once or twice." Mr. Keene rubbed his jaw. The jewel on his finger winked at Luke from within the lacy folds of his cuff.

Luke shook his head, finding it difficult to contain his anger. "To a proper lady, a kiss is nearly equal to a proposal of marriage." But guilt tightened his gut at the thought of the kisses he'd shared with Miss Channing. How was he any different from Mr. Keene?

Mr. Keene looked incredulous. "You can't possibly think I could limit myself to a single lady when there are so many delectably ripe fruits from which to pick?" He waved a hand over the crowd, and his gaze froze on a particularly succulent fruit smiling at him from the corner. "If you'll excuse me, gentlemen." And off he went in a flourish of satin.

Luke followed him with an angry gaze, remembering the look of agony in the woman's eyes moments ago.

Biron crossed his arms over his chest. "A dangerous man, that one. At least to the ladies. And he's a mite old to be playing such games."

Luke nodded. At one and forty, the man still presented a handsome figure. Yet his age gave the incorrect impression of maturity and stability. "He should take care with the sentiments of others."

"In truth, he reminds me a bit of you, Captain."

"Me?" Luke said. "Bite your tongue, man."

"How many hearts have you broken in this town?"

Biron's words struck Luke like a frigid wind. He could always count on the blunt assessment of his friend. Yet, in truth, Luke had never actually considered it. Hadn't he spent his life flitting from woman to woman, never landing on one long enough to form an attachment? Suddenly, dozens of tear-filled eyes—just like the eyes he'd seen on that young lady—paraded across his vision.

At the time he had brushed them off as overemotional females. Now, he understood their pain—felt it himself down to his core. Shame soured in his stomach. In fifteen years, would Luke end up like Mr. Keene, a flashy, pretentious philanderer whose only skills included cards, drink, and meaningless trysts with wanton women? At six and twenty, he was well on his way. Or he *had* been until Miss Channing had given him a chance to better himself. Until she had given him the desire to be a better man.

"I'm not like that anymore," he announced, raising his empty glass with a frown.

"I'm glad to hear it." Biron gave him a knowing look before his eyes latched onto an elderly woman standing beside a much younger one at the edge of the dance floor. "Now, if you'll excuse me. I see the lady I've been looking for."

Luke watched as his old friend wove his way through the crowd to stand before the older woman as the younger wandered off to dance. She smiled and dipped her head in agreement to whatever he was saying. The scene brought a glimmer of joy to Luke's otherwise dour mood. Turning, he started for the refreshment table in the next room when the shimmer of an emerald gown hooked his gaze, drawing it toward a red-haired beauty across the dance floor.

*Cassandra. . .*Miss Channing.

What was she doing here? Had she found someone else to escort her? Jealousy twisted in his gut. She stood beside Marianne and Miss Rose, the trio of heads drawn together in some covert feminine scheme. Her burgundy-colored hair fell in ringlets around her neck and sparkled like garnets when she moved. Mesmerized by the sight of her, Luke forgot where he'd been going. Then she turned and glanced across the room as if looking for someone. Her eyes met his and her smile faded. He lifted his empty glass toward her in a salute as Miss Rose leaned and whispered something in her ear. Marianne grinned, and Miss Channing turned her back to Luke once again.

What was he thinking? Of course she'd found another escort. She was a beautiful woman who possessed manners and charm and intelligence and courage.

MaryLu Tyndall

And the kindest heart he'd ever known.

With a huff, he turned and slipped through the door into the next room in search of two things: Noah and a drink. The sooner he aided his friend in getting rid of Mr. Snyder, the sooner Luke could leave this ostentatious ball and head toward the tavern where he belonged. So much for his promise to Biron. He found Noah standing next to the man in question—Mr. Snyder—who was relaying some lavish tale to the mayor, General Smith, and two other councilmen. Noah gave Luke a nod to carry out the plan they'd spoken of earlier.

Selecting a glass of wine from the oblong refreshment table set against the wall, Luke reached for the bottle of laudanum inside his coat pocket and poured a hefty amount into the glass. He handed it to Noah, who handed it to Mr. Snyder. Three glasses later, the man had not slowed a breath in his fervent speech. Finally, the mayor made some excuse to leave, and the party broke up. Mr. Snyder, with a barely perceivable stumble, made his way to Miss Rose across the room. Cassandra stood beside her.

Much to her apparent dismay, Mr. Snyder grabbed Miss Rose's arm and dragged her into the other room toward the dance floor where a Virginia reel was just beginning. Noah and the ladies followed, leaving Luke with no recourse but to join them. Not that he minded. Though Miss Channing would not grace him with even a glance, Luke relished their close proximity.

Taking his wife's arm, Noah swung about and faced Miss Channing. "If you would honor Mr. Heaton with a dance, Cassandra, it will help us keep an eye on Snyder."

Luke started to protest, not wanting the woman to be forced to taint herself with his touch, but she agreed before he could utter a word.

"For Rose," she said and lifted her gloved hand.

An unavoidable grin on his face, Luke placed it within the crook of his elbow. He must thank Noah later.

Her hand was stiff on his arm as he led her to a spot in the line of women and took his position across from her. The music began and the couples bowed toward each other then stepped together. "I can see how it pains you to be close to me." Looping his elbow through hers, he swung her about.

"I will endure it for my friend's sake." Her voice was as sharp as glass.

They retreated and waited as the head couple sashayed down the middle of the line. "How noble." He gave her a spurious grin.

She pursed her lips and lifted her chin. "What would you know of nobility?"

The couples surrounding them began to stare.

Infernal woman. They came together again at the head of the line. Luke lifted his hand, but she hovered hers atop his as if she loathed to touch him. He escorted her down the line of dancers. "About as much as you know of forgiveness, miss."

Her eyes narrowed into shards of emerald. She opened her mouth to say something when beside them, Mr. Snyder emitted an odd giggle and began to sway. All eyes shot toward Rose as she attempted to keep the man from falling.

Disappointment weighted Luke's shoulders. The laudanum had worked too soon. Yet what did it matter? His conversation with Miss Channing had been nothing but an exchange of insults. She turned to her friend, her rigid features of only a moment ago softening as she helped Rose and Mr. Snyder from the floor. Noah gave an approving nod to Luke.

Mr. Snyder took up a harried pace through the press of people, nudging them aside as he went and sputtering words in some sort of tirade. Finally, collapsing into a chair, he lowered his head into his hands.

Critical whispers collected behind fans, riding upon looks of repugnance. Finally the butler at the front door announced the entrance of a new actor to this mad play. "Mr. Alexander Reed."

Everyone's heads swerved.

Including Miss Rose, who stumbled backward in shock. Mr. Snyder slumped to the ground. Luke dashed to him, pulling him up by one arm while Noah grabbed the other.

Miss Rose, her brow lined with concern, leaned over her unconscious escort.

"He'll be all right, Miss Rose." Luke winked. "He just needs to sleep it off." Then, with great difficulty, he and Noah dragged the councilman through the parting crowd, out into the gardens, up the stairs, and into a room they'd previously purchased.

"Heavy old bugger." Noah chuckled as they deposited Mr. Snyder on the bed and swung his feet up on the coverlet. "That should hold him for a couple hours." Noah slapped his hands together.

"I still don't see why you're doing this for that British lieutenant."

Luke stared at the drooling councilman.

"Miss Rose seems to find favor in the man. Besides, he's going back to his ship tonight."

"To terrorize and murder more Americans?" Luke growled. "We could be hanged for allowing him to escape." Even as he said it, he realized his own hypocrisy.

"Aye, I realize that." Noah crossed his arms over his chest. "But there's nothing to be done for it. It would break Rose's heart. Besides, Mr. Reed is an honorable man who regrets his part in this war."

Luke gazed at Mr. Snyder. "Honor. A quality sorely lacking in the councilman."

The two men left the room, closing the door tight, and returned to the ballroom. Upon seeing Marianne, Noah excused himself, leaving Luke alone once again. He scanned the room but saw no sign of Cassandra. It was just as well. He had no desire to see her in another man's arms.

Turning to leave, Luke nearly ran into Mr. Crane, his face an expanding mass of red angst.

"How dare you, sir?"

"How dare I, what?" Luke huffed and raised a brow.

Mr. Crane's lips twisted in disgust. "How dare you escort Miss Channing to this ball and then abandon her." He jerked his head to the left, and Luke glanced over to see the object of their discussion, standing along the back wall, forlornly watching the dancers float across the floor. Oddly, Biron stood beside her.

Luke longed for a drink. "I neither escorted her, sir, nor abandoned her."

Mr. Crane's face crumbled. "Then, why is she here? Why are *you* here?"

"As to the first, you may ask her yourself. As to the second, I shall remedy that immediately." Luke dipped his head to the shorter man and brushed past him and out the door.

❖

Cassandra eyed the weathered seaman beside her. As soon as he had approached, she recognized him as Mr. Heaton's first mate. "Are you enjoying yourself, Mr. Abbot?"

"Aye, I am, miss," he said. "I don't attend functions like this very often, but I was finally able to purchase a suit to wear from my earnings aboard *Destiny*."

"Well, you look very handsome, sir." She smiled and glanced at the dancers twirling and gliding over the floor like lilies on a swirling pond, happy to see Noah and Marianne enjoying themselves.

Mr. Abbot shuffled his shoes and shifted his glance between her and the crowd.

"Did you wish to speak to me about something, Mr. Abbot?"

He sighed. "Aye, it's about Luke. . .Mr. Heaton."

"Did he send you?" Just then she spotted him across the room talking with Mr. Crane. Odd.

"I thought you should know," Mr. Abbot said, "how terrible he feels about not remembering the ball."

"I'm quite sure." *Sure that he's an unfeeling sot.*

"He thinks quite highly of you, miss. He's got much on his mind lately."

His many other lady friends, no doubt. "Just not me, apparently."

"Beggin' your pardon, that's where you're wrong, miss."

Cassandra could hear no more. "I know you must think me some vain shrew, Mr. Abbot." Actually, she wasn't sure why she was behaving in such a way. "I know privateering is not easy business, and I imagine it's quite harrowing and dangerous at times, but a gentleman's word is a gentleman's word." And she had been so excited, so hopeful that she could depend on the word of that particular gentleman, if she could refer to him by that title. Even so, when Luke had shown up at the ball anyway, she thought perhaps she might give him another chance. Then she realized he'd only come to help Noah, not to see her. And she'd been crushed all over again.

"He hurt you." Mr. Abbot cocked his head.

She lifted her chin. "Don't be silly. It would take much more than the broken word of a cad to distress me."

"He has more than privateering on his mind," he said. "A private matter that eats away at him. I thought you should know."

Cassandra's traitorous gaze swept back to Mr. Heaton, still speaking with Mr. Crane. What problems could the man possibly have that surpassed her own? He had only himself to care for. And only his drinking and gambling habits to fund. Yet, she had sensed a hint of sorrow about him in the solarium that night.

Finally, Mr. Heaton and Mr. Crane separated, and the latter headed toward her. "Oh, bother."

"And I thought you should also know"—Mr. Abbot dipped his head at a passing elderly lady—"that he kept his word to you about not partakin' of rum out at sea."

Cassandra studied the old sailor. A wisdom she had not expected to see intensified his eyes, while his words about Luke befuddled her mind. Why would he honor such a difficult promise and yet forget all about the ball? "Mr. Abbot, you are a loyal friend to Mr. Heaton. He doesn't deserve you."

As Mr. Crane approached, his frown transformed into a sickly smile. "Miss Channing"—he bowed—"how lovely to see you. I have just heard from Mr. Heaton that you are here without an escort."

Mr. Abbot groaned, excused himself, and walked away, Mr. Crane's glare following him through the mob.

"That is true, sir." Her voice snapped his attention back to her.

"May I have the pleasure of the next dance?"

Cassandra eyed the man—the slight quiver of his bottom lip, the anticipation in his eyes. But her mind swam with what Mr. Abbot had said, and her heart was drawn out the door where Mr. Heaton had disappeared.

"I thank you, Mr. Crane, but I'm afraid I only came to help a friend. I am not in the mood to dance tonight."

His face fell and fury filled his eyes. "I see your privateer has returned." He gestured toward the door where Luke had exited.

"Indeed."

"With more prize money?"

"That is none of your concern."

A frown folded his lips. "But what is my concern, Miss Channing"—with raised brows, he leaned toward her, his cologne unable to mask his inky smell—"is how the man manages to slip past the British blockade. At least three times now, is it? When men of far greater nautical skill either do not attempt it or get caught in the process."

"What are you saying, sir?" Although Cassandra knew precisely what he implied—had entertained similar questions herself.

"I'm not saying anything, miss." He brushed dust from his shoulder. "Just speculating."

Cassandra's jaw tightened. "Well, I'll thank you, sir, to keep your speculations to yourself until you have evidence to back them." The hypocrisy of her defense of Mr. Heaton, when only moments before she accused him of being dishonorable, was not lost on her.

Mr. Crane's eyes narrowed. He appeared to be having trouble breathing. And frankly, Cassandra found her tolerance of his company waxing thin.

"If you'll excuse me, Mr. Crane. . ." Clutching her gown, she hurried away, weaving a spiraled path amongst the crowd. All she could think of was catching up to Mr. Heaton. Had she misjudged him? Had she even given him a chance to explain? Cursing her selfishness, she dashed from the room into the garden. Stopping only long enough to ensure he was not there, she pushed her way through the throng that mobbed the front stairs and dashed out onto the street. Muggy air, filled with the fragrance of sweet magnolia, stole the odor of tawdry perfume and tobacco smoke from her nostrils. Taking a deep breath, she scanned the street in both directions. Thank goodness they had lit the lanterns on Light Street or she'd not be able to see very far. As it was, she spotted a lone man, dressed in black, walking toward the harbor. She knew that confident gait.

Ignoring the myriad eyes staring her way, she darted down the street, her slippers clacking over the cobblestones and her heart racing in her chest.

"Mr. Heaton!" she shouted when she thought he might be able to hear her.

He didn't turn around.

"Luke!"

Still, he continued on his way.

Her chest heaving, she halted, tears forming in her eyes.

Then as if sensing her distress, he stopped.

And slowly turned to face her.

❖ CHAPTER 27 ❖

S ensing, rather than hearing, someone following him, Luke turned around. He shook his head at the vision that met his eyes—Miss Channing floating on a cloud of green satin, haloed in golden light from the street lantern above her. He rubbed his eyes. Surely, he hadn't consumed *that* much alcohol. Yet instead of vanishing like all the good things in his life, she moved toward him, growing more real and lovely with each passing moment.

Only when her scent of gardenias tickled his nose did he truly believe she had followed him.

"You shouldn't be out here alone."

"I'm not alone now, Mr. Heaton."

He could not fathom why she had chased after him. She'd been nothing but churlish all evening. He gazed into her eyes and swallowed at the yearning and affection he saw within them. "Come to whip me with more angry retorts?"

She lowered her chin. Her creamy chest rose and fell beneath the gold trim of her gown. "I spoke with your first mate, Mr. Abbot."

A landau clattered past, laughter spilling from within onto the cobblestones.

"Indeed. I saw you together," Luke said, uneasy at what the foolish old duff might have told her. Yet she wouldn't be standing here now—

adorable, shy, inviting—if he'd told her the truth of his actions.

A gentle smile graced her lips. "You inspire loyalty among your crew."

Luke huffed and pushed a strand of hair behind his ear. "A fact that shocks me as much as I'm sure it does you."

She gazed past him as a breeze from the harbor frolicked in her delicate curls. Luke longed to do the same, but instead he locked his hands together behind his back.

"Perhaps I was a bit hasty in my anger, Mr. Heaton."

He cocked his head. Had the poor woman taken to drink as well? "I was a cad to forget the ball. I deserved your anger."

She searched his eyes as if looking for something. "Something troubles you, some travesty."

A bell rang from the harbor. Hot, muggy air moistened his neck and forehead. "Is that what Mr. Abbot told you?" Luke untied his cravat, allowing the white silk to hang down upon his coat.

"I fear my thoughts have been only for my own hurt pride." She swallowed and looked away but then met his gaze once again. "So what troubles you, Mr. Heaton? Is there something I can do to help?" The concern pouring from her eyes set him back. It took all his strength to keep from taking her in his arms.

"It is a private matter, Miss Channing. One I must deal with on my own."

Music and laughter bubbled out onto the street from the Fountain Inn. A horse with a rider clip-clopped past.

"Very well." She bit her lip.

Luke shifted his stance. He wanted more than anything for her to stay. But he did not want her pity. "Was there something else?"

She smiled. "Only that I formally accept your apology."

Luke chuckled, drawing fire from her eyes.

She placed a gloved hand on her hip. "Did you or did you not beg my forgiveness, Mr. Heaton?"

"It would please me greatly if you'd call me Luke." He grinned.

"That would hardly be prop—"

Luke lowered his lips to hers. He could stand it no further. He delighted in her fervid response. . .her scent of gardenias. Her taste. And the way her curves molded against him. No other woman had affected him so. His world spun and he wanted nothing but her in his arms. Forever.

Withdrawing, she pushed back, her chest heaving. Glancing over her shoulder at the ladies and gentlemen clustered around the inn, she raised a hand to her lips. "We shouldn't."

Luke brushed his thumb over her jaw. Soft, delicate, like the petal of one of her gardenias. She closed her eyes. He eased his hand down her neck, finally fingering her silky hair as he had so often longed to do. He drew her close to him once again.

"I love you, Cassandra," Luke whispered in her ear, no longer caring what she thought, what her reaction would be. He could no longer contain the secret—a secret so important, so wonderful, it could never be kept within the heart of a man.

She gazed up at him, her breath heavy and ragged. A moist sheen covered her eyes.

Then hardened into glass. "How many other women have you said that to?"

Luke frowned. "None." He spoke the truth.

She lowered her gaze.

Lifting her chin with his finger, he leaned toward her and stared into her eyes. "None, Cassandra. I do not speak those words lightly."

The glass in her eyes dissolved into liquid emeralds. She pressed down the folds of her gown and stared into the darkness.

Luke fingered the scars on his hand. Baffling woman. He had no idea what she was thinking. Feeling. Or why she even remained. "I've offended you with my bold affections. Forgive me."

"No."

"You will not forgive me?"

"No, you have not offended me."

Luke flinched as hope began to rise within him. "Then what troubles you?"

She gave him a coy smile, even as her eyes took on a mischievous sparkle. "That I have fallen in love with the town rogue."

Heart bursting, Luke engulfed her in his arms. He kissed her forehead as she snuggled against him. "You make me not want to be a rogue anymore. You make me want to be honorable and good and dependable."

She pushed away from him. Her gaze shifted across his. "Can you be those things, Luke? If not, I fear you will break my heart."

At the thought of his traitorous activities, guilt trampled Luke's joy.

"I would never wish to hurt you, Cassandra. As long as I live, all I want is to protect and cherish you."

A tear slipped down her cheek. She fell against him again.

Yet, as Luke held her, a battle waged within him. Now that he had won the love of such an exquisite, wonderful woman, how could he expect to keep it when he was betraying his city, his country, and most of all her?

❖

Crane stormed back into the Fountain Inn, his jaw clenched so tight it hurt. Shoving his way through the crowd, he entered the side room, grabbed a glass of punch wine, and tossed it to the back of his throat, ignoring the gasps of a few ladies nearby. When he lowered his glass, it was to the curious gaze of Lieutenant Abner Tripp.

"Something vexing you, Mr. Crane?"

"Yes, indeed." He tugged the lieutenant to the side, out of the hearing of curious ears. "You told me that if I confiscated Miss Channing's prize winnings, you'd take care of Mr. Heaton for me." Setting his empty glass on the tray of a passing butler, he grabbed another full one. "And I just saw him in a rather passionate embrace with the lady outside."

The lieutenant's eyes narrowed. "Yes, it seems my initial plan failed." He gazed across the chattering crowd. "Though I cannot imagine why. The man should have been caught by a British warship or sunk."

Crane sipped his drink. "But instead, he sails into town on that heap of wood and tar with more earnings. How am I to impress upon Miss Channing her need to marry me when that tavern mongrel"—he growled—"continually feeds her money and charm. And the woman soaks it up like the gullible hussy she is."

"Indeed, I quite agree." Lieutenant Tripp rubbed the scar on his face. "It is inconceivable that the man continues to have so much success at sea. And in such a short amount of time. And I daresay, I find his avoidance of the blockade quite baffling."

Crane drained the remaining wine from his glass. "So, we have established that the man is a good privateer. How does that work in our favor?"

"Because, kind sir, I do not believe he is as skilled as he pretends. No"—the lieutenant leaned closer to Crane, lowering his voice—"I suspect foul play."

"I am of the same mind, sir!" Crane shouted, happy to find a partner in his suspicions, but quickly slammed his mouth shut at the lieutenant's look of censure.

Tripp smiled at a passing couple then shifted his slitted eyes around the crowd. They halted on a man hovering over the refreshment table. "Ah, and there is the solution to our problem, sir."

Crane's muddled vision found the dandy in question, a man the lieutenant had pointed out before as Mr. Keene, the boatswain aboard Mr. Heaton's ship. "What does it matter, sir? All Heaton's vermin are loyal to him."

"Perhaps, yes. But I've heard Mr. Keene likes his drink. And I've also heard his tongue loosens considerably the deeper into his cups he becomes."

Crane smiled. "What do you say we set up a meeting at a nearby tavern with the man?"

❖

Stretching, Cassandra pushed aside the curtains and sat in the window seat, peering down at her solarium. Laughter shifted her gaze to the back garden where Hannah and Darlene held hands and twirled in a circle, singing "Ring around the Rosie." She smiled. Sunlight coated her in warmth, and she drew a deep breath of the fresh dewy morning. An odd sensation over came her. One she hadn't felt in years.

Happiness.

After Mr. Heaton's. . .*Luke's* declaration of love two nights past, she'd hardly slept a second. Closing her eyes, she pictured him standing in the moonlight, a loose strand of his black hair grazing the stubble on his jaw. The look of adoration in his eyes. The tender love in his kiss. The feel of his strong arms around her. He loved her! And he had vowed to change.

Perhaps she was a fool to trust him. But she couldn't help it. She'd never been more sure of anything or anyone in her life.

Opening her eyes, she hugged herself and smiled. She had enough money to provide for her family and was being courted by the most fascinating, strong, capable man.

"You're in love, miss." Margaret's voice jerked Cassandra from her daze, tossing her heart into her throat.

"Sorry to startle you. I knocked but there was no answer." The perky maid flitted into the room, carrying a pitcher of water and a grin on her rosy face.

Cassandra slid off the seat. "What did you say?"

"You are positively glowing this morning, miss. You must be thinking of him."

"Why, whoever are you referring to?" Cassandra gave her a coy look.

"Why"—Margaret lifted her brows—"Mr. Heaton, of course."

Cassandra moved to her bed and grabbed the post. "Yes. I admit it. I do love him." She touched Margaret's arm, stopping her. "Have I gone mad?"

"Love is never madness, miss." Margaret continued to the dressing table and poured water into a china basin. She began humming a hymn.

Cassandra clutched the folds of her white nightdress. "But his reputation. . ."

"We have all made mistakes. People change, miss."

"I hope you're right." Cassandra settled onto her bed. "But what will Mother think?"

"Your mother will accept him, in time."

Cassandra wished she harbored the same confidence.

Her maid's eyes flashed. "Perhaps God has not abandoned you after all?"

"Perhaps." Cassandra flipped her long braid over her shoulder. Yet she was not quite ready to concede on that point. "We shall see. But do help me get dressed, Margaret. Luke is coming to call, and I want to look my best."

Two hours later, a knock on the front door sent Cassandra's heart spinning as she sat in the parlor reading a storybook to Hannah and Darlene.

Her mother looked up from her crocheting. "Whoever could that be? We aren't expecting anyone."

Before Cassandra could answer, Mr. Dayle, with a smirk on his face, announced Mr. Heaton. The handsome privateer stepped into the room. He had combed his hair and tied it neatly back and even shaved for the occasion. Cassandra lifted a hand to her cheek, remembering the scratch of his stubble on her skin.

An unavoidable smile flirted on her lips, no doubt noticed by her mother.

Frowning, she tossed aside her crocheting and rose from her seat. "Mr. Heaton. This is most unexpected."

But his eyes were on Cassandra. His smile warmed her. Turning, he dipped his head toward her mother. "Your daughter invited me to call, Mrs. Channing."

Her mother's incredulous gaze sped to Cassandra.

"Do sit down, Luke." Cassandra gestured toward the sofa. "Forgive me, Mother, I forgot to mention it," she lied. In truth, she didn't know how to tell her mother that she and Mr. Heaton were courting.

Leaping from the sofa, Darlene barreled into Luke. He swept her up into his arms. "There's my little runaway." Darlene giggled and gestured for Hannah to join her.

"Hannah, this is Mr. Heaton," Cassandra said. "He's the captain of the privateer I've hired."

The little girl inched toward him, thumb in her mouth. She curtseyed and mumbled something that resembled, "Pleased to meet you, sir."

"I'm happy to see you well, Miss Hannah." Luke smiled down at the little girl. "I heard you were ill."

Hannah plucked her thumb from her mouth. "Miss Margaret says God healed me."

Bending over, Luke set Darlene down and held out his hand to Hannah. Much to Cassandra's surprise, the little girl didn't hesitate to reach for him. He placed a kiss upon her hand. "You are both as beautiful as your older sister."

They giggled, and Hannah gave him a wide grin.

Cassandra shook her head. His charm on women held no boundaries.

Luke faced her mother, who stood staring at the display as if the devil himself had just charmed her daughters into selling their souls to him. "Mrs. Channing, a vision of loveliness as always." He gave her that beguiling grin that had melted a thousand hearts.

It softened the look of horror on her mother's face. "You flatter me, sir." She looked away. And for the first time, Cassandra saw a blush rise on her mother's cheeks. Had she ever seen such a reaction to her father's attention? Luke's blue eyes found Cassandra again, and a look of affection stretched between them. Her heart fluttered like a thousand birds in flight.

Out of the corner of her vision, Cassandra could see her mother pick up her handkerchief and wave it about her flushed face, eyeing them with suspicion.

"Didn't you say, dear, that you need to go to the chandler for some more candles? You should gather Margaret and go before the heat becomes unbearable."

"Mother, we have a guest. I can go anytime."

Resigned, her mother sank back onto her chair.

Mrs. Northrop entered with a service tray and slid it onto the table. "Mr. Dayle suggested you'd be wanting tea for your guest, miss." She poured three cups and scurried away.

Luke lowered himself onto the sofa.

Darlene slid beside him, but Hannah squeezed in between them and gazed up at him curiously. "Are you a pirate?"

Luke smiled and a chuckle escaped his lips. Twisting his face, he hunched over and growled. "Arg, ye be right about that." Sending both girls into a fit of giggles.

"Oh my." Her mother heaved a sigh. But Cassandra blinked at the sight, unable to reconcile the town ruffian with this man who appeared so at ease with children.

"Do you ever fire your cannons?" Darlene battled Hannah for a spot beside him then finally moved to sit on his other side.

"Girls, this is hardly appropriate conversation." Mrs. Channing's sharp tone pierced the joy that had infiltrated the room.

"Fire my guns? Why, all the time." Luke's eyes beamed as he picked up his tea. The china cup appeared ill placed in his large, tanned hands. "Perhaps I'll let you come aboard and fire one sometime."

Darlene's face lit in excitement. "I'd like that very much."

"Me too! Me too!" Hannah jumped up and down, nearly spilling the tea in Luke's cup. He set it down on the table.

A loud bark preceded Dexter, who romped into the room on all fours. The massive dog charged toward Luke and tossed his front paws onto Luke's lap before he could move out of the way. Not that he would have done so, for he seemed to welcome the dog as he chuckled and ran his fingers through the animal's fur—even allowing Dexter to lick his face.

Shocked, Cassandra stood. "Get down, Dexter." She dashed toward them. "Luke, please forgive him. He's not normally so affectionate with strangers."

"Oh, my head." Grabbing her bell, Mrs. Channing, shook it, sending a *ding ding ding* bouncing over the walls.

Luke rose to his feet, shifting the animal from his lap. "It's no bother."

Dexter barked and leapt onto the spot on the sofa that Luke had just vacated. Darlene and Hannah began wrestling with the animal.

Ignoring the mayhem, Cassandra stared at Luke, longing to be alone with him. "When are you setting sail?"

"In two days."

"So soon?"

"I'm afraid so." His blue eyes adored her. "The war takes no respite."

Mrs. Northrop stomped into the room and turned expectant eyes to Cassandra's mother, who stopped ringing her bell and waved toward the cyclonic havoc occupying the sofa. "Please take that unruly beast out to the garden," she ordered.

Clutching Dexter by the collar, Mrs. Northrop led him away with a huff.

"Hannah, Darlene," her mother barked. "Both of you settle down as well or you'll be joining Dexter."

Much to Cassandra's surprise, both girls sat back and folded their hands in their laps.

"Did you hear the musket shots last night?" Her mother's attempt at breaking the spell that kept Cassandra's and Luke's gazes locked on each other was obvious.

Severing the connection, Luke faced the elder woman. "I've heard rumors of British troop movements to the south. Some say they are heading for Washington." He lowered himself to sit between Hannah and Darlene, stretching his booted feet out before him.

"Surely they won't attempt to capture our capital?" Cassandra took her seat again, envious of her sisters' close proximity to Luke.

"Who can know?" He shrugged. A strand of hair that had loosened during the chaos slid over his jaw. "But General Smith has the fort on alert and has ordered the entire militia to be on the ready."

"What is militia, Cassie?" Darlene asked.

"They are citizen soldiers, sweetheart."

An unsettled silence permeated the room.

Her mother eyed Luke as if she wished she could summon Mrs. Northrop to take him out back as well. She took a sip of tea. "What is the purpose of your call, Mr. Heaton?"

Cassandra squeezed her hands together and cleared her throat. She had best just blurt it out. "Mother, you should know that Mr. Heaton and I are courting."

Mrs. Channing dropped her cup with a clank on its side, spilling her remaining tea into the saucer. "Oh my." Closing her eyes, she raised a hand to her brow. "What of Mr. Crane?"

"What *of* Mr. Crane, Mother?" Anger overcame Cassandra's concern for her mother's nerves.

"He's made his interest in you quite clear, my dear."

"That he has," Cassandra said. "But I hardly think that mentioning it in front of Mr. Heaton is appropriate."

"But Mr. Crane is. . ." Her mother opened her eyes and shook her head as if trying to shake off the words she'd just heard. "He's. . ."

"Much more respectable than I? Much more stable? Honorable?" Luke leaned forward on his knees and cocked his head. "Is that what you intended to say, Mrs. Channing?"

"Since we're being forthright, sir. Yes. That is precisely what I was going to say."

"Really, Mother!" Shame burned Cassandra's neck, followed by an apprehension of how Luke would respond to such an affront.

"But, Mama." Darlene thrust out her chin. "Mr. Heaton saved my life. He is a hero."

Hannah's uneasy gaze swept over all of them before she plunged her thumb into her mouth.

"I agree with you completely, madam." Luke's statement jolted Cassandra and folded her mother's brow.

"I am in no way deserving of a woman like your daughter." His eyes flitted to Cassandra. "But I promise I shall make every endeavor to alter that fact, as well as your opinion of me."

Disdain burned in her mother's eyes. "We shall see, Mr. Heaton. However, let me be clear. I do not approve of you calling on Cassandra. But she's never listened to me or taken my advice, so it would be pointless for me to protest."

"Come now, Mother." Cassandra sighed. "Surely you understand why I wish to choose whose courtship I accept."

"No, I do not understand, Cassandra." Anger tightened the lines around her mouth. "Not when our family's future is at stake." She slowly rose. "I fear I do not feel well. If you'll excuse me, Mr. Heaton." She faced Cassandra. "Do not forget to purchase candles."

"Can we go with you?" Darlene's face lit in expectation.

"Yes, take the girls, dear. I could use some quiet," her mother said as she left the room.

Cassandra started to chase after her. To apologize. To console her. But what good would it do? Cassandra would never be able to make her understand.

Luke approached and laid a hand on her arm. He gave her a sympathetic look, but then his eyes filled with a yearning that sent an odd swirl through her belly.

"I'd be happy to escort you as far as the chandler." He eased a lock of her hair behind her ear. Her breath caught.

She stepped back. "We would love that, Mr. Heaton." Tearing her gaze from his, Cassandra glanced at her sisters, astounded to find them still sitting politely on the sofa. "Wouldn't we, girls?"

Their calm facade faded beneath happy yelps of agreement.

As soon as Margaret and Mr. Dayle joined them, Cassandra grabbed her reticule and followed Luke and the girls out the door. Squinting at the glare of the sun off the stone walkway, she tugged on her gloves. Ahead of her, Luke scooped Hannah into his arms, and then he reached down to grab Darlene's hand.

Emotion clogged Cassandra's throat. Would this man never cease to surprise her? The last thing she would have expected was that he would be so tender, so caring with children. How could Cassandra have so misjudged him from the start?

Hot air blasted over her. Dark clouds bunched on the horizon, churning and broiling as they made their way up to steal the light of the sun.

Misjudged, indeed. Yet as she stepped out from her porch, she couldn't help the niggling feeling that things were not as they seemed.

❖ CHAPTER 28 ❖

Luke allowed the hot August sun to melt the chill of Mrs. Channing's icy reception. He had expected her disdain. Always expected it from polite society, but that never seemed to dull its sting. Now, as he strolled down the street, Cassandra and her sisters by his side, it seemed as though they were a family. A happy family. And suddenly—if he could only rescue John—life held the possibility of a hope and joy he'd never thought possible.

Until he remembered that he was a traitor.

And if Cassandra ever discovered his nefarious activities, this happy moment would dissipate along with all his dreams. Even if she could excuse his behavior given his brother's abduction, how could she ever forgive him for allowing her to spend money dripping with the blood of Americans?

Luke shifted his shoulders, hoping to shrug off the morbid fear settling on him as thick as the storm clouds roiling across the horizon. If his next plan to rescue John worked, no one need know of his treachery at all.

He bent his arm toward Cassandra and was pleased when she slipped her hand within the crook of his elbow and smiled, a sweet smile, full of possibilities. It sent a thrill through him. On his right, Darlene gripped tightly to his other hand, while Hannah clung to Cassandra's on her other side. Together they strolled down South Street, drawing the critical gazes of the town's gossips.

"I fear your reputation is at stake, Miss Channing." Luke gestured toward a cluster of elderly ladies across the way, heads bent together, tongues clacking.

"Your company is worth the risk." She lifted her pert nose.

Enamored by her words and by the gleam of ardor in her eye, Luke fought the urge to take her in his arms and kiss her right there.

But Mr. Dayle's and Margaret's footfalls behind them reminded Luke that Cassandra's chaperones would never allow him to take such liberties. Besides, there were children present. Adorable creatures so full of life. Just like their sister.

Darlene pranced beside him as if she were actually proud to be seen with him. Amazing. She smiled up at him, and he gave her hand a squeeze.

A breeze, ripe with the sting of rain and salt, wafted over them. Somewhere fiddle music played, floating atop the hum of conversation, the *clip-clop* of horses' hooves, and a bell chiming in the distance.

Lifting his face to the warm sun, Luke could never remember feeling such joy. Such hope for the future. *God, if You're there and responsible for this, thank You.* He shocked himself at the prayer, but since he had opened up the conversation, he might as well add, *And please help me rescue John.*

He heard Cassandra groan, and he lowered his gaze just as she bumped into a man exiting the butcher's with a wrapped package of meat in his hand.

"Oh, Mr. McCulloch, pardon me," she said. "Good day to you, sir."

The customs agent tipped his hat as his eyes shifted from her to Luke. "Good day, Miss Channing, Mr. Heaton. How fares the privateering business these days?"

Margaret and Mr. Dayle stopped behind them.

A curious look twisted Cassandra's expression. "Surely you know, sir, since Mr. Heaton has no doubt declared his prizes in your office."

The agent's face seemed to fold in on itself. "Miss Channing, I fear you are mistaken, for I've never done business with Mr. Heaton."

Ice coursed through Luke's veins.

Cassandra's emerald eyes bore into him. "Pray tell how, Luke, do you declare the cargo you confiscate? And the ships?" She released her hold on his arm.

The air chilled. Luke shifted his stance, feeling the loss of her touch like an anchor in his gut. "At other ports," he explained.

Dark clouds captured the sun, casting the street in gray shadows.

Cassandra cocked her head. "Yet since you've been able to slip past the blockade, why not sell them here?"

"I certainly cannot sail a prize British ship through the blockade." Luke forced a smile, not meeting her gaze. The anchor clawed his insides.

No doubt bored with the conversation, Hannah released Cassandra's hand and poked Darlene from behind, giggling.

"Stop it!" Darlene shouted. "Cassie, Hannah hit me."

Grabbing Hannah, Cassandra handed her off to Margaret.

Mr. McCulloch's brows scrunched. "How *do you* slip your ship past the blockade, Mr. Heaton? I, for one, am enamored at the skill of those few privateers able to accomplish such a feat."

"He's the best captain in the world," Darlene exclaimed, still clinging to his hand. "That's how he does it."

Luke smiled at the girl. Would that her elder sister believed the same. He faced the customs agent. "That's all it is, sir, I assure you. Skill with a bit of luck mixed in."

"Hmm." Mr. McCulloch did not seem satisfied. "Well, I must be going. I need to get this pork home to the cook." He tipped his hat again and ambled away.

Thunder rumbled across the sky, portending Luke's doom. He tried to shake it off but the look of suspicion glazing Cassandra's eyes confirmed his fears.

"I should be going as well," Luke said, anything to avoid the censure pouring from Cassandra. "I have much to do to ready the ship to sail."

"Of course." She smiled, but the light was gone from her eyes.

Darlene tugged on his hand. "May I come and help?"

Luke knelt and Hannah stormed into his embrace. "Not this time."

Darlene pouted. Luke hugged both girls and stood, risking a glance at Cassandra. "May I call on you when I return to port?"

"You may."

Seizing the flicker of affection in her eyes, Luke kissed her on the cheek then nodded toward Margaret and Mr. Dayle and marched down the street. He hated lying to Cassandra. The sooner he put an end to this deceit, the better. He would appeal to Captain Raynor's honor. He would load up his ship with as many goods as he could carry, offer to give them as a gift to the British captain in return for his brother and Luke's vow to never again attack British ships.

Any man possessing an ounce of decency would agree to it.

Trouble was, Luke wasn't sure the British captain possessed an ounce of decency.

❖

Hoping to escape for a few moments' peace, Cassandra slipped down the stairway and headed toward the back door. Hannah's and Darlene's screams shot through the house like deviant trumpets, accompanied by the incessant clanging of her mother's bell. How could anyone think in the midst of such clamor? And thinking was precisely what Cassandra needed.

The nagging feeling she'd had yesterday as Luke escorted them into town had burst into a suspicion as hot and dense as the muggy air that suffocated the city. Though it was certainly possible for Luke to sail his prizes and goods into other ports, it left him precious little time to spend here in Baltimore. And how did he slip past the blockade unscathed on so many occasions? Mr. McCulloch's questions had awakened doubts that had been squashed beneath her rising infatuation of the handsome privateer. To make matters worse, Mr. Crane's prior accusations reappeared above the waters of her denial, reeking more of truth than jealousy. In fact, the more she thought about it, the more impossible it seemed that Luke could sail out of Baltimore, capture a prize, sail into another port, sell the goods, deal with customs, and sail home in the short duration of his recent voyages.

But how else could he be making money? He'd sent her a fair amount in the post before the ball, along with the paperwork. Though not as much as before, the funds would last Cassandra and her family almost a year. Opening the back door, she braced herself against the sizzling heat, grabbed her skirts, and made her way around the corner of the house. Each strike of the hot sun jarred her reason awake and plunged her heart into fear.

By the time she entered the solarium, her spirits were as heavy as the air that surrounded her.

A yelp brought her heart into her throat and her gaze up to see Mrs. Northrop standing with Cassandra's open chest in hand.

Terror streaked across the housekeeper's wide eyes. "I thought you were in town, miss."

Marching toward the woman, Cassandra tore the chest from her grasp then grabbed the key from her hand. "What on earth are you doing with my personal belongings? How dare you?"

Mrs. Northrop's swallow ran down her long neck. "I'll be going now, miss." She started toward the door.

Cassandra grabbed her arm and spun her around. "You will do no such thing. I demand to know what you were doing looking through my father's chest!"

"Nothing." She stared at the ground.

Closing the lid, Cassandra set the chest down on the bench and fingered the key in her hand. Her mind swam in the confusing horror of betrayal. Then the realization hit her.

"You." She gaped at the woman. "You stole my money."

Mrs. Northrop backed away, wringing her hands. She bumped into a gardenia bush. "It was Mr. Crane. He made me do it, miss."

"Mr. Crane?" Cassandra shook her head. Why would the man do such a thing? Her legs weakened, and she sank onto the stool. "He wanted my family to be beholden to his charity," she spoke her thoughts aloud. "He wanted me." Cassandra stared at the trembling housekeeper. "Why would you agree to this?"

"He paid me a good sum, miss. An' I wasn't getting my due from you."

"You should have come to me."

Mrs. Northrop's eyes misted. "What are you going to do, miss?"

Drawing a deep breath, Cassandra squared her shoulders and stood. "You are dismissed at once. Gather your things and leave this house by nightfall. Is that clear?"

Tears wove crooked trails down Mrs. Northrop's cheeks.

"Where is the money?" Cassandra demanded.

"I gave it to Mr. Crane. I didn't keep any of it, miss. I swear."

"Very well." Cassandra gestured toward the door. "Get out."

Mrs. Northrop's bottom lip quivered. Clutching her skirts, she tore from the solarium.

An hour later, with the sun's hot rays forming beads of perspiration on her brow and neck, Cassandra hurried down Liberty Street on her way to the *Baltimore Register* to confront Mr. Crane. Fortunately, for him, he was not there when she arrived. "But I expect him to return in a few hours, miss," his clerk had declared. "May I give him a message?"

"Indeed." Cassandra waved her fan about her face. "You may inform

Mr. Crane that I know he stole my money, and he will return it or face charges of thievery."

The poor clerk's face had blanched considerably at her statement, but she hadn't stayed to witness any further effects. Now, hurrying down Pratt Street, Cassandra was exhausted and overheated, but too angry to care. Darkness cruised the city, absconding with the light. She needed to get home.

Unable to resist, she stole a glance at the wharf where *Destiny* was docked, hoping for a glimpse of Luke. She wasn't ready to talk to him. Wasn't entirely sure what he was up to. But certainly a glimpse would do her no harm. It might even help her recall how much she cared for him. Though, in that regard, her heart needed no reminder.

What she saw halted her on the spot. There on the wharf, which sagged beneath its weight, were dozens and dozens of barrels, crates, and sacks ready to be loaded onto Luke's ship. And still more came, carried by workers trudging down the dock. Luke's crew scrambled across the ship as Mr. Abbot stood atop the bulwarks, directing the men in bringing the supplies aboard, whilst Mr. Sanders—if she remembered his name correctly—stood by his side, scribbling on a paper in his hand. Luke was nowhere in sight.

Why would a privateer need that many supplies? Enough to feed dozens of privateers for a month, by her estimation. Though they did not know how long they'd be at sea, certainly stuffing the hold would allow no room for the goods they'd confiscate from the British.

It made no sense.

A surge of torrid wind clawed at her bonnet and stole the breath from her mouth. She gripped the brim of her hat, standing her ground.

What was Luke up to? If she confronted him, she couldn't be sure he would answer her. She'd accepted that he was a private man. She'd accepted that something heavy weighed upon him as Mr. Abbot had told her. What she couldn't accept was him doing anything subversive with her money.

Since he was to set sail on the morrow, there was only one way to find out the truth. And that was to stow away on his ship and see for herself.

❖

But Luke did not set sail the next day. Or at least Cassandra hoped he hadn't. By the time she had arrived home that night, rumors rampaged through the city that British troops were marching into Washington, DC. Warning bells rang incessantly as terror held the city in its tight grip through the long hours of the night. And although some citizens bravely stood on Federal Hill to watch the distant glow of fires raging through the capital, Cassandra had stayed home to comfort her mother, who was enduring a fit of nerves at the unhappy tidings.

Then, the following day, before anyone could recover from the tragedy and discover the fate of their great nation, the storm hit. Winds as fierce as any Cassandra had experienced stampeded over the house, seeking entrance into their shelter and flinging spears of rain at their windows. In the glow of candles, Cassandra, her sisters, mother, servants, and Dexter had huddled at the center of the house, waiting to be blown away.

But after a few hours, the winds abated, the rain ceased, and the clouds withdrew, leaving behind toppled trees, torn-down fences, and the joyous news that the British had retreated from Washington. Margaret, who had been appealing to God all through the afternoon, gave praise for His mighty deliverance.

Cassandra was not so sure.

Nor was she sure why Mr. Crane had not been by to answer her accusation. Nor why Luke had not come calling to see if she and her family had suffered any injuries from the storm.

After spending the rest of that day and most of the next one cleaning up the wreckage and helping neighbors do the same, Cassandra now stood before her dressing glass in her chamber as evening tossed shadows upon the unusually quiet town.

"Miss, I don't think this is a good idea." Margaret's reflection behind Cassandra was one of anxiety. Her normally rosy cheeks had gone pale, and her eyes sparked with fear. Cassandra gazed at her visage in the mirror. Baggy gray breeches stuffed in oversized boots, a white cotton shirt covered in a gray waistcoat and black overcoat. A red neckerchief rode high upon her neck. Atop her head a cocked hat perched. Noting a rebellious curl peeking out from the side, she stuffed it back in place, giggling at the sight.

"Even with the bandages around your chest and the dirt on your jaw and chin, you still look like a woman, miss." Margaret touched Cassandra's arm. "Please don't do this. It's far too dangerous."

"Oh, bother, Margaret. You fret too much," Cassandra said. "I'm far safer wandering about town looking like this, than dressed as a lady."

"What if he has already set sail?"

"Then I shall come home." Though she knew Luke hadn't left yet—had heard just today from Mr. Dayle, who had ventured out for supplies, that *Destiny* had survived the storm unscathed and was preparing to leave that night.

"I'll sneak on board Mr. Heaton's ship before anyone sees me. No one will know I'm there."

Margaret shook her head, the normal luster gone from her eyes. "But what if you are at sea for weeks, months even, before you discover what you wish to know?"

"You mean that the man I love might be a traitor to our country?" Cassandra tugged her hat farther down on her head as the last rays of sunlight withdrew from her chamber. "I'll find out the truth soon enough. Mr. Heaton doesn't seem to be gone for more than a week or so at a time." Which also didn't speak well for his innocence. "If too much time passes, that will prove my suspicions wrong. Then I shall reveal myself and beg his forgiveness. I'm sure he'll bring me home immediately."

"What will you eat and drink?"

"I have enough food and water to last four days in my knapsack. Plus, I imagine there's plenty of stored food belowdecks."

"What of the rats?" Margaret shivered.

Cassandra's belly gurgled in queasiness. "I shall have to endure them."

"I do not see why you cannot just ask Luke."

Cassandra swung around. "Do you think if he's betraying his country—and me—that he'll tell me the truth?" She walked to the window, nearly stumbling in the awkward boots. "No, I must find out for myself. This is the only way. I cannot"—she swallowed down a lump of heartache—"I cannot give my heart to a man who is a liar and a traitor." She plopped down on the window seat. "All my life, I only wanted someone to depend on."

"You can depend on God, miss."

Cassandra smiled. "Such a saint you are, Margaret." Rising, she grabbed a piece of foolscap from her dresser. "If I do not return tonight, give this letter to Mother tomorrow. It will explain everything." At the look of horror on her maid's face, Cassandra took Margaret's hands in hers. "Never fear, I shall return soon. Tell the girls to behave. And do watch over them now that Mrs. Northrop is gone, will you?"

"Of course." Margaret nodded. "What if you discover Luke *is* a traitor and he. . ." Margaret looked away. "He. . ."

"Luke wouldn't hurt me. I don't believe that. Fear spiraled through Cassandra, pricking at her resolve. Perhaps she should just call off the courtship and let it be. But if her suspicions were true, how could she go on spending money gained by the blood of her countrymen? No, she must find out for sure.

"Now, go make sure no one is below so I can make my escape."

Margaret stopped at the door. "God go with you, miss. I shall pray for you every day."

Twenty minutes later, with head lowered and a knapsack strung over her shoulder, Cassandra did her best to march like a man down the muddy street. In her trek to the wharves, not a single person stopped her, most barely gazed at her: ladies with children hurrying home; groups of merchantmen; the chandler, Mr. Sikes, who didn't seem to recognize her. One gentleman had even bumped into her and offered no apology. Cassandra smiled beneath the shadow of her hat, even as an odd feeling of being ignored settled on her. Odd because wherever she went she usually drew quite a bit of attention. It had never occurred to her that some people drifted through life like shadows, their presence rarely acknowledged. Pondering this, she hastened to the wharf where *Destiny* was anchored. She knew Luke usually set sail close to midnight and since it was no later than eight, she hoped only a few crewmen were on board.

What she didn't expect was the swarm of workers and sailors hauling all manner of crates and barrels onto the ship. Again. Perhaps they'd been forced to unload everything during the storm. Halting near the dock's entrance, she searched for Luke, but he was nowhere in sight. However, in the light of several lanterns hanging from the main and fore masts, she spotted Mr. Abbot and Mr. Keene marching across the deck, bellowing orders.

Now, how to get on board?

Across the bay, the retreating glow of sunlight quivered over frolicking dark waters. Bare masts rose like spires of defeat into the bowl of night descending upon the city. Only Luke's ship was a plethora of activity.

Cassandra's heart thundered against her ribs. It wasn't too late to turn around and go home, sleep in her own warm bed. But if she did, she would be more fool than coward. And she would not be made a fool of, nor abandoned by some man who was even better at lying than charming the opposite sex. Or perhaps the two went together.

Taking a deep breath as if she could inhale courage, she picked up a box that was sitting atop a barrel and hefted it onto her left shoulder. Though it wasn't too heavy for her, the sharp edges bit through her coat as she eased into the line of men heading toward the ship. Keeping her head behind the box, she followed the man in front of her, hoping she didn't trip on her way onto the ship. Already her boots—borrowed from Mr. Dayle—rubbed the skin on her ankles to soreness. Ignoring the pain and the fear screaming in her head, she stepped onto the teetering plank, watched it bow beneath the weight of the large man before her, then leapt onto the deck with a thud. Pain shot up her legs, and she stumbled for a second as the ship rocked.

"Hurry up, there, boy!" the man behind her yelled, shoving her forward. Thankfully before Mr. Abbot saw her. Navigating down the companionway ladder was no easy task, especially with one's hands full. Alone, she may have toppled into the darkness below, but the burly men before and after her cushioned her against a fall.

Following the men down another level, Cassandra squinted into the darkness of the hold where only a single lantern swayed from a hook on the deck head. Across a vast expanse of muck and crates, empty-handed men ascended another ladder above. A putrid stench rose up from the depths like some viper to strike her, filling her nostrils and lungs with the smell of mold and waste and something else indescribable. She coughed. Some of the men looked her way. She lowered her head. A man she recognized as one of Luke's crew, Mr. Sanders, directed the men where to deposit their loads. Cassandra scanned the shadowy hold. Toward her left, beneath a low beam, was a section where the light did not reach. If she could slip away undetected, she could find a place to hide.

Mr. Sanders stopped two of the workers and demanded they lower the crate they carried. "Open it. I want to see what it contains." His squeaky voice echoed over the waterlogged hull.

Cursing, the men slammed down the container. The screech of the lid being pried off sent a tremble through Cassandra.

While the rest of the men stopped to watch, Cassandra inched backward into the shadows.

"What is this? Bolts of fabric! We did not purchase this, nor have we need of it. Take it away." Mr. Sanders waved his hand then made a mark on his document.

Cassandra continued backing up. Fear prickled her skin. Her boot struck something hard, sending a thud through the air and an ache through her feet. She halted. But no one looked her way. Setting down her box, she retreated into the darkness at the rear of the ship and ducked behind a large crate.

Hours later, after the men had left and the hold groaned with a full load of supplies, Mr. Sanders grabbed the lantern and ascended the ladder, leaving Cassandra in a darkness so thick it seemed to ooze over her. Two questions began to weigh heavy on her mind. Had she lost a grasp on all good sense and reason? And what was she going to do about the pattering of little feet advancing toward her?

❖ CHAPTER 29 ❖

Light from the lantern high up on the foremast flickered over the signal flags flapping from *Destiny*'s gaff. Signal flags that gave Luke and his crew free passage through the British blockade.

Flags that marked him as a traitor.

He gripped the quarter railing. Frustration and anger bunched a tight knot in his jaw. Hot wind sped past his ears, tainted with the fury of yesterday's storm. He gazed upward. No stars dared to peek at them from behind the black curtain that hung over a sea transformed into molten coal.

"We've brought enough supplies for near the entire fleet," Biron commented as he leapt onto the deck beside Luke. "Let's pray we find Captain Raynor in a good humor."

Luke tightened his lips. "If not, I can think of no other way to rescue John without putting him in danger."

"You can't blame yourself for this, Luke." Biron placed a hand on Luke's back.

"Who can I blame for it, God?" But no, Luke wasn't the sort to blame God or anyone else for his failings. It was his own fault.

Biron frowned. "It was God who saved our grand capital yesterday."

"Lud. You refer to the sudden storm?" Luke snorted. "Not that unusual of an occurrence."

"But one that just so happened upon Washington when she was being burnt to the ground." Biron chuckled.

Luke rubbed his ear. "A mere coincidence." He thought of Cassandra and wondered how she had fared through the tempest. It had taken all his strength to keep from calling on her. But Luke didn't want to face her again as a traitor. No, the next time he faced her, he wanted to be the man of honor he saw reflected in her eyes.

"I've discovered"—Biron lifted his hat to scratch his head—"that many of what we call coincidences are actually God's mighty intervention."

The hull of a ship loomed several yards off their port bow. Part of the British fleet. Despite having passed through the blockade several times, Luke could not shake his uneasiness at the sight. "Coincidence or not, at least the Almighty spared *Destiny* in the storm." He couldn't say the same for many of the ships anchored in Baltimore Harbor.

"Quick thinking on your part, Captain, to move her away from the other ships and tie her to multiple pilings with lines long enough to handle the surge."

Luke nodded. He'd learned from the best, Noah Brenin.

"God spared us, indeed." Biron sighed.

Luke gave his friend a disbelieving glance. "If God spared us, then why did He allow the storm to destroy many of Washington's buildings?"

Biron shrugged. "Still, the British were sent packing. And Washington is in American hands again."

"Indeed." Luke folded his hands across his chest. "And now they are more angry than ever. Which gives me little hope for my negotiations with the infamous Captain Raynor."

Whom he would see within four days at their normal rendezvous spot two miles off the coast of Virginia. *Destiny's* sails thundered as they caught the windy remnants of the harrowing storm, sending the ship careening over a wave. Bracing his boots on the deck, Luke snapped the hair from his face and took a deep breath of salty air. Somehow, he knew deep in his soul that this was his last chance. His last chance to end his traitorous activities.

His last chance to rescue John.

❖

Cassandra had lost track of time. And days. Her world had morphed into nothing but undulating darkness, creaks and groans of madness, a stench that made her toes curl, and the constant assault of rats. The fresh water in her knapsack had run out yesterday, along with the dried beef and bread she'd brought. Willing to risk getting caught rather than dying, she had finally ventured out of the hold late last night when the cessation of footfalls and voices told her that most of the crew was abed.

She hadn't realized how much she missed the wind and the air and the sky until she stepped onto the upper deck and made her way to the port railing, sinking behind the small boat latched to its moorings on the deck. There, she had gorged on a dried biscuit she'd found in the galley. It sank like a brick into the stale water mixed with beer she'd previously poured down her throat. Regardless of her pathetic meal, she wished she could have stayed on deck all night, but it was too risky. After a few hours of breathing in the fresh sea air, she had slumped below to her putrid abode.

Now, as she crawled to sit atop the highest crate she could find, she wondered at the sanity of her decision. What if they were to get into a real sea battle and cannon shot pierced the hold, flooding the ship and sending her to a watery grave?

The thunder of footsteps above, along with the peal of a bell, told her that another day had dawned. Another day of hunger clawing at her belly, thirst scraping her throat. Another day of kicking away rats while she sat on her hellish throne. Another day in which her mind dove deeper into madness.

Luke's authoritative timbre drifted down from above, sending a traitorous leap through her heart. She longed to go to him, feel his arms around her, and hear him reassure her of his innocence. But she couldn't. She couldn't allow her affections to take root until she knew the truth. Bringing her legs to her chest, she laid her head on top of her knees and prepared for the heat that accompanied the rising sun. Already perspiration formed on her brow. She wiped it away and tried to concentrate on the *whoosh* of water against the hull, a soothing sound in its constancy and bland melody.

But suddenly the sound lessened. The purl of water transformed into jarring splashes. And the plod of feet and the shout of men increased above her. Cassandra sat up, tilting her ear toward the deck. More shouts. Luke's powerful voice filled the dank air, and the ship slowed even more. Why were they stopping? Shouldn't they speed up at the sight of a potential prize? Or perhaps they sailed back into Baltimore. She wished it were so. Because that would mean Luke was no traitor and she would soon be home! Finally, after several minutes, the ship came to a near stop. Only the gentle rise and fall of the deck and the sound of waves lapping against the hull told Cassandra they were still at sea. She was about to descend from the crate when something thumped against the ship, nearly toppling her to the floor. Something massive. A groan echoed through the hold. The timbers creaked in complaint.

Men's voices grew louder as dozens of footfalls thundered down from above. Cassandra leapt from her perch and dove into the shadows just as light filled the hold and a group of sailors descended, one of whom hooked a lantern on the deck head. Peering from her hiding place, Cassandra watched as the men hefted crates, barrels, and sacks onto their backs and climbed back up the ladder.

Confusion twirled her crazed mind into a frenzy, unwilling to land on the only possible explanation. Blood pounded in her ears. Her heart refused to settle. Just as well. Because if it did, Cassandra was sure it would break in half. An hour passed as she waited and watched while the crew carried all the cargo up the ladder. Men's voices, including Luke's, crowded the air above her. She had to know what was going on. She had to make sure her suspicions were true.

On shaky legs, she ascended the ladder, nearly falling twice in her weakened condition. Continuing past the sailors' berth, which was empty, she made her way up the companionway ladder onto the main deck. Bright light brought her hand up to shield her eyes as she scanned the scene. *Destiny* floated hull-to-hull alongside a larger ship, grappled together with tight lines. Lifting her gaze, Cassandra saw the Union Jack flying from the head of the larger ship's main mast. A British frigate. The air escaped her lungs, and she leaned on a nearby barrel to keep from toppling to the deck.

"What is all this?" A distinguished-looking man standing at the frigate's railing waved a hand over the barrels and crates crowding *Destiny*'s decks. His British accent grated over Cassandra's ears.

"I propose a new bargain, Captain." Luke's voice responded from somewhere atop the frigate's deck. Confirming Cassandra's fears. Anger scoured through her—searing, thrashing, all-encompassing anger. Anger at Luke's betrayal. Anger that she had fallen in love with a traitor. Anger that he had made her an accomplice in such a despicable deed.

She barreled forward, weaving through the maze of cargo and shoving aside sailors who stood in her way.

❖

"A bargain?" Captain Raynor laughed. "I don't bargain with rebels."

Luke grimaced and glanced at John, who stood just below the quarterdeck ladder. He looked well, tired and thinner, but well. Facing the captain again, Luke resisted the urge to punch the supercilious smirk off his face. "Yet you have already bargained with this particular rebel, sir. Hear me out, I beg you."

The captain glanced at his first and second lieutenants, flanking him on the main deck of the frigate, and huffed his impatience. He gave Luke a look of boredom. "Make it quick."

"All of these supplies, which are enough to feed you and at least five ships like yours for more than a month, including several hundred bottles of rum, I offer you entirely without cost." Waves, slapping the hull, laughed at Luke's offer.

Captain Raynor studied him. "Unless you have come to your senses and wish to throw your lot in with the victors of this war, I cannot see why you would make such an offer, sir."

"I make it on the following conditions." Luke tried to steady his voice, tried to drown out the urgency screaming in his head. "That you return my brother to me, and I give you my word I will quit privateering."

Captain Raynor gave a scoff of surprise as if Luke had asked for a chest of gold. "Your word, sir?" This time the lieutenants as well as some of the crew standing nearby chuckled. "What is the word of an American worth?"

The frigate rose over a swell. Luke adjusted his footing, refusing to answer the man's absurd question.

Captain Raynor grimaced and tipped his cocked hat against the rays of the rising sun. "Besides, what is to stop me from absconding with all of these supplies and keeping your brother as well?"

"Nothing but your honor, sir." Luke hoped that Captain Raynor held his honor in high esteem, or at least his pride. For the captain certainly wouldn't want to be seen breaking a gentleman's oath in front of his entire crew.

Captain Raynor narrowed his eyes.

Hope began to stir within Luke. He was about to restate his terms when a familiar female voice sprang over the frigate's bulwarks like a grappling hook.

"You are a traitor, Luke Heaton! A traitor and a cad. How dare you sell supplies to our enemies?"

Luke closed his eyes, wishing the voice away, hoping it came from his tortured conscience and not from the source that frightened him the most. Scuffling sounded from below on *Destiny's* deck. Then Biron's disbelieving groan confirmed Luke's worst fears. Opening his eyes, he approached the railing and peered over the side. There, struggling in Biron's and Mr. Keene's grasp, stood Cassandra—in breeches and shirt, of all things—her auburn hair flailing in the breeze, and her eyes pointed at Luke like two loaded cannons.

Captain Raynor grinned. "Friend of yours, sir?"

Shock stiffened Luke, followed by terror. How did she get on board? Why was she dressed like a man? But there was no time to find out.

"Yes. . . No," Luke mumbled, facing Raynor. "She's the ship's cook. Ignore her. She's quite mad." He leaned over the railing. "Mr. Keene, if you would escort Miss Channing below."

The boatswain nodded and headed toward the companionway with Cassandra in tow when she tore from his grasp and shoved her way toward the rope ladder.

"Bring the woman up here. I'd like to meet her." Captain Raynor's words fired into Luke's gut.

Luke waved a hand through the air. "She's nobody, Captain, ignore her." He cringed at his own pleading tone.

A tone not missed by the captain of the HMS *Audacious*—he grinned. "Yet she seems to be quite surprised at your nefarious activities, no?"

Luke saw Cassandra's red hair pop above the bulwarks as she hoisted herself over the railing. She landed on the deck with a determined thump. Catcalls rang across the ship before the master's mate silenced the men. Ignoring them, Cassandra approached Luke, her icy stare lancing him before she scanned the assembly of British officers, sailors, and marines crowding the deck.

Did the woman fear nothing?

Spotting the captain, she charged toward him. Two midshipmen grabbed her arms before she got too close.

"Is this man selling you goods, Captain?"

Luke's throat closed. Heated wind slapped him in the face.

"Why, yes, madam, he is." The captain seemed to be enjoying himself immensely.

Tearing free from the midshipmen's grip, Cassandra marched toward Luke. Raising her fists, she pounded on his chest. He allowed her. He deserved it. Each blow caused his heart to shrink a bit more until he wondered if there was anything left.

The crew of the *Audacious*, however, found the scene much to their amusement, as laughter bounced through the air.

Finally, after her anger was spent, Cassandra bent over in a sob.

Luke grabbed her arms and drew her close, whispering in her ear. "This isn't as it seems, Cassandra. Go back to the ship." But she jerked from him, too disgusted to even meet his gaze.

"Very good. Very good." Captain Raynor clapped his hands together as if applauding a performance. "And who, may I ask, are you, miss?"

Sweat slid down Luke's back. *Do not tell him. Keep your mouth shut.* His gaze found John, still standing by the quarterdeck, and looking as frightened as Luke felt.

Drawing a breath, she lifted her shoulders and faced the captain. "I am Cassandra Channing from Baltimore."

Luke shook his head. The ship groaned over a swell, mimicking his silent moan within.

"Ah," the captain said. "And might I assume you weren't aware of this man's. . .activities?"

"You assume correctly, sir." She grimaced and pointed a finger his way. "For I would have shot him myself rather than allowed him to trade with the likes of you."

"Gentlemen"—the captain gestured toward Cassandra—"behold the ill-tempered shrews these colonies breed."

The men seemed more than happy to obey the order as all eyes took Cassandra in as if she were the feast at a royal ball. Only then did Luke notice that the breeches she wore revealed far too much of her feminine curves.

Captain Raynor smiled. "As it happens, I've been in dire need of a decent cook for quite some time. Mr. Milner over there"—he flicked a hand toward a man on his right—"can't boil a chicken without making it taste like tar."

The grimy cook lifted one shoulder and smiled.

A metallic taste filled Luke's mouth. The sun beat down on him, lashing him for failing once again.

For the first time, fear took residence on Cassandra's features, as if she'd only just awakened from a dream. "I am no cook, Captain."

"Indeed? Regardless, you would make a lovely addition to our ship." Pompous victory rang in the captain's tone. "And from the look in Captain Heaton's eyes, you are much more than a cook to him."

"She is nothing to me," Luke growled, desperate to say anything to save her.

Cassandra shot him a pained glance as Biron eased over the railing to join them.

"Then you won't mind if I borrow her?" Removing his hat, the captain dabbed a handkerchief over his forehead. "All the more incentive for you to return with more supplies. I do say, my men and I are becoming quite accustomed to eating fresh food."

Grumbles of assent thundered through the crowd.

Luke clenched his fists. His fingernails dug into his skin. "John is more than enough incentive."

Cassandra backed toward the railing. "You cannot kidnap me, sir. I am neither a privateer nor in the military. I am but an innocent citizen of Baltimore."

"There are no innocents in that haven of pirates!" Captain Raynor barked then stuffed his handkerchief inside his coat. "I can take whatever I wish to take. When the subjects of our great and glorious king defy his laws and resist his rule, they lose all rights."

"She's just a lady, sir." Biron shared a harried glance with Luke.

Luke reached for the hilt of his sword out of habit, meeting dead air. He stepped in front of Cassandra. "Take me instead. My crew will still do as you say."

"I don't quite agree, Captain. The woman ensures your return. Besides, it's been a long time since I've had female companionship." Raynor smiled at the lieutenant standing to his right, who returned his grin with a chuckle.

Loose sails flapped above them.

Cassandra's eyes took on a haunted look. Gone was the anger, the hatred, replaced by sheer terror.

Luke's blood pulsed in his head. He must do something. But what? He was outmanned, outgunned, outwitted.

"No. I will not allow it!" He charged toward the captain, no longer caring what happened to him. The metallic chime of a sword screeched over his ears before the tip landed on his chest, halting him.

Cassandra gasped. John screamed, "No!"

The captain grinned.

Luke stared at the marine holding the sword. The hatred in the man's eyes sent a chill through Luke. Settling his breath, he took a step back. He couldn't help Cassandra and John if he were dead.

"Oh, and by the by," Captain Raynor added with a smirk. "We found the note you gave the lad, so I wouldn't be trying that pathetic ploy again if I were you." He gazed up at the sun and frowned. "Infernal heat of these colonies!" Then with a flick of his finger, he gestured for the purser to step forward. "I wish to purchase only what we agreed upon, Captain Heaton. Take the rest home. We shall see you two weeks hence."

And with that, he swung about to speak to his first lieutenant. Two sailors grabbed Cassandra's arms and led her away. The last thing Luke saw was her pleading gaze before she dropped belowdecks.

❖

Cassandra couldn't feel her feet. Couldn't feel her hands as the men led her below. Was her heart still beating?

"Put her in the warrant officer's cabin, Mr. Windor." The marine on her left released her to the other man, who then ushered her down a narrow hall, lit by intermittent lanterns swaying with the movement of the ship. Halting before a door, he opened it and shoved Cassandra into a cabin not much bigger than a coffin. A wooden plank attached to the bulkhead and covered with a straw tick formed the bed. Beside it, a tiny desk and chair filled the rest of the space. Uniforms hung from hooks on the opposite wall. The sailor lit the lantern then backed out of the room, his eyes hungrily roving over her. He shut the door, and the lock clicked.

Cassandra stood there, numb and empty and alone. She heard the cargo being loaded on board, the shouts of men, the boatswain's pipe, the thunder of sails flapping to catch the wind. But not until the ship jerked and began to move, did she fall to the bed in a heap.

What have I done? She began to sob as stories Marianne had told of her impressment aboard the HMS *Undefeatable* rose in Cassandra's memory to torture her. Stories of endless days cleaning and polishing and scrubbing and catering to the every whim of a mad British captain with no rescue or end in sight.

The ship yawed to starboard, and Cassandra clung to the bed frame to keep from falling. Every inch they sailed over the sea sped her farther away from her home, her family.

Why had she been so foolish? Fury had dulled her reason. She slammed her fist against the bulkhead. Pain burned up her wrist. She should have known better. She should have contained her rage.

Even now, despite her terrifying predicament, that rage stirred to life within her. Or maybe because of it. It was Luke's fault she was here. If he hadn't been a traitor, hadn't lied to her, hadn't broken her heart, she would never have snuck on board his ship.

Drawing her boots up on the bed, she curled into a ball and hugged herself, trembling. Fear battled heartache for preeminence as tears poured down her cheeks onto the burlap coverlet. An hour or two passed. Or maybe more. The sun, like an apathetic actor, passed over the stage of her porthole until it disappeared beyond.

Finally the latch lifted, and the door creaked open to reveal a boy around nine or ten years of age, holding a tray of food. Unkempt dark brown hair fell around his face and nearly reached his shoulders. Gray eyes twinkled above a smile that reminded Cassandra of Luke. She looked away. She didn't want to be reminded of Luke. The boy slipped inside and set the tray on the desk.

"Captain sends his regards, miss. He thought you might be hungry."

Cassandra eyed the steaming tea and plateful of apple slices and cheese, but her stomach lurched at the sight. "You may inform the captain I've lost my appetite."

The boy gave an understanding nod. "It's not so bad here, miss. You'll get used to it."

"I don't want to—" Cassandra stared at the boy. "Are you a prisoner too?"

He nodded. "For a month now, as well as I can guess. At first, I was real scared like you are now, but"—he shrugged—"most everyone's been nice to me, though they do make me work all the time."

The ship bucked, and he stumbled, favoring one of his legs.

"I'm John." His kind smile eased over Cassandra's nerves.

"A pleasure, John." She nodded. "I'm Cassandra." She studied him. "How did you get here?"

"Same as you, miss. I was taken from Luke's ship."

Frowning, Cassandra rubbed her forehead. Nothing made sense anymore. "What were you doing aboard Luke's ship?"

The boy beamed with pride. "Why, miss, don't you know? I'm his brother."

❖ CHAPTER 30 ❖

Luke paced across Noah's library, the thump of his boots on the oak floor hammering his guilt deeper and deeper into his gut until he felt he would implode.

"You did what?" Noah leapt from his chair behind his desk, his eyes blazing, his hand reaching for the sword strapped to his hip. "Are you drunk?"

Luke shook his head. He wished he was. He wished all that had transpired was merely a rum-induced nightmare.

Mr. Reed, standing by the cold hearth, turned with a groan, his dark brow furrowed.

Luke halted, still not believing he'd finally said it out loud. He'd admitted to being a traitor to his country. Yet instead of feeling relieved, all remaining hope dissipated beneath the look of disgust and disappointment on Noah's face. "They captured John."

"John," Noah repeated, his voice spiked with shock. "Your brother?"

Clawing a hand through his hair, Luke took up a pace again. "Yes."

"Upon my word, how did the British get ahold of your brother?" The enemy's accent throbbed in Mr. Reed's voice.

Grinding his teeth together, Luke faced Noah. "Does *he* have to be here?"

One brow of censure rose over Noah's sharp eyes. "He is my houseguest and engaged to Miss Rose. And you will treat him accordingly." His captain's voice gave no room for argument.

"Engaged?" Luke stared at the British lieutenant. "I thought you were reporting back to your ship."

"God had other ideas." Mr. Reed gave a slight chuckle then grew serious and took a step toward Luke. "I've joined the Americans."

Before Luke could process the information, Noah's harsh voice blasted over his ears. "And exactly *whose* side are you on, Luke?" His friend circled the desk, sliding his hand over the walnut top and landing inches from his pistol.

Pain seared Luke's heart at the thought that his friend would ever use the weapon against him. But how could he blame him? "Shoot me if you wish. Turn me in if you want. But I had no choice. They would have killed John."

The tight lines around Noah's eyes softened. A hint of relief freed the breath in Luke's throat. But it caught again when he remembered he had yet to inform them about Cassandra.

"How long has the boy been there?" Mr. Reed asked.

"A month." Luke shook his head. Fury fisted his hands, and he fought the urge to punch something, anything, if only to release the rage within him.

Noah sat on the edge of his desk and crossed his arms over his chest. "And you've been supplying them ever since?"

"What other choice did I have?"

Mr. Reed's mouth quirked in disgust. "The choice to not be so rash, sir. To seek aid instead of putting others at risk with your own self-pitying stubbornness."

Enough from this pompous Brit! Luke charged the man, raising a fist in the air. Taking a step back, Mr. Reed raised his own, preparing to fight. But Noah darted between them, grabbed Luke's wrist in midair, and shoved him back.

"Confound it all! Fighting is not the answer. Mr. Reed is right. You should have come to me sooner." Noah's face flamed. "We could have figured something out."

Seething, Luke retreated. He should leave. If Noah would even allow him to, now. Unclenching his fist, he rubbed the scars on his palm. "Yes, of course," Luke said with a smirk. "We could have sent my schooner and your brig against a Royal Navy frigate. Even if we managed to fire a broadside at them, my only brother is on board." *Not to mention the woman I love.*

"Instead, you chose to suffer alone and betray your country," Noah growled. "Blast your pride, man!"

"Don't you think I've been trying to get him back?" Luke snapped. Noah's eyes narrowed. He shook his head in disdain.

Perhaps, Luke had made a mistake in coming here. Perhaps, friend or not, Noah would summon General Smith immediately and have Luke hauled off for treason.

Tugging on his coat, Mr. Reed took a stance of authority as he'd often done when they'd been his slaves aboard the HMS *Undefeatable*. "So, why now? What has humbled you enough to seek help?"

Luke backed away and sank into a leather chair. "Something else happened. I met the frigate four days ago to offer the captain my entire hold full of supplies for free if he'd release my brother."

Mr. Reed frowned. "Unlikely any British captain would agree to that."

Luke swallowed. "As I discovered. But it was my last hope."

"And?" Noah studied him, apprehension on his face.

"Turns out I had an unexpected stowaway." Luke prepared himself for the pain it would cause him to simply say her name. To admit what he'd done. "Miss Channing. They took her."

Mr. Reed released a moan that—based on his intimate knowledge of the happenings aboard a British warship—did not bode well for Cassandra's future.

"Cassandra?" Noah winced. Eyes wide, he stumbled backward. "What was she doing on board your ship?"

Luke grimaced. "I imagine she suspected my activities."

"I cannot believe it." Noah pinched the bridge of his nose and closed his eyes. "We must not tell Marianne. It would vex her overmuch."

Luke dropped his head into his hands. "This is my fault. I don't know what to do." He raised his gaze to see Mr. Reed, hands fisted at his waist, staring into space as if in deep concentration.

"Do you know this Captain Raynor?" Luke asked.

"Only by reputation." Mr. Reed rubbed his chin. "If it helps, he isn't the erratic ogre Captain Milford is."

Luke drew in a deep breath. "You offer me little consolation, sir. Now, offer me a way to get Cassandra and John back. These treacherous mongrels are your people. You know how they think. I beg you"—Luke hesitated, wondering if Reed would help him after Luke had nearly assaulted him—"tell me you have an idea."

"I do." The Brit's eyes sparkled.

"Egad, Alex! Let's hear it." Noah's tone was anxious.

"I still have my uniform." Mr. Reed grinned. "All we need is a small ship, a British ensign, and forged papers ordering Captain Raynor to release the prisoners into my custody."

"Will that work?" Luke asked, afraid to entertain the hope sparking within him.

"With courage, wit, and God's help, it just might," Mr. Reed replied.

Luke shook his head. Though warmed by the Brit's offer to help, it was too much to ask. "No, I cannot allow it. You risk too much." He glanced at Noah. "Both of you."

"You risked the same for me," Alex said. "When you arranged for me to see Rose at the ball."

Noah gripped Luke's arm. "Allow me to choose my own risks."

"But if we are caught, we'll quite possibly all be hanged as traitors."

"Perhaps." Noah's brow rose. "Or perhaps we'll be hailed heroes for rescuing an innocent American woman and child."

"And I'll be hanged when the story is revealed of how they came to be captured." Luke released a ragged sigh. "But that is no more than I deserve."

"God will decide such things, Luke. Will you take the risk? Will you trust Him?" Noah asked.

Luke's eyes burned at his friend's loyalty. "Trusting God, I cannot promise. But laying my life down to save my brother and Cassandra, that's a risk I'll gladly take."

❖

Lieutenant Abner Tripp poured more brandy into Mr. Keene's mug. "I daresay, I do admire a man who can hold his liquor."

Mr. Keene laughed and lifted the mug to his lips. "And I, sir, admire any man who buys me a drink."

The door to the tavern opened and three rugged-looking fellows entered. Wind snaked in behind them and stirred the flame of the candle on the table. It flickered in Mr. Keene's glassy eyes as he took another sip.

"To what do I owe the pleasure of such a distinguished officer's company?" Mr. Keene's words finally began to garble.

Finally. Tripp had been buying him drinks and telling him jokes for nearly an hour. The stench of tallow, sweat, and alcohol burned in Tripp's nose. He doubted he'd ever get the smell out. Yet still the fop avoided answering questions about Mr. Heaton. Unable to converse with Mr. Keene at the Fountain Inn Ball before he'd left, Tripp's search of the city's taverns the past two weeks had finally paid off when he happened upon the ostentatious fat wit here at Payne's Tavern engaged in a game of Gleek.

Now, the bumbling fool insisted on flirting with every doxy who passed by while drinking away Tripp's meager wages without giving him a scrap of information in return.

"Another one, Mr. Keene?" Tripp grabbed the bottle and poured another swig into the glass. "I find privateering absolutely fascinating. What exactly is it that you do aboard *Destiny*?"

"I'm a boatswain. Directing the sails and such." He sipped his drink, slumped back in his chair, and waved a jeweled hand, framed in lace, through the air.

"Indeed? I assumed a man of your years and intelligence would be the captain or at least the first mate."

Mr. Keene smiled then hiccupped. "Kind of you to say, sir."

"Privateering agrees with you and your captain, I'd say. Word is you've had plenty of coin to spend on every gentleman's pleasure available in the city."

"Indeed I have, sir. Easiest coin I ever made." A tavern wench sashayed toward the table and deposited another bottle of brandy in the middle. Though it was Tripp who dropped coins in her outstretched palm, her eyes swam over Mr. Keene.

"Still meeting me later tonight?" she asked, her painted lips forming a red bow.

Grabbing the edge of the table, Keene struggled to his feet, swayed for a moment, then leaned over to whisper something in the woman's ear. Giggling, she darted off, blowing a kiss at him over her shoulder.

He plopped down into his chair with such force, it nearly tipped. Waving his arms through the air like a demented bird, he steadied himself.

Tripp restrained a groan of disgust. *Ah, the vermin Mr. Heaton surrounds himself with!* But what did Tripp expect? He leaned in with a wink. "I admire any man with enough business sense to make money during wartime."

"I quite agree, sir!" Keene's expression grew serious. "If we must fight a war, let the wisest and shrewdest of us profit."

Now Tripp was getting somewhere. After glancing around them for prying ears, he gave Keene a sly look. "I, for one, intend to use this blasted war to line my pockets with gold."

"Aye, we are of the same mind." Keene tossed the remaining brandy to the back of his throat. His eyes shifted over the dark tavern but seemed unable to focus.

"Here's to ill-gotten gains!" Tripp lifted his mug.

Mr. Keene blinked in slow motion. Grabbing his drink, he managed to strike empty air three times before finding Tripp's mug. "To ill-gotten gains."

Disgust bittered Tripp's mouth.

Nearly dropping his cup, Keene settled it on the table and leaned forward on his elbows. His gaze wavered over Tripp as if he couldn't determine which one of him to focus on. "Let me tell you about ill-gotten gains, sir."

❖

Pressing down the folds of the oversized silk gown that the captain insisted she wear, Cassandra made her way down the companionway to the stern of the ship. Flickering lanterns perched at intervals afforded the only light in the otherwise gloomy narrow hall, making Cassandra feel like a mouse trapped in a maze. Raucous male laugher blaring from behind the door halted her, but the marine behind her nudged her forward with the barrel of his pistol. Why the man thought he needed the weapon was beyond Cassandra. Standing at just over five feet, she couldn't do much damage to anyone—well, unless she had a brick in hand.

Or her parasol, of course. She smiled.

The marine brushed past her, their bodies touching. A lecherous smirk lifted his lips before he knocked and opened the door at the gruff "enter" that came from within. Then all but shoving her inside, he closed the door behind her. The smell of roasted duck and sweet butter instantly filled her nose as the flickering of a dozen candle flames struck her eyes. An oblong wooden table centered the captain's quarters, upon which perched two silver candelabras, platters of steaming food, pewter mugs and plates, silverware, and glittering goblets filled with some type of drink that contained nutmeg. The eyes of seven men lighted on her above smiles, some salacious in nature, others filled with hate, while a few held nothing but casual admiration.

"Do come in, Miss Channing. I hope you don't mind dining with a bunch of old crotchety sailors." Captain Raynor stood and gestured toward a chair at the far end of the table.

"Do I have a choice?" She took her seat, surprised to see a clean serviette beside her plate. Taking it, she slipped it into her lap, threw back her shoulders, and met their gazes with a boldness she did not feel within. If she had to endure imprisonment aboard this ship, she would endure it with grace and courage and show these sanctimonious, ill-bred Brits the real spirit of America.

That her countrymen weren't backward, ignorant ruffians cowering beneath their beds. That Americans were strong and smart and courageous and boasted of more honor than any British could lay claim to.

"You have a choice to eat or to starve, Miss Channing," the captain said, shifting his jaw. "But if you choose the former, I'm afraid you'll have to endure our company."

Cassandra gave him a tight smile. Better to eat and maintain her strength, not to mention have a chance to overhear some valuable information. "Gentlemen," the captain gestured to her with his hand. "May I present Miss Cassandra Channing, American rebel from Baltimore."

Cassandra poured herself some of the peach-colored liquid. "I prefer *patriot*, Captain."

"I suppose it all depends on your perspective," a chubby man, sitting on her left, said.

Nodding to him, she took a sip of the rum-laced tea and coughed.

"Perhaps you'd prefer the fresh water your. . .your. . ." A look of feigned consternation claimed the captain's face. "Now what shall we call Mr. Heaton, your paramour?"

Heat sped up Cassandra's neck. The men chuckled.

Captain Raynor cocked his head. "Your beau? Your friend? Your—"

"He is none of those things." Cassandra cut him off, longing for a fan to wave back the blush that was surely evident on her face. "And yes, I would prefer water."

The captain snapped his fingers to a steward who stood against the bulkhead, sending the boy out of the cabin. The men, three lieutenants and two midshipmen, if Cassandra's assessment of the buttons and epaulettes adorning their uniforms was correct, began piling food onto their plates. A platter of roasted duck, bowl of rice, corn, boiled potatoes in sweet cream, and biscuits passed by her.

She took a small portion of each, though her appetite had abandoned her—just as Luke had done.

But dare she admit that the revelation of Luke's reasons for his traitorous activities—in the form of the sweet, young boy she'd met earlier—had softened her anger considerably? For she knew, without a doubt, that if Hannah or Darlene had been thus kidnapped, she wouldn't hesitate to do whatever it took to rescue them unscathed.

The steward returned, pitcher of water in hand, and poured some into her mug. She thanked him. Smiling, he returned to his post. So young. Not much older than John. She wondered if he had chosen to be on this ship, in the Royal Navy. Had his parents arranged the position for him, proud to send their son off to a grand career at sea, or was he impressed as they were?

The men proceeded to eat with more civility than Cassandra expected, but then again they were officers. Talk of the sea, the operation of the ship, and longing for loved ones back home dominated the conversation, but their words blended into a nonsensical drone as Cassandra nibbled at her food and gazed out the stern windows into the darkness beyond. From the slight rock of the ship, she'd guessed they'd all but stopped for the night. Barely perceptible stars winked at her like devilish sprites, reminding Cassandra of her desperate situation.

Not that she needed reminding. A massive cannon guarding the captain's berth, a sentinel of the strength and superiority of the British navy, along with a row of glistening swords, knives, and axes, hanging on the bulkhead, did a sufficient job of scrambling the contents of her stomach.

"Do tell us how life is in Baltimore these days, Miss Channing?" The captain's grating voice brought her gaze forward. Candlelight blazed a mischievous glint in his eyes.

Stirring Cassandra's anger.

"As you have heard, Captain, Baltimore is the largest thorn in your side. Its people are brave, determined, and well armed. Our fort is impenetrable, and we have sent out more privateers to nip your heels than any other American port city." She regretted the words instantly as anger contorted the captain's face. Yet the chuckles of two of his lieutenants seemed to soften his expression.

"She is goading you, Captain," one of them said. "What do women know of such things?"

Captain Raynor dabbed his lips with his serviette then tossed it onto the table. "And what, pray tell, are the defenses of this impenetrable fort?" He snorted, sharing a look of annoyance with his officers. "Stones and sticks, no doubt?"

"Why, as you know, I can hardly divulge such secrets, Captain. Besides, what do women know of such things?" She gave the lieutenant a smirk.

The captain sipped his drink and leaned back in his chair, lacing his hands over his belly. "We shall see what the good citizens of Baltimore think when our ships sail into her harbor and reinstate British rule."

The food soured in Cassandra's stomach.

One of the lieutenants, a gruff man with more hair on his eyebrows than on top of his head, slammed his mug onto the table—giving Cassandra a start. He gazed at his comrades as excitement filled his tone. "If the task is to be as easy as the taking of the rebel capital, we should place British boots on Baltimore's streets within a fortnight!"

The men raised their glasses in a toast of impending success.

Cassandra's throat felt as though it had been stuffed with sand. "Are you to burn Baltimore down as well?" What would become of her sisters? Her mother?

The captain plopped a piece of duck meat into his mouth. "If need be, I suppose."

Her empty spoon fell to her plate with a *clank*. "What need could there be, Captain, to destroy shops, homes, and libraries and force people onto the street? I see no honor in that."

"Honor!" Spittle flew from Captain Raynor's lips. "You speak to me of honor when it is you and your rebels who have turned against our sovereign king."

Cassandra stood, her anger squashing what was left of her fear and her reason. "Whenever a government becomes abusive and destructive, it is the right of the people to alter or to abolish it. To institute a new government—a government where man rules himself, where his rights—which are life, liberty, and the pursuit of happiness—come from God and not from man, not from some pompous, uncaring monarch."

The captain's brows scrunched together. "What sort of gibberish is

272

this? And here I thought you would provide my men and me with a pleasant diversion. I tire of your company, Miss Channing."

"Let her stay, Captain. I find her zeal exhilarating," the hairy-browed lieutenant said with a wink in her direction.

"And quite comical." One of the midshipmen chomped on a biscuit.

"Are all American women so brash?" The chubby man to her left did not direct the question to her, but rather addressed his bumbling friends.

"I dare say, sadly, I've heard it is the case," a midshipman across from him answered.

"Then 'tis no wonder the American men prefer war. It keeps them away from the shrews at home."

The officers broke into a fit of laughter.

"How dare you!" Cassandra's voice faltered in the boisterous revelry.

When the laughter subsided, the captain's hard eyes latched on her. "Nevertheless, Miss Channing, you have depleted my patience." He waved her off. "Mr. Olsen!" His shout brought a marine back into the room. "Take Miss Channing back to her cabin."

"Captain." Cassandra tried to steady her voice. "If I displease you so, send me and the boy home. You have no use for us here."

"On the contrary, I have every use for you. To procure supplies." He gave her a sordid smirk. "And after we've won, perhaps I'll keep you as an example to all shrewish women in the colonies that they should submit not only to their husbands, but to their new rulers."

❖ CHAPTER 31 ❖

Cassandra wrung her hands together and took two steps across her tiny cabin before the bulkhead barred her way. She swung around. Two steps fore and two steps aft. That was the extent of freedom left to her. Instead of granting her more independence, every decision she had made in the past six months had limited it. Investing all her money in a dubious venture had put her family at great risk and restricted her options. Not storing her prize winnings at the bank had left them near destitute. And now, stowing aboard Luke's ship had made her a prisoner, possibly for life. How would her family manage without her? Instead of helping them, she had only put them in more danger.

Instead of aiding her country, she had unwittingly been aiding the enemy.

The ship bucked, tossing her against the frame of her bed. Pain radiated through her knee. She no longer cared. She'd grown used to the bumps and bruises that marred her arms and legs from constantly being thrashed about. It had been six days since her altercation with the captain in his cabin. And he'd not summoned her since. Not that she wanted to spend another moment with the implacable blackguard, but neither did she wish to remain entombed in her cabin.

Twice a day, a marine escorted her on deck for an hour, during which time dozens of piercing gazes and vulgar comments assailed her, making her feel like a dancer on stage in a bawdy saloon. Even so, as she stood at the railing and stared at the sea, the hour went by far too quickly before she was given access to the captain's private privy and then locked in her cabin once again. Meals, consisting of biscuits, fish, water, and an orange or lemon, were brought to her twice a day by a man with a permanent stoop and a pungent body odor that would ruin anyone's appetite. Nevertheless, she thanked him and tried to eat the food as best she could, even remembering now and then to ask God's blessing on it. She smiled, knowing her mother would be pleased, but more than that, in her present predicament, Cassandra was thankful for anything she received.

For she knew her life and her future rested in the hands of this British crew.

When asked why they kept her locked up, the marine mumbled something about another lady prisoner who had been able to do much damage to a British ship. Smiling, Cassandra wondered if they referred to Marianne.

A knock on the door froze her in place. The jingle of keys and clank of the latch reverberated through the room, and the door opened to reveal young John with a smile on his face and his hands behind his back.

"Only a minute, boy." The marine behind John shoved him inside and slammed the door. Sweeping his arms out, the boy presented her with a leather-bound book.

Upon further inspection, a rather holy book. "A Bible?" Cassandra didn't take it.

"One of the sailors gave it to me, miss. I thought you could use it about now." He stretched it toward her.

She waved it off. "I thank you, John, but keep it. It has never done me much good."

Sadness tore the smile from his face. "Then you need it much more than I thought, miss." He shoved it toward her again. She took it this time, if only to be polite, then sank onto her bed and gazed at the frayed pages and weathered leather binding. "Unless this will sprout wings and fly me back to shore, I don't see how it will help."

"Perhaps it *will* sprout wings." John's eyes danced. "God can do anything He wants. He is with us, Miss Channing. I've felt His presence ever since I boarded."

Cassandra flattened her lips. "I believe what you're feeling is dread."

He chuckled, and the curve of his mouth reminded Cassandra of Luke. Heaviness settled on her chest. Would she ever see him again?

"Fear doesn't bring hope, miss. Only faith and love do."

Cassandra lifted a skeptical brow. "And you have hope we'll get off this ship?"

"Yes, I do."

Envious of the joy and assurance in his eyes, Cassandra lowered her chin. "God abandoned me long ago."

The deck canted. Stumbling, John gripped the door frame and adjusted one of his legs. He winced.

Cassandra reached out for him. "Are you all right? Have they harmed you?"

"No, miss." He lifted one side of his breeches. An odd metal contraption hooked around his ankle, extending to a brace that disappeared up his leg.

At her look of astonishment, he said, "I have rickets."

Concern for this poor boy flooded Cassandra. She stared at him, unsure of what to say. All this time, Luke not only had a brother he cared for, but an ill child.

"It's not serious, miss. Besides, Luke was able to purchase this new brace with his prize money." He released the pant leg, once again hiding his withered leg.

Just as the outward appearance of man often hides the evil intentions of the heart. Cassandra's thoughts sped to Luke—a loving heart loyal to family yet hidden beneath a rough exterior. And what of Mr. Crane? A black heart hidden beneath the prim polish of a wealthy newspaper owner.

Rays from the setting sun peered in through the porthole and bounced over the back of the door with each move of the ship. Up down, up down, as if the light were restricted from going beyond certain boundaries.

"Luke sounds like a good brother."

"He's the best, miss. Been taking care of me since I was a baby."

"Yes, I heard your parents were killed. I'm sorry."

John's eyes grew vacant as he glanced out the porthole. "I don't remember them." Then his face brightened. "But I'm sure I'll see them in heaven."

Cassandra smiled. "I would have never known you wore a brace."

"Not everything is as it seems." John snapped his hair from his face, reminding her once again of Luke. "Which is why we must believe God has a plan."

She studied him. "How can you say that when you've been trapped here for a month?"

He shrugged. "God doesn't want me to leave yet. When He does, I will." A whistle sounded from above, followed by the *clang clang* of a bell.

John nodded toward her, his eyes widening. "And God has something for you to do as well."

"Me?" Cassandra nearly laughed. Such childlike faith. But Cassandra wasn't a child. She was a grown woman who had experienced enough of life to know that faith in God was for pastors and children and the simpleminded.

A knock pounded on the door. "Boy!"

John frowned, but then his eyes took on a sparkle. "Oh, I nearly forgot." He reached into a pocket in his oversized breeches and brought out a piece of foolscap, a tiny bottle of ink, and a quill pen.

"What are these for?" Cassandra asked.

"If you want to write a note to Luke or someone back home, I can try to slip it to him next time he comes. I thought it would help pass the time."

"Thank you, John." Cassandra took them and set them aside. Then grasping his hands, she squeezed them. "Be careful, John. These men are our enemies."

"I know." Stepping toward her, John embraced her. "Be careful as well, miss."

Startled by his affection, Cassandra wrapped her arms around him as her memories drifted to Hannah and Darlene. Sorrow threatened to overwhelm her.

"Hurry up, boy!" The shout sent John reaching for the door handle.

"You remind me of your brother," Cassandra said. "Though smaller and kinder and not so angry."

The statement brought a huge smile to the boy's face. "You're the woman he talked about, aren't you?"

"One of many, I am sure."

"No. He told me you were special. One of a kind. A true lady."

Initial elation gave way to sorrow as Cassandra realized that, just like everyone else in town, she had not believed that Luke was anything but a rogue. If she had, if she had shown faith in him, maybe he would have trusted her and told her the truth. Then maybe she could have helped him think of a way to rescue John.

"I'll come back as soon as I can." John opened the door, and the marine tugged him out before Cassandra could say good-bye. Gathering the pen and ink, she lifted her skirt and tucked them inside the pocket she'd sown in her petticoat. No doubt if that stiff marine saw them in her cabin, he'd take them from her. The boy's infectious faith remained in the cabin long after he left, giving rise to a yearning within Cassandra—a yearning to believe she was not alone, that everything that had happened was part of a plan, for a purpose, and that her life and the world were not spinning chaotically out of control toward some final destruction.

With the Bible snug in her lap, Cassandra sat for hours and watched as the sun's rays withdrew from the door and slid over the deck head until finally disappearing out the porthole, taking with them the last trace of hope left by John's presence.

Despair took its place. It crowded in her throat and threatened to fill her eyes with tears. Unless she could figure out a way for her and John to escape—or by some miracle Luke rescued them—she'd be stuck on this ship forever. In this cabin all alone, or worse. . .

What would become of her mother and sisters? They had only enough money to last a year. Would her mother be frugal enough to stretch the funds beyond that? And what of Darlene and Hannah's upbringing? Aside from Margaret and Mr. Dayle, they had no decent instructors in life. Without a firm hand, Darlene would only grow more unruly with each passing year. Who knew what trouble she would become entangled in with her rebellious, carefree spirit?

Like you.

Me? Cassandra glanced over the shadows burgeoning from the corners of the cabin as memories assailed her of all the times she'd disobeyed her mother and father. All the times she'd left home without permission, snuck food into her bedchamber, put spiders in Mrs. Northrop's bed, garden snakes in the stew, ink on her brother Gregory's teeth while he slept. The list went on endlessly, bringing a smile to her lips. Her rising shame quickly transformed it into a frown. Each time she'd been caught for one of her seditious deeds her father had coddled her, rescuing her from her mother's wrath. Yet now, Cassandra wondered if he had done her more of a disservice.

"I'm different now. I've grown up," she said out loud to the creaking timbers of the ship.

But visions assaulted her: how she traipsed about town at night with a large-summed banknote in her reticule, invested in a privateer against her mother's wishes, and dressed like a man and sneaked aboard Luke's ship.

All reckless acts that had led her to her current dire situation.

"Oh, bother." She hung her head as her eyes filled with tears. She had never really changed, had she? She had always done exactly what she wanted, went her own way, caused her parents grief. And not trusted anyone. In particular, God. And where had it gotten her?

Doomed to a life of slavery.

"But I wouldn't have done those things if You hadn't left me, God. I had to take care of my family."

I never left you.

A chill struck Cassandra. Hugging herself, she sent a wary gaze about the tiny cabin. No doubt the many hours she'd spent alone were causing her to hear things. She set the Bible on the desk and stood to light the lantern hanging from the deck head. Its glow chased the shadows back into hiding as the room filled with the smell of whale oil.

Yet if God was speaking to her, if He was listening, she had some things to tell Him. Her jaw hardened. "But You took my father, my brothers."

Silence.

As she thought. God wasn't there.

Sails thundered above and the bell rang again, followed by the pounding of feet. The change of a watch, no doubt. The smells of some kind of stew permeated the thin walls, making her stomach growl. She rubbed it, regretting that she'd stubbornly turned down her noon meal. It would be at least an hour before the sailor brought her supper.

Stubborn pride. She knew it well. Had seen it mirrored in Darlene. It was the kind of pride that made Cassandra refuse to rely on anyone else—forced her to accomplish everything herself. For if she did not trust, she would never be hurt, abandoned, or disappointed. Would she?

Distant thunder hammered the evening sky. Or was it cannon fire? Standing on her tiptoes, Cassandra peered out the porthole at the undulating sea. Coral and crimson fingers stretched over the indigo waters in one final caress of the sun. The ship jolted. Staggering, she fell back on her bed. The lantern flung shifting silhouettes of shadow and light across the bulkheads. Dark and light, good and evil, faith and unbelief. Life was full of choices.

Cassandra hadn't realized until now how important those choices were.

She opened the Bible. She didn't know why. She'd heard plenty of passages read in church, hundreds of sermons. Flipping through the pages, she landed on James. Her eyes idly scanned the text until the word *proud* seemed to magnify on the paper.

"God resisteth the proud, but giveth grace unto the humble. Submit yourselves therefore to God. Resist the devil, and he will flee from you. Draw nigh to God, and he will draw nigh to you."

Had God resisted her because of her pride? And her unbelief? Was it too late to draw near to Him? Would He still answer her prayers? Or had her arrogant rebellion formed an impenetrable wall between them?

Releasing a heavy sigh, she sifted through the pages, seeking answers, stopping in Hebrews.

"But without faith it is impossible to please him: for he that cometh to God must believe that he is, and that he is a rewarder of them that diligently seek him."

Instead of seeking God, Cassandra had been running from Him, thinking He was not worthy of her trust. That He, like everyone else, had abandoned her. Hope peeked out from her despair. If she diligently sought God now as His Word said, would He reward her? Would He come to her aid?

Hadn't Reverend Drummond told her that God would never leave her and would always provide? And what of Margaret? Still loving God. Still trusting Him after He took her only child.

Confusion sent Cassandra's convictions into a whirl. Bad things, terrible things still happened. And God could have prevented all of them. She glanced over the shadowy room.

"Why didn't You? Why did You let Papa die and my brothers leave us?"

They chose.

"But You could have stopped them."

Silence, save for the creaks and groans of the timbers.

Seek Me. Trust Me.

The ship rose and crashed over a swell, and somewhere a fiddle began to play.

Closing the Bible, Cassandra pressed it against her chest. This time it felt as though she held holy words in her hands. For she knew without a doubt that God had spoken to her.

"I want to trust You." To know she was never alone. To know that Almighty God would always be there to help her, protect her, love her. It was too much to hope for. Too good to be true. Too much to believe. Wasn't it?

I Am.

Wiping the tears from her face, she glanced over the room. An explosion of joy and peace filled the air, permeating every crack and crevice. Gooseflesh ran from her head down to her toes.

And she knew God was there.

"I'm so sorry, Lord." Dropping to her knees, she set the Bible on her bed and leaned her head on top of it. "I'm sorry I've been proud, resisting You, not believing You loved me. I'm sorry I've been running from You." Tears trickled down her cheeks, dropping onto the leather. "I've been a fool."

I love you, precious daughter.

Several minutes passed. When she opened her eyes, moonlight spilled through the porthole, forming milky arms that curled around her in a warm embrace. And for the first time since she arrived on this abominable ship, Cassandra curled up on the bed and fell into a deep sleep.

❖

Laying his coat, sword, and pistol onto the table in the foyer, Luke entered the sitting room. Mrs. Barnes sat in her chair by the fireplace, knitting. Where she'd been nearly every minute since John had been kidnapped. Luke had even caught her sleeping there many a night.

She glanced up, and a sad smile lifted the corner of her lips. "Do you think your plan will work?"

"It has to." Luke huffed and glanced out the window at the darkening sky. All was in place. They'd spent the past two days disguising *Destiny*: removing her name, painting her hull, changing the position of her cannons. Noah had managed to garner two British naval uniforms from the fort—discards from prisoners of war—and Mr. Reed was putting the final touches on forged orders for the transfer of prisoners.

Mrs. Barnes returned to her knitting, and Luke's gaze drifted to her open Bible on the table beside her. "We could use your prayers." He could hardly believe he was asking such a thing. *Creak, creak, creak.* The rhythmic rock of her chair echoed through the room. Though the sound usually soothed Luke's nerves, tonight it raked over them with claws of guilt and failure.

"I *have* been praying," she said. "We'll have John back soon. I know it."

Marching to the window, Luke peered at the tumble of clouds forming on the horizon. "I wish I had your confidence." He snorted. "Both in myself and in your God."

"Two things that must be remedied before you can truly succeed," she said. "The latter before the former."

Her words stirred an odd desire within Luke for both.

"You have good friends," she said. "Mr. Brenin and Mr. Reed. They risk much for you."

"Not for me. For Cassandra and John."

Turning around, he strode to the sofa and took a seat across from her. Her hands dipped and shifted over needle and yarn like a conductor before an orchestra.

"I don't think I've seen you stop knitting for weeks now."

She laughed. "Better to work than to fret." She spread the product of her efforts over her lap. A beautiful tapestry of white and black thread formed delicate patterns in graceful symmetry.

"Did you intend for it to turn out so beautifully?"

"Why yes, of course." She stroked it lovingly. "I planned it from the beginning. It's a blanket for John when he returns." Her eyes sparkled assurance.

Luke shook his head. He had not expected to see such an exquisite coverlet come from Mrs. Barnes's harried movements. Order from chaos, beauty from simplicity, dark and light molded together in a meaningful pattern.

Could God do the same? Luke wondered.

Could God use chaos and darkness to create beauty and light?

Shaking the silly musings from his head, he rose.

Mrs. Barnes's sharp eyes found him. "I've smelled no rum on you lately."

"I need a clear mind." He glanced at the clock, ever stuck at 9:13. "We should get that fixed someday."

"When John returns. But perhaps God is telling us something. Perhaps it's not a time, but a date? It is September thirteenth in three days. . ."

Stifling a chuckle at the woman's delusions, Luke knelt before her.

She set down her knitting, and he took her hands in his. "I'll do my best to get him back, Mrs. Barnes." He fell short of promising something he had no reason to believe he could do. Maybe he should appeal to God, after all, for it would take Almighty intervention for their plan to work.

The prayer sat idle on his lips when a *pound pound pound* drew his gaze to the front door. Mrs. Barnes's face knotted in concern. Luke stood, wondering who it could be. He'd told Noah and Reed to meet him at the ship by ten, but that was at least an hour from now.

Stomping to the door, he swung it open to a cold chill and the sight of Lieutenant Tripp, a bombastic smirk on his face and two armed privates by his side.

Luke had no time for his theatrics. "What do you want?"

"I have come to arrest you, sir."

Mrs. Barnes gasped.

"On what charge?"

"On the charge of treason."

❖ CHAPTER 32 ❖

A loud *clank* barged into Cassandra's sweet sleep, stirring her to consciousness. Ignoring the sound, she drew her wool blanket up around her neck and sank back into the oblivion of her dreams.

Until firm hands gripped her arms and shook her.

With a scream, she jerked to a sitting position, forcing her eyes open to see the red coat of a marine standing over her. "Captain's orders, miss. He wants to see you immediately." The shiny brass hilt of his sword winked at her in the first rays of dawn angling through the porthole.

Of all the times for the captain to summon her, he had to choose the first time she'd been able to sleep in days.

Yet even as she started to grumble, terror gripped her at what the man could possibly want.

"Now." The marine stood erect. The urgency of his tone threatened to dissolve Cassandra's newfound faith.

Tossing the blanket aside, she scrambled to her feet, rubbed her eyes, patted down the wrinkles of her gown, and lifted her chin. "Very well."

As she followed the marine onto the main deck, Cassandra couldn't help but notice that a mood of apprehension, even excitement, had settled over the ship. Squinting at the sun rising on the horizon, she spotted the yards overhead, full of men unfurling sail. Shouted orders from lieutenants on the quarterdeck sent the remainder of the sailors scampering over the decks.

Something was happening. Something important.

Whatever it was did not bode well for her—or for America. As she made her way down the companionway to the captain's cabin, dismal thoughts tortured her. Were they setting sail for England, where she'd be forever separated from her country and her family—and Luke? Or were they about to attack some American ship or worse, America itself?

On trembling legs, she entered the main cabin. Captain Raynor, sitting behind his desk, barely peeked at her from above the document he was reading. But it was John who drew Cassandra's gaze. Turning from his position standing before the captain, he smiled at her, sending a wave of relief over her tight nerves.

The marine stood to attention just inside the door.

"Miss Channing, you and the lad are being moved to an American truce ship." The captain tore the spectacles from his nose.

Hope jolted her heart, though she didn't dare allow it to grow. "Truce ship?"

"Aye." Tossing down the papers, Captain Raynor rose to his full ominous height.

"Then"—she gulped—"we are free?"

"Hardly, madam. You will be guarded well. And when we succeed in our plans, you and all the citizens of your fair city will once again be subjects of the Crown."

Cassandra grimaced at the man's arrogance. She squared her shoulders. "And just what *are* your plans, Captain?"

He grinned, his eyes lighting up with malicious glee. "Why, my dear, we are attacking Baltimore from both land and sea. You and your city don't stand a chance."

❖

Bands of light coursed over Luke's eyelids, like slow-moving waves at sea, passing in swells of warmth and cold. Shouts beckoned to him, jarring his memories. He moved his hand. Moist stones scraped his fingers. Something bit his neck. He swatted it. A bugle sounded. The pounding of drums thundered in his head. Snapping his eyes open, he struggled to rise, ignoring the ache in his back from sitting all night against the wall of his cell in the guardhouse. Making his way to the tiny window, he gripped the iron bars and peered into the inner courtyard of Fort McHenry.

Soldiers from various Maryland regiments, muskets in hand and haversacks tossed over their shoulders, darted across the dirt and out the entrance of the fort. One soldier dropped his canteen and stopped to pick it up.

"What's happening?" Luke shouted.

The man, who could be no older than eighteen, flung his canteen strap over his shoulder and stared at Luke. "It's the British. They've landed at North Point and are marching toward the city." His voice held a fear that registered on his face before he sped away as if it occurred to him that perhaps he shouldn't be speaking to a prisoner.

Which was exactly what Luke was. A prisoner. A traitor.

Sinking back into his dank cell, he took up his daily pace. He hadn't seen Lieutenant Tripp since the man had tossed him in here two nights ago. Last night after spending a sleepless night and an entire day listening to the pounding of soldiers' boots and the harried shouts of officers outside his window, Luke grew desperate for news. So when a young boy brought him a crusty piece of stale bread and a mug of putrid water, Luke had begged him for information. Hesitant at first, the lad finally told Luke that some fifty British warships had sailed up the Patapsco River and anchored just three miles from the fort.

The news had driven a knife into Luke's gut. He'd been unable to sleep yet again, unable to do anything but pace his cell until exhaustion had pulled him to the ground in a heap. Now, the additional news of a land invasion sealed the tomb on Luke's hope. The British were making their move. A full assault by land and sea. And although General Smith had made extensive enhancements to the fort, how could Baltimore survive against the greatest military and naval power in the world?

Luke's thoughts drifted to John and Cassandra. Had Noah and Mr. Reed carried out their plans to rescue them without Luke? He hoped so. It was the only thing that had kept his heart from sinking into despair— believing that they were both safe at home. The first rays of the sun made a courageous effort to shine but were soon subdued by thick, ominous clouds broiling across the sky. Stifling air, heavy with moisture and the smell of gunpowder and fear, settled, rather than swept into his cell. Thunder roared as if God was angry at the invasion. Luke hoped that was the case. For maybe the Almighty would finally intervene. Soon, rain began to fall, offering some reprieve from the torturous heat of the day. It slashed at the roof and battered the mud, mimicking the march of boots. Muffled shouts drifted to his ears, but Luke could no longer make out the words.

Minutes stretched into hours, and hours stretched into the early evening. Luke felt like a caged animal, rage and fury churning within him. Fury at Mr. Keene for his betrayal. Though at first Luke hadn't wanted to believe Tripp's revelation of the man's disloyalty, he knew there was no other explanation. How could Mr. Keene have been so careless? Drunkenness was no excuse for a loose tongue, especially when lives were at stake.

He slapped another mosquito on his arm. Yet how often had Luke done foolish things when he'd been deep into his cups? He halted and rubbed the sweat from the back of his neck. In truth, Mr. Keene and Luke had more in common than Luke cared to admit. And watching his faults play out before him sickened Luke to the core. But no doubt, Mr. Keene was already paying dearly for his betrayal. He, along with Luke's entire crew, had most likely been rounded up and tossed in prison as well. Luke longed to talk to Biron. His old friend always had a wise word of comfort. And Sam. Poor Sam. So young. With so much promise. The foolish lad had longed to emulate Luke in every way. Now, tossed in prison as a traitor, his wish had come true.

Luke moaned. Was there no one in his life who had not been harmed by his foolhardy actions?

Lightning lit his cell in bursts of eerie gray. Gripping the iron bars, Luke peered across the yard. Rain slammed against the stone window ledge and sprayed his face. He shook the water off as a band of soldiers marched by. Mud oozed down their once-white trousers, and the *squish squish* of their boots filled the muggy air with a determination that could be seen on their expressions. A hint of fear quaked in their voices as they waited for the first bombs to strike. Across the way, Luke spotted Major Armistead speaking to a group of officers. Earlier, Luke had overheard the man's urgent orders to transport his pregnant wife out of Baltimore. The general probably feared he'd never see her again.

Just like Luke would never see Cassandra. Thunder rattled the bars. Daylight retreated beneath the encroaching darkness. He stepped away from the window, wondering where she was and what horrors she must be enduring. Was she still angry at him for what he had done? Or, upon meeting his brother, did she understand his actions? Were she and John allowed to speak? A smile, the first one in days, taunted his tight lips. John would lift her spirits and encourage her. It was his way. Small consolation though it was, Luke was pleased to think that the two people he loved more than anything in the world were together.

A cannon boomed in the distance, followed by a spray of musket shot. Luke wondered how the troops had fared that day. He wondered why the British fleet had not attacked the fort. He wondered where Lieutenant Tripp had gone.

Most of all, Luke wondered if he'd ever get out of this cell.

He thought of Noah's and Reverend Drummond's words that God had a plan. He snorted and ran a hand through his hair. Not a plan for Luke. No, there was no divine purpose for his life. Luke was a failure. And he infected everyone he touched with his disease.

He spun around and barreled the other way, striking the wall with his fist. Pain lanced up his arm. He rubbed it as he stared at the rainwater pooling on the stones by his feet. Storming toward the door, he pounded on the thick wood. "Let me out!" But no one came.

Thunder shook the timber and stone. Sweat streamed down his back. This cage was as fitting a place as any to die, he supposed. For he felt as though he'd been in a cage his entire life—a cage of emptiness and failure. A cage he'd built from each bad decision and wayward deed, a prison that kept him trapped in an empty existence.

Darkness as thick as tar rose from the corners and slithered on the floor. Luke watched it with detached curiosity. He was either going mad or dying. He preferred the latter.

Failure, failure.

Worthless, worthless.

The voices stabbed him like a thousand devilish prods. A cold mist enveloped him. He sank to the floor. Rainwater seeped into his breeches. And he knew.

He knew that if he gave in to the darkness he would die.

He closed his eyes. "God, help me." But thunder muted his voice. Exhaustion tugged at him, and he felt himself falling into an empty void.

God, if You're there, help me.

Seconds passed, minutes maybe, as rain pounded above and wind whistled past his window, laughing at him. But then, a warm glow illuminated his eyelids. Luke looked up. A man—no, some otherworldly being—stood just inside the door. White light rippled out from him in glittering waves. Luke's blood turned cold. Holding up a hand to shield his eyes, he tried to make out his face, but the glow was too bright. Yet. . . recognition struck him. "I know you."

The man nodded.

"Who. . .who are you?"

The being drew a massive sword from a scabbard at his hip, sending a chime ringing through the air that was instantly set aglow.

Luke shrank back against the cold stones. His ear began to throb. He rubbed it as flashes of memories filled his mind.

One in particular—the shining man with his sword drawn, standing in front of a burning house.

Luke stared at the man aghast. "You were there."

Again the man nodded. And sheathed his sword with a resounding scrape of metal.

Gripping the stone wall behind him, Luke inched his way to standing. Flames filled his cell, devouring his family home. Little John in his arms. His mother's scream and. . . "You stopped me. You cut me!" Luke grabbed his ear.

"You were persistent." The man's voice sounded like the rush of a waterfall, drowning out the sound of the storm.

Luke's skin grew clammy. His breath escaped him. He had not failed to save his parents! Their deaths were not his fault. The revelation gripped him, breathing life into his soul. Yet anger took the place of fear. "Why?" he cried out. "Why did you stop me?"

"To save you and John. It was not your time."

"And it was my parents' time?" Luke fisted the wall.

The being nodded. "Their task was complete. Yours and John's were not."

"What task?"

"Good works which the Father predestined for you to do before you were born."

Now Luke knew he had surely gone mad. "Me? Good works? You got the wrong man."

The glowing being said nothing, but Luke thought he saw a smile on his blinding visage. "The Father wants you to know you are greatly loved."

Thunder bellowed. The stones quaked, and Luke closed his eyes. The glow dissipated. Jerking alert, Luke glanced over his cell. All was dark again. A dream. Just a dream.

Greatly loved.

The words shot through the hard crust around Luke's heart, dissolving it.

No, not a dream.

"You're real, God." Luke swallowed. "All this time, You've protected me and John. You stayed with me through all my wanderings. All this time, I thought I failed my parents. But it was meant to be. Everything was meant to be." Clenching his fists, he hung his head. "I'm sorry for not believing, for not seeing."

Dawn's glow showered in through the tiny window and surrounded Luke in glittering light. Where had the night gone? What seemed only minutes must have taken hours. A presence filled the cell. A strong sense of peace and love.

The squeaking of a rusty hinge met his ears. He looked up to see the door of his cell ajar. Thunder bellowed. No, not thunder. He knew that sound. It was a cannon blast. The menacing whine of an incoming shell flew overhead.

Before an explosion rocked the fort.

❖ CHAPTER 33 ❖

Clutching her skirts, Cassandra followed John up the ladder and emerged onto the main deck of the sloop *Minden*. Ever since they'd boarded the American truce ship the morning before, heavy rains had kept them cooped up below. Cassandra hadn't minded. Together, she and John had read the Holy Scriptures and talked about the things of God and Cassandra's newfound faith. They'd also talked of Luke, how John and he had lost their parents in a savage fire, and how Luke had been forced to care for John since he was but a babe. Every story John told Cassandra about Luke, about his love for John, the way he'd provided for him and their housekeeper all these years, flew in the face of her initial impressions of the man. Though she didn't completely understand why Luke had taken to drinking, gambling, and womanizing, John's obvious admiration and love for his brother spoke volumes as to the man's heart. Though lately, she needed no aid in attesting to the same.

Heavens, she had no idea he even had a brother. Neither Marianne nor Noah had mentioned it. If they had even known. And a crippled brother at that. Though now as she watched the lad ascend the ladder, hobbling slightly, she realized his physical impediment had not limited him nearly as much as her spiritual one of rebellion had limited her.

She stepped onto the main deck to a burst of rain-laden wind and drew a deep breath, hoping to rid her lungs of the musky air below. Black clouds churned above them, mimicking the dark waters of the Patapsco River that slammed against the hull of the tiny ship. Throwing out her arms to catch her balance on the teetering deck, she peered into the gloom. Surrounding them, dark hulls rose like dragons from the deep, the sharp teeth of their masts stabbing the low-hanging clouds.

The British fleet in all its majestic and terrifying glory wound tight like a pack of ravenous wolves ready to spring on innocent Baltimore.

John took her hand and led her portside, where her fellow prisoners huddled in deep conversation. She gripped the wet railing. A chill seeped through the moist wood into her hands and up her arms. In the distance, the massive stars and stripes billowed proudly above Fort McHenry, daring the British onward. Daring them to try to steal the freedom represented in that grandiose flag.

Sorrow burned in her throat, her eyes, her gut. She could not bear to see her country fall. And would she ever see Luke again? Would she ever be able to tell him she understood why he'd betrayed his country? And that she loved him more than anything? She sighed. That was in God's hands now. She was no longer alone. Her life and the lives of her loved ones were in the capable hands of Almighty God. Ah, such sweet comfort even in the midst of troubling times.

Troubling indeed—and harrowing—confirmed by the British marines, resplendent in their red coats and white breeches, with long muskets in their hands as they lined the deck of the *Minden*. Though an American ship originally, the sloop had been seized by the British and all those upon it were now prisoners of this horrid war. As their punishment, they were being forced to watch the British attack their country, their city. Helpless to do anything.

Terror seized Cassandra's throat. Bowing her head, she whispered a plea to God to spare her city and her country.

A man eased beside her. "I see we are of the same mind, madam. Only divine intervention can save us now."

Opening her eyes, Cassandra stared at the modishly attired man. "How did you know I was praying?"

"The look on your face, pleading yet peaceful, reflecting heaven's glow." He smiled.

Cassandra felt a blush rising.

"Forgive me, I've embarrassed you. Allow me to introduce myself. I am Sir Francis Scott Key." He bowed elegantly. "At your service, madam.

I had heard a woman prisoner had come aboard."

"A pleasure, sir." Cassandra put a protective arm around John. "I am Cassandra Channing of Baltimore."

He dipped his head, and his eyes lowered to John. "Your son?" He gazed up at Cassandra. "No, you are far too young. Brother?"

John giggled. "No, sir, I am John Heaton, brother to the great privateer Luke Heaton."

"Ah, a privateer! Courageous fellows, all! We owe them the highest gratitude."

Distant musket fire splintered the air, drawing Cassandra's gaze to the stretch of land alongside the Patapsco River.

Mr. Key followed her gaze, worry twisting his features. "Word is our American troops have retreated from North Point."

"God be with them," Cassandra said.

"Indeed." He faced her again. "Pray tell, how is it you and John find yourselves prisoners of the British navy?"

Cassandra proceeded to relay their harrowing tale, with John piping in now and then filling in the more colorful details.

"Fascinating, indeed." Mr. Key rubbed his chin. "A most daunting position. I cannot say I wouldn't have done the same thing in Mr. Heaton's shoes."

Lightning flashed silver over his somber expression.

"And how did you come to be here, Mr. Key?"

"Ah, not so adventurous a tale as yours, miss, I'm afraid." He took a step back and motioned for two men, who had been conversing to his left, to come forward. He introduced them as Dr. William Beanes and Colonel John Skinner, an American agent for prisoners.

"Colonel Skinner and I boarded this ship, raised a white flag of truce, and went in search of our dear friend Dr. Beanes, who had been taken prisoner," Mr. Key explained. "As it turns out we found him on board Admiral Cockrane's eighty-gun flagship, the HMS *Tonnant*."

"Indeed?" Cassandra turned to Dr. Beanes, a humble-looking man of small stature. "You are not a military man, sir. May I ask why the British kept you prisoner?"

He cocked his head. "For the crime of tossing some rather unruly British soldiers in jail." His gentle smile gave no indication of the hardship he had no doubt endured.

Thunder quivered the gray sky. The ship canted. Clinging to John,

Cassandra gripped the railing as a foam-capped wave slapped the hull, showering them both with salty spray. Wiping the moisture from her face, she turned to Mr. Key. "I see your mission was somewhat successful." She wondered what magic they wielded to achieve such a feat when Luke had tried everything in his power to free a boy who had done nothing.

"At first not," Mr. Key said. "But we were finally able to persuade General Ross, a rather reasonable fellow as far as the British go." His features sank. "I heard the poor man was killed at North Point." He sighed. "Nevertheless, we seem to have managed only to move Dr. Beanes from one prison to another. And got ourselves captured as well."

Colonel Skinner gazed toward Baltimore. "And now we're forced to witness the invasion of our country."

Musket fire popped in the distance. Thunder shook the tiny ship as she rode upon another swell. Cassandra glanced over the morbid scene.

"I wonder where Luke is," John said.

She drew the boy close. "Pray for him, John. And pray for our country."

Shouts echoed through the gloom from the British ships. Cassandra could make out the shapes of sailors scampering about the deck, hovering over cannons like bees over nectar—deadly nectar.

They were preparing to fire on Baltimore.

❖

Luke stared at the open cell door, too shocked to move. Had the angel opened it or had the explosion jarred the lock? Either way, Luke knew he had not been dreaming. He had seen the angel, heard his words, and through them, God had released Luke from a different kind of prison— one Luke had created for himself out of unbelief and failure.

Another thunderous explosion shook the building, and dust showered him from above. Darting from his cell, down the gloomy hall, he emerged into the empty guardhouse then out into the courtyard of the fort. Officers brayed orders. Soldiers stomped across the ground, mud flinging from their boots, their faces masks of fear and torment. Militiamen and citizens stormed in and out of the open front gate.

Open, with no guard in sight.

In the mayhem Luke would have no trouble slipping out unseen. Ducking into the shadows beneath the building's overhang, he lowered his head and started toward the entrance. Yet with each thud of his boots, something tugged at his heart, urging him to stay. To fight. Even if it meant his death.

Hadn't the angel said Luke had important works, good works to do? Perhaps this was one of them. Perhaps everything that had happened was meant to bring him to this spot.

At this time.

He halted. He was tired of running. Tired of running from God, tired of running from himself. And tired of failing. Anger stormed through his veins. The British had impressed him into their navy, whipped his back, stolen his brother, made Luke into a traitor, kidnapped the woman he loved, and now they were intent on stealing his freedom.

And he was not going to let them succeed without a fight.

Searching the yard for someone in authority, he spotted a colonel standing by the bunkhouse directing a band of militiamen. Fear surged through Luke. Would the man recognize him? Yet, some invisible force nudged him forward even as peace registered in his heart. He must do this. He couldn't explain it, but he knew he was supposed to help defend the fort. Regardless of whether they tossed him back in his cell, he had to try. Snapping the hair from his face, Luke dashed into the rain and halted before him.

"What can I do to help, Colonel?"

The man's eyes narrowed as another explosion split the sky. "Who are you, sir?"

"Luke Heaton, privateer."

"Very good, Mr. Heaton." The man dismissed the militiamen. "Can you handle an eighteen-pounder?"

"Aye, sir." Relief brought a smile to Luke's lips.

"Then report to Captain Nicholson and the Baltimore Fencibles on the shore battery."

Luke hesitated, thinking of the incoming British fleet. "Have you sunk any ships in the bay to bar their passage?"

The colonel huffed. "Where have you been, man? We sunk several merchant ships yesterday. I assure you, the Brits will get no farther than they are, at least not by ship."

With a nod, Luke started off, glad to be helping, glad he had not been thrown back in his cell. As he marched out of the fort, over the moat, and around to the battery, rain stung his face. White-hot lightning etched across the gray sky.

Please, God, give me strength and wisdom and protect this fort and this city. Though his whispered prayer felt odd on his lips, peace as he'd never known washed over him. Approaching the man he assumed to be Nicholson, he glanced at the ominous barricade of British warships perched in the dark waters just three miles from the fort—like a line of soldiers, well armed, their faces like flint, their determination unyielding. He wondered if Cassandra and John were among them. Sorrow crushed his heart as an orange flash shot out from the lead ship, followed by a thunderous boom. Soldiers across the field froze. Some ducked. A splash of water flung toward the sky where the shot fell short of land.

Luke reported to Nicholson and was immediately put to work loading and priming an eighteen-pound messenger of death. At least he hoped it would deliver that resounding message to the Brits. The next several hours passed in a melee of commands, screams, and explosions. Giving up on its single shots, the British fleet began firing several bombs into the air at once, raining deadly hail upon the fort and the men defending it. Fortunately, most of the shots missed the fort. Yet their impact on land and sea did not fail to shake the ground as well as Luke's nerves. And though he and his crew returned fire as rapidly as they could, their shots always fell short of the row of ships.

British mortar bombs continued to pound them even as the wind and rain assailed them from all sides. Hours passed as Luke, sweat laden and sore muscled, went through the methodical motions of working the gun. Bending over to catch his breath, he inhaled a gulp of smoke-laden air. It stung his nose and throat. He backed up, coughing, and bumped into a passing soldier.

"Luke." The man's incredulous voice spun Luke around. Noah stared at him, eyes brimming with shock from within a soot-encrusted face. Blackthorn stood by his side.

"What in the blazes are you doing here?" Noah asked.

"I could ask you the same," Luke said, gripping his friend's arm. "Did you rescue John and Cassandra?"

A group of militiamen stormed past. Shouts filled the air.

Noah shook his head, sorrow filling his eyes. "Without you, we had no idea where to meet the frigate."

Of course. Luke released his friend. He hadn't thought of that.

"Blackthorn and I came to help the fort." Noah scanned Luke as if he expected him to disappear at any moment. "I'm very glad to see you alive, my friend."

Blackthorn ducked beneath another explosion. "We heard you were arrested."

"You heard correctly," Luke shouted and ran a sleeve over his forehead, marring the white cotton with soot. He leaned toward them. "Do not worry, neither of you were implicated."

Noah's brow folded. "How did you get free?"

"God set me free, my friend." Luke gestured above.

The eerie whine of a bomb sailed overhead.

"It's a long tale." Luke ducked as the explosion shook the ground. "For another time."

A passing corporal pointed toward Noah. "Brenin, Blackthorn, with me!"

Noah clasped Luke's arm. "Take care, my friend."

"You too." Luke returned his grip.

After Noah and Blackthorn rushed off, Luke faced the British fleet. More shots fired from the ships in rapid succession, pummeling both land and sea, like an angry giant pounding on a door. Behind him, one of the bombs met their mark on one of the fort's buildings. The ground trembled. Luke crouched as a shower of stone stung his back and screams of agony battered his ears. When nothing but raindrops struck him, Luke rose, swiped off the debris, and returned to his duties.

The sergeant in charge of the gun Luke was assigned to lowered his scope. "They have rocket launchers on board their sloop. How are we to withstand such a force?" His eyes grew vacant with terror.

"We keep fighting, sir." Luke hefted another iron ball into the mouth of the cannon. He faced him with a look of defiance. "We do not give up."

The sergeant nodded and released a ragged sigh. "Indeed." He glanced down at an empty bucket. "Mr. Heaton, go fetch some more powder bags."

Grabbing the container, Luke headed toward the fort when a firm hand on his shoulder flung him around.

Lieutenant Tripp. With black smudges on his face, rain dripping from his chin, his uniform torn, and a look of shocked abhorrence twisting his features. "What are you doing here, Heaton?" he shouted over the noise.

Luke's stomach folded in on itself. "I'm helping to fight, Lieutenant."

Explosions thundered the sky. Rain slammed down on the mud, skipping over the puddles. "How did you get out of your cell?" The lieutenant's eyes seethed hatred. "It doesn't matter, you will come with me now!" he barked.

An eerie whine coiled around Luke's ears. He glanced up to see the flame of an incoming shell. Too close. Far too close.

"Get down!" He shoved Tripp. Eyes wide, the lieutenant's arms flailed as he tumbled backward several feet before toppling to the ground. Leaping, Luke dove and covered his head with his hands.

The bomb landed on one of the battery guns. Mud and pebbles quivered against Luke's cheek. A scream of torment rent the air. Scraps of iron and flesh lashed his back.

After a few seconds, Luke raised his head. Two men lay dead, another severely injured, and the gun they'd been using was nothing but a smoking pile of sheared metal. Men swamped the scene, attending to the dead and injured. The shouts, the blasts, the pounding rain—every sound seemed to drift into the distance beneath the thumping of Luke's heart and the ringing in his ears. He shook his head.

Three yards to his right, Tripp struggled to his knees, brushing mud from his shirt. Their eyes met. Blood sliced a red line on his right sleeve. Gripping his arm, the lieutenant nodded begrudging thanks to Luke and then ambled back to his post.

❖ CHAPTER 34 ❖

S taring at the same spot she'd been looking at since the shelling began, Cassandra gripped the railing of the sloop until her knuckles whitened. Though the sun had long since set, darkness could not hide the constant bursts of orange and scarlet flaming from the British fleet, nor the arc of glittering fire that spanned the sky and exploded in showers of red-hot sparks above Fort McHenry.

Her legs ached from balancing so long on the heaving deck. Her head throbbed from the endless roar of cannons. Her throat and nose stung from the incessant smoke that filled the air. But most of all her heart broke for the lost lives of the brave soldiers at the fort.

John slipped his hand into hers. "It will be all right, miss." His comforting tone did nothing to assuage her fears.

"I don't see how."

Beside her, Mr. Key and his companions' shouts of defiance and victory had long since faded into shocked silence, broken only by groans of defeat.

It didn't help that every time it appeared that a British bomb had hit its mark, the marines guarding them shouted "huzzahs!" of victory, making Cassandra feel attacked from both front and rear.

"Egad, how much can the fort take?" Mr. Key exclaimed. "They've been firing rockets at them for nigh on twenty-three hours!"

"I didn't realize the British could house so many bombs aboard their ships," Dr. Beanes added.

The third man, Colonel Skinner, grabbed a backstay and slunk down to sit on the railing with a moan.

Cassandra took up a pace. "It is unbearable to sit idly by and watch our city, our country under attack." A blast of wind engulfed the ship in smoke. Gunpowder stung her nose. Coughing, she batted away the fumes.

"I quite agree, miss." Mr. Key propped one boot on the railing and held a handkerchief to his nose. "But we must not give up hope."

Boom boom boom caboom.

Another barrage thundered the air. Violent flames surged from the fleet, flashing a sinister glow upon the British ships before darkness swallowed them up again. Bombs riding on streams of fire sped toward the fort. Explosions, barely distinguishable from the thunder growling its displeasure from above, rocked the peninsula.

"What is to become of us?" The deck tilted, and Cassandra hugged John, drawing him close. He trembled, and she knew he was thinking of Luke. As was she. "Never fear. You know how resilient your brother is. I'm sure he is all right."

She hoped he was. Prayed he was. John said nothing.

Cassandra could not imagine living under British rule. Though her grandparents had suffered during the Revolution, and her mother was but a child during the fighting, Cassandra had been born into freedom. The freedom to elect those who would represent her in government, the freedom to speak out in defiance of injustice, the freedom to choose her own way. She sighed. Perhaps she had taken that freedom for granted too long.

Another round of rockets roared through the air. One crashed onto the ground—either near or on the fort, she couldn't tell which. The deafening explosion plunged a dagger into her heart. She hugged John tighter as Mr. Key offered her his hand. "Shall we pray for our country, Miss Channing?"

Wiping her tears, she slid her hand into his and bowed her head.

Hours later, Cassandra leaned back on a barrel one of the men had rolled over for her to sit on. John stood by her side, while Mr. Key and his friends lined the starboard railing, frozen in shock. Each bomb bursting over the fort reflected the red glow of horror on their faces. Cassandra's hope had long since given way to despair. She placed a hand on her aching back. There was no way Fort McHenry could survive such an onslaught of rockets. So many she'd lost count. Hundreds, even thousands. Yet neither the darkness nor the distance allowed them to determine how much of the fort had been destroyed.

Or how many men had lost their lives.

Fierce wind whipped around her, tearing her hair from its pins and thrashing the wet strands against her neck. She didn't have the strength to brush them away. The sloop rose over a wave. Gripping John, Cassandra clung to the barrel as she dropped her sodden shawl into her lap. She no longer noticed the chill that iced her bones.

Only the chill that penetrated her heart.

"I wonder about the land invasion," she said absently.

Mr. Key turned toward her. Lantern light oscillated over his haggard features. "I've heard no musket shot for some time."

"What if the Brits are ravaging Baltimore as we speak?" Cassandra's voice cracked. She fought back tears. What of her mother and sisters? And Marianne and Rose and poor little Jacob? What would the monsters do to them?

Approaching her, Mr. Key took her hands. "We do not know that. We must trust God and not speculate on the worst."

"I agree, Miss Channing," John said. "God is in control. Besides, Luke is in town. He won't let those nasty Brits come anywhere near his friends."

Cassandra smiled at the boy's trust. "But what can one man do?"

"One man and God can change the world, Miss Channing," Mr. Key said as another volley of cannon fire drew their gazes to a fiery glare arching over the black sky. He shifted his shoulders beneath his coat, dripping with rain. "Besides, the fact that the ships are still firing is a good sign."

"How so?"

"It means they have not taken the fort."

"Of course." Cassandra hadn't thought of that.

"It's when the bombing stops that we need to be concerned." He rubbed the back of his neck.

Cassandra peered into the thick darkness. Though the storm had subsided, a light mist settled in the air, cloaking the scene in a surreal gray mirage. Above them, the heavens revealed a sparkling serenity of stars that defied the proceedings below. Even so, the night dragged on interminably, and Cassandra began to wonder if she'd ever see the light of day again.

Another broadside from the fleet released its fury.

The ship teetered, creaking and groaning as if it were just as tired as they of the nightlong onslaught.

"Look." John pointed east. "Dawn is coming."

Cassandra lifted her chin to see a brushstroke of golden light paint the horizon.

Dr. Beanes approached the railing. "We shall know soon enough, then."

Slowly rising, her eyes locked upon where she knew the fort stood, though she still couldn't make it out.

Several minutes passed. Cannon fire punched the air. All coming from the British fleet. Silence hung over the fort. But what did that mean? Were all the Americans dead? The guns destroyed? Had the British landed and stormed through the town?

Nothing but the creak of the ship and the chuckles of marines playing cards answered Cassandra's frenzied questions.

Grabbing a halyard, Mr. Key leapt up on the bulwarks, straining to see in the distance. "Look for which flag flies above the fort. If the Union Jack, we are doomed."

Cassandra swallowed. Her breath crowded in her throat. She drew John to her and together, they focused their gazes into the darkness.

A darkness that soon transformed to gray. Shadowy objects formed in the distance. The warble of birds greeted the dawn as if no slaughter had taken place overnight.

Boom! The British ships fired again.

Cassandra's heart seized. She felt John tense beside her.

Then the sun burst over the horizon in all its glory, chasing away the darkness. All eyes peered toward the fort, whose buildings now formed before them.

Mr. Key laughed. Then he chuckled, ecstatic joy bursting in his throat. "I see her! She's sodden and limp, but yes, 'tis the stars and stripes!"

He leapt down and grabbed Cassandra's shoulders. "We've held them off!"

Stunned, Cassandra could only stare at him. The air thinned in her lungs as tears of joy filled her eyes.

Mr. Key embraced his friends.

"I told you, Miss Channing." John looked up at her and smiled.

She brushed wet strands of hair from his forehead. "Yes, you did, John. Yes, you did."

"Colonel Skinner," Mr. Key said. "Go below, if you please, and find me a pen and something to write on."

"Of course. Whatever for?"

Mr. Key gazed at the fort. "I must write about this. A poem, a song, explodes in my head, I can hardly contain it."

Within minutes, the colonel returned. "There is no pen to be found, sir. I did find this envelope, but no pen."

"No pen?" Mr. Key looked stricken.

The colonel shook his head and frowned.

"Blast it all!" Grabbing the envelope, Mr. Key spun around.

A faint remembrance jarred Cassandra. Turning her back to them, she lifted her skirt and reached into the pocket of her petticoat for the quill pen and ink jar John had given her. Amazed, she smiled at John and handed them to Mr. Key.

"Where did you get these?" he asked.

Cassandra swallowed as the realization struck her. "God provides, Mr. Key."

"Indeed, He does." He kissed her on the cheek then laid the envelope on top of the bulwarks, dipped his pen in ink, and began to write.

❖

Luke sank to his knees as the first rays of light shot over the horizon, scattering the gloom and stirring the mist hovering over the water. Wet mud seeped into his breeches. He wiped the grime and sweat from his brow with his torn sleeve as he noticed the splatters of blood on the fabric. Not his. But the blood of the injured he had carried to the infirmary. How many, he had lost count. Wind slapped strands of his hair against his cheek. He jerked them away and glanced up at the American flag hanging proudly over the fort.

They had won!

They had repelled an invasion from the greatest naval power in the world. And Luke had been a part of it. As the sun crested the horizon, he bowed his head and thanked God for the victory and the privilege.

"Luke Heaton praying?" Noah chuckled as he and Blackthorn came

MaryLu Tyndall

up on either side of him.

Struggling to his feet, Luke smiled, despite the fact that every muscle and bone in his body screamed in agony. "Miracles do happen."

Noah raised his brows. "War brings many men to their knees."

"It was long overdue." They exchanged a knowing glance.

Before Luke could stop him, Noah clutched him in a manly embrace. "I'm glad to hear it."

"An' me as well," Blackthorn growled. Removing his hat, he slapped it against his leg.

"They are sailing away!" A shout came from the tower, and one by one, the men who had sunk, exhausted, to the ground where they stood, rose to their feet and inched toward the shore.

White sails, gleaming in the sunlight, appeared on the yards of the British ships like snowy clouds. And within minutes, the ships grew smaller in size.

The fort's morning gun fired, sounding rather dull compared to the onslaught that had met Luke's ears throughout the night. Above them, men lowered the storm flag and raised the massive American ensign above the fort. A band began playing "Yankee Doodle."

Luke glanced at his friends covered in mud and ashes, their shirts and breeches torn and sopping wet. "Aren't you both a sore sight?"

Tossing his arms over both Luke's and Blackthorn's shoulders, Noah drew the trio together. "Aye, but we are alive. And God is good to give me such friends."

Uncomfortable with the emotional exchange, Luke backed away as "hip hip hurrays" trumpeted from the exhausted troops. Hats flew into the air and congratulations abounded over the shore battery.

Luke glanced at the departing British fleet. Even amid the triumph and gaiety that surrounded him, his heart collapsed in pain. What of Cassandra and John? Were they still on the HMS *Audacious,* and if so, where was the ship? He had failed to rescue them, and they were lost to him forever.

Noah laid a hand on his shoulder. The joy on his face faded to sympathy, and something else. Determination. "We'll find them."

Luke nodded, though he saw no possibility of that now. Especially if he was locked up and tried for treason. He scanned the crowd. No sign of Lieutenant Tripp. But he would have to face the man sooner or later. And be tossed in his cell once again. No less than Luke deserved. He should

304

be grateful to God he'd been allowed to help defend his great city. To pay a small recompense for his traitorous deeds.

"What of my crew?" he asked Noah. "Were they rounded up?"

"No." His friend shook his head. "I'm told your Mr. Keene made a deal with Tripp. Only you were to be charged."

Another thing to thank God for. Though Keene's betrayal stung Luke hard.

The sun shot ribbons of golden light over the murky waters of the Patapsco River, dividing the mist like the Red Sea. Luke squinted. *Oh God, please save Cassandra and John. And, whether locked up or free, have Your will in my life.* He could hardly believe he prayed such a prayer. That he could submit his future to a distant God. No, not distant. He rubbed the scars on his hand. Always with Luke.

Blackthorn shifted his stance. "I've never seen so many shots. I thought it would never end."

"I spoke with Major Armistead." Noah tugged his muddy cravat from his neck. "Last count, near eighteen hundred bombs were fired our way. Four hundred landing within the fort."

"How many dead?" Luke was afraid to ask. "Only four." Noah blew out a sigh. "Can you believe it? Several wounded, but only four dead."

Blackthorn shook his head. The brawny man touched a wound on his forehead and winced. "It's a miracle."

"Indeed," Noah said, squinting into the rising sun. "Against such overwhelming forces, only God Almighty could have prevailed."

Shifting his boots in the mud, Luke followed Noah's gaze, though he was blinded by the light. He thought of the angel. He thought of destiny. Of freedom and God's love. And he realized that he'd been living in the darkness for far too long.

Noah gestured beyond the fort. "Let's go home, shall we?"

Luke swallowed as his old familiar friend—failure—begged entrance into his soul. "I don't know if I can."

Noah flattened his lips. "Let us find out."

They made their way around the side of the fort where Major Armistead and several of his officers stood together looking like a pack of sopping stray dogs. Yet despite their disheveled appearance, relief softened the taut lines on their faces. At the edge of the group stood Lieutenant Tripp, mud streaked over his uniform, one boot missing and the epaulette on his left shoulder hanging in tatters.

Bile churned in Luke's empty belly.

Noah swung an arm over his shoulders. "Better to face him now."

Luke knew his friend was right. He must face the consequences of his actions and allow God to decide his fate. Time to stop running. Flanked by his friends, he threw back his aching shoulders and pressed on. They halted before the officers, drawing the gaze of Major Armistead.

"Well done, men. I owe you all a debt of gratitude for coming to fight alongside my troops." The major's voice brimmed with sincere appreciation. "Have we been introduced?"

Luke studied Tripp, expecting him to draw his sword and drag Luke back to his cell, but the infernal man would not meet his gaze.

Noah cleared his throat. "No, sir. Forgive me. I am Noah Brenin, privateer." He gestured toward Blackthorn and introduced him as his first mate. Then the major turned to Luke.

"Heaton, sir. Luke Heaton." Would the major recognize his name as the traitor who had been locked in the fort's guardhouse? Lieutenant Tripp's eyes finally landed on Luke. Surely he would say something now. But the man's mud-strewn expression carried no trace of the arrogance and anger that usually simmered in it.

"Very good, Mr. Heaton." Major Armistead clasped the hilt of the sword hanging at his hip as confusion claimed his face. "Ah, Heaton. Wait a minute. That name *does* sound familiar."

❖ CHAPTER 35 ❖

Luke's gut twisted in a knot as Major Armistead's unyielding gaze fixed on him. "Yes, I have heard your name before. But where?"

The major gripped the hilt of his sword even tighter, and Luke braced himself for the inevitable arrest.

Instead, the major's eyebrows rose. "Ah yes." He dipped his head toward Tripp. "I understand you saved the lieutenant's life?"

Luke blinked. An odd look of surrender settled on Tripp's expression.

Major Armistead chuckled. "Come now, don't be modest, Mr. Heaton. The lieutenant regaled me with the tale himself."

Tripp lifted his chin. "I owe you my life, sir." He tugged Luke aside and leaned toward his ear. "Mr. Brenin told me of your brother," he whispered. "And the paperwork of your arrest seems to have disappeared in the mayhem." Then stepping back, he winked at Luke before he rejoined the group. Luke numbly followed him.

"Shall we call our accounts settled then?" Tripp cleared his throat.

Luke stared dumbfounded at the man for a moment before he nodded. Yet surely this was some cruel joke. He braced himself for the laughter that was sure to come before they hauled him away.

"And we have just received word"—Major Armistead glanced over his men with glee—"that the British advance was halted at North Point as well. So, off with you, men. Go home. Kiss your wives, your sweethearts.

Your country thanks you for your service and your courage."

Luke shared a look of shock with Noah. He hesitated. They weren't going to arrest him? He was free?

Grabbing his arm, Noah dragged Luke away as the major's final words penetrated his heart. *Service and courage.* Reverend Drummond had said Luke had a destiny. But Luke had never considered it would be such an important one.

❖

Cassandra hugged herself. Morning mist hovered over the river, slipping over the sides of the small boat and swirling about her feet. John leaned his head against her shoulder and she looped an arm around him and drew him near.

"Where are they taking us?" he whispered.

She kissed the top of his head. "I don't know." Recognizing the fear icing her voice, she added in a more cheerful tone, "Perhaps home."

His shoulders loosened and he smiled.

The splash of paddles and squeak of oarlocks echoed through the fog, scraping over Cassandra's nerves. She and John had been ushered off the truce ship in such haste, they'd been unable to say good-bye to Mr. Key and his friends. A dozen terrifying possibilities crowded her thoughts. Though they'd seen the American flag over the fort, perhaps their celebration had been premature. Perhaps Baltimore had been taken by the British. Perhaps she and John were being escorted to a city she would not recognize. A town occupied by the enemy. Or worse, perhaps she and John were to be executed

For treason against the Crown.

But surely the British would have done the nefarious deed aboard their fleet? Why head into town?

And what would happen to Mr. Key, Dr. Beanes, and Colonel Skinner? Why had they not been brought along?

Cassandra rubbed her head. Too many questions. And none of them had answers that helped settle her nerves.

Sunlight angled through distant trees, chasing away the mist and revealing land up ahead. Her heart tight and her mind reeling, she hugged John tighter and lowered her head to pray.

Please protect us, Father. Please protect Baltimore and our country. And whatever Your will is, please give me the grace to accept it.

No sooner had she raised her gaze than the tiny craft struck the shore, nearly tossing her from the thwarts. Birds chirped a cheerful melody while the smell of cedar and pine wafted over her. The marines leapt into the shallow water and tugged the boat farther onto the sand.

One of them held his hand out for her, his unyielding expression offering no indication of her fate.

Staggering to her feet, she took his hand, noticing her that her own were trembling. Thankfully, John took her other hand then splashed into the water beside the marine.

Cassandra's oversized boots sank into the sand as she and John plodded onto dry land.

A splash and creak of wood turned her around. Both marines hopped back into the boat and made ready to leave.

"What is happening, sir?" she demanded.

One of them looked up as he swung the oar backward and plunged it into the water.

"You and the boy are free to go."

❖

Luke wove his way through the throng of cheerful citizens, singing and dancing in celebration of their victory. Boys dashed between adults, sticks in hands, playing mock battle. Little girls, in flurries of lace, whirled to the sound of fiddles and pianofortes chiming from taverns. Church bells rang. Men slapped each other on the back while women embraced. Luke plowed through them, unaffected by their giddiness. How could he join in the celebration when every passing moment sent Cassandra and John farther away?

Not that he wasn't grateful God had freed him from the noose. Luke rubbed his neck at the thought. *Yes, Father, more grateful than I can say.* Only newly committed to God, and already the Almighty had performed a miracle. Several this day, in fact.

But now, if Luke was to rescue Cassandra and John, he needed another one. And fast.

"What do you intend to do?" Noah caught up to him, breathless.

"I intend to go after them."

"The entire Royal fleet?" Clutching his arm, Noah spun him around. "Are you mad?"

Luke clenched his jaw. "Go home to your wife, Noah." Blackthorn had done as much as soon as they'd entered the city.

Turning down Pratt Street, Luke ducked and dove between clusters of revelry makers and passing carriages. He spotted *Destiny*'s bare masts jutting into the morning sky at the end of the long wharf and breathed a sigh of relief. She hadn't been sunk in the effort to keep the British from advancing.

Noah kept pace at his side. "Think, man. Even if you could navigate past the sunken merchant ships, what do you intend to do? Sail up to the British fleet in your small schooner and beg their leave?"

Luke ground his teeth together as he forged ahead.

Noah groaned. "Do you expect them to be in a generous mood after their humiliating defeat?"

"All the more reason why I must rescue John and Cassandra as soon as possible." Luke continued, slower this time, as he searched his mind for a solution.

Noah stopped him. "Haven't we missed your last rendezvous?"

"Yes, but what does it matter? I am sure he has no further interest in making our appointments." A gust of wind blasted over them, sending a chill through Luke's wet clothes.

"The captain knows he still holds something of extreme value to you." Noah's calm tone held a wisdom Luke envied. "Perhaps he is greedy enough to seek an exchange."

Luke huffed. He rubbed his eyes, thankful for his friend's level thinking.

"Let's go home," Noah said. "Get a good night's sleep and something warm in our bellies. Then tomorrow at dawn, we'll head out to my ship at Elizabeth City and sail to the rendezvous spot. Perhaps this Captain Raynor will show up."

Luke was about to agree when a female voice shouted Noah's name. Spinning around, Noah rushed to Marianne who held Jacob in her arms. Behind them, Miss Rose and Mr. Reed approached. Noah showered his wife and son with kisses in such a display of exuberant affection that Luke tore his gaze away at the intimacy. His eyes landed on Miss Rose. She smiled in return before gazing up at Mr. Reed. Luke could not help but see the affection that strung between them. Raking a hand through his damp hair, he approached his friends.

"We simply could not wait another minute to see you, Noah." Marianne brushed tears from her face. "I was so frightened you'd been injured. We were on our way to the fort when we saw you standing here." She scanned him. "Are you injured?"

"No, just tired and"—he gazed down at his torn filthy attire—"and quite dirty, I'm afraid." Noah pointed toward her gown, where evidence of their embrace smudged over the cotton fabric. "I've ruined your gown."

"Do you think I care about that?" Marianne handed Jacob to Noah and fell into his arms again. The baby flung his hands up and down, giggling.

Rose stepped toward Luke. "We heard you were arrested. We were so frightened."

"Indeed," Luke said. "But God worked all that out."

"God?" Miss Rose cocked her head, studying him.

Luke nodded toward Mr. Reed. "Congratulations on your engagement."

Red blossomed on Rose's face as she slid her arm through Mr. Reed's. "Thank you. We are very blessed."

The Brit leaned down and planted a kiss on her forehead.

Though happy for his friends, Luke turned away from viewing yet more affection he would never experience. Sunlight cast a smattering of glittering diamonds over the bay. Without Cassandra, the beautiful sight seemed empty. Exhaustion tugged on him as agony weighed his heart. Noah was right. There was nothing to be done at the moment to find John and Cassandra. Nothing but pray. Yet, hadn't he proved, of all the things he could do, prayer was the most powerful?

Please help them, Lord. Bring them home to me.

Bells of jubilee rang through the streets.

An odd sensation traversed his back, as if someone was looking at him. A sensation of delightful foreboding that sent pinpricks down his spine. Shaking it off to his exhausted state, Luke turned and scanned the crowd nonetheless. Nothing unusual.

A soldier led a weary horse down the center of the street. Behind him, on the saddle perched a woman and a young boy, their faces hidden in the folds of the soldier's cloak. The man pulled his horse to a stop then reached behind to help his passengers dismount.

A crush of people passed in front of Luke, blocking his view.

His heart thrashed against his chest. Why, he couldn't say. But there was something. . .

He forged toward them, gently nudging people aside, peering

through the throng, desperate, yearning, hoping.

Then he saw her.

Cassandra, hand in hand with John, craned her neck over the mob. Their eyes met. She stopped. Her chest rose and fell. A tiny smile crept over her lips.

The throng of people parted, their movements slowing. The clamor of voices and music faded, and all Luke could hear was the wild *thump thump thump* of his heart.

"Luke!" Breaking free from Cassandra, John flew into Luke's arms. Bending over, Luke swallowed him up and spun him around and around, laughing. His heart felt as though it would burst. He set the lad down. "How did you get here?"

"The British released us early this morning, and that nice soldier gave us a ride on his horse." Gripping his brother's arms, Luke shook him, if only to make sure he was real, uninjured, whole. "You look well."

"I am. Miss Channing took good care of me."

"More like the other way around." Her sweet voice eased over Luke's ears like a soothing ballad. Rising to his full height, he gazed into emerald eyes, glistening with tears.

But before he could utter a word, Marianne and Rose crowded around Cassandra, taking turns hugging her.

"You'll never believe what your mother told me." Marianne pulled away and smiled. "Apparently Mr. Crane found the money that was stolen from you. And he has returned it all!" She squeezed Cassandra's hands. "She came to tell me two days ago before the fighting began, and also to see if there was any word about you or Luke. She's been out of her mind with worry."

Cassandra exchanged a smile with Luke. "That is good news, indeed. I will go see her soon."

"John." Noah drew the boy away. "Come tell us of your adventures." He took his wife's hand, pulling her from Cassandra. Rose followed them.

But Luke hardly noticed, so mesmerized was he by the love beaming from Cassandra's face.

He took a tentative step toward her. Wind danced through her auburn hair, half-torn from her pins and hanging down her back. Her petite curves were swallowed up in an oversized pink gown that dipped too low in the front. Sunlight glistened over her skin. Muddy boots covered her feet and dark shadows curved beneath her eyes.

Luke thought she was the most beautiful woman he had ever seen.

He reached to touch her. Worried she was only a dream. Worried she would not welcome his caress, but needing to touch her anyway, needing it more than anything. He brushed a thumb over her cheek.

Leaning into his hand, she smiled. "John told me everything, Luke. I'm so sorry I doubted you."

"Sorry?" Luke snorted. "Lud, woman. I'm the one who should be sorry."

She swallowed. "You did what you had to. I should have trusted you." A tear spilled down her cheek.

Luke brushed it away. "I gave you no cause." He reached for her hand, hoping it wasn't too late to win her heart. "But if you'll give me a chance. . ."

❖

A chance? Cassandra nearly laughed. She would give anything to own the heart of this honorable, courageous man. In fact, her own heart had not ceased to dance wildly in her chest since she'd spotted him, standing by the docks: dark hair hanging in his face, open shirt flapping in the breeze over his muscled chest, the sharp cut of his stubbled jaw, his flashing blue eyes the color of the sea he loved so much, and stains of blood and dirt smudging his clothes.

Earlier today, she thought she'd never see him again. And now she knew she could never live without him.

Blood! Alarm snapped her gaze to his arm. She touched the stains on his sleeve. "Are you injured?"

He cupped his hand over hers and drew it to his lips. "No. It's not my blood. I was at the fort."

"During the bombing?" Cassandra could hardly believe anyone could survive what she had witnessed all night.

He nodded, kissing her hand. Warmth spread up her arm. He entwined his fingers with hers and stared at her, caressing her with his eyes, drinking her in as if she were a deep pool after crossing a desert.

Flustered and overjoyed at his perusal, she lowered her gaze. "Thank God you weren't kill—"

His lips touched hers. Moist, warm, gently caressing. He drew her close. Pressed her against him. She felt the heat through his damp clothes. A tempest swirled in her belly, a pleasurable tempest she hoped never to dissipate. Then he withdrew slightly and leaned toward her ear. "Marry me, Cassandra." His whispered breath caressed her neck, sending shivers down her back. Delightful, glorious shivers.

Air escaped her lungs. She couldn't speak. Couldn't move. Didn't want this moment to end. But then he backed away. A breeze filled the space between them. She wanted him back. Wanted to dwell in his arms.

But uncertainty clouded his face.

"Marry the town rogue?" She gave him a coy smile, hoping to brighten his mood. "Surely, you jest."

Lowering his chin, he stepped back. "Forgive my presump—"

She placed a finger on his lips. "Yes."

A devilish glint sparked in his eyes. "Yes, you'll forgive my presumptuous behavior?"

"No, you fool. Yes, I will marry you."

One side of his lips cocked in that beguiling grin of his, before he hoisted her into his arms and flung her around. Their laughter mingled in the air above them.

Soon, clinging to Luke's arm, Cassandra led him to their friends. As they approached, wide grins and knowing looks met them as congratulations were passed all around. John could hardly contain his glee.

Another boom of victory sounded from the fort, drawing Cassandra's gaze. Throwing one arm around her and his other around John, Luke drew them both close. Overcome with thankfulness at what God had done, Cassandra glanced at her friends: Marianne and Noah stood arm in arm, Jacob perched on Noah's shoulders; Rose leaned back on Mr. Reed's chest, his hands folded protectively in front of her.

All of them gazed with pride at the massive flag flapping in the wind over Fort McHenry.

"God had a great destiny for us all in this war," Marianne said.

"Destiny and love," Rose added, exchanging a glance with Mr. Reed.

Cassandra gazed up at Luke then lifted her face to the light of the sun. "He did indeed. And I don't think He's done with us yet."

❖ HISTORICAL NOTE ❖

At noon on September 11, 1814, the British fleet sailed to the mouth of the Patapsco River and anchored off North Point, just fourteen miles from Baltimore. Arrogantly spurred on by their successful march into Washington, DC, three weeks earlier, the British planned to attack the "Nest of Pirates," as they called the city, from both land and sea. Early in the morning on September 13, while British troops advanced on land from North Point toward Baltimore, five bomb ships and several other warships maneuvered into a semicircle two miles from Fort McHenry. Just after dawn, the bombing commenced.

Major Armistead, commander of the fort, would later estimate that in the next twenty-five hours, the British would hurl between 1,500 and 1,800 exploding shells at them. A few never hit their mark, but most exploded directly over the fort, showering destruction on the defenders. One bomb exploded on the southwest bastion, destroying a twenty-four-pounder, killing Lieutenant Levi Claggett, and wounding several men. Soon after, another shell crashed through the roof of the gunpowder magazine. By the grace of God, it did not ignite. Major Armistead soon ordered the barrels of powder removed and stored elsewhere.

While the British land invasion was failing due to the courage and preparation of Baltimore's militia, the bombardment of Fort McHenry continued throughout the long night. Finally at 7:00 a.m. on September

14, the shelling ceased, and the British fleet withdrew. Major Armistead immediately brought down the dripping storm flag that flew over the fort and hoisted in its place the forty-two-by-thirty-foot flag sewn by Mary Pickersgill, the action accompanied by the fort's band playing "Yankee Doodle."

Eight miles away, aboard an American truce ship, Sir Francis Scott Key, overcome with emotion at the sight of the flag, penned what would become our national anthem, "The Star-Spangled Banner." Miraculously, Baltimore successfully defended itself against an attack by the greatest military and naval power on earth. The humiliating defeat suffered by the British changed the course of the war, and three months later, on Christmas Eve, Britain made peace with the United States at Ghent. In Baltimore, the *Niles Weekly Register* announced the news with the headline: "Long live the Republic! All hail! Last asylum of oppressed humanity!"

May it ever be so!

"The Star-Spangled Banner" Lyrics
By Francis Scott Key 1814

Oh, say can you see by the dawn's early light
    What so proudly we hailed at the twilight's last gleaming?
Whose broad stripes and bright stars through the perilous fight,
    O'er the ramparts we watched were so gallantly streaming?
And the rockets' red glare, the bombs bursting in air,
    Gave proof through the night that our flag was still there.
Oh, say does that star-spangled banner yet wave
    O'er the land of the free and the home of the brave?

On the shore, dimly seen through the mists of the deep,
    Where the foe's haughty host in dread silence reposes,
What is that which the breeze, o'er the towering steep,
    As it fitfully blows, half conceals, half discloses?
Now it catches the gleam of the morning's first beam,
    In full glory reflected now shines in the stream:
'Tis the star-spangled banner! Oh long may it wave
    O'er the land of the free and the home of the brave!

And where is that band who so vauntingly swore
    That the havoc of war and the battle's confusion,
A home and a country should leave us no more!
    Their blood has washed out their foul footsteps' pollution.
No refuge could save the hireling and slave
    From the terror of flight, or the gloom of the grave:
And the star-spangled banner in triumph doth wave
    O'er the land of the free and the home of the brave!

Oh! thus be it ever, when freemen shall stand
    Between their loved home and the war's desolation!
Blest with victory and peace, may the heav'n rescued land
    Praise the Power that hath made and preserved us a nation.
Then conquer we must, when our cause it is just,
    And this be our motto: "In God is our trust."
And the star-spangled banner in triumph shall wave
    O'er the land of the free and the home of the brave!

Dexter

Other books by MaryLu Tyndall

SURRENDER TO DESTINY SERIES

Surrender the Heart
Surrender the Night

CHARLES TOWNE BELLES

The Red Siren
The Blue Enchantress
The Raven Saint

THE LEGACY OF THE KING'S PIRATES

The Redemption
The Reliance
The Restitution

The Falcon and the Sparrow